Dr. Greyson

BROTHERS PARADISE

A Novel

by:
Grace Maxwell

Brothers Paradise: Dr. Greyson/Grace Maxwell — 1st edition

One

Greyson

I stand at the nurses' station in the emergency department at Paradise General Hospital, flipping through a chart. The end of my shift is in sight, but the morning's been dragging its feet like molasses in winter. After work, I'm driving to Vancouver to catch a ferry to Victoria. It won't be much longer, but for now, I'm here with a queasy teen clutching a bucket—likely a victim of last night's expired takeout—and a screeching toddler. That's an ear infection, no doubt.

My phone is full of unread messages in the family chat, and while I have a moment to breathe, I scan through them. They're mostly my father and younger sister, Tarryn, arguing over the effects of last year's nearby forest fire and the late frost last week. Tarryn says the pinot grapes might not survive. Dad insists they will.

I scroll through, noting the tension in Tarryn's clipped

responses. Elise Anderson, her best friend and our vintner's daughter, wouldn't let Tarryn make that statement lightly. Elise is preparing to take over when her father retires. The thought nags at me. If the grapes don't bounce back, what does that mean for the vineyard? For our family's legacy?

I shove the phone back into my pocket. I don't have time to unpack all that now.

"Dr. Greyson," calls Vivian Daniels, a nurse in the emergency room, snapping me from my thoughts with her velvety voice. "You're looking sharp today." She leans against the counter, one eyebrow cocked playfully. I glance over the rims of my glasses, catching the twinkle in her eye.

Vivian and I tangled in the sheets ages ago — a mistake wrapped in tequila and poor judgment — but that ship has long sailed. I don't do encores, a rule that's kept my life uncomplicated.

"Thanks, Vivian. I'm off to Victoria this afternoon for the MedTalks conference."

She nods. "That's right. You're speaking there. Beckett said it was a big deal."

Beckett, known as Dr. Beckett, is my younger brother and a cardiologist here in the hospital. There are too many doctors in our family for us to go by our last name at work. He's always one of my biggest cheerleaders and was excited when I was asked to share my experiences in emergency medicine with clinicians from around the world.

I'm about to return to endless paperwork when the intercom crackles to life.

"Dr. Greyson, we've got a bus en route," the nurse in charge announces. "Three patients, collision with farm equipment over at Black Bear Vineyard."

I fight the urge to curse. *The Dempsey family.* The name is like a splinter under my skin. Memories of the last time our families stood toe to toe at a wine council meeting flash through my mind — Dad's voice rising, me trying to mediate, and old man

7

Dempsey walking out in a huff. I shove it aside.

There's no room for grudges in the ED. These are lives in my hands, and no family feud will stop me from giving them everything I've got. Still, I can't help my visceral reaction.

Vivian's eyes meet mine, flirtation now replaced with professional resolve. "Looks like our break is over," she says, her tone all business.

"Wouldn't want it any other way," I reply.

I slip into a paper gown, its crinkle a prelude to urgency. With Vivian beside me, the team converges around us, a swarm of focused energy ready to combat the chaos about to burst through our doors.

"Let's go," I murmur, and we fall into the rhythm of preparation. Gloves snap against wrists, and an electric current of anticipation runs through my veins. Moments later, I hear the wail of the approaching ambulance.

The bay doors fly open with a bang, and we push forward, ready to receive. "What've you got?" I call.

Warren Sweeny, EMT and familiar face in times of crisis, emerges from the back of the ambulance. A gurney rattles out. "Thirty-seven-year-old male," he reports. "Hit by a dirt bike out in the vineyard. BP is ninety over sixty. Pulse one-ten." Even as he speaks, my eyes sweep over the patient — the pallor of his skin, the crimson that stains the gurney sheets.

"Head trauma," Warren continues, pointing to a swath of bandages attempting to hold back the bleeding. "Looks like a possible concussion."

"Got it." My response is automatic. "On it, Warren." I motion to Will Stewart, one of our new doctors. "Take the head trauma," I instruct, meeting his steady gaze. He nods and wheels the man to bay four for a CT, leaving blood droplets on the shining floor in his wake. He'll assess for serious brain injuries like bleeding or skull fractures.

"Let's keep moving, people," I urge, scrubbing the sight from my mind. There's more to be done. The dance of emergency medicine never stops; it only changes tempo.

The ambulance bay doors shudder open again, and Warren rolls in another gurney. This one holds a kid who looks barely into his teens, his body slack but face oddly animated. "Fourteen-year-old male," Warren barks. "On the dirt bike. BP one-forty over ninety."

"Jesus, that's high," I mutter, inspecting the boy as we snip away his protective pads. The unmistakable flush of adrenaline — or something more illicit — paints his cheeks a vivid rouge, and his eyes are dilated. "Matthew Dempsey, right?" I lean in, trying to pierce the haze of his intoxication with my gaze.

He flails an arm, nearly clipping my jaw. "Nah, man, I ain't done nothing."

"Sure." My voice is flat, unconvinced. "Bloods, tox screen, and keep Narcan on hand." As I rattle off orders, he snickers, lost in whatever chemical joyride he's on.

Dr. Regina Prince strides over to manage the gurney, her short frame buzzing with energy. But no one here is deceived by her size. She's the kind of doctor who commands respect from the moment she opens her mouth. "Saline, now," she barks, her tone sharp but calming, a paradox I've never been able to figure out.

The kid flinches, his bravado cracking. *Good.* Regina will handle him, no matter what he's on.

"His parents?" I ask, already pivoting to the next crisis.

"Right behind us," someone assures me.

I leave Matthew in Regina's capable hands and turn to find Warren gesturing helplessly toward a young woman cradling her midsection. I recognize her as Josie Dempsey, her features twisted in pain. "She's hypotensive, same as the first guy," Warren says. "Dazed and confused after the collision."

"Josie, talk to me," I say, easing her onto a gurney. "Where does it hurt?"

"Everywhere," she breathes, her voice trembling as her hands hover protectively over her abdomen. "It was just — so fast.

Enrico's mower came out of nowhere, and then Matthew on the dirt bike…" She trails off, wincing as pain overtakes her words. Her hands clench the gurney rails. "I didn't even see Matthew."

The frustration in her voice is tinged with fear, and I quickly order Demerol to take the edge off, knowing we're only just beginning. Inspecting her, dread coils in my stomach. The way her abdomen distends isn't right. I lean down. "Josie? Are you pregnant?"

"God, no." She moans. "Unless it's immaculate conception."

I smile at her reply, but I can see she's scared and hurting.

She chokes back a sob as we cut through her T-shirt. "This was my favorite concert."

"Coldplay will be around again," I assure her, attempting a smile. I know distraction is feeble comfort when fear has its claws sunk deep.

The needle I'm handed feels like lead in my grip, but I wield it deftly, pulling fluid from her belly. It's blood — too much of it. Josie's eyes roll back, her body surrendering to unconsciousness.

"Ana!" My shout pierces the clamor, summoning the surgeon on call. Dr. Ana Williams appears, calm and unflinching despite the blood already streaking her scrubs.

As she whisks Josie away to surgery, I take a moment to regroup. The scent of antiseptic and blood fills the air, and the adrenaline in my veins feels both familiar and suffocating.

The name *Dempsey* rings in my ears. I can't help but wonder if this surgery will save Josie or become another in our families' long history of shared tragedies. "Dammit," I whisper to no one. But there's no time to dwell.

"Dr. Greyson, when are you off?" asks my nurse, Linda, her eyes scanning for the next crisis even as she speaks to me.

I flick my wrist, the watch face glinting under harsh fluorescent lights. "Two hours ago," I admit with a rueful chuckle.

"Go," she urges, looking past me to the next task at hand. "Before we get another wave of patients."

"Will do," I promise. "And hey, I'll grab you those chocolates from Victoria if I have a chance." Her grin is brief but genuine. We've worked together for years now, and I know those are her favorite treat.

"Thanks. Have fun at the conference," she says, her attention already turning back to the fray. "Knock 'em dead with your talk."

A nod and a wave are all I manage as I pivot on my heel, striding to the locker room. The hot spray of the hospital's staff shower does little to wash away the day, and by the time I'm slipping into fresh clothes, the volume of what I'm leaving behind has begun to weigh on me—Josie's pale face, the young teenager's bloodshot eyes, Dad's terse messages. It's all there, a quiet storm in the background of my thoughts. But I take a deep breath.

My ten-year-old Range Rover waits patiently in the parking lot like an old friend. The drive to Victoria will be a welcome escape this afternoon—five hours without interruption or emergencies.

Still, as the hospital fades in my rearview mirror, I feel a twinge of guilt. Is it that I should stay and help or that I feel badly about how much I want to leave everything behind for a few days in Victoria? Either way, it's fleeting, gone with the first rush of open air through the window. *No need to worry about that now*, I tell myself. Right now, I'll focus on getting through this drive and finding a place where nothing feels like it's waiting on me.

Two

Greyson

I coast into the ferry terminal just before nine o'clock, the engine's purr subsiding as I maneuver into the last spot on the evening vessel bound for Victoria. With a satisfying click, I kill the engine and gather my belongings — keys, wallet, and the stack of medical journals that's been taunting me from the passenger seat.

Stepping out into the brisk coastal air, I take a moment to stretch, rolling my shoulders to relieve the tension that's nestled there after hours hunched over the steering wheel on my five-hour drive from Paradise. The ferry, a hulking mass of steel, will cut through the Strait of Georgia around multiple islands to deliver us to Vancouver Island. I make quick work of the distance between my car and the passenger entrance, eager for the solitude the ferry's upper deck promises.

Inside, I navigate through clusters of families and tourists. Their excited energy is a world away from the serenity I crave, and I push forward until I find an empty row of seats tucked away near a window with a view that even in darkness could steal your breath if you let it.

I absolutely love British Columbia. Spring has arrived, bringing gentle rains that nourish the vibrant landscape, and the sun now lingers until nearly seven thirty in the evening. As summer approaches, we'll be playing golf under golden skies that stretch well past ten p.m. It's a place of breathtaking beauty, by far the most stunning spot in the world.

I claim my spot on the aisle, sinking into the padded seat with a sigh of relief. The medical journals land on my lap, and I'm just about to delve into an article on cutting-edge surgical techniques when the familiar ping of my phone beckons my attention.

Tarryn: We've received a formal invitation to the International Wine and Spirits Competition in London in November.

In a series of additional pings, my three brothers congratulate her and Dad. The two of them have now taken the family vineyard, Paradise Hill Family Estate Winery, international. We are a fourth-generation winery, founded by our great-grandfather, who established the vineyard during the Temperance Act to produce sacramental wine in the town named after our ancestor. Today, we proudly carry on the family legacy — though we've expanded our offerings — with eight generations of our family calling the beautiful town of Paradise and Black Bear Valley in central British Columbia, Canada, home.

My eyes skim over the details Tarryn sends, a spark of interest igniting within me at the thought of representing our family's wine on such a prestigious stage. Thumbs hovering over the screen, I type my own congratulatory response, already envisioning a fun trip to London. But before I can press send, a voice, soft yet confident, pulls my attention away.

"Excuse me, is this seat taken?"

I glance up, and time seems to pause, or maybe it's just my breath. A woman stands before me, her presence commanding. She's undeniably beautiful, with an allure that's not just her appearance but in the way she holds herself — a mix of grace and self-assuredness that's impossible to ignore.

"Uh, no," I manage to reply. "Please, have a seat."

She offers a smile, one that hints at conversation I hadn't planned for but am now entirely open to having. As she slides gracefully into the seat beside me, I pocket my phone, the unfinished message to Tarryn forgotten for the moment. Right now, something tells me this unexpected encounter might be worth putting everything else on hold.

The journal on my lap garners her attention almost immediately. "Are you attending the MedTalks in Victoria?" she asks.

"Yep, I am," I respond with a nod, careful not to divulge my role as one of the speakers. It feels too much like bragging. "And you?"

"Yes. I'll be there. It's my first time attending one of these, and I'm very excited. It's been ages since I've been to Victoria. I feel like I'm on a school trip or something…"

She's charming and bubbly and disarmingly attractive, like a classic Hollywood starlet with her friendly demeanor and Marilyn Monroe-esque curves. There's an ease to our conversation that surprises me, her flirtatious manner quite alluring. It's been a long time since I've talked to someone without second-guessing their intentions, and it feels like a breath of fresh air.

We talk about everything and nothing during the hour-and-a-half sail, and before I know it, the intercom announces our impending arrival in Victoria.

"We should probably head down to the cars," I suggest reluctantly.

"Sure thing," she says.

I realize I haven't formally introduced myself amidst the shuffle of disembarking passengers. So I extend my hand. "Greyson Paradise."

"Greyson, nice to meet you." My name rolls off her tongue for the first time as we make our way to the parking deck. "Trinity Blaine," she offers with a wink.

We part with a wave, promising to look out for one another at the conference.

As I sit in my car, waiting for my turn to exit the ferry, thoughts of Trinity occupy my mind. Will I see her again? The possibility seems simultaneously hopeful and daunting. MedTalks draws a huge crowd, and Victoria is swarmed with attendees. Every hotel room is claimed. We should have exchanged numbers.

Pulling out my phone, I'm hit by a pang of guilt. I forgot to finish my message to Tarryn when Trinity joined me. As I open the family chat, it seems Tarryn has asked for help, but Beckett can't make November, and Ryker will go only if no one else can attend. My oldest brother Kingston is virtually a hermit these days as he works on his own company, so he has also declined. Beckett and Ryker then moved on to jesting about me picking up a woman on the ferry since I haven't responded. A wry smile tugs at my lips. They're not entirely wrong.

Me: Sorry. I got caught up. Barely made the ferry. Congratulations, Tarryn and Dad. I can join you in London as long as I can swing the time off.

With one last glance at my phone, I pocket it and focus on the path ahead. This MedTalk I'm giving could be a game changer, and that thought tugs at something deeper. What if it is? What if the world does take notice, and the opportunities I've avoided for years finally catch up to me? Dad always says we have a duty to the vineyard, to the family, but I followed our mother into medicine. I've always enjoyed the vineyard, but I've found my purpose in the ED. As I stare out at the dark waves, the question lingers — can I keep both worlds afloat, or will I eventually have to choose?

The ferry's ramp lowers with a mechanical groan, and as one of the last to get on the ferry, I'm also one of the last off. Once I'm finally free to drive into Victoria, the trip to the hotel is brisk, the city lights blurring past as I navigate the route. Pulling up to the Delta Hotel & Conference Center, I park and gather my belongings with an eagerness I can't quite tame.

As I make my way to reception, there she is — Trinity, her hair catching the golden light of the lobby chandelier. She spots me too, and our eyes lock in a brief but charged acknowledgment before decorum demands we look away.

"Made it without getting lost, I see," she jokes as I approach.

"Only because I was following your lead," I reply.

Our conversation is cut short by the call of two front desk clerks, requesting our attention to complete the check-in process.

We both get our keys, and together, we step into the elevator. She pushes the seventh-floor button, which happens to be my floor too. I keep my eyes forward as the digital numbers climb steadily until they ding at our floor.

As we exit and walk down the corridor, Trinity turns to me casually. "Want to grab a drink in a little bit? Maybe downstairs in the lounge?" she asks.

"Sounds great," I respond, "as long as you don't mind if I fit in a late dinner?" My stomach reminds me it's been hours since I've eaten, and the thought of good food paired with her company is more than appealing.

"Perfect. I could use a bite to eat. I have to follow up on some emails from my office. Would thirty minutes work?" She smiles.

"Thirty minutes. We can meet at the bar," I confirm, and we part ways, the promise of the evening ahead making every step toward my room feel light.

Once inside my temporary sanctuary, I place my bag on the bed and pull out my phone, noticing a new message on the screen. It's from Griffin Martin. A rush of excitement runs through me. Griffin's been a steadfast friend since our med school days.

Griffin: Where are you? We're all here at the hotel, downstairs at the bar. Get your ass down here.

I should be thrilled but, instead, feel a twinge of reluctance. I had conjured a quiet, intimate evening with Trinity, not a boisterous reunion. Yet how can I pass up the chance to reconnect with friends I rarely get to see?

Me: Give me a few. I just checked in. I'll be right there.

Taking a moment to freshen up, I examine my reflection in the mirror, straighten my shirt, and run a hand through my hair. With that, I pocket my phone and head out the door. This will give me a few minutes to catch up with old friends before I meet Trinity for dinner—and before whatever might unfold with her after that.

Downstairs, I stride into the bustling hotel bar, the clink of glasses and laughter already filling my ears. Scanning the crowd, my eyes land on a familiar group huddled around a high-top table, their heads thrown back in mirth.

"Greyson!" A voice booms, and Griffin Martin emerges from the throng, his arms open wide. We embrace like brothers.

"Man, it's been too long," I say, grinning at the faces of our med school pack. Roman Quinlan is here, too. He lifts a half-full beer.

"Too long indeed," Griffin agrees, clapping me on the shoulder. "Still dividing your time between the ED and the vineyard?"

I nod. "I try to help out the family on my days off. What

about you?"

"Thankfully my oldest brother and youngest brother have the family business under control."

Griffin's family own Canada's largest communications company—newspapers, television stations, radio stations, and the largest mobile phone provider.

"Speaking of which, I ran into your brother Kingston a few weeks ago, and he seems busy with his medical technology company. How are Beckett and Ryker?" Griffin asks with an arched brow.

"Stuck back in Paradise," I reply with a sigh, knowing full well our respective siblings would love nothing more than to be here with us, though likely just to hang out and cause problems. "And yeah, Kingston's business is really doing great."

I look over Griffin's shoulder and spot his older brother, Davis, a pediatric cardiologist. I wave to him. Conversation flows, filled with catching up and inside jokes. Yet even so, part of me is clock-watching, anticipating Trinity's arrival.

Just when the teasing about old flames reaches its peak, I turn to see her approaching. She's a vision—professional yet undeniably sexy, her jeans and sweater hugging her curves and commanding the attention of every eye in the room. Her pink lip gloss makes me want to kiss it off right this instant.

"Guys," I interrupt, and my voice fills with a pride I didn't see coming, "this is Trinity Blaine." I turn toward her. "Trinity, meet some of the best damn doctors—and troublemakers—I know." I gesture to introduce each friend in turn, their smiles welcoming.

"So nice to meet you," she says.

"Should we grab that dinner?" I suggest, eager to peel away from the group and focus solely on her.

"Absolutely," Trinity replies.

After I agree to meet my friends in the morning, Trinity and I make our way to an open table on the other side of the bar. We sit across from each other, studying our menus as a candle flickers between us, casting soft shadows on Trinity's face. I make a quick decision about food, something not too heavy but that will satisfy the beast in my stomach.

That decided, I set the menu aside. "I never asked earlier, but where do you work?" I say to Trinity.

"North Vancouver General," she replies as she eyes the server heading our way.

"Must be a busy place."

"Never a dull moment," Trinity replies with a laugh, tucking a strand of golden hair behind her ear. "I love it, though. Keeps me on my toes. And there's something about working with people in their most vulnerable moments. It makes you appreciate life in a way nothing else can." She pauses as the server approaches and takes our order.

When he scurries off, her smile softens. "What about you? Where do you practice your medical wizardry?"

"Paradise General," I reply. "Emergency medicine. It's chaotic, but there's nothing like it. Every second counts, and the stakes couldn't be higher. I've seen things most people only read about, and every day feels like it matters."

"Emergency, wow. You must thrive under pressure."

"Something like that," I admit.

"Tell me about it," she says, and from there the conversation ebbs and flows from playful banter to deeper revelations. I told her something I've never admitted to anyone. I hate working nights, though sometimes my job requires it. Something about her just draws out honesty, and time dissolves in her presence.

The server comes and goes, bringing food and drinks, and as we finish our meal, I lean forward, resting my elbows on the table, not wanting the night to end, though we're quickly moving into early-morning territory. "Trinity," I murmur with a boldness fueled by wine and her company. "Would you like to come back to my room?"

She doesn't hesitate, her lips curving into a smile that

could lead men to war. "I thought you'd never ask."

After I charge the meal to my room, we stand, and I offer my arm, feeling like a character in an old-fashioned romance as we stride toward the elevator.

The elevator doors slide shut, enclosing us in a quiet cocoon of charged air. My pulse quickens as I turn to her. Trinity leans casually against the wall, but her eyes betray her. There's a glint of something daring, something that mirrors the fire simmering in my veins.

I take a step closer, hesitating for just a moment, long enough for her to tilt her chin up and meet my gaze. Her lips part, the barest invitation, and I'm drawn in, the pull magnetic and irresistible.

My breath mingles with hers, but the kiss isn't rushed. It's exploratory, deliberate, each second a test of boundaries. Her fingers thread through my hair, anchoring me, and my hand finds the curve of her waist, pulling her closer.

By the time the elevator dings, signaling our floor, we're already lost in the rhythm we've created. The doors slide open, and for a heartbeat, we stand there, breathless and unwilling to pull apart. But then the hallway beckons, my room promising privacy and the chance to let this moment unravel into something even more consuming.

We move together down the corridor to my room, and I swipe my keycard, the door clicking open. Before it fully shuts, my back hits the wall and Trinity's lips are ravaging mine with a fervor that leaves me gasping. My fingers slide into her jeans, finding the lace edge of her panties. She's wet, ready.

"Tell me what you want," I groan between kisses.

"Hard and fast," she breathes, her chest heaving.

"Your wish," I murmur, lips trailing down her neck, "is my command."

I grasp the edges of her sweater, and the buttons slip free, one by one, revealing soft skin beneath. I slide the garment off her shoulders, letting it fall to the floor, forgotten. "You can tell me to stop if it becomes too much," I whisper, even as every fiber of my being hopes she won't utter those words. My fingers dip into her bra to find her nipples, teasing them into hard peaks. I watch, fascinated by her reactions as I twist and tug gently, testing, exploring her boundaries.

But Trinity is full of surprises. She goes to work at my belt, undoing the buckle with eager haste. Before I can process it, her hand is inside my pants, her grip firm around my cock. A surge of heat floods through me as she strokes, her voice a sultry plea for more. I pull my shirt off and drop it to the floor.

"Greyson..." she begs, and the sound of my name on her lips is my undoing.

I drop to my knees, an act of worship as much as it is a prelude to pleasure. Sliding her panties off, I then hook her leg over my shoulder, my face inches from the center of her desire. The scent of her arousal is intoxicating, and without hesitation, I dive in, tasting her. She's sweet and heady, and I drink her in like a man dying of thirst.

Her moans are music to my ears, a symphony of appreciation that spurs me on as my tongue dances over her folds, lapping at her warmth. My fingers play a more daring tune. Three find their way inside her, stretching, filling, moving with intent. My mouth claims her clit, sucking deeply, savoring the pulsing nub between my lips.

"Greyson!" she cries as her body tenses, then shatters, her climax washing over us both in waves of pure ecstasy. Her name is a prayer on my tongue as I continue to worship at her altar, committed to every note of pleasure that escapes her lips.

When she's nearly boneless, I lick my fingers clean, the taste of her lingering as I rise and gaze into her eyes. "Get on all fours and face the mirror in the corner." My voice is thick with desire as I point to the bed. She complies, and I admire the curve of her ass as she positions herself. My pants hit the floor with a soft thud, and as I roll a condom down over my length, I lean in close. "Is this okay?"

"Yes," she breathes.

"You're absolutely stunning," I murmur, my hand coming down in a gentle spank that causes her to gasp, a sound that sends heat straight to my groin.

A shiver runs through her body, and I watch, mesmerized, as a drop glistens at her entrance, betraying her readiness. "You're such a turn-on," I confess as I position myself behind her. With one smooth motion, I push inside, and we both groan at the contact. She's tight around me, warm and enveloping like a velvet blanket that's been heated by the sun. It's perfect.

The room fills with the rhythmic slap of skin against skin, a primitive drumbeat to our carnal dance. I grip her hips as I thrust harder, faster. Her serene expression tells me she's lost in the sensation, and it drives me wild. Heat coils low in my belly, an intense pressure signaling the impending release.

Reaching around, I find her clit, strumming with urgency. She's responsive under my touch, and I revel in her pleasure, the way she tilts her hips back to meet each of my thrusts. Then, with a cry that echoes off the walls, she cascades over the edge again, her body clenching tight around me. The sensation tears my own climax from deep within, a surge so powerful it leaves me breathless. Together, we ride the waves, united in a moment of pure ecstasy.

We collapse on the bed, a tangle of limbs and heavy, satisfied breaths. My arms instinctively encircle her, pulling her close against my chest. The rise and fall of her back against me gradually slows as our breathing synchronizes.

She whispers into the silence of the room, "You're incredible."

The words wash over me, a wave of warmth in the afterglow. I press my lips to her cheek, a silent thank you for the shared passion. We don't speak further, but words are unnecessary. Our bodies entwined, we drift into sleep, exhaustion claiming us both.

Three

Trinity

Sometime in the early light — not all that long after we went to sleep — I slip out of the hotel sheets, the silence in the room amplifying my heartbeat. It's steady, purposeful, as if it's trying to convince me that leaving is the right choice. The soft rhythm of Greyson's breathing lingers in the air like a ghost I can't shake, tugging at me with a warmth I can't afford to feel. I dress quickly in the bathroom.

Out in the hallway, the air is crisp, a sharp contrast to the warmth I left behind. I take a deep breath as the door to Greyson's room closes softly behind me, letting the chill settle my frayed nerves. *It's for the best*, I tell myself. One night, one mistake, neatly wrapped up and walked away from. I don't need to let him distract me. I'm at this conference to learn what I can and take it back to my hospital.

It's not until I'm sipping coffee at the hotel breakfast spot that the truth crystallizes for me. *Greyson Paradise.* From the town of Paradise. When my parents left Vancouver, that's where they retired and where my father passed away just after Christmas. Greyson's family's legacy looms as large there as the mountains that cradle the town. They named it, and later, they poured their soul into earth and vine to bottle the essence of that place.

A chuckle bubbles up through my nerves. I'm sure he assumed I was a doctor. Maybe I should have clarified, but he never asked, so I didn't. I'm in hospital administration, and one day, I'm going to be CEO. I'm what makes our hospital run and ensures the employees get paid. I'm orderly, meticulous, and controlled. Last night was an aberration, a single point of convergence never to be repeated. Despite being at the same conference, I doubt I'll even see Greyson again. We're just two people in an ocean of faces here at MedTalks. There are multiple events every hour and tens of thousands of people in attendance. And I need to get going if I'm going to get a good seat in the first talk this morning.

I toss my cup and follow the signs through the building to the conference room reserved for "The Ripple Effect of Small Acts in Medicine," the first presentation I'll attend. When the session begins, the presenter's East Indian accent curls around each concept, and she seems to really understand that effective medicine requires administration to work *with* clinicians. We're not on opposite sides of the street. That's a welcome perspective.

Because it's not merely about medicine — not for me. It's about every cog in the healthcare machine, every administrator who feels invisible, or worse, who acts as a barrier amidst the gleaming scalpels and stethoscopes. All of us in healthcare can be catalysts for change, our decisions and directives rippling outward to touch patients' lives.

I scribble notes, capturing my thoughts before they can drift away. My team will love this. We'll brainstorm, we'll strategize, we'll implement. Subtle shifts in policy, gentle nudges in process — we'll be the unseen force guiding the hospital safely.

When she's finished, the speaker receives her due applause, but within me, the applause is for the future, for the potential of my hospital and the reason I came to MedTalks.

As the crowd files out and disperses for lunch, a new determination settles in my chest. I am here on a mission. I am here to improve how the hospital works and, of course, our bottom line.

I balance my plate carefully as I navigate to the only available seat at the lunch table I've been assigned to. I nod at those already seated and begin eating the rubbery chicken, listening as each of the ten people at the table expounds about specialties that range from neurosurgery to pediatric oncology and swap stories. The air is thick with medical jargon and anecdotes of miraculous surgeries.

When the expectant eyes finally turn to me, I offer a smile. "Trinity Blaine," I say, clearing my throat. "And I specialize in administration." The words dangle awkwardly in the air, like a misplaced puzzle piece. A beat passes, then two, and the previously animated conversation stalls into an uncomfortable silence.

The man to my right shifts in his chair, the sound of his fork against his plate sharp enough to turn heads. He clears his throat, and I brace myself for what's coming. "Administration." His voice drips with disdain. "In my experience, administration knows nothing about medicine except how to ruin it." He stands abruptly, and his napkin flutters to the table.

My cheeks burn. "Excuse me?" I ask, trying to keep my voice steady, though my pulse races with anger. "We're the ones who keep the lights on and the bills paid. You wouldn't last a day without us."

But he's already gone, leaving behind an uncomfortable silence.

Heat floods my cheeks. "That is not at all the case," I say firmly, though my voice catches at the edges. I look around the table, desperate for even one ally, but their eyes slide away like

I'm contagious.

This isn't new, I remind myself. I've seen that look before — doctors who think administrators are little more than parasites, feeding off their "real work." Only this time, it stings. Because it's not just about me. It's about every administrator who keeps the lights on, every policy that gives the doctors space to save lives.

I force a smile and take another bite of the rubbery chicken, though it tastes like ash in my mouth.

This cold reception isn't what I expected here, but maybe I've just been ignoring reality for too long. I force myself to sit straighter, keeping my face neutral even as my stomach knots. *"Symbiotic, not adversarial,"* I've often said in board meetings, staff seminars, and even to myself on those long nights as I work on my current software migration project. The entire province is transitioning to a unified electronic medical records system, which will ensure that any doctor you visit already has access to your health information. My job is to transfer data from the old system to the new one, making the process so smooth that no one realizes just how complex it really is. Sitting here, surrounded by people who won't meet my eyes, I can feel how little they think of me.

I push back the rising sting of rejection. They don't know me. They don't know the sleepless nights I've spent making sure no one at the hospital notices a change or glitch. They don't know how our office has fought to keep programs running when funding cuts loomed.

"We're on the same team," I once explained to a resident who mocked administration in a meeting.

He'd smirked and replied, *"Not if you're cutting our paychecks."*

I still remember the bite of those words.

And now, with the glares and silence at this table, I'm right back there again, scrambling to prove I belong. The clinical teams provide the critical care — like chefs creating a life-saving recipe — while hospital administration ensures the kitchen is stocked, the tools are sharp, and the environment runs smoothly. Together, we deliver the care patients need to thrive, ensuring the entire system survives and succeeds.

"Look," a woman across the table says, "I'm not interested in leaving my hospital, so save your recruitment spiel." Then she turns away, rejoining the fragmented discussions around us.

"I'm not a recruiter," I murmur.

As the meal continues, I might as well be invisible. By the end, I'm left alone at the table.

"Mind if I ask what you said to scare everyone off?" A curious voice breaks through my thoughts.

I glance up to find a man standing over me, his expression open and a hint of humor dancing in his eyes. "Just the truth," I reply with a shrug as I rise and collect my things. "I work in hospital administration."

"Ah..." He nods knowingly before extending a hand. "That would do it." He extends his hand. "Carl Gordon, also in the unenviable world of administration."

He leads me across to a corner where a group huddles together. They greet me with smiles as Carl introduces them — pariahs, as he playfully dubs us. As we exchange administrative stories, I find solace. Without us, they agree, doctors would drown in paperwork and financial chaos.

Pleased with this newfound alliance, I move with several from the group to our next session, "Why Every Second Counts: Lessons from the Emergency Room." This is the presentation that convinced me to come to this conference.

I settle in a seat between Carl and a woman he introduced to me as Karen. I leaf through the program, skimming for the umpteenth time over sessions on cardiac breakthroughs and neuroplasticity. My mind wanders, envisioning streamlined triage processes and reduced wait times, a dream scenario for any hospital administrator tasked with overseeing an emergency department.

Then a hush falls over the crowd, and my gaze lifts from

the glossy pages to the stage. The moment the speaker steps into the spotlight, my heart stumbles. *Greyson Paradise*. The man who whispered promises to me under the cover of night is now center stage.

I used to dream of standing up there myself, speaking to a crowd about leadership in healthcare. Now, I know administrators don't get applause.

Yet already, Greyson owns this room with his easy charm. And he looks good in his chino pants, a crisp button-down shirt, and his big watch and fancy shoes. He hasn't even spoken yet, and his confidence is palpable. That stokes my frustration to burn hotter.

My fingers tighten on the program as his voice fills the room, smooth and authoritative. There's no hint of the man who traced circles on my back as we lay tangled in hotel sheets. Instead, he's the golden boy, effortlessly respected by the very people who turned their backs on me at lunch. And as much as I want to roll my eyes, I can't tear them away.

"Please welcome Dr. Greyson," announces the moderator, "head of the emergency department at Paradise General Hospital here in British Columbia."

Applause erupts like a thunderous wave, and a playful voice calls, "Fancy Pants!"

Laughter ripples across the audience, and even Greyson's lips curve into a smile. My pulse races, and my thoughts return again to last night and the time we spent together. How did I miss his name, emblazoned right here in the schedule? I meticulously planned every session I'd attend, strategically pinpointing each talk for maximum benefit, yet I overlooked the name of the man I spent last night with. How could I have been so unaware?

As the chuckles subside, Greyson steps forward, ready to impart his wisdom. I'm still reeling from the revelation, trying to regain my composure as he leans into the microphone, a wry smile playing on his lips.

"Ah, Fancy Pants," he says, "a moniker given to me by my

dear friend, Griffin Martin, back in medical school." He rolls his eyes with a touch of feigned exasperation. "Though leaving behind the hijinks of our academic youth wouldn't be the worst thing."

Laughter flutters through the audience once more, and I shake my head, even as I feel the corners of my mouth tug upward. The camaraderie among medical students is something I've only observed from the sidelines, but their bonds seem unbreakable.

Squaring his shoulders, Greyson shifts gears. "Now, let's dive into the heart of why we're all here today." He pauses, sweeping a glance over the crowd, and for a split second, I fear his eyes might find mine. But he continues, and the moment passes.

"My hospital serves over a dozen communities," he says, gesturing with his hands as if painting the picture. "We have retirees enjoying their golden years, retail workers who keep our local economy buzzing, professionals who spend their days in offices, and farm workers who till the soil that nourishes our town — and make a little wine." The crowd laughs.

I listen, intrigued. It's a clever way to frame the talk, grounding us in the realities of a diverse patient population. Yet notably absent from his introduction is any mention of the Paradise name being his legacy, not merely the town's. I catch my breath, realizing this omission isn't accidental. He's likely glossing over that detail as a way to avoid seeming privileged or disconnected from the grassroots level of healthcare delivery. Nonetheless, he probably plays by very different rules than the rank and file.

He's good at this, I begrudgingly admit to myself as his talk continues. As Greyson speaks, weaving narratives of community and care, I find myself drawn in, not just by the content, but by the realization that there is more to him than even I've glimpsed beneath the dim lights and sheets. And whether I like it or not, I'm curious to learn what drives this man who both infuriates and fascinates me, this man who doesn't flaunt his lineage like some would expect but rather seems to shoulder it as a quiet responsibility.

"At Paradise General Hospital, we see an average of sixty-five-thousand patients a year," he explains. "In the emergency department, each doctor handles between one-point-eight and five patients every hour."

I glance around, catching a sea of nodding heads, acknowledgments of a shared struggle. The numbers mirror the volume at my hospital.

"When I took over, wait times were as long as thirty-three hours," he says, and a ripple of disbelief travels through the crowd.

That is an average wait time at my hospital as well, because like so many, we're understaffed, not just with doctors but with nurses and lab workers and radiology techs, and then there's just the lack of space. We run CT scans twenty-four/seven, three-hundred and sixty-five days a year.

Greyson's next words pique my interest further. "Our focus has been on decision-making under pressure. It's not just about medicine. It's the implications for life beyond our hospital walls."

He's talking about leadership, strategy — my world, where every choice trickles down into someone else's reality.

"By adopting rapid assessments and prioritizing emergencies effectively, we've managed to decrease our longest wait time to twenty hours, with an average of six hours." Greyson's voice is tinged with pride, and rightly so. "And in our mind, that is still too slow. We still have work to do."

That kind of improvement is monumental. My mind races. *Could we implement something similar? What barriers would I face in my department?*

"And we've streamlined the process of admissions," he continues.

My ears perk up. Streamlining, the holy grail of

administrative efficiency. How did he manage it? Does his facility possess resources mine lacks, or was it simply innovative thinking?

"We did this by cutting down administrative redundancies and focusing on what's essential for patient care." He smirks and rolls his eyes.

Suddenly my brain is stuck, frozen on those words. *Administrative redundancies? There are no redundancies in our administration. He's blaming wait times on my department? How about the government requirements?* My pulse thrums.

"Split-second decisions," he says, "they're not just critical in the ED. They resonate through every facet of life, every business model. The key is to trust your instincts and act decisively."

Instincts? As long as his department can document and my department can bill, instincts are fine. But there is no room for experimentation. It's not like we can just wing it.

"Improving our emergency-response systems isn't just a local challenge; it's global. Lives depend on it, and we all have a part to play." His gaze sweeps the crowd, a sea of intent faces.

A moment later, he opens the floor for questions, and my hand shoots into the air like an arrow. Greyson's eyes find mine, and for a split second, the world tilts on its axis. Surprise flickers across his handsome features. He points to me. "Trinity."

At least he remembers my name, though I'm still fuming that he threw hospital administration under the bus.

I want to ask him if it was so easy to make changes at his hospital because his name is on the door, but I refrain. "Can you elaborate on how you've streamlined the admittance process while ensuring all healthcare coverage information required for reimbursement of costs is captured?" I ask instead.

Greyson clears his throat. "My team started with the admittance form," he says. "In our case, and perhaps in many others, it asked for the same details multiple times, which can lead to contradictory data. As you are likely aware, in Canada, the essentials are a patient's social insurance number, address, and name." He pauses, looking over the crowd before adding, "What truly matters to the physicians, however, are allergies and medical history — information likely *already* stored in our electronic medical records, as long as we have the required essential information to access it."

My irritation flares. "Redundancy?" I ask. "Is that what you're saying? You mean the national requirements that keep hospitals from being sued into oblivion? That enable services to be paid for?"

Greyson's gaze flicks toward me, unreadable, but he doesn't falter. "I'm not dismissing their importance," he says smoothly, "but there's always room to make things more efficient."

Efficient. The word grates on me. It's easy for him to criticize when he's standing up there, basking in applause. I cross my arms tightly, feeling solidarity with every dismissed administrator in the room. He doesn't understand — none of them do — that our work is the foundation their miracles rest on.

From across the room, the woman who dismissed me at lunch raises her voice, "This is precisely how hospital administration hampers medicine!" Her words draw eyes — and judgments — from every corner of the amphitheater.

Greyson's gaze briefly meets mine before he turns to acknowledge another eager participant. It stings, this dismissal, not just from him but from an entire profession that fails to see the necessity of each cog in the healthcare machine.

When the session ends, I stand at the side of the amphitheater, arms crossed, as Greyson is swarmed by admirers. They buzz around him, eager bees to the honey of his words and charm. He spares me a fleeting glance, one that skims my face without truly seeming to see me. My lips press together tightly, a barrier holding back the torrent of words clawing up my throat.

I can't watch this any longer. I turn on my heel and exit up the aisle.

"Trinity!" Carl calls, hurrying to catch up. But I don't slow down until I'm through the hotel lobby and outside, the briny harbor air cooling the fire under my skin.

"Are you okay?" Karen asks.

I let out a breath, forcing a laugh that doesn't quite land. "Fine. Just tired of being the *enemy*."

Carl gives me a knowing look. "They'll come around one day."

I want to believe him, but as I stare out at the shimmering water, all I can see is Greyson Paradise standing at the front of that room, untouchable and unbothered. And I hate how much I care. After making the sort of changes he's made, I would hope he'd see things differently. I can't believe I slept with that guy.

"Hey," Carl's voice breaks through my internal storm. "What do you say we head out for a drink?"

Karen nods in agreement.

"Sure," I reply.

"Trust me, you'll love the Empress Martini at the Fairmont," she assures me as we make our way down the sidewalk. "It's absolutely to die for."

The thought of anything *to die for* feels ironic considering my current mood, but I nod, grateful for the change of scenery. We stroll along the harbor as the late afternoon sun dips lower, casting a warm glow over the water, softening the edges of my irritation.

Carl and Karen chat animatedly, discussing the day's seminars and speakers, but their words float past me. My mind remains back in that room, fixated on the condescension directed toward hospital administration like an unshakeable stigma. How can they not see that what they call red tape—forms and protocols—are what keep the system from spiraling into madness?

"Are you okay?" Karen's voice cuts through my ruminations.

"Hmm?" I turn toward her, forcing a smile. "Yeah, just

thinking about the conference."

"Let it go for now," she advises. "Enjoy the moment. Enjoy the martini."

Four

Greyson

The steering wheel is cool under my palms as I navigate the familiar bends leading to the vineyard. It's been only a few days since I returned from Victoria and my MedTalk. It was a great conference, but Trinity was both a surprise and a disappointment. I don't know what I did that ran her off before morning and then had her barking at me during my talk. Then again, I don't know why it matters. We had an evening together, and a phenomenal one at that. Since when is there more I need?

Anyway, I'm off to see my family for the first time since I got back. Sunday dinners are sacred for us, unless the emergency department demands my presence. The ritual soothes something fundamental within me, a touchstone of normalcy in my otherwise frenetic life.

As I drive, I marvel at how so many of the farms from my

childhood have been sold to developers. Homes now butt up against our five-hundred acres of land on several sides, along with some smaller vineyards.

As the car hums along the road, my thoughts drift to Trinity again, as they have often in the previous days. Her face, etched with indignation, flashes before me. I can still hear the sharpness in her voice in that crowded auditorium, the way her words seemed to cut through the applause. Did I push too hard during our night together? Did I cross a line without realizing it? Or was it something I said, or didn't say, that made her so angry during my talk?

Her question about streamlining I expected, particularly from physicians in Canada, but her anger I did not. I worked *with* admin to get it done and meet their needs while helping physicians get more quickly to our requirements for treatment.

Most of all, the memory of her leaving that morning after without a word gnaws at me. She didn't owe me an explanation, but why didn't she stay? We didn't exchange information, and I thought we both had a great time.

Either way, it shouldn't matter. But for some reason, it would seem it does.

I turn onto the quiet street that leads to my childhood home, still lost in my thoughts. The path ahead constricts with a swarm of visitors to our vineyard, their cars lining the street as they meander between tasting rooms and pop-up stalls, arms laden with bottles and whimsical wine-themed trinkets. I'm annoyed by the traffic but remind myself that their enthusiasm for our wines is a gift to my family. It's what has transformed us from a regional, family-run operation into a name whispered reverently by connoisseurs.

I finally turn onto the private gravel road that will take me to the house, leaving the tourists behind. No sooner have I killed the engine than I'm surrounded by the pack of our family dogs. Pinot, Fizz, Vinny, and Barrel bound toward me, a blur of wagging tails and excited yips.

"Hey, boys!" I exit the car and kneel to greet them, scratching behind ears and ruffling fur. Each dog vies for attention, noses nuzzling against my palms with sloppy affection.

"Looks like you've got quite the welcoming committee there." My father's drawl carries over from the porch where he stands, a pillar of rustic charm in his muddy jeans, rubber boots, and beaten straw hat shadowing his rugged features.

"Wouldn't be home without it," I reply, standing and brushing off the dog hair that clings to my pants.

"You're the first to arrive. You beat your brothers this time, though not your sister, of course." He chuckles because my sister, Tarryn, lives in a cottage on the other side of the vineyard. But then the twinkle in his eye quickly shifts to something more probing. "Saw your MedTalk on the internet. Who was that woman who called you out?"

I shift uncomfortably, taken aback by his directness. "Honestly, I'm not too sure," I deflect with a white lie, doing my best to keep my tone light. The last thing I want is to delve into that particular sore spot, especially when I'm still parsing it out myself. "Just someone with a bone to pick about administration."

Dad gives me a long, searching look, but then he nods and tips his hat back, a silent gesture that says he'll let it go, for now. Grateful for the reprieve, I pat Pinot's head one last time and follow my father into the house.

I step into the kitchen, the scent of roasting beef and herbs filling my nose. Mom stands at the counter, maneuvering between pots and pans with the grace of a conductor orchestrating a symphony. She looks up, her face lighting with a smile reserved just for these family occasions.

"Greyson! There's my star." She wipes her hands on her apron before pulling me into a tight hug. "I watched your MedTalk, you know. You were brilliant, as always."

"Thanks, Mom." I try to match her enthusiasm.

"Such a shame I couldn't be there," she continues,

releasing me to check on something in the oven. "Did you meet anyone special?" Her eyes gleam with hope, always the matchmaker.

I chuckle as I lean against the countertop, watching her work. "It was a conference full of medical professionals. What do you think?"

"Right, right," she says. She knows better than to pry too much but can't help herself sometimes. She's dying to be a grandmother.

"Can I help with anything?" I ask, eager to redirect the conversation.

"Would you set the table for nine? Everyone will be home tonight, plus your uncle Maximus and cousin Zane will join us." She points to the dining room with a wooden spoon.

"Is this going to turn into one of those *meetings* disguised as dinner?" I inquire, dreading the possibility of business talk overshadowing the meal.

"Absolutely not," she says, shaking her head. "No business until after dessert, if at all. And that's only if it comes up naturally. Tonight is about family."

"Good to hear."

She always says that, but we talk about the business all the time. This is our only chance to be together.

"Go on then," Mom urges with a gentle nudge toward the dining room.

"Got it," I say, pushing away from the counter to gather the necessary utensils. Setting the table gives me a moment to clear my head before the rest of the clan arrives, each with their own dynamic and drama.

I shuffle the silverware in my hands, laying each piece with meticulous care. As I straighten a knife, my gaze drifts through the floor-to-ceiling windows. Outside, the pinot vines are stubbornly refusing to bloom. Summer fires last year, extreme temperatures, and an early frost have taken their toll on these old plants. Though the lush greenery of the rest of the vineyard still forms a beautiful backdrop, and Black Bear Lake lies cradled at the valley's base, shimmering amidst our cultivated rows of chardonnay, pinot gris, and riesling vines.

For a moment, I'm a child again, racing through those vines with my brothers, laughter pealing louder than any bell. We were invincible then, kings of our verdant domain.

"Greyson!" Ryker's voice snaps me back to the present as he strides into the dining room. "You're going to make a great wife one of these days."

"Not likely," I reply, turning from the window as he heads into the kitchen. I catch snippets of his conversation with Mom, the serious tone that always accompanies talk of their patients, as Ryker is yet another doctor in our family. Mom's trying to retire, and Ryker is going to take over her practice. His latest charge is a brittle diabetic, and Mom's input seems invaluable as they bounce ideas off one another. Their dedication to the people in this valley is inspiring.

I hear Beckett before I see him. "Just so you all know," he announces, "I'm on call tonight."

"Seriously?" I ask, smirking. "How do you plan to fight your way through the tourist traffic over the bridge to the hospital if they need you?"

As if on cue, the distant whir of helicopter blades cuts through the air. That's likely Kingston making his grand entrance. We step outside to watch, and a few moments later, his two-seater bird touches down with precision on the back lawn where we used to play soccer.

Beckett's grin stretches wide. "Like that," he boasts, jerking his thumb toward the settling dust.

Our sister, Tarryn, strolls up and leans against the porch railing, rolling her eyes dramatically. "And what about your car? You plan on abandoning it here?"

"Please…" Beckett scoffs. "The ladies will be lining up to drive me back here to get my car. They're always eager to show their gratitude."

Tarryn mimes gagging, her disgust theatrically overdone. "You better hope you haven't slept with anyone I know, Beckett. Despite what you think, you're not God's gift to women."

"Maybe I have," Beckett shoots back, a wicked glint in his eye. "Maybe I've already charmed them all."

Her glare could slice through steel. "Gross."

I shake my head, amused despite myself, and return inside to finish the task at hand. The family dynamic never changes, but it's these moments — the teasing, the laughter, the debates over medicine and wine — that bind us together.

I step back into the house just as Dad strides in with Maximus and Zane in tow. He's lost the muddy boots, but he still smells like he's been working in the fields. Mom declares dinner is ready, and I glance over the spread she's put on the table. A giant roast beef commands center stage, surrounded by an array of vibrant vegetable side dishes and golden roasted potatoes.

"Ah, someone's opened the cabernet," Dad says, his eyes lighting up at the sight of a dark red liquid breathing in the glass decanter.

"Magnum bottle," I offer with a nod.

Glasses find their way into every hand, and Dad raises his with a proud smile. "Let's toast to Tarryn, for all her hard work with the International Wine and Spirits Competition. We're going to shine in London come November."

We all raise our glasses, but Maximus's toast comes out half-hearted at best. "The best wines are *my* blends," he mutters under his breath.

I catch Tarryn's eye and give her a subtle nod of solidarity. She's more than earned this moment. She's worked so hard to market our wines internationally. If she didn't, Maximus would only be able to work here part time, and Zane would only work during the picking season.

"Thank you, Dad. And thanks to everyone. It's been a team effort, through and through," Tarryn responds graciously.

As we dig into the feast, I watch Kingston, who sits quietly at the far end of the table. He's living alone in that grand house on the Black Bear land that he built for his wife, but then she left him for his best friend a few years ago. I worry about him. He wasn't always like this. I remember when Kingston was the loudest voice at this table, debating Dad about grape varieties or challenging Beckett to impromptu soccer matches on the lawn. Now, he sits at the edges, his thoughts seemingly a world away.

I make a mental note to visit him soon, but the thought comes with a pang of guilt. How many times have I vowed that before and let life get in the way? Kingston doesn't ask for help, but maybe that's the problem. He shouldn't have to.

A new voice breaks my train of thought. Zane, ever the opportunist, leans close to Tarryn, likely pitching some venture or another. "It could really put us ahead of the curve," he insists.

Tarryn folds her arms, her brow furrowing. "I'm not convinced it aligns with our current business strategy. We've spent the last two years stabilizing after the frost nearly wiped out the Bordeaux yield. I won't gamble on a risky venture when we're still recovering."

Zane's smile falters for a moment, but he presses on. "Recovery is exactly why we need this. Playing it safe won't get us ahead." His voice carries a hint of impatience, his eyes darting toward Maximus as if seeking reinforcement.

"Is it worth endangering the family legacy?" Tarryn's response is calm but steely. She folds her arms, meeting Zane's gaze head-on. "If you're so confident, Zane, why not back it yourself?"

Maximus clears his throat, the sound deliberate. "That's enough," he interjects smoothly, though his tone is anything but neutral. "We're here to discuss ideas, not to shoot them down before they've been explored."

I catch Tarryn's jaw tightening, along with her grip on the silverware. Maximus's words carry weight, but not the kind that earns respect. It's a warning, thinly veiled as reason.

"Yeah, come on," Zane adds. "If you're going to take over

managing the vineyard, you have to explore all options." He waves a dismissive hand toward the window and the flowerless pinot vines. "Especially with twenty-seven percent of our yield at stake."

"Zane, I—"

"Maybe we need to discuss whether you're the right fit for the job," he interrupts, his voice laced with challenge.

"Enough, Zane," I cut in sharply, unable to mask my irritation. "Tarryn knows more about these vines and this land than any of us. She was chosen to take over for our dad for a reason."

Zane's face tightens, but he falls silent. For now.

"There's no business talk at this table until dessert," Mom says as she glares at our father.

I sit back, feeling the weight of the disagreement as I observe the dynamics at play around the dinner table. Tarryn's eyes tighten every time Max cuts her off mid-sentence. Her smile never wavers, but her eyes are alight with a fire that's all too familiar. Zane, ever the self-appointed savior, leans into the conversation with a confidence that grates on me. He speaks as if he's the linchpin holding the vineyard together, and it sets my teeth on edge.

Tarryn manages this tension with more grace than I ever could, but that doesn't make it fair. Every time Max needles her or Zane questions her competence, I feel the pull to step in, to help. But there's only so much I can do. I've always wanted to be a doctor like our mother. So I come over on my days off, and I'm here when Tarryn needs me—a shoulder to cry on, a person to throw ideas at, and a helping hand when someone doesn't show up for a shift and I'm not working.

Eventually, Mom brings in the dessert. It's a decadent chocolate torte that momentarily distracts us from our conversations. But the reprieve is short-lived. Max announces, with a flourish, that he's enlisted an outside consultant to assess our operations, a blatant jab at Tarryn's competency.

She doesn't miss a beat. "How thoughtful of you, Max. We'll be eager to hear their insights."

I stifle a laugh, disguising it as a cough into my napkin. The audacity is almost admirable. Dad, however, doesn't share my amusement. "Decisions like that are for Tarryn and me to make, but thank you, Maximus, for your…generosity." His look toward my uncle holds a finality that everyone at the table understands.

Without a doubt this "generous contribution" will evaporate by morning, filed away with the rest of Max's ill-fated suggestions. Uncle Max has always felt slighted that his father didn't give the vineyard to my dad *and* him. Family history dictates that it's always been passed to the firstborn son. Dad's always shared it with Max and made him an important part of the business but as an employee.

As for my generation, my oldest brother, Kingston, made it clear that he was going into medicine when we were very young, and my two other brothers have done the same, as have I. Consequently, after Tarryn graduated with a degree in viticulture from the University of British Columbia, Dad announced that she would be the heir to the vineyard. That was quite the dust up, but it was a happy surprise. She'll be the first female CEO of Paradise Hill Family Estate Winery.

Once the dessert has been consumed, Max's departure is swift, with Zane trailing after him like a shadow. No sooner are they out the door than I move to Tarryn, wrapping my arm around her shoulders. "You're doing an incredible job." I pull her in tight. "Don't let Max or Zane rattle you. You've got Dad's savvy, and all of us are backing you up."

From the kitchen, Mom's voice carries through, "And don't forget about me!" Her tone is light-hearted, but the undertone of fierce protectiveness is unmistakable.

The room erupts in laughter, and Tarryn's posture relaxes ever so slightly. "Thanks, Grey." She gives me a grateful squeeze. "I won't forget."

"Good," I say, releasing her to stand. "I've got the six a.m. shift. I need to get some rest."

"Drive safe," Dad says, his eyes following me as I collect my jacket from the hook by the door.

"Sleep well, dear," Mom adds, emerging from the kitchen with a tea towel in hand.

I step over and give her a kiss on the cheek. "Will do," I reply, pulling on my jacket and opening the front door to step into the cool night air.

I slide into the driver's seat, turning the key in the ignition. As the engine purrs to life, Trinity moves once again to the forefront of my mind, as if she's just been here in the car waiting for me. But right now, I need rest. Tomorrow's early shift looms over me, a twelve-hour dance with fate in the emergency department.

As I roll back down the quiet road, the vineyard fades in the rearview mirror. "Let's hope for an uneventful drive," I murmur to myself, the road stretching out before me as I head back to my condo and the world I've chosen to navigate on my own terms.

Five

Trinity

I stride into my manager's office for our scheduled post-conference debrief, the late-afternoon sun casting long shadows across his cluttered desk. My eyes fall to his name plate as I take a seat across from him, the leather chair cool against my skin. *Andy Keshan*, it reads. I wonder why they didn't use Andrew.

"What did you think about the conference?" He opens his notebook, ready to jot notes. After all, I was sent to bring back insight for all of us.

"MedTalks was an eye-opener," I begin, hesitating only briefly as I collect my thoughts. "You could've given me a heads-up about the cold shoulder from the doctors. They see admin as the enemy."

Andy leans back in his chair, a sympathetic grimace on his face. "I know it's rough, but did you meet other hospital admins there?"

I watch the rain fall nonstop outside his window. "I did find my people eventually, and they were a great support."

"I'm grateful you went. You have no idea how much I dread those conferences." He shudders theatrically, and I smile.

"Get this," I say. "One pompous guy actually claimed in a talk that he rewrote his hospital's emergency room intake paperwork himself. Evidently, it was all the administration's fault that things were so redundant."

Andy's laughter fills the room. "He can't have done that all on his own. The paperwork is set by the government if the hospital wants to be reimbursed for care. But you know what can help with intake? Your project. That provincial-wide electronic medical record system is going to revolutionize paperwork for us. No longer will patients be asked the same question four times. It will be asked once, and we can populate it everywhere it's needed."

Pride swells at his mention of the work that has consumed my life for the past three years. "We'll be ahead of the curve as one of the first hospitals to implement the new software," I point out, allowing myself a moment to envision the eventual completion of the project. Just a few more months now. "Once that happens, I'm taking a week off. Hawaii, maybe. Just me, the beach, and absolutely nothing else."

"Sounds like paradise," Andy says. "You'll deserve every second of it. Just be warned, your next project might not be as thrilling."

I nod, already mentally sifting through emails and spreadsheets, the promise of sandy shores a distant but beckoning light at the end of the tunnel. Then I refocus on my notes and take Andy through a rundown of the insights I picked up at the conference. Mostly my experience confirmed that we're moving in the right direction, and we might even be leading the way.

The meeting with Andy comes to a close with an

unexpected twist. "We're celebrating Janie's newfound freedom tonight," he tells me, referring to one of my coworkers. "She signed her divorce papers last night." There's a twinkle in his eye, which makes me wonder if he's particularly invested in Janie's single status. "You should come."

"Thanks for the invite, but I've got plans," I tell him as I rise to leave, thinking of my best friend Liz and the catch-up session we've scheduled.

He tells me I'm always welcome if anything changes, and I return to my office to finish up the day. After checking through the last of my emails, I tidy up my desk, thoughts of post-work revelry pushing away any residual stress.

I bundle myself into my raincoat, and in no time, I'm crossing the Lions Gate Bridge as rain dumps into the water below. Despite the wet weather, downtown Vancouver is buzzing with life, and I drink it in, feeling the shift in energy from the hospital's sterile hallways to the vibrancy of Gastown.

Liz is already at the Pourhouse when I arrive, her laughter reaching me before I see her. She's chatting with some tall guy who looks like he walked out of a cologne advertisement. I hang back, not wanting to intrude just yet, but she spots me, and the guy seems to get the hint, excusing himself.

Sliding into the booth across from her, I'm greeted by the mouthwatering sight of two smashburgers, which have arrived at the perfect time. The Pourhouse has this secret sauce that clings to your taste buds, making you swear there's something to it beyond mere culinary expertise.

"Drinks will be right up," our server promises with a smile, disappearing into the throng once more.

Leaning in, I ask, "What did we get?"

Liz gives me a wink, all mischief and excitement. "Got you a Widow's Kiss," she says. "And for me, a Sidecar."

"Classic choices." I grin, ready for the evening to unfold with one of my oldest and dearest. We've been friends since high school, and these days Liz works as a physiotherapist. She's the one who actually saw the job posting at the hospital when she was working on her practicum a few years back and dropped my resume off with Andy.

I pepper Liz with questions as we eat, and she entertains me with stories of her patients and her family. But by the time I'm picking at the remnants of my smashburger, the tangy sauce lingering on my fingertips, Liz is ready to turn the tables. She leans forward. "So, spill it. Did you meet someone at the conference?"

I stab a fry with my fork and try to skirt around the truth. "Oh, you know, just the usual networking."

But Liz has always been able to read me like her favorite novel, worn pages and all. "I can see there's more. Out with it."

Taking a deep breath, I surrender to the inevitable. "Okay, fine. There was someone, but it was kind of a mess." I recount the luncheon fiasco, how the doctors scattered when they learned I was *admin*. Each word is a reminder of the sting, the isolation. "And I think Greyson was the worst. He dissed administration during his talk about efficiency in the ED. It was humiliating." I sigh and look away. *Not that he knew I was admin…*

"Greyson?" Liz quirks an eyebrow, a silent prompt to continue.

"Yes." My cheeks flush with irritation and something dangerously close to longing. "We met on the ferry on the way there, and he had entertained me the night before. I didn't realize I'd be listening to him the next day."

"Ouch." Her empathy is as quick as her curiosity. "Was he awful?"

The memory rushes back, a tide of sensation that makes me squirm in my seat. "Actually, it was…incredible," I admit begrudgingly. "He seemed to anticipate my every need, like he was in tune with me or something. It was kind of mind-blowing."

"Nice." Liz's smile is teasing but not unkind. "So could you maybe overlook his attitude and just have fun?"

I shake my head, pushing away the plate. "He lives in

Paradise. And besides, respect is a big deal for me. I can't be with someone who doesn't value what I do, even if the sex is earth-shattering."

"Earth-shattering?"

I look around the bar at the guys we see all the time. "Unfortunately."

She nods. We're cut from the same cloth in this regard. Respect is non-negotiable. We fall into silence. Inside, I'm anything but settled, the ghost of Greyson's touch still haunting me.

The server weaves through the crowd, balancing a tray with our drinks. Her smile is apologetic as she sets them down. "Sorry for the wait. These are on the house."

"Really?" Liz beams, and I feel myself smiling as well. We offer our thanks and clink our glasses together.

"Here's to being single and ready to mingle." Liz's eyes sparkle.

I raise my glass, joining her toast, and then shift the conversation back to her. "What's the latest with you and Carson?" They've been on and off for the past few months. It kills me that she doesn't just kick him to the curb.

She rolls her eyes. "I caught him sexting another woman. She sent him a photo of her…assets." She uses her hands to mimic large breasts, and I shake my head. "Very large, very fake."

"Ugh, I'm so sorry." I squeeze her hand. "You deserve so much better."

"Thanks. It stings, but I try to console myself knowing it's better to find this out now than after we'd married."

"Yes! He's a pig, and if she wants a lying cheat, she can have him."

"That's right. Because once a lying cheat, always a lying cheat."

"Absolutely."

She leans forward, lowering her voice. "And remember, the best way to get over a man is to get under a new one."

We both laugh, and I raise my glass to that sage advice.

Just then, the guy Liz was chatting with earlier saunters over, a hopeful gleam in his eye. "Did I just hear an open invitation?" He's bold; I'll give him that. He also has excellent hearing.

Liz tilts her head, sizing him up with a smirk. "Only if you're prepared to devote the next four hours to licking pussy."

He doesn't miss a beat, grinning and glancing down suggestively. "I'm more than ready." The bulge in his pants is noticeable.

"Looks a little small for such big promises," Liz counters. "We're only interested in receiving tonight, honey."

His face falls, but he manages a chuckle. "Can't blame a guy for trying."

"Move along," Liz says, and he retreats back into the crowd.

"Men," I mutter, shaking my head but unable to suppress a grin.

"Like moths to a flame," Liz agrees, raising her glass once more. "To independence and better days ahead."

"Cheers to that," I echo.

Liz leans back in her chair, twirling her glass between her fingers. "You know, Vancouver is like a giant cereal box," she declares with a laugh.

"Full of fruit, nuts, and flakes?" I finish for her, chuckling at our running joke.

"Exactly!" She slaps the table. "Trying to find a decent guy is like searching for a prize at the bottom—lots of digging through the crazy."

I nod, sipping the last of my Widow's Kiss, the bittersweet liqueur leaving a lingering warmth on my tongue. "A prize that probably doesn't even exist."

"Speaking of prizes," Liz says with air quotes so exaggerated they almost knock over her Sidecar glass. "Are you planning to *run into* Mr. MedTalk if you visit your mom in

Paradise?"

I snort. "Not a chance. That ship has sailed. And speaking of sailing, Mom's off on a cruise to Hawaii with her bestie right now." I picture them lounging on deck chairs, tropical drinks in hand.

"Good for her. She deserves some fun," Liz says. "And you do too. We should do something wild this weekend."

"Between the raindrops?" I tease, but I'm already imagining us trying out a new hiking trail or hitting up a street festival, anything to shake off the drudgery.

"Exactly! A little water never hurt anyone." Liz grins.

A little while later, we wrap things up and part ways outside the Pourhouse, promising to text each other ideas for the weekend. The cool evening air feels refreshing after the warmth of the bar, and as I walk back to my apartment, I cycle through the work waiting for me tomorrow. Reports to review, emails to answer — perhaps I should get a jumpstart tonight.

But when I get home, the silence of my small space wraps around me like a comforting blanket, and I make a different choice. I kick off my shoes, change into my comfiest pajamas, and crawl under the covers with my laptop.

"Time for some real Netflix and chill," I murmur as I scroll through the romantic comedies until one catches my eye — a story about a second chance at love.

"Perfect," I say, settling deeper into the pillows. Work can wait. There's plenty of my project left. But tonight, it's just me, the warm glow of the screen, and the promise of a feel-good ending.

Six

Trinity

The shrill ring of the phone wrenches me from sleep, and for a moment, I can't remember where I am. I fell asleep while running some numbers for work, but after a moment, I realize I'm at home in my bedroom.

I try to leave my duties at the office, but in the last few months, since I returned from the MedTalks conference, really, my work on the electronic medical records project has picked up. This puts me behind on some of my other duties, and I have to catch up when I can.

I take a deep breath, my heart thumping against my ribs as if it already knows that calls like these mean bad news. Fumbling in the dark, I grasp the receiver, my voice a raspy whisper. "Hello?"

"Trinity, it's Daisy Crandall, your mother's next-door neighbor." Her words tumble out, tinged with panic. "An ambulance just left with her, but before that, I heard a crash outside my door. I think she fell. She seemed confused and was in her nightgown. I think... It might be a stroke."

I'm bolt upright, adrenaline clearing the cobwebs of sleep. "Which hospital?" My mind races, planning steps ahead.

"Paradise General," Daisy says.

"Thank you, Daisy. Seriously, thank you." I hang up, not waiting for a response. The neon digits of the clock glare 2:07 at me. Quick math tells me I can make it by eight if I hustle. I throw clothes into a bag, essentials only, my movements automatic.

In less than fifteen minutes, I'm behind the wheel, winding down the streets toward the highway. Paradise is a five-hour drive on a good day. I press the accelerator a little harder. I hit speed dial for the office voicemail and call my boss.

"Andy, it's Trinity," I say when the line connects. "There's been some sort of incident, and an ambulance took my mom to the hospital in Paradise. I'm driving there now and will work remotely until I know what's going on. I'll have my phone, so call if you need me. Thanks!"

With that managed, I shift my mind to what lies ahead. Thinking about Paradise's hospital reminds me that I know someone who works there. The thought of seeing Greyson Paradise again twists my stomach into knots. But it's a large regional hospital with a massive staff, the biggest employer in Paradise. The chances of running into him are practically zero. Plus, that was three months ago. I'm sure he's forgotten all about me.

A few hours later, the first light of dawn tints the horizon as I pull over for coffee. The adrenaline has worn off, and the four hours of sleep I got weren't nearly enough. Nonetheless, I'm back on the road within minutes, the paper coffee cup a small comfort in my hand.

Finally, Paradise looms before me, and I cross the giant bridge over Black Bear Lake. At eight thirty, I burst through the ED's sliding doors and head for the front desk, where I explain who I'm there to see.

A nurse nods, her face a mask of professional sympathy. "Come with me," she says, leading me through the labyrinthine corridors to the curtained bay where my mother lies sleeping or unconscious—I can't tell which. The sight of her so vulnerable, so small against the sterile white sheets, sends a pang of fear through me.

"I'll let the doctor know you're here," the nurse murmurs before slipping away.

I take my mother's limp hand in mine, the constant beep of the heart monitor intruding on the silence. Questions bubble up, each one a tiny terror. For now, all I can do is wait and hope that the updates will be good, that my presence can somehow anchor her back to reality.

I'm tapping my foot, a nervous rhythm against the cold linoleum, when the curtain swishes aside. My eyes close because, *of course*, none other than Greyson strides in. My breath catches. Of all the doctors at Paradise General, it has to be him.

"Trinity? What are you doing here?" he asks, eyes wide.

"Greyson," I breathe. "I—I'm here for my mother." I gesture to the gurney as my words tumble out in a rush. "She's had an episode. I drove from Vancouver as soon as I got the call."

He studies me for a moment. "You drove through the night?" There's an edge to his question, a slight disbelief that needles at my already frayed nerves.

"Yes," I snap, suddenly aware of my disheveled hair and the coffee stains on my shirt. Of course, he has to see me like this—unpolished, unraveled.

"Dr. Paradise," I say, the title sharp on my tongue as I try to steady myself, focus on the matter at hand. "I need an update on her condition."

He doesn't flinch, his gaze steady and clinical. "Actually, it's Dr. Greyson," he corrects.

I snort, the sound bitter. "Right, because the weight of your last name is too much to bear."

His eyes narrow slightly, but he doesn't take the bait. "It's practicality," he says. "My family is full of Dr. Paradises. Using our first names keeps things simple."

For a moment, I see the man I met months ago, the one who made my heart thump and my body glow. Then the moment is gone, and we're back to this awkward, tangled mess.

I realize I'm being snotty without cause. *Why am I lashing out at him?* It's not his fault that life has thrown yet another curveball my way.

"Sorry, Dr. Greyson," I mutter, tugging self-consciously at my rumpled clothes. "It's been a long night."

His fingers dance across the keyboard, and he swivels the laptop around. The images — gray and white shadows that should mean nothing to me — somehow convey everything I fear.

"Your mother arrived just after two-fifteen this morning," he says, his voice clinical yet not unkind. "The MRI revealed ischemic changes with evidence of cerebral tissue damage and structural abnormalities." His finger hovers over the image. "These findings are consistent with multiple lacunar infarcts."

I hold up my hand. "Can you say that in regular English? I'm not a doctor."

His brow furrows. "You're not a doctor? You said you worked at North Van General Hospital."

I nod. "I do, but I work in administration."

His eyes grow wide. "Well, what I said means the MRI confirmed brain tissue damage and abnormalities." His finger indicates a cluster of ominous spots. "These are indicative of several brain bleeds that we call a hemorrhagic stroke."

My gaze moves over the screen.

"This is an active brain bleed," he continues, tapping another area. "That's what we're currently addressing with intravenous medication."

"Is she...?" My voice trails off into the void of uncertainty.

"We've consulted with the on-call neurologist," he assures me, closing the laptop with a gentle snap. "She'll be admitted as soon as a bed becomes available, and she's scheduled for an echocardiogram to check for blood clots that may have traveled to her brain."

The hospital buzzes around us, but in this bubble, it's just Greyson, me, and the weight of his words. "What does this all mean for her, realistically?"

He regards me with those too-perceptive eyes. "If we can manage the bleed and she demonstrates cognitive stability in her tests, she might go home. Otherwise, she'll need assisted care."

Tears betray me, welling up before I can stop them. I mumble a choked thank you and slide my chair closer to my mother's still form. Her hand is warm, deceptively strong in mine, and I cling to it like an anchor.

I can't lose her too. Not now. The thought of becoming an orphan at twenty-eight paralyzes me, even as I realize it's ridiculous, because adults don't become orphans. But if I lose her, what am I then? She's more than my mother. She's my compass, my confidant.

"Is your dad here?" Greyson asks.

I shake my head. "He passed away just after Christmas," I mumble.

"I'm sorry to hear that," he replies. "Once we schedule her tests, someone will be here to take her." And with that, Greyson leaves.

"Mom," I whisper, knowing she likely can't hear me. "Please be okay."

But the room offers no answers, only the steady beep of the heart monitor, an indifferent witness to my unraveling world.

Then I feel my mother's hand slipping away as her eyelids flutter open. "Ellen?" she murmurs, her voice hoarse.

"Mom, it's me. Trinity," I correct gently, but my heart sinks like a stone in deep water. Ellen is her sister who passed away a few years ago. The blank look in my mother's eyes isn't just confusion. It's a fracture in the foundation of who she is. Who we are.

I've always thought of her as indomitable, my north star.

But now that star feels impossibly distant. What does it mean to lose someone piece by piece? To become the caretaker instead of the cared-for?

"Trinity?" she echoes, searching my face with bewildered eyes.

"Your daughter," I remind her gently.

"I wasn't aware I had any children."

A lump forms in my throat, thick and suffocating. I fight to keep my composure, swallowing back the surge of emotion. "It's only me. You only have a daughter."

Her gaze drifts away, uncomprehending, and I'm left clutching at the frayed edges of hope. I stand abruptly, my legs unsteady, and step outside the curtain. A nurse hurries past, and I catch her arm. "My mother's awake," I tell her. "Please let the doctor know."

"Of course," she replies before disappearing down the corridor.

I step back inside and sink into my chair, the chill of the hospital seeping into my bones. Time blurs until Dr. Greyson reappears, his presence a strange comfort despite everything.

"That's good news that she's awake," he says. He then engages in a brief, one-sided conversation with my mother before a technician appears and she's wheeled out for her echocardiogram.

"Here." Greyson hands me a clipboard laden with hospital paperwork, his tone oddly gentle. Paper. My hospital migrated away from paper a few years ago. "Take your time with this. It's thorough."

"Thanks." I manage a small smile, accepting the task.

He nods and leaves me to it.

The questions on the paperwork blur together, medication lists, emergency contacts. I flip through them, leaving blank spaces where answers should be. None of it is unfamiliar, but I don't have all the details. They're tucked away in Mom's apartment, in her purse, somewhere out of reach.

Greyson reappears, his frown deepening as he scans the forms I hand him. "These aren't complete," he says, his tone all business.

My patience snaps. "I know! But this is all I have. I'll get the rest when I go to her condo."

He points to the date I've put in at the top of the form. "This information is two years old. Our electronic medical records will have most of this, except if she's never been admitted here before, we'll need her personal health number to access the records."

"Great," I bite out, my voice rising. "I'll find that at her condo too."

His expression hardens, but he doesn't reply. Instead, he steps back, letting the frustration hang heavy between us. For a moment, I hate him—for being right and for making me feel small when everything already feels impossible.

Panic flares up inside me. "I just need to run to her condo, get her social insurance card, her personal health number, and her medical file."

He glances at his watch. "Thirty minutes," he says firmly. "Otherwise, we'll have to reschedule her test."

"All right." I rush from the room, my mind racing faster than my feet can carry me.

What should be a quick drive across the lake in morning traffic is slower than I would have expected for a town this size. Mom lives in a five-story condo building with a stunning view of downtown across the lake. I realize her condo is close to Greyson's family vineyard. I park crookedly in Mom's second parking place and race up the stairs to her front door.

The key scrapes in the lock, and I twist it hard and burst inside. My hands fumble through her drawers, flinging contents aside until her purse and medical file are secured under my arm. The clock is ticking.

I weave back through traffic, each red light an eternity. When I finally skid to a stop again at the hospital entrance,

Greyson's there, arms crossed, and I brace myself before his disapproving gaze.

"Late," he says, as if I'm a tardy intern instead of a woman grappling with her mother's health.

"Traffic," I snap back, brushing past him, my pulse pounding. He follows me to the waiting area where I hastily complete the forms, the pen scratching aggressively against the paper.

Greyson leans over my shoulder. "These medications you listed don't match our records."

"What? Did I put them down wrong?" I thrust the sheet from her file toward him. "This is what she had at home."

He studies the date on the corner and points to it. "The information you provided is out of date. This is why electronic medical records are crucial, and it's a waste of your time to fill out all these forms."

"I know that," I snap. "But unless someone fills out that ridiculous form, the province won't cover the hospital bills." My voice rises, frustration boiling over. "Not everyone can rely on a family fortune to pay like you can."

I stand and head back toward where I last saw my mother, leaving him standing with his perfect hair and impeccable coat. *Why is it so easy for him to unravel me?* I return to my mother's bay just as they're wheeling her back in. A man in scrubs introduces himself as Dr. Mark Chappell, the neurologist. His words echo Greyson's previous report, adding a thin strand of hope that her memory might return with time. And he thinks it won't be long now before there's a room open for her to be admitted.

"Thank you, Dr. Chappell," I whisper, my throat tight.

I sit with my mother for hours. Occasionally, she stirs, but mostly, she just sleeps, and I try to accomplish a few tasks to distract myself. When night falls, a nurse, her kind eyes shadowed by exhaustion, suggests I go home to rest. She assures me they'll get my mother into a room eventually. It seems wrong to leave, but I feel myself nodding mechanically, and soon, I'm retracing my steps out to my car and back to my mother's place. When I arrive, the condo feels alien, haunted by what was once familiar.

I open the freezer and a chill escapes, revealing rows of frozen corn stacked with eerie precision. The fridge is no better, half-empty, its shelves holding a few cartons of milk — all but one expired, and a forgotten jar of pickles.

How long has it been like this? Had her memory been slipping before this happened? Hidden behind carefully rehearsed conversations and polite deflections? I talk to her daily, but seeing this is completely different. Was this not her first stroke?

The distance between Vancouver and Paradise suddenly feels insurmountable, a five-hour gap that's now grown wider. How do I bridge it when every corner of this apartment whispers of neglect I should have noticed?

I sink to the floor, the cold seeping through my jeans, and for the first time since the phone call, I allow myself to completely let go and cry.

Seven

Greyson

On Friday afternoon, my shift is over, and I'm headed to the gym for my regular pick-up basketball game with my brothers. It's our ritual as often as we can pull it off. Since I saw Trinity again yesterday, I can't shake her from my mind, her fiery eyes blazing with that intensity I remember from three months ago. She was an intense but fleeting connection, someone I wasn't supposed to think about after the conference ended. She made that clear enough. Yet now, she's back, bristling with the same energy that pulls and frustrates me in equal measure. I remind myself that I don't do repeats.

Still, she's not like anyone else I've met—sharp, unyielding, and completely unimpressed by my name or title. Maybe that's why she sticks in my head. Or maybe it's because for the first time in years, I don't have the upper hand in our conversation. She's unpredictable, and I don't know if I like it or hate it.

It feels as if fate is toying with me. I glance down at my watch. Damn, I'm late.

"Greyson!" A voice dripping with suggestion pulls me from my thoughts as I step into the gym. Amanda Lambert, a woman I've known since high school, leans against the doorframe like she's modeling for a men's magazine, all bright purple leggings and cleavage. In Paradise, you run into people you've known your entire life everywhere. She's practically thrusting herself at me with an eagerness that makes my skin crawl. I remember the high school drama and Tarryn's stories about Amanda's spiteful antics. She's trouble with a capital T.

"Hey, Amanda," I manage, keeping my tone neutral as I sidestep her obvious display. Her laugh follows me, tinged with a promise of things I have no intention of exploring.

The squeak of rubber soles on polished wood greets me as I enter the court. There, amidst the rhythm of bouncing balls and brotherly banter, are Beckett, Ryker, and Kingston. They don't notice my arrival, too caught up in their own world. So I scoop up a ball and dribble toward them, turning my back on the distraction at the door.

"About time you showed up!" Ryker calls, wiping his brow with the back of his hand. His face is flushed from exertion—and probably stress. He's working as hard as he can to keep up with our mom and her legendary work ethic.

"How are you doing, Ryker?" I ask. "You seem to have worked up a sweat."

"Well, this is exercise," he scoffs. "But Mom's schedule's insane," he adds a moment later between shots. "She remembers every detail about her patients. How does she do it?" He shakes his head, a touch of overwhelm in his eyes.

"Genetics, maybe?" I suggest, trying to lighten his load. "Or maybe she's just superhuman."

"Definitely the latter," Beckett chimes in, sinking another basket.

"Where are Penn and Phillip?" I ask. Penn and Phillip Cole are brothers and longtime family friends. Penn is my best friend, and Phillip is Ryker's.

"Can't make it. Wedding planning," Ryker explains.

I groan. "I love Frankie, but I hope she doesn't start restricting his basketball games."

"I think you're fine," Ryker replies as he bounces the ball three times, shoots, and whooshes it through the net. "This was a meeting at the church and the only time that worked."

"Don't tell Mom, but that is never going to be on my radar," I promise.

Ryker laughs, and for a moment, the tension lifts from his shoulders. "Amen to that."

The ball slams against the polished floor, an echo of my thumping heart. I catch it on a rebound and pivot to face Beckett, who's already set in a defensive stance. His eyes are shadowed, a flicker of something dark passing over his features before he masks it with a determined glare.

"Rough day?" I ask, knowing the answer even before he nods.

"Lost one on the table," he says, voice clipped. "A bypass. It happens, especially in a community with so many retirees."

"Comes with the territory," I murmur. Black Bear is a picturesque town, a haven for those seeking an affordable place to live with plenty of activities for their golden years. But every paradise has its shadows.

I dribble past Beckett, taking advantage of his momentary distraction, and make the shot. The ball swishes through the net, though that does nothing to lighten the mood.

Kingston catches the ball as it bounces back into play. He's a fortress of a man—solid, dependable, and unerringly quiet unless he's got something important to say.

"Good news on my end," Kingston offers, holding the ball under his arm. "The new joint design's getting approved all across Europe."

"Following in the U.S. FDA's footsteps." I nod.

It's impressive, even if he won't say it himself. The guy's struck gold with his invention, and now, he's sitting pretty as one of Canada's richest—and most eligible—bachelors. You'd never hear that from him, though. If anything, it's made him a hermit. Well, that and his vicious ex-wife. There's another reason never to marry.

"Congrats, man," Ryker says, tossing Kingston a towel. "You're going to revolutionize the field."

"Already has," I add, clapping him on the back.

But he shrugs off the praise. "Let's keep playing," Kingston suggests, and we dive back into the game.

This court is our sanctuary, a place where we can shed the weight of our last name and just be ourselves—no titles, no expectations, no constant comparisons. We're all carrying something—a loss, a frustration, pressure—but out here, it doesn't matter. For a little while, we're just brothers, chasing a ball like we're kids again. As we trade points and playful insults, I find myself grateful.

I snatch the ball from Beckett's grip, dribbling it with a focused rhythm.

"I heard you ran into Trinity at the hospital yesterday," he comments.

"Isn't that the woman from the MedTalk conference?" asks Ryker.

I dribble the ball without looking at them. "Yes."

"Ah," Beckett grins, bouncing on his heels with an annoyingly knowing look in his eyes. "The plot thickens. You've mentioned her several times since you got back. I thought she lived in Vancouver."

"She does," I reply.

"Is she stalking you now?"

"Hardly. She'd probably take me out if she could," I say, faking left before shooting right. The tension I felt seeing Trinity again dissipates slightly with the familiar whoosh of the net and the thud of the ball against the court.

"Why does she hate you so much?" Kingston asks.

"Honestly, I have no clue." I catch the rebound and run it to the other side of the court, though I miss my basket. "At the conference, I thought she was a doctor, but it turns out she works in admin."

"That's easy then," Ryker says with a shrug. "You totally dissed admin during your talk. Even our admin are upset at you."

I stop mid-throw. "Why are they mad?"

"Because you've made it seem like with a stroke of a pen, you got rid of all the paperwork. They've been fielding calls from across the province."

"That's not what I did." I jump and throw, but it misses again.

Ryker catches the rebound and shoots and makes it. "How do you know she's not here for you?"

"Her mom was admitted early yesterday morning, and she drove all night to be here," I explain. "She did not seem pleased to learn I was her mom's doctor."

"Come on. I've never met anyone who didn't like you." Ryker swipes a towel over his forehead. "If they start off cold, you charm them right into your fan club."

A laugh almost escapes me, but I smother it down. "Believe it or not, Ryker, there's a long list of people who can't stand me." A three-pointer arcs gracefully from my fingertips, finally hitting nothing but net.

Ryker shakes his head, tossing the ball back to me. "They don't know you then. Either that or they're just jealous, man."

I catch the ball and line up another shot. "Jealousy or not, I'm pretty sure Trinity's disdain for me isn't about to change."

I focus on the hoop, but all I see is her fiery stare, challenging and unforgiving. It's unsettling how much I want to sway her opinion, though I didn't do myself any favors yesterday. I felt entirely unsettled at seeing her, so I leaned into being a stickler for protocol. *But again*, I tell myself for probably the millionth time, *it shouldn't matter*. What's done is done. And once her mom gets settled, she'll return to Vancouver anyway. She has some administration job at North Vancouver General.

Kingston's voice cuts through the banter. "Are we here to chat or play ball?" His eyes glint with a competitive fire.

"Let's go." I dribble to center court, waiting for the sloths to catch up.

We play hard, muscles straining and sweat sheening our skin. Laughter bursts forth to mix with the scuffs of sneakers and the swish of the net. Ryker's quick reflexes have him stealing the ball, Beckett's height gives him an edge in defense, and Kingston, ever silent, communicates with precision passes. I fake left, then go right, sinking a basket and earning hoots from my brothers.

"Nice one!" Beckett yells.

"Man, am I glad we do this," I pant after another aggressive round.

My brothers all nod, equally drenched in the satisfaction of a game well played.

"Time to cool off at your place?" Ryker suggests, still bouncing the ball absentmindedly.

"Sounds good. I'll meet you there." I lead the way out of the gym. The fading light of dusk casts long shadows as we walk to my condo building. It looms over Black Bear Lake on indigenous land that was sold for a steep price to our developer. Eventually, there will be other buildings, but for now, it's only a dozen owners with a spectacular pool. Our footsteps echo in the vast underground parking garage as we make our way to the elevator.

As I adjust my gym bag on my shoulder, I spot her. Trinity's at the elevator, wrestling with an overnight bag and a paper grocery bag that looks ready to burst. Suddenly, the bag topples, and her groceries are on the ground. I race over, leaving my brothers behind, and pick up a canned soup, then chase an orange that seems to be running away.

"Thank you." She reaches for a box of my favorite chocolate-covered cookies and looks up, her eyes widening as she realizes it's me. "What are you doing here?"

"I live here, and you live in Vancouver. Shouldn't I be the one asking why you're here?"

She stumbles slightly. The weariness in her movements is hard to miss, and something twists in my chest. Then she straightens, her eyes flashing with defiance, and the moment of softness evaporates.

"This is my building," I tell her, reaching for another can. "I live here. Let me help you."

Her eyebrows knit together before she retorts, "Well, so does my mother. Fourth floor."

I exhale and nod. "I've never met her before. I don't meddle with the homeowners' council or anything. I keep to myself."

"And you didn't notice her address was the same as yours?"

"I don't see her address on my computer." I look at the groceries still on the ground and turn to my brothers, who parked in the visitor's area and are just now catching up. "Can you grab the reusable bags in the back of my truck?"

Ryker opens his mouth but then takes in the broken grocery bag and heads to my car.

"That's not necessary." She starts loading her purse with bananas and apples. She puts the oranges in her pocket.

"Let me at least help you." I stack up some frozen meals. "You actually like these?" Immediately, I wince. It just came out of my mouth without any thought.

"Just..." She snatches them from my hand. "I told you. I don't need any help."

Ryker arrives with two cloth bags. I take them from him with a nod. "Here." I turn back to Trinity and start loading things into the bags. "You can hang on to these."

We stand there, an awkward truce between us as she takes

the new bags with her groceries. My brothers exchange looks but wisely choose to stay silent. Despite everything, despite the way she bristles at my every word, something about Trinity still pulls me in, like gravity, like fate, and I can't shake it off.

I step back, holding my key fob in the air with a mock bow. "Ladies first," I tell her.

Her wary eyes make it clear she's not impressed by the gesture. With a reluctant sigh, Trinity lifts her own fob, and the green light blinks our permission to enter the elevator. I follow suit with my brothers in tow, and the doors slide shut with a soft whoosh, sealing us into the confined space. The fourth and fifth floor light up.

"My mother said there was only one unit on the fifth floor," Trinity notes.

I nod. "That's correct."

"Your mother," Beckett pipes up, "how is she doing?"

Trinity sighs. "Not much has changed." She puts the bags down on the elevator floor and stretches her fingers. "Visiting hours were over, so I picked up some groceries. She doesn't have much at home."

"Tomorrow," I hear myself promise, my words surprising even me, "I'll stop by and check on her." I'm not her doctor now that she's been admitted, but for some reason, I either feel invested in how her mother is doing or I'm trying to impress Trinity. I'm not really sure.

The elevator chimes at the fourth floor. "Thanks for the bags. I'll leave them for you at the hospital." Trinity slips out without a backward glance, and she's out of sight before the doors close again.

"Anyone else feel that?" Beckett breaks the silence as we ascend, his eyebrows raised in a knowing arch.

"Feel what?" I play dumb, but Kingston's rare interjection pulls a smirk to my face.

"Chemistry," he states simply.

"Doesn't matter," I grumble, shaking my head. "She hates

me."

The elevator opens into my unit. We spill out into my living room, and shortly thereafter, I sink into the buttery leather of my couch, a cold beer in my hand. The guys sprawl around me, and we turn on the Blue Jays game. But I can't forget the electricity that lingered in the elevator with Trinity.

"Man, she's got you twisted up, doesn't she?" Ryker teases, elbowing me lightly as he reaches for his beer.

I let out a noncommittal grunt, not ready to admit anything, especially not the fact that her defiant eyes keep appearing in my mind.

"Grey," Ryker continues, undeterred by my silence, "I bet you could win her over. Hell, make her fall head over heels for you."

The idea is ludicrous, and I bark out a laugh. "Ryker, even if we have—*had*—our moments," I say cautiously, acknowledging the connection without giving away too much, "there's no way she'll fall for me. I can hardly get her to talk without going off on me."

Trinity isn't just a woman with a sharp tongue and a defiant glare. She's someone who could unravel more than just my pride. As I lean back, waiting for the pizza to arrive and trying to focus on the game, a small twist of anticipation—or is it dread?—settles in my stomach. It seems she's going to be around for a while and closer than I ever expected. What have I gotten myself into?

Eight

Trinity

On Saturday morning, I rub the sleep from my eyes in the hospital parking lot. My hand is wrapped tightly around my cardboard coffee cup, heat seeping into my palm, the rich aroma promising a semblance of alertness. I take a sip, savoring the bitterness that cuts through the fog in my brain. "Nectar of the gods," I mutter with a wry smile as I exit the car and push through the sliding doors into the antiseptic brightness of the hospital. Mom finally has her own room, and I'm anxious to get an update.

The familiar beeps and murmurs guide me to her room, where I find Mom propped up in bed, a scowl on her face. "This breakfast is atrocious," she declares, pushing the tray away with more strength than I've seen in days. Cold scrambled eggs ooze on the plate beside half-eaten squares of melon. Her distaste for both is no secret, and her complaint, though passive-aggressive, floods me with relief. If she's griping, she's feeling better.

"Hey, Mom." I pull up a chair and settle in. "How was last night?"

She ponders for a moment, eyes scanning the room before settling back on me. "I need my book," she says.

"I'll go get that for you. Where is it?"

"On my bedside table. The new Danielle Steele."

Surprise flickers through me; I didn't see it last night. "Of course. After the doctor visits, I'll run home and grab it."

Her lips twitch in a faint smile, and I cling to this small victory. A book might not be much, but if it can tether her, even slightly, to the world she inhabits, it's worth every effort.

The door swings open with a whisper, and Dr. Chappell enters in his white coat. He greets me with a nod before turning his attention to Mom, who seems to brighten under his clinical gaze.

"Good morning, Mrs. Blaine," he says, "Can I call you Joy?"

She giggles like a schoolgirl, and I think I just threw up in my mouth. There are some things in life children shouldn't witness, and a flirting mother is one of them. I shudder.

He unfolds his stethoscope from around his neck. "How are we feeling today?"

"Not so bad," she quips.

Dr. Chappell chuckles, encouraging her humor as he checks her pulse, her pupils, and asks a few questions that test her memory — what did she have for breakfast, what's her name. When he asks who I am, she just stares at me. I listen, half-distracted by the rhythm of life-saving machines, until Mom mentions something that snags my full attention.

"It's good to see you have a visitor." Dr. Chappell looks at me and smiles.

"George stopped by this morning before work," she says casually, tapping an invisible watch on her wrist. "You just missed him."

My heart lurches. Dad's been gone for six months, taken swiftly by a heart attack. Alarm tightens my chest, and I glance at Dr. Chappell, searching his face for a reaction. He meets my eyes briefly, a silent understanding passing between us. He knows my father wasn't here.

"Joy," he says gently, redirecting the conversation. "Tell me about your daughter."

"She works in a hospital in Vancouver, and she's very important. She's single, and I'd fix you up with her if you weren't married."

"I've been married twice," he teases.

"Marriage is the best," she says. "George is my soulmate. We met when we were young. I'm so lucky. We just clicked. He's a dreamer, and I was so serious. We bring out the best in each other."

I wipe a tear away. We both miss him so much. I take a deep breath and look at Dr. Chappell. "When do you think you'll be releasing her?"

"It will be a few days. If you'd like to bring her a robe and slippers, that would be fine."

"Oh great. Would you like that, Mom?"

"Sure." She nods.

"When I grab your book, I'll get some things from home. Maybe your toothbrush and your favorite powder. And maybe some outside food? Something better than cold eggs? That is, if I can bring in outside food." I turn again to Dr. Chappell.

"It's against hospital policy, but the meals here aren't very good, so just don't let the nurses see it." Dr. Chappell types on his laptop. "And keep it healthy."

"Healthy," I repeat, filing away the list in my head — nightgown, bathrobe, slippers, reading material, and real food.

We exchange farewells as Dr. Chappell finishes his exam, but I excuse myself and follow him out into the hallway.

"Doctor," I call, catching up to his brisk pace. "My father — he passed just after Christmas. Is it normal for her to — ?"

"Confuse things?" he supplies. "It can be. The brain bleed has stopped, thankfully. So now we wait to see the extent of the damage. She's much more alert now, but it's possible some memories might not return." His voice is soothing, but the truth is a jagged pill to swallow.

"Thank you," I manage, watching him stride away. There are still so many questions, but I have no choice but to return to Mom's room. Back at her side, I smile reassuringly. "I'll go get your things — and that book you wanted."

"Thank you, sweetheart," she says, her attention already drifting.

I head out, and as the elevator doors close, I cling to hoping she gets better.

A little while later, I pull into Mom's parking spot. I don't even remember driving here. I look up at the concrete ceiling and wonder how safe I am if I can't remember anything about my drive. My phone pings, grounding me in the present.

Unknown Number: Are you coming in to see your mom today?

Me: I just left. I'll be back shortly. Who is this? Is my mom okay?

There's no immediate response, so I tuck my phone back into my pocket and make my way to Mom's condo. Inside, I fill an overnight bag with necessities. My plan is to work from her room, so I snatch my laptop from the desk and make my way back to the front door.

As I'm walking out, I realize I forgot Mom's book. A quick scan of her room yields no sign of it. Frustration nips at my calm as I survey the shelves, lined with an eclectic mix of literature. She's always loved to read almost everything, but romance seems to be her favorite. With reluctance, I pluck a Danielle Steele novel from the collection. I can always go to the bookstore at the mall if this doesn't work for her.

The lake glints in the midday sun as I drive back to the hospital, stirring memories of summers spent here, carefree and untouched by the responsibilities I now carry. But even as nostalgia tugs at my heartstrings, the sight of charred land from last summer's wildfires brings me back to the present.

Over the years, Paradise has morphed into something almost unrecognizable. The vineyards that once sprawled across the Black Bear region's west side are now hidden behind burgeoning housing developments. Yet despite the changes, there's a quaint charm to this place I still appreciate.

I pull over at a bustling fruit stand, wooden crates brimming with the season's bounty. I gather a generous assortment of strawberries, peaches, raspberries, and blackberries — their colors unbelievably vibrant. These will be for the nurses on Mom's floor. Working in a hospital, I'm intimately aware of the tireless dedication each nurse pours into the care they provide. It's a small gesture, but recognition goes a long way.

"Thank you," I say to the vendor, handling the bags of fruit gingerly as I head back to the car. They deserve this and so much more. Making a final stop at a bakery, I pick up a scone with some clotted cream. *This is a healthy snack.*

I haul everything I've collected — the bursting bags of fruit, Mom's overnight bag with her book tucked inside, my work bag, her snack, and my purse — through the hospital parking lot. I must look like a Sherpa making my way to the top of the mountain. Thankfully, the automatic doors slide open with a soft whoosh, but I struggle to balance all the packages while pressing the elevator button. When the doors part, I step in and immediately feel the need to rush, as if time is slipping away with each floor the elevator ascends.

"Need a hand?" A nurse enters on the next floor just as I fumble with the bags. She steadies them with a smile, and relief washes over me.

"Thanks," I reply. "I'm a bit of a pack mule."

She chuckles and exits the elevator with me, assisting me to the nurses' station where I deposit the colorful bounty. Their faces light up. "Thank you for taking such good care of my mom," I tell them.

"Dr. Greyson was asking about you earlier," one of the nurses mentions casually. "He's quite the looker, isn't he?"

I look at her name tag. *Samantha Marks.* "Is he?" I manage half a smile, the memory of tangled sheets flashing briefly before I push it aside. "He was Mom's doctor when they brought her into the emergency department. Did he say what he wanted?"

She shakes her head, curls bouncing. "Nope. He might swing by again, though."

I nod, curiosity lingering, but I have more pressing concerns. I continue down the hall to my mother's room.

"Mom, I brought you your favorite scone. I thought you might be hungry." I step into the quiet space, holding out the offering along with the book.

She glances at the pastry, then back at me, her expression distant. "I've eaten already."

"Really? Did they bring you another tray?" I ask as confusion clouds her features. She seems agitated. What happened while I was gone? "Did Dr. Greyson stop by?" I ask, trying to direct our conversation to something tangible.

Her eyes widen, a flicker of fear passing through them, and my heart tightens.

"Mom?" The question hangs between us, unanswered. Her eyes bounce around the room, and I can tell her anxiety is ratcheting up.

With a sigh, I step back into the hallway and walk down to the nurses' station. "Can someone check on my mom? She is upset and isn't able to tell me why."

Samantha volunteers for the task.

"Thank you. Do you know if anything happened with her while I was out?"

"Nothing on our end," Samantha replies, though she looks a bit concerned. "Wait out here. Let me see what I can determine."

"Okay, thanks." I lean against the cool wall for a moment, gathering strength as I try to listen as Samantha talks to Mom.

"Who was that woman?" Mom asks when she enters.

"The tall blonde?" Samantha asks.

Their voices drop low, and my mind is a pinball machine, pinging through questions. *Is she asking about me? No. It can't be.*

After a moment, Samantha emerges from the room, her hand finding my arm in a gesture of comfort. "She's all right," she says softly. "Just some confusion is all."

"She didn't recognize me?" The question slips out, barely a whisper, but the weight of it crashes down like a landslide.

If she forgets me, who am I without her? The thought is selfish, but I can't help it. For so long, my mother has been my anchor, the person who believed in me even when I doubted myself. Watching her slip away feels like losing a part of myself, piece by piece, with no way to stop it.

There's a moment's hesitation before Samantha responds. "Memory issues can be sporadic after a brain bleed. It might just be a momentary lapse." She gives my arm a reassuring squeeze, but it feels like a bandage on a gaping wound.

"Thank you," I manage to whisper, plastering on a smile. As she walks away, I steel myself and step back into the room, where Mom is now reading. To anyone else, she might look content, absorbed in Danielle Steele's world, but to me, she's adrift at sea.

"Hey, Mom." I move the scone and clotted cream closer to her. "The nice nurse brought you a snack?"

"Uh-huh," Mom murmurs without looking up. "Very sweet of her."

As I sit down at the foot of the bed, the whiplash of emotions makes it hard to focus. There is nothing for me to do but be here. "Do you mind if I do some work?" I ask.

She doesn't answer.

When I open my laptop, an email from my boss blinks urgently at the top of my inbox. His words are kind and supportive, but essentially, he wants to know how long I think I'll be gone. And he needs an update on the systems migration project, stat.

I take a deep breath because I can't reply to his questions with firm answers.

Andy,
My mom had a stroke. There isn't much for me to do right now but sit by her side and be here for the doctors, but it feels important to be present. I don't know how long I'll be here, but I'm connected and working and keeping up with all my duties.

We're sorting out the kinks in the new electronic medical records system with the beta team, and we're on track for a hospital-wide rollout in five weeks. I'm happy to hop on a video call if you need me.

Trinity

Send. I skim through the other emails, responses from vendors mixed with internal queries. Everyone wants a piece of me, but right now, my mother needs my attention.

The click of the door interrupts my thoughts, and I look up to find Greyson standing there. His dark hair is perfectly tousled, and his white coat drapes over broad shoulders. Doctor or not, he looks more like he stepped off a magazine cover than a hospital ward.

"Dr. Greyson," I say. "What brings you here?"

He steps in, looking over at mom. "I checked in on your mom earlier, and you weren't here," he explains, "so I thought I'd come back by to see how you're navigating things. Maybe go over what Dr. Chappell mentioned about her condition?"

My defenses rise instantly. "Why would you do that?" I challenge.

For a moment, he looks taken aback, but then his expression softens. "I check in with most of my patients' families when they're admitted," he says gently. "It's important to ensure everyone feels supported during the transition from emergency to the wards."

Mom doesn't look up from her book.

"Right," I murmur, not entirely convinced but grateful nonetheless. That's certainly not how it works at my hospital back home. I remind myself to stay focused on the present. "Thanks, Dr. Greyson. That's...thoughtful of you."

"You can just call me Greyson," he insists, with a hint of the charm I recall so vividly. "We know each other outside the hospital walls."

I nod, though I'm not ready to cross the line from patient's daughter to anything else. "I appreciate it." Suddenly, I remember I have his reusable grocery bags. "Here. I was going to drop these off on my way down."

He looks at them and smiles. "You can keep those. I have more."

"I have dozens at home in Vancouver, and Mom has a healthy stack in her closet. Thank you for your help."

He nods but doesn't take the grocery bags. Instead, he pulls out his computer. "Let's see what Mark put in your mother's chart."

I narrow my eyes, still not ready to buy into the friendly-doctor routine. "Dr. Chappell explained everything well enough," I assure him.

"Have you started looking for a care home?" he asks casually, as if discussing the weather and not my mother's future.

My heart skips a beat. "A care home? Why would she need that?" The words tumble out, laced with panic.

"Trinity," he begins gently, but the softness of his voice does nothing to cushion the blow. "She won't be able to go home immediately. She's going to need time and rehabilitation. Her motor skills have taken a hit. She's not walking well. And the memory issues will make it difficult for her to be on her own."

The room seems to tilt, a carousel of emotions spinning me around. Dr. Chappell hadn't painted such a dire picture. "This... This isn't what he told me," I stammer, feeling lost.

Mom flips the page in her book.

Greyson nods, understanding etched in his features. "I've got a list of recommended care homes," he says, his tone calm, almost too calm. "I'll get it to you today and can make some calls if you'd like."

There's something in his voice that catches me off guard. It's not concern, exactly, but understanding. Perhaps this isn't just another case for him.

"Why are you doing this?" I ask before I can stop myself. "Is this what you do for everyone?"

He meets my gaze. "Because I can. And because you don't have to do this alone, Trinity."

"Is this your way of trying to...?"

But Mom has put her book down and is listening intently. The accusation trails off, born of old hurt and new fear.

He shakes his head, a sad smile touching his lips. "You know, Trinity, Vancouver might have jaded you a little. Here in Paradise, we look out for each other."

"Stop arguing with the nice doctor," my mother chimes in.

"Thank you," I manage, the words sounding hollow. "Your help is appreciated."

As he turns to leave, a memory flashes—a tangled mess of limbs and white hotel sheets. My body responds with an involuntary shiver as if his touch lingers on my skin.

"Are you cold, dear? Do you need a blanket?" Mom asks.

"No, Mom, I'm fine," I reply, rubbing my arms as if I could wipe away the memories along with the chill.

Greyson exits with a nod, leaving me to grapple with all of this—my past and Mom's future.

Nurses, doctors, and a few therapists come and go from the room all afternoon. I watch, listen, and learn. Mom is not the same strong woman she was when I was growing up, and I'm becoming alarmed.

After dinner, a nurse peeks her head into the room. "Visiting hours are almost up."

I nod, forcing a tired smile, and glance at my mother before packing my things. I close my laptop with a soft snap, the screen darkening as I do so. My gaze lingers on Mom's sleeping form, her chest rising and falling. Quietly, I gather my bag, my thoughts still churning with the news Greyson dropped like a bomb.

The air outside has cooled, bringing with it the scent of pine and the faintest hint of grilled meats from a nearby restaurant. I order my favorite comfort food, tacos, for pickup and begin the trek back to Mom's. For a while, I'm focused on my meal, but as I pull out of the restaurant's parking lot, my grip on the steering wheel tightens. The weight of Greyson's words lingers. *A care home?* The words feel like betrayal, even if I realize it might be necessary.

Back at the condo, I eat the tacos mechanically, barely tasting them as I replay our last conversation. The way Greyson's gaze never wavered, his earnestness… That was real, wasn't it? Shaking off the thought, I clear away my mess and continue down the hall to the guest room, which still smells faintly of Mom's lavender perfume.

I get ready for bed and settle between the sheets. My fingers brush my e-reader to life, a particularly steamy scene bookmarked and waiting. As I read, heat unfurls within me and I conjure images of Greyson's hands, his mouth electrifying my skin. A shiver runs down my spine, and I reach for the silver bullet hidden in my suitcase, a secret indulgence I packed on impulse.

Lying back against the cool sheets, I let the vibrator hum to life. With every touch, I imagine it's Greyson's tongue, wicked and insistent, tracing a path along my thighs. As the fantasy builds, another image intrudes — the way his gaze softened when he spoke about care homes, the steady resolve in his voice.

My breath catches, and the tension coiled in my body shifts, an ache blooming deep within me that isn't just physical. It's longing, yes, but also fear — fear of wanting something real, something that could break me if I let it in. Greyson said I don't have to do this alone, but letting someone help feels so vulnerable. Everything about me is raw and exposed right now.

Refocusing, I chase my release, desperate to quiet the emotions threatening to overwhelm me, but I can't quite get there, the ache remains — a reminder of everything I can't control. "God, Greyson," I whisper into the silence of the room. If he were here, he'd know exactly how to push me over the edge, how to draw out each sensation until I was a quivering mess beneath him. But would he want to? Or is his interest purely in my mother's care?

The fantasy builds, coiling tight. Just for now, I want to lose myself in the memory of us — entwined, abandoned to desire, and far away from the sterile walls of the hospital and the weight of decisions yet to be made.

I'm teetering on the edge, breaths shallow and quick as pleasure builds within me. The silver bullet's hum is a sweet promise. *I'm so close.* His dark eyes that see right into my soul...the sound he made as he climaxed... I pinch my nipple.

The sudden ring of my phone shatters the moment. I groan, snatching it with a trembling hand. I'm out of breath.

"Hello?" I gasp.

"Trinity? Did you sprint for the phone?" Greyson's voice drips with amusement, and frustration tightens my chest. My climax is sprinting away, fading into the distance.

"What do you want, Greyson?" I snap, my other hand still gripping the vibrator.

"I pulled some strings and found a bed for your mom. It's the best care facility in town," he says. "I have tomorrow off, so I can join you for a walkthrough. What time works for you?"

I hesitate, hovering in the limbo between the need simmering inside me and the cold reality of duty. I can hear the clucking sounds he's making, mocking my hesitation, questioning my self-control. With a loud sigh, I push back against my desires. "I can handle it myself."

"Thing is," he continues, "they're holding this bed specifically for me, so I need to be there."

"Fine," I relent. "Whenever you're ready in the morning."

"Great. Let's leave here at eight," Greyson replies, a hint of triumph in his tone. "It's a date." And the line goes dead before I can protest.

"Arrogant..." I mutter.

The silver bullet in my hand feels alien now, its purpose lost. I toss it aside, feeling every bit as spent as if I'd followed through. Lying back, I try to find sleep, but Greyson's image haunts me — those washboard abs, that cocky grin, the way his body once moved against mine. It's etched into my memory, a standard no one else could meet.

"Damn you, Greyson," I whisper into the dark. My eyes close, but there he is, seared onto the backs of my eyelids, an indelible mark of pleasure and torment.

Nine

Trinity

The next morning I stare at the faded lines on the parking garage floor, my mind racing with thoughts of Mom and the tour ahead when I hear footsteps approaching. I glance up to find Greyson leaning casually against my car, the sleeves of his shirt rolled up to reveal forearms I remember all too well. In each hand, he's holding a paper cup, steam curling lazily from their plastic lids.

"Hey," he says, pushing off the car with a smile that's all charm and trouble. "Didn't know what you liked, so I got a latte and an espresso. You can choose."

My hand gravitates toward the latte, fingers brushing his as I take it. The warmth seeps into my palm, comforting yet unsettling as I recall the heat of his touch. I bring the cup to my lips and find the latte is flawlessly crafted — just the way I like it. My heart skips, but I mentally scold myself. *Don't fall for this guy,*

Trinity. It's just coffee.

"Thanks," I murmur, tucking a strand of hair behind my ear. My gaze drifts past him to the parking lot beyond, where a Land Rover stands out like a relic among the sleek, modern vehicles. The SUV has seen better days, its once-khaki paint dulled by time, but there's something solid and dependable about it.

"Shall we?" he prompts, gesturing toward the Land Rover with a raised eyebrow.

"Is that yours?" I ask, unable to mask my surprise. The exhaust pipe is curiously positioned next to the windshield. It's an old design, meant for function over form. This isn't what I expected from a doctor who comes from family money.

Greyson smiles, a hint of pride in his eyes. "Yeah, she's not the latest model, but this baby can handle anything. Perfect for emergencies, especially if there's flooding, and she was fantastic in the fires last summer with all the smoke and heat. Can get to any situation, any time."

I hide a smile behind another sip of my latte. Of course, the man who lives life on the edge would choose utility over luxury. It's strangely endearing, reminding me that beneath that suave exterior lies a man dedicated to helping others, no matter the situation. *That's what brings us here today.*

"Practical," I concede, taking a final glance at the sturdy vehicle before returning my gaze to Greyson.

He waits.

"Let's go," I say, squaring my shoulders for what comes next.

The Land Rover's engine purrs as we navigate through town. We're not far from the hospital when Greyson slows, steering the vehicle toward a sight I wasn't prepared for—a grand Victorian house standing proudly on the waterfront, its yellow façade gleaming with white trim. The lawn is impeccably manicured, stretching out like green carpet.

"Wow," I murmur, my heart fluttering at the thought of

Mom here. She'd spend hours on that porch, sipping tea and gazing at the lapping water's edge. "This place is gorgeous."

Greyson doesn't respond, but I catch him watching me. He parks the Land Rover, and we step out into the fresh air. It's peaceful, tranquil—the kind of place that promises rest and care.

We enter the reception area, a warm and inviting space filled with antique furniture. Soft, classical music plays in the background.

"Greyson Paradise!" The voice cuts through the quiet ambiance, and I turn to see a tall, beautiful redhead striding toward us with open arms. Frankie Peterson, according to the nametag pinned to her blouse, beams up at Greyson. Her hair is like a flame, vibrant and full of life, and it seems to match her personality perfectly. "How have you been?" she asks him. "Penn always keeps you to himself. And your family? How are Kingston, Beckett, Ryker, and Tarryn?" she asks.

"Everyone's good," Greyson replies. His gaze shifts to me. "Frankie, this is Trinity Blaine. And Trinity, this is Frankie Peterson, fiancée to my best friend, Penn, and the executive director of Lakeview Assisted Living. As I told you, we're here to discuss Lakeview for Trinity's mother."

"Of course, of course." Frankie turns to me with a professional smile. "Welcome to Lakeview, Trinity. Let's get started with a tour, shall we?"

I nod, feeling overwhelmed. *This is happening.*

"I'll be right here when you're done," Greyson assures me. He steps back, shoving his hands into his pockets.

I nod again as Frankie leads me down the hall.

"Tell me about your mother," she prompts.

I take a deep breath. "We lost my dad right after Christmas. They'd just celebrated their thirty-fifth wedding anniversary. She was alone for the first time in her life, but she was managing."

"I'm so sorry to hear that," Frankie sympathizes.

"Before her stroke, Mom was vibrant," I continue, my

throat tightening just a bit. "Or at least I think so. I live in Vancouver, so I wasn't here to see for certain. But we spoke often on the phone, and she traveled with her best friend just a few months ago. She loved reading — was busy with a book club. She painted watercolors that could steal your breath away, and her home always smelled like cookies or fresh bread. It's..." I swallow hard. "It's tough seeing her like this."

Frankie's eyes soften, a hand reaching out to squeeze mine. "She sounds like a wonderful mother," she says, and I can only nod, fighting the prickle of tears behind my eyes.

She leads me through gleaming hallways, pointing out various features and amenities. The staff's smiles and the cozy common areas should comfort me, but the knot in my chest only tightens as we approach the memory care section.

"Here at Lakeview we have twenty-two beds," she explains as we pass a cozy common room where a few residents are gathered around a puzzle.

It looks nice, and it would just be for the care Mom needs until she can move home. She can see her condo across the lake from here. That might be good motivation.

"This is our memory care unit," Frankie says when we pause again. "Your mother will be staying in our rehab section, but should her memory deteriorate or she wanders at night, she would be moved to this part of our home," she continues. "It's designed especially for safety *and* comfort."

I hesitate at the entrance, noticing the security measures in place. "If she's moved here, she'd be locked in?" I ask. She's an adult. She doesn't need to be locked down.

Frankie hurries to reassure me. "It's not like that," she says quickly. "See, to exit, one simply has to push this button and then pull the door. It's easy for us, but for those with severe memory issues, remembering to do both can be challenging." She pauses, gauging my reaction. "It's for their safety, Trinity. To prevent wandering and ensure everyone is looked after properly."

I watch as she demonstrates, pressing the button, the door

obeying with a soft click. It looks simple enough, yet the thought that my mother would be beyond these doors, potentially struggling with such a basic task, sends a pang through my chest.

"Okay," I whisper. I wonder if it's like this at all assisted-living facilities. Safety first, even if the thought of her being confined in any way would be agonizing.

We enter, and outside each door are collages of photos and mementos with name plates. I could wander and stare at these for hours. What a wonderful gesture.

"We usually have a waiting list, but two of our patients were able to go home recently, and Greyson called in a favor. You're really lucky to have his support. You two must go way back."

Frankie and I stop to look out at the stunning gardens. A nearby window is open, and the smell is heady.

"Actually, we met a few months ago at a medical conference, and then I got a call in the middle of the night that Mom had been rushed to the hospital," I explain. "I came here from Vancouver, and Greyson was her doctor."

"You're not dating?"

I shake my head. "Noooo…" Then it dawns on me. "He doesn't do this for all his patients who needs rehab care?"

"Your mom is the first one he's ever called me about."

I feel my eyes go wide. I don't know how to respond to that.

Frankie leads me down a corridor lined with vibrant paintings, each canvas a burst of color that seems to dance in the soft lighting. We stop by a room where a handful of residents are engrossed in a pottery class. The air smells faintly of earth.

"Your mother could join classes like these," Frankie says. "Art therapy is wonderful for stimulating the mind."

I nod, imagining my mother rediscovering her love for watercolors among new friends. It's a comforting thought.

We end the tour outside, in the lush garden that seems more fitting for a grand estate than an assisted-living facility.

Roses bloom in wild abundance, and the gentle sound of a fountain provides a serene soundtrack to the beauty around us. "It's stunning," I admit.

"Isn't it?" Frankie agrees. "A perfect place for reflection and peace."

The practical side of me resurfaces, and I clear my throat. "How much does all this cost?"

"During rehab, everything is covered by provincial healthcare," she explains, and relief washes over me. "Should your mother stay beyond the twelve weeks the government pays, we charge half of her monthly pension, and the province takes care of the rest."

"Thank you," I say, truly grateful. My worry about finances has been a constant weight, and this news lightens it considerably.

We return to the reception area, and Greyson is leaning against the counter. He straightens when he sees me.

"So? What do you think?" he asks.

"This seems like a great place," I respond, emotions catching in my throat.

"Good." He smiles.

Frankie reappears then, a tablet in hand, and suggests I take a seat to fill out the forms. She and Greyson strike up a conversation, and their laughter drifts toward me, light and easy, as a knot tightens in my stomach. I hear wedding talk, and she's trying to schedule a fitting for Greyson.

Suddenly my overwhelm returns. *I'm not ready to make a decision this minute. This place seems nice, but what are my options?*

I consider asking questions, but instead, I type my mother's information into the tablet, trying to focus on the task at hand. Their flirtatious tones tug at me, irking me more than I want to admit. I remind myself Frankie is engaged to Greyson's friend, but it doesn't soothe the irritation.

This is moving too fast.

"Will next Saturday work for you?" Frankie asks Greyson.

"Saturday's perfect," he confirms. "And thank you again for making a space for Joy Blaine."

My stylus pauses mid-signature. They're taking for granted that I'm doing this.

"Trinity?" Frankie prompts.

"Sorry," I mumble. "Just thinking." I finish digitally signing the documents and rise to return the tablet to Frankie.

"I'm sorry the intake paperwork is so fierce," she says.

"She likes paperwork," Greyson teases.

"No one likes all the monotonous paperwork. It just has to be done." Frankie rolls her eyes at Greyson before smiling at me. I'm grateful for someone who understands the value.

"Thanks," I say, gathering the paper copies of the document I've just signed. "I appreciate everything. And I, uh, I guess I'll let you know?"

I look toward the exit, eager to escape the tangle of feelings I've been forced to confront today. Greyson catches my eye, a question lurking in his gaze. But I can't decipher that now, not with the unease of making such a large decision so quickly.

"I'm not sure when she'll be released," I say, uncertainty swirling within me.

"Don't worry. The bed will be ready for Joy whenever she needs it," Frankie assures me.

"Thank you," I murmur.

We step back out onto the porch of Lakeview Assisted Living, and Greyson guides me back to his Land Rover. As we settle inside, the scent of leather mixed with his cologne floods the air around me, a distraction I don't need right now.

"Nice place," he comments, starting the engine.

"Yep," is all I manage, looking out the window. Does he think this is a done deal? He just took over, practically made the decision for me. How does he not see that?

"Where to?" he asks.

"Home."

Greyson takes us back toward the condo building as the

minutes tick by. He hasn't said much since we left Lakeview, but his silence isn't comforting. It's like a pressure building, waiting to crack wide open. And I don't know how much longer I can keep my mouth shut.

He glances at me as he drives, his hands relaxed on the steering wheel. "So," he says finally, his voice careful. "What did you think?"

"What did I think?" I echo. I turn in my seat to face him, my arms crossed tightly. "I think I walked into that place completely unprepared. I think I stood there nodding while you had everything figured out for me. I think I didn't get a say in where my mother is going to live. Everyone seems to think the decision has been made."

His jaw tightens, but he keeps his eyes on the road. "That's not true. I wasn't trying to cut you out. I was trying to help."

"Help?" I say, my voice rising. "You call this help? You made all the arrangements, Greyson. You got her bumped to the top of the list. You walked me through like all I had to do was sign the damn paperwork. You didn't even ask me if this is what I wanted or if this was the right fit for my mom."

His hands grip the wheel a little tighter, his knuckles paling. "You said you didn't know where to start. I was trying to make things easier for you."

"Easier for me? Or easier for you?"

He glances at me, his eyes dark with frustration. "What's that supposed to mean?"

"It means you swoop in and take over because you think you always know what's best. This isn't about you, Greyson. This is about my mom."

"I know that," he snaps, his voice sharp now. "But she needs care, Trinity. Lakeview is the best option. I wanted to make sure you didn't waste time on places that couldn't give her what she needs."

"But how do I know that's the right place?" I fire back. "How do I know what's best for her if I haven't even seen anywhere else? You didn't give me a choice. You made the decision for me."

He pulls the car onto the shoulder, the tires crunching against gravel as he shifts into park. He turns to face me fully, his expression hard but not unkind. "I wasn't making a decision for you," he says evenly. "I was giving you an option. One I thought would be the best for her and for you."

"And what if it's not?" I ask, my voice trembling. "What if I don't feel ready to make this decision? What if I'm not ready to accept that she might never come home?"

His expression softens, but the tension doesn't leave his shoulders. "You think I don't get that?" he asks. "I know this isn't easy, Trinity. You don't live here, and rather than you having to spend a week walking in and out of a dozen different assisted-living locations, I saw a way to get you a spot at one of the few places I'd send my own parents. I was trying to take some of the weight off your shoulders."

"And instead, you made me feel like I don't have a say," I whisper. "Like this isn't my decision to make."

For a moment, neither of us speaks. I look away, my gaze fixed on the horizon, where the sun reveals all the various colors of green that paint the hills around town. "I know you're trying to help," I say finally, my voice quieter now. "But you don't get to decide what's right for me. Or for her."

He exhales slowly, his hands loosening on the wheel. "You're right," he says after a long pause. "I should've talked to you first. I just… I didn't want to see you struggling anymore."

I glance at him, his shoulders slightly hunched, his eyes softer than before. For the first time, I see it, the fear behind his actions, the way he's trying so hard to fix things because he doesn't know how else to help.

"I'm not asking you to fix this, Greyson," I say, my voice steady now. "I need you to let me figure it out in my own way. Even if that means making mistakes."

He nods slowly, his gaze meeting mine. "Okay," he says

quietly. "I'll back off. But if you need me...I'm here."

His sincerity makes my chest ache, and for a moment, I can't speak. I nod, turning again to the window as he pulls back onto the road. The tension lingers, but something else settles between us too, something softer, quieter.

A few minutes later, we're back at the condo building. Once he parks, we exit and walk to the elevator, still in silence. It quickly dings its arrival, and the doors slide open with a smooth whisper. I reach for my fob, but before it can graze the sensor, Greyson spins me to face him, his hands framing my cheeks. His kiss is sudden and ferocious, claiming me, demanding every ounce of attention I have. The soft moan that escapes me is drowned by the intensity of his lips moving against mine, igniting a wildfire that races through my veins.

As quickly as it began, the kiss ends, leaving me breathless and burning. "No. Stop." I wipe my mouth with the back of my hand. "I hate you."

"You didn't kiss me like you hate me."

I need to get out of this tiny space.

"Do you even know why you hate me?"

"Yes! You insulted my work in front of thousands of people. You don't respect what I do."

"I—I what?" He studies me a moment and I can almost see the pieces clicking into place. "I didn't insult your work. I insulted the work the province requires. The government. Not you. You're doing your job. And by the way, I got a lot of grief from my own admin team for not admitting how instrumental they were in changing the paperwork so it would still meet provincial requirements."

"I'm still mad at you." There's no anger in my voice.

"Then I'll keep kissing you until that's gone."

He leans in to kiss me, and I give myself freely to him.

The elevator doors glide open at his condo, and without breaking eye contact, he pulls me into his home by the hand, leading me with an urgency that matches the pounding of my heart.

"Strip," he commands.

For a moment, I hesitate, caught between defiance and desire. Then the memory of our night together in Victoria floods back — the heat, the connection, the escape it provided. Maybe this isn't just about following orders. Maybe this is what I need too. I hesitate, a storm of emotions inside me. This isn't just lust. It never has been. With Greyson, it's more complicated, more dangerous.

But the way he's looking at me now makes me want to forget all the reasons I shouldn't. I unbutton my blouse, each movement deliberate, until the fabric slips from my shoulders and falls to the floor. Greyson's sharp intake of breath tells me he feels it too, This is more than just desire. This is surrender.

Ten

Trinity

I stand naked before him, the air prickling against my skin as Greyson circles me like a predator assessing its prey.

"Stand behind the couch and bend over," he commands, his voice a low rumble.

For a moment, I hesitate, the weight of his order pressing against the boundaries I usually maintain. But something in his voice makes me move. My heart races as I step into place, anticipation coursing through me.

There's something undeniably thrilling about this man taking charge. As I lean forward, resting my palms on the leather surface, he traces a path down my back, over my curves, lingering on my ass before slipping lower. A shiver runs through me as his fingers probe between my legs, finding me wet and ready.

He whispers, his breath hot against my ear, "You're very turned on."

A small nod is all I can muster.

"Trinity," he begins, "you left my hotel room without permission last time." He pauses. "Did we do something that upset you?"

"No," I breathe, the truth of it simple and clear. I liked it too much, and I couldn't tell him that.

Without warning, a sharp pinch to my nipple jolts me from my thoughts. His words follow. "I'm going to spank you for being so naughty." But then he adds, "If it becomes too much, just tell me, and I'll stop."

I nod again, granting permission and accepting the punishment. Then comes the first slap, a nice, hard smack against my ass cheek. I gasp at the sensation, a mix of pain and pleasure that throbs through me. Greyson's touch is quick to soothe, caressing away the burn.

One, two, three more spanks land across my flesh, alternating sides, each one sending waves of both agony and ecstasy crashing through me. My groans fill the room as he slides two fingers inside me once more, stretching, filling me.

"See? I know how much you like this," Greyson says, reading my body like an open book, every reaction laid bare for him to interpret. And he's right, I do. Every part of me is screaming for release, begging for the sweet climax I know he can give.

But I also know it's not mine to take, not until he decides I've earned it.

My breath hitches as he stretches me farther with a third finger, his free hand finding my clit. His fingers dance inside me while his thumb circles in a rhythm that sends shockwaves through my core. I'm teetering on the edge of something explosive, but just as I'm about to tumble over the precipice, he stops.

"Naughty girls can only come when they're given

permission," he reminds me. His words send a jolt through me, but it's more than just desire. It's the intoxicating mix of trust and surrender, of letting someone else take the reins for once.

I hate how much I crave it. How much I crave him. Because needing anyone has always felt dangerous, like stepping onto a bridge you're not sure will hold. And yet, here I am, giving him control, as if it's the most natural thing in the world.

A whimper escapes my lips, and I turn to look at him, a silent plea in my eyes, but Greyson is unyielding.

"Get on your knees," he commands, and I descend to the floor. The sound of his zipper reverberates, and when his cock springs forward, my body responds with an instinctive hunger. "You're going to suck my cock," he tells me, and my nipples pebble against the cool air.

I envelop him, taking him deep, and I feel him at the back of my throat.

"Damn you look hot with my cock down your throat," he murmurs. "Now look at me. Show me how much you love my cock."

Lifting my gaze, I lock eyes with Greyson, setting a brisk pace as I worship him with lips and tongue. My hand wraps around the base, stroking in time with the movements of my mouth, while my other hand sneaks down to play with my clit, desperate for some relief.

I'm so close, hovering on the brink of ecstasy, when Greyson captures my wrist, pulling it away from my center. "You don't have permission to come yet," he says gruffly.

Denied once more, I focus all my attention on pleasuring him, determined to earn the release held just out of reach. He pulls his cock from my mouth with a loud pop.

"Stand up," Greyson orders, a hint of satisfaction in his voice as he steps back. I rise to my feet, shaky and flushed with arousal. He takes my hand, leading me down the dimly lit hallway to his bedroom.

"Get on all fours," he instructs.

I position myself obediently, facing the large mirror that dominates the room. In it, I see both of us—my anticipation evident in every line of my body, his dominant presence looming behind me. This reminds me of our first time together. He strips down, each article of clothing sliding from his body as a promise of what's to come.

There's a glint in the mirror on his right nipple. *Is that a piercing? How did I miss that last time?*

Greyson grabs a handful of condoms from the nightstand and unwraps one. The sight of him rolling it onto his impressive length sends a surge of pleasure through me, and before I can stifle it, a small climax shudders through my body.

"Did you just orgasm?" Greyson's brow arches in the reflection.

I nod, breathless. "I couldn't help myself."

He shakes his head, not with disappointment but with a restrained hunger that makes my core clench. Greyson positions himself behind me, and as he pushes in deep, the sensation is overwhelming—so big, so full—I feel him against my cervix, and I have to bite my lip to keep from crying out.

"Remember, no orgasm without my permission," he reminds. But then he adds again, "Tell me if it becomes too much."

I don't want less. I crave more, every thrust, every nuance of pleasure. I watch him move, powerful muscles flexing with every pivot, and the reflection in the mirror only amplifies the intensity. My need coils tight. "Harder," I groan.

"You're so fucking beautiful as you unravel."

He jackhammers in and out as my eyes track every move.

"Touch yourself," he urges, and my fingers dart down to my clit, circling with desperate urgency. I'm so close now, teetering on the edge of oblivion, when suddenly his thumb presses against my asshole. A shockwave of sensation blots out everything else. All I see is white, pure and blinding.

"I'm going to come," I announce.

He thrusts even faster.

The climax hits like a storm, fierce and all-consuming. My entire body seizes, and I am suspended in time, freefalling over the precipice into a sea of ecstasy. I hear my own release as if from a distance, a keening cry that echoes in the room.

"Trinity," Greyson groans as my pussy clenches around him, milking him for all he's worth. For a moment, we are nothing but sensation and desire, two beings fused by the most primal of connections.

I collapse onto the bed, my limbs splayed in sweet exhaustion, breathless from the storm of sensation that just ravaged through me. Greyson's name pulses in my veins like a sacred mantra. After a moment, he strides to the bathroom, leaving me in silence.

When he returns, there's a tenderness in his eyes. A warm washcloth glides over my skin, soothing and intimate, erasing the remnants of our fervor. He cleans me with careful precision, his touch gentle in a way that feels almost foreign after the intensity of what just happened. And yet, even as I find comfort in his care, a quiet voice whispers in the back of my mind. *What happens when this tenderness is gone? When this version of him, soft and steady, gives way to the man who always has to be in control? Not just in the bedroom, but in life…*

I push the thought away, burying it beneath the warmth of his embrace. Yet the question lingers, unresolved.

He pulls me close, his arms holding me tightly against his chest. His heartbeat is a steady drum, grounding me as I try to regain my sense of self after being so thoroughly undone.

"I should get going," I murmur. "Need to see my mom and check in." It's a feeble attempt at responsibility, but even as I say it, I long to remain ensconced in this cocoon of warmth.

Greyson's grip tightens infinitesimally, his body pressed flush against mine. "Not yet," he commands. "You will stay right where you are." There's no room for argument in his tone, and honestly, I don't want to anyway.

Just for now, I tell myself. Because reality can wait a little longer.

Eleven

Greyson

Later that afternoon, I lean against the cold granite of my kitchen counter, a half-hearted attempt at making coffee abandoned, the mug I'd set out for Trinity still empty. She's gone to see her mom in the hospital, she said. It's well past three, and I know she hasn't been there yet today. The thought twists in my gut. I should have insisted on feeding her before she left—a decent meal after all our exercise.

I made her promise to come back after visiting hours. *Why?* I scrub a hand over my face, the prickle of stubble a reminder of this morning's haste. I had it all planned—get her out of my system with one more go. *Damn it, that wasn't enough.* Not even close. There's something about her that lingers. She's sharp, independent, and infuriating in all the best ways.

It's not just her body I crave. It's the way she makes me feel, unsettled, like I'm playing a game where she knows the rules and I don't. I've never let anyone get under my skin like this, and it both terrifies and thrills me.

My mind wanders to earlier—the way her eyes clouded over with surrender when I took control. As someone who's built her life on self-reliance, the relief in letting go seemed to wash over her, soften her. I need to see that look again, find that crack in her armor.

I'm not used to this—wanting seconds. And thirds. But I want more from her, more *of* her. I push away from the counter to pace the length of the room. Rational thoughts try to claw their way in. Once her mom is settled, Trinity will return to Vancouver. But this could be a once-a-year thing, when she comes down to Paradise to visit. *Yeah, that could work.*

But deep down, I know it's a lie. Despite my current predicament, I don't do repeats, annual or otherwise. I tried it once when my previous relationship fell apart a few years back, but it soon lost its luster. I didn't see the point of living in limbo. Better to keep things uncomplicated.

I can't spend the rest of the day mooning about. So I shower and dress quickly in a pair of dark jeans and a crisp white shirt. Then I'm out the door with an urgency that's not entirely born from concern for the winery. Trinity's image still lingers in the back of my mind persistent and distracting.

The drive up to Paradise Hill Family Estate Winery is short but gives me enough time to shift gears mentally. By the time I park and stride into the cool dimness of the barrel room, business is all that occupies my thoughts. The scent of oak and fermenting grapes is a familiar comfort as I spot Tarryn deep in conversation with Elsie. She seems upset.

"Hey," I call, my voice echoing among the rows of huge steel vats.

Tarryn turns. "Greyson? What are you doing here?"

"Can't stay away from the family business too long," I say with a grin. "What's going on?"

She exchanges a glance with Elsie, who looks equally troubled. Elsie steps forward, her hands clasped tightly together.

"We've got trouble. One of the chardonnay vats has been tampered with. We think it's sabotage."

The word hits me like a punch. Paradise Hill Chardonnay is a well-loved label and a major moneymaker for us. A ruined batch could mean thousands of dollars in losses.

"Are you sure?" I ask, my stomach knotting.

Elsie nods. "Absolutely. Everything was on track until two weeks ago. Now the pH balance is all wrong. It's turning to vinegar."

I search the room around us. "Is this the only one?"

"Thankfully," Tarryn replies.

"Damn," I mutter. I trust Elsie's expertise implicitly. Only her father, our vintner, knows wine better. If she says something's off, then it's off.

"Who could be behind this?"

Tarryn shakes her head. "There have a been a few other minor incidents. Dad and I have been talking about cameras. Maybe he'll finally agree."

"Maybe," I concede. "We'll get to the bottom of this." My mind races ahead, plotting, planning. This is more than just a spoiled batch of wine. It's a threat to our family legacy, and I'll be damned if I let it slide.

"Let's gather everyone and figure out our next steps," I suggest. I need to shake off the restlessness that's been plaguing me since Trinity left earlier, and throwing myself into the winery's troubles is just the distraction I need.

For now, at least.

I wrap my arm around Tarryn's shoulder as her tears threaten to spill. I can feel her trembling. "Hey," I murmur, holding her close. "This isn't on you."

"Greyson, Dad's going to freak out when I tell him," she whispers.

"Maybe not," I counter. "What if we pivot? Could we make this a…unique batch of chardonnay vinegar instead?" My chemistry knowledge might be rusty, but desperation breeds creativity.

Elsie, who has been quietly analyzing charts and data, looks up. "We discussed it," she says, brushing a strand of hair behind her ear. "We'd have to outsource the bottling since our lines are not configured to take anything other than our wine bottles. It could work, but I need to confirm what was added to the vat before we commit to anything."

"Get it to the lab, then. The sooner, the better."

"Can you grab your father and meet us at Dad's office, Elsie? We need to strategize our next steps," Tarryn says.

She's recovering from the disappointment. That's good.

"Of course," Elsie agrees. She walks out with the walkie-talkie on her hip as she calls for her father.

With Elsie dispatched, I turn back to my sister, catching the fresh sheen of tears in her eyes. "Talk to me. How's everything else going?"

She lets out a shaky breath. "I'm fighting battles on too many fronts. Vendors are challenging me, pushing for Dad because they don't like my answers. Sometimes..." She swallows hard. "Sometimes I wish he'd just tell them they have to deal with me, not run to him."

"Would it help if I had a word with Dad? A subtle nudge to show more public support?" I offer.

Her eyes find mine. "Maybe? I don't know."

"You're doing great. Dad knows it, too. He just needs to show it." I squeeze her hand.

"I'm okay if you can't talk to him," she says, but I hear the unspoken plea. She needs this win.

"Let's worry about that later," I say, giving her another hug. "Right now, we've got vinegar to make—or at least to consider."

"Thanks for being the awesome big brother you are," she murmurs, and I feel a swell of protectiveness.

"Always." I straighten my shoulders. Tarryn doesn't need to carry this alone. My brothers and I may not be working in the day-to-day of the vineyard, but it's ours too.

We converge in Dad's office, Mitch and Elsie in tow. The door swings open to reveal Dad behind his desk, his expression a mix of curiosity and concern. "Why the party?" he asks.

"Someone's sabotaged vat three — a chardonnay," Tarryn reports, her voice steady.

Dad's eyes narrow, a silent request for more information. "Are you sure?" His question is directed at Tarryn, but it's Elsie who steps forward.

"Positive. The pH has dropped from three-point-four to two-point-seven since last week."

"Damn Dempseys," Dad mutters, shooting a glance at Mitch. "They just bought that plot in Appleton for their own chardonnay vines. Can't be a coincidence."

I feel a flicker of anger at the thought of sabotage, and my fists clench. Then the strategizing begins, a torrent of ideas on salvaging what can be saved from the vat, if anything at all.

As they delve into discussions, I scan the room. Determination lights up Tarryn's eyes now, replacing the earlier uncertainty. With Elsie's support and Dad's seasoned input, they've got this handled. It's clear my presence isn't necessary.

"All right, I'll leave you to it," I say, offering a reassuring nod to Tarryn before slipping out the door. There's an unspoken promise in our exchange. I'll handle Dad later and give Tarryn the backup she deserves.

The late-afternoon sun kisses my skin as I step outside. I love spring when our days begin to get longer and the air is filled with the sweet floral fragrance of grape flowers in bloom, my favorite scent in the entire world. Though Trinity is quickly becoming my second. As I leave the winery, my thoughts drift back to her. The day's chaos — the sabotage, the tension in Tarryn's voice — now feels lighter as I anticipate seeing Trinity again.

By the time I reach the butcher shop, my focus has shifted entirely. Tonight isn't going to be about the vineyard or the

Dempsey family. It's about Trinity and cooking her a dinner she won't forget.

The bell over the door jingles as I enter. "Hey, Greyson! How are things going?" Jim, the butcher, asks immediately.

I offer him a wave. "Not bad. I can't complain."

"What are you in the mood for?" He steps behind the cooler full of various fresh meats.

"I'll take your best lamb chops and whatever side dishes you've got prepared," I respond, and a smile tugs at my lips.

"Got a special night planned?" Jim teases.

"Something like that," I reply, keeping the details to myself.

Jim wraps my order, and his chuckle follows me as I exit. Jim went to school with my older brother, and the butcher shop is a hub of gossip, so I'm not about to tip my secrets to him. Plus, this is only going to last a few weeks at most. Trinity doesn't even live here.

But none of that matters now. Tonight I'm ready to craft a meal worthy of the woman who's managed to captivate me, twice.

An hour later, back at my place, "Greyson's Grille" is in full swing. The kitchen is my domain, where every spice and utensil knows its place. The hockey game plays low on TSN, background noise to my culinary performance. I glance at the screen just as my phone buzzes on the marble countertop.

Trinity: I'm just stopping at my mom's place to clean up a bit. I can't wait to taste what you're cooking.
She punctuated with a winking emoji.

Trinity: What can I bring? Wine? Dessert?

I find myself grinning like an idiot. It's unlike me, but then again, so is wanting someone more than once. With Trinity, it seems, the rules are different. My thumbs dance across the screen.

Me: Nothing you need to bring but yourself...and leave the panties at home.

A bold move, but if there's one thing I've learned about Trinity, she doesn't shy away from boldness.

Her reply comes quickly, charged with that same electric playfulness that drew me to her back at MedTalks.

Trinity: Might need to use my silver bullet to take the edge off.

I shake my head, amazed. She says exactly the right thing.

Me: Bring the silver bullet with you.
I add a devilish smirk emoji.

It's a suggestive dance we're in, two steps forward, no steps back. There's a part of me that wonders what happens when we reach the edge? The push and pull between control and surrender, the way she looked up at me, eyes dark with trust and something wild. It was raw, intimate, and it's left a craving in me that goes beyond physical. It's a challenge, a connection. I want to unravel the enigma that is Trinity, layer by layer. *Am I ready for that?* The thought lingers as I shift my attention to the lamb chops sizzling in the pan.

Whatever the evening holds, first I'll feed her, show her a side of Greyson Paradise that isn't just about dominance and desire. Tonight, I'll offer nourishment for the body, and perhaps, if she's willing, for the soul too.

The rich aroma of a well-aged cabernet wafts up from the decanter. I've chosen one of our best bottles, one that promises layers of flavor to complement the meal I've prepared. I adjust the table setting one last time, ensuring everything is in its perfect place.

My phone buzzes, her text lighting up the screen.

Trinity: At the elevator now.

The anticipation zings through me, and I pocket my phone as I head to the elevator doors, making the short journey to greet her.

The elevator dings its arrival, and the doors slide open. There she stands, radiance personified, her sundress hugging her waist, the full skirt swaying gently, teasing me with its every movement. Her eyes meet mine, sparkling with mischief, and then drift downward, prompting a flush of heat to course through me. "Down boy," she teases, her laughter like music to my ears.

"Hard not to stand at attention when you look like that," I reply as I gesture for her to step out of the elevator.

Trinity enters, clutching a bag against her side. Curiosity piqued, I nod toward it. "That your infamous silver bullet?"

"Among other things," she grins, revealing the can of whipped cream and caramel sauce nestled beside it. "Thought we could indulge in some creativity."

"Maybe dinner should wait," I suggest. The idea of exploring every inch of her with those sweet and sticky additions stirs something primal within me.

She shakes her head, firm yet still flirtatious. "That's dessert, Greyson. Patience."

"Fine by me," I concede, unable to mask the eagerness in my tone. "But I also have something I want to talk to you about a little later, an idea that's been brewing since you left this morning."

Her curious gaze locks with mine, and I recognize the spark of intrigue. It's an opening, a chance to delve deeper than before, beyond the rawness of our physical connection. And I'm intent on seizing it.

Twelve

Trinity

I watch closely, marveling at Greyson's cooking abilities as he takes six small lamb chops out of their marinade, stirs garlic mashed potatoes, and checks some kind of vegetables that are being roasted. "I'm impressed."

He smiles. "I spent a lot of time when I was growing up in the kitchen at the vineyard's Paradise Grill. But here I can't take credit for anything other than the lamb chops. I went to the meat market and bought the mashed potatoes, roasted vegetables, and crème brulée for dessert.

"I'm even more impressed that you're honest about that." I grin at him.

"I wouldn't want you to think I'm perfect at everything. I mean, we know I'm smart, a fantastic lover—"

I laugh. "You have a giant ego."

"See? I'm not perfect."

"And the jury's still out on the lover thing. Don't get me wrong, but it could be beginner's luck that you did so well the first couple times. And that third time was a tossup." I grin so he knows I'm teasing.

He shrugs casually. "I'm up for proving it over and over again."

Feeling myself blush, I step away from the counter to admire the panoramic view through the floor-to-ceiling windows. It steals my breath. Black Bear Lake lies tranquil, its surface a glassy mirror reflecting the fiery hues of the setting sun. The Paradise suspension bridge arches gracefully over the water, an elegant silhouette against the crimson sky. On the lake, boats glide by, trailing water skiers and jet skis that dance on the waves like sprites at play.

"Wow," I murmur.

Greyson glances over. "It never gets old," he says.

With a nod, I turn back to the interior of his industrial chic space. Exposed-brick walls juxtapose with warm wood floors. It's spacious, a testament to success and style, yet it's the outdoors that truly captivates. Beyond the windows in the other direction I can see that half of the roof has been transformed into a park perched high above the world.

My surprise must be evident because Greyson chuckles softly. "Didn't expect a small park on the fifth floor of the building?"

Shaking my head, I follow him out to where he's fired up the grill on the terrace. "How long have you had this place?" I ask.

"About three years now," he replies, placing the chops on the grill.

"That's around the same time my parents moved in. They were one of the first to take residence once the building was finished."

"Really? So was I."

I'm intrigued by this connection. "What made you decide

to live here?"

"My buddy from school was the developer for this building," he says, a wistful note in his tone as he watches the flames lick the meat. "I needed to leave the guest house on the family vineyard. I wanted to give myself some distance so my father wouldn't convince himself I went to medical school just to help run the vineyard."

"Practicality meets opportunity," I muse aloud, leaning against the railing.

"Indeed," he agrees, offering me a sly smile. "I have a cab that's probably breathed enough to drink, or I have a full bar."

"The cab sounds good," I say.

He springs into action to fill me a glass, and I follow him back inside.

"This is my favorite," he says as he offers it to me.

I perch on a high stool at Greyson's kitchen island and take an experimental sip.

"What do you think?" he calls as he returns outside to plate the lamb chops. When he brings them in, the scent wafts toward me, rich and savory, making my mouth water.

"It's fantastic," I tell him, raising my glass in salute.

We move over to the table, and he brings out the potatoes and vegetables. Everything looks so beautiful, and the breeze blows gently from outside. I'm glad someone cooks in this situation because it's definitely not me.

We take our seats and toast to this bounty of food, and then Greyson urges me to dig in. "So, Trinity, tell me about your life in Vancouver," he says after his first bite. "Where do you live?"

"North Van," I reply, letting the familiarity of home wash over me for a moment. "Not too far from the hospital. On clear days, I walk to work. It's nice, the way the morning air feels…brisk."

He nods. "I went to medical school in Vancouver. North Van is a pretty hip spot. What do you do for fun?"

I take a bite of the perfectly seared lamb before answering. "Fun? Well, I'm not exactly the life of the party. Dinner with friends, movies now and then. Occasionally we hit a club, but mostly, I'm focused on work." I shrug, feeling suddenly dull.

"Work can be fulfilling. What drew you to hospital administration?" Greyson leans his elbow on the table.

"Initially, I wanted to be a doctor." I twirl the stem of my wine glass. "But then I studied biology at McGill in Montreal and realized med school wasn't for me. Nor was pharmaceutical sales." A chuckle escapes me as I remember those days of uncertainty. "I didn't know what to do with my biology degree, so I took a job at a hospital, just to get by, you know? Turned out, I loved it. Went on to get my MBA at UBC part-time while I was working. Now, I'm overseeing the implementation of province-wide electronic medical records."

"Quite the journey," he comments with an approving nod.

Our easy conversation continues, laughter mingling with the clinking of cutlery. He tells me some wild tales from the ED and paints a picture of life here in Paradise. As dinner winds down, Greyson's gaze lingers on me, warm and inviting. "How long do you think you'll be staying in Paradise?" he asks.

I lean back, considering. "Hard to say. I need to get my mom settled. She's only going into assisted living temporarily. At least that's my hope. So I want to stay close." I glance at him, trying to read his thoughts. "For now, I can manage my job remotely. We're almost through the toughest part of the project I'm working on."

"Sounds like a lot to balance," he says.

"It is," I admit, grateful for his empathy. To think it's been in there all this time, despite his anti-admin exterior. "I'll have to go back to Vancouver for the next rollout. I'm not sure for how long. Maybe a few weeks, maybe longer. Depends on how things unfold with Mom."

"Here's hoping for smooth sailing, then," he toasts, our glasses meeting with a soft chime.

"Cheers to that," I echo, savoring the taste of the wine and the company.

Greyson reaches out, his fingertips grazing mine, sending a charge through my skin. "Did you enjoy our time together earlier?" he asks, his voice low and husky. "What did you say it was? A tossup?"

My lips curl into a smile. "Judging by the fact that I'm not wearing panties and brought along my silver bullet..." I lean in just enough to keep it intimate. "I'd say I enjoyed myself immensely."

His grin widens. "It seems we have a lot in common," he muses. "Here's what I wanted to ask you about. Given that your stay here isn't permanent, would you be interested in seeing each other regularly while you're in town?"

The proposition thrills me. It's just sex — exciting, uncomplicated, and exactly what I need right now. I nod. "Are you okay with casual monogamy?"

He nods. "That's what I was thinking." He pauses, his gaze appraising. "I don't want to lead you on. I don't do long-distance relationships, and I'm not leaving Paradise."

I appreciate his candor. "No commitment, no love, the occasional date, and this lasts until I return to Vancouver or we decide we're done?"

He smiles wide. "Yes. Great. We're on the same page. Is there anything you don't like?"

"Everything we've done so far has been...to my liking," I reply.

Satisfied, he stands, walks over to my bag, and retrieves the small vibrator.

"Show me how you use this," he commands gently, taking my hand.

My heart pounds in my chest as I rise. I've never performed for a man. But I suppose Greyson has seen all my crazy sex faces, so there isn't much more that can embarrass me. With a surge of daring, I decide to embrace the moment, to throw caution to the wind.

"All right," I say, my voice tinged with a nervous excitement. I take the vibrator from him. "Right here next to the porch?"

He looks around, and across the patio, we can see someone in the next building. "Maybe we take this back to my bedroom. In there, we can see out, but they can't see in."

My nipples pebble with anticipation as I follow him down the hall. In the bedroom, I perch on the edge of the bed, my heart racing as Greyson settles into a chair opposite me. I lift one leg onto the mattress, my knee bent, and lie back as I open myself to him—literally and figuratively. With deliberate slowness, I raise the hem of my sundress, revealing the slick heat of my arousal. A part of me balks at the vulnerability of this moment, the way I'm laying myself bare—not just physically, but emotionally. Trust doesn't come easily to me, yet here I am, surrendering to his gaze, his presence, his request.

What scares me isn't the act itself. It's how much I want this. How much I want *him*. Wanting means risking, and risking means I could lose it all. Even with these guidelines we've agreed to, this is uncharted territory for me.

Greyson's sharp intake of breath is audible, a sound that sends a thrill spiraling through me. My fingers trace the dampness at my core, a gentle exploration that has me biting my lip to stifle a whimper. I watch him, noting the unmistakable bulge rising in his pants, and it fuels my courage. *It's just sex*, I remind myself. An indulgence between two consenting adults who happen to share a voracious appetite for pleasure.

The metallic chill of the bullet in my hand contrasts with the warmth pulsing from within as I switch it on. I run it across the fabric covering my breasts, watching as my nipples respond, puckering into tight buds. I close my eyes, allowing myself a moment of pure sensation, letting the vibration awaken every nerve ending it touches.

A soft moan escapes me as I guide the bullet downward,

over my stomach, and then to the center of my need. The sensation is electric, a direct current straight to my pleasure centers. My body moves instinctively, hips tilting to meet the persistent buzz. *This is for me*, I think, even as I feel his gaze like a caress, hot and heavy, upon my skin.

My eyelids flutter open, and there he is — Greyson, bold and unashamed, his hand wrapped around his impressive length. He strokes himself in a rhythm that mirrors the pulse of my own desires, watching me intently. The sight sends a jolt of heat through me. "Do you like what you see?"

"Very much," he replies. "Don't stop."

Emboldened by his words, I guide the silver bullet inside myself, where the slickness of my arousal makes it easy to slide deep. I move it in and out, setting a slow, deliberate pace that soon has me groaning with pleasure. I slip the strap of my dress off my shoulder, exposing more skin, and my fingers twist and pull at my nipple.

Our eyes lock, and his gaze amplifies each sensation, making my body sing with every touch. Then, craving more, I reach for the caramel in the bag he's brought along with us to the bedroom. I drizzle the sticky sweetness over my breasts, watching as it trails down my skin.

"Would you mind licking the caramel off?" I challenge.

Without a word, Greyson drops to his knees between my legs, his eyes blazing with a hunger that matches my own. His mouth closes over one caramel-drenched nipple, and he sucks hard, drawing a sharp gasp from me. I arch into him, wanting, needing more, the silver bullet forgotten.

And he obliges, his tongue leaving a warm, wet path down my belly until he reaches my clit. There, he feasts with an intensity that sends me spiraling toward climax. My fingers grip the sheets, my back arches, and I'm lost in the sensations, crying out as waves of pleasure crash over me. In this moment, with Greyson's name on my lips, I'm consumed by a bliss that obliterates everything else. It's just us, the connection, the intimacy, and this shared dance of desire. Panting, I catch my breath and feel the sweet aftershocks of pleasure ripple through me.

Greyson's voice pulls me from my daze. "Turn around," he instructs. I swivel to face the full-length mirror that reflects our tangled forms, my skin still glistening with the remnants of fevered passion.

As he rolls on a condom, he mutters, "We need to talk about this, condoms…"

I watch him in the mirror. "I'm clean," I assure him, catching my flushed cheeks in the reflection. "And I'm on birth control too."

Without another word, he aligns himself behind me, and I brace against the force as he enters. A deep groan escapes my lips as I feel impossibly full, his presence engulfing me from the inside out. In the mirror, I watch him move — a powerful, rhythmic dance that has my breasts swaying with his every thrust. His hands weave into my hair, pulling slightly, tilting my head back to meet his gaze in the glass. The intensity in his eyes sends a thrill down my spine, amplifying the delirious sensation of being utterly possessed by this man.

His hand snakes around me, fingers finding my tender clit, and he pinches with a precision that catapults me over the edge. My second climax crashes over me, fierce and blinding, and I cry out, gripping the edges of the bed. As if my release triggers his own, Greyson follows, his body tensing as he spills himself into me with a series of guttural groans.

Afterward, we collapse on the bed, a tangle of exhausted limbs. Greyson's chest rises and falls, his arm draped around my waist. "Your birth control — what are you on?" he asks after a moment.

"The shot," I reply, tracing idle patterns on his forearm.

"I've never gone without a condom before," he admits after a moment, almost to himself. "But with you…I want everything." He pauses, his fingers trailing lightly over my side.

"It's strange how easy it feels. But easy doesn't mean simple. I don't do this—let people in. Not since..." He trails off, shaking his head as if to banish the thought.

His vulnerability hits me like a lightning bolt. It's not just his words; it's the way he says them, like he's balancing on the edge of something.

"Me too," I breathe.

I wait for his reply, but instead, as if the night's escapades have sapped all his energy, Greyson's breathing evens out, his hold on me loosening as he drifts into sleep. I lie there, still enveloped in the warmth of his embrace as my mind wanders over the contours of the evening—the thrill, the connection, the unabashed pleasure—and for now, I let myself sink into the quiet contentment of the moment.

I nestle into the crook of Greyson's arm, the thrum of his heartbeat beneath my ear a soothing lullaby. His chest is a broad expanse of warmth against my cheek, and I inhale deeply, taking in the scent of him. How can I not fall for this man who makes me feel such a whirlwind of emotions, who stirs up a storm within me and calms it all at once?

But I know the rules. We'd both set them, clear as crystal. Sex and the occasional date. No strings attached. Exclusivity. It's for the best, isn't it? Life is complicated enough without adding feelings to the mix. Yet, every time he looks at me, there's a tenderness that feels entirely out of place in our arrangement. How can I keep the lines from blurring? When the time comes to walk away, will I be able to?

My life is hectic enough without the complexities of a full-blown relationship. And yet, there's a whisper of longing that refuses to be stifled, a yearning for something more than fleeting passion and casual conversation over dinner. But I'm getting ahead of myself.

Enjoy it. Just while it lasts.

For now, this moment is mine. Tomorrow can wait.

I close my eyes, the thoughts drifting away, carried off by

the rhythmic cadence of Greyson's breaths. I'm safe here, wrapped in his strong arms, cocooned in a haven of warmth and security. For now, that's all I need, all I want.

Thirteen

Trinity

The last week and a half have been nonstop, but I've eked out a bit of a routine. I work most of the day from Mom's hospital room and spend my nights with Greyson. Today, however, we're moving Mom to Lakeview Assisted Living. In the end, it was indeed the best option. I feel a little silly about the way I reacted initially, but I needed to see for myself what the choices were for Mom. And I wanted to make an informed decision. But after lots of web surfing and calls, and even another visit, it turns out there weren't that many places with anything open, and none of them was as nice as Lakeview.

I dodge around the work crap I've spread out on my mother's living room floor, looking for where I put my keys. My Zoom meeting ran long, and now, I have to hustle if I want to be there when they release her from the hospital.

In the middle of all of this, my phone rings, but I have to

smile when I see my best friend's silly face on the screen.

"Girlfriend!" Liz's voice crackles through the phone when I answer.

My heart lifts at the sound. "Liz? I miss you like crazy," I tell her, balancing the phone between my shoulder and ear as I lift a pizza box to find where my keys are hidden. I slip them into my pocket and head out the door to the car.

"Good! Because I'm driving over for the weekend, as long as you're okay with it."

"Yes, please come. I could use the company. And honestly, I think I need someone to help me figure out…all of this."

"All of what?" Liz presses.

I hesitate, focused on the elevator buttons as I descend to the parking garage. "Everything. Mom, work…me."

"Sounds like I'll need to bring wine," Liz quips, but her voice softens. "Don't worry. We'll figure it out."

I step out into the garage and head for the car. "Thanks. Mom has moved on to the rehab portion of her recovery. They kept her in the hospital longer because her heart started doing funny things and they were worried, but they decided it was the meds and adjusted those. Today, she's moving to a temporary living arrangement where she can continue to get stronger."

"I can't wait to see her. We'll have a great time. We're single and ready to mingle, right?" I can almost see her flirty wink through the phone.

"Well, not so single, but I'll give you all the details over drinks here at my mom's." I pull out of the garage and start my trip to the hospital.

"Interesting…" she notes. "Either way, I need a change of scenery. How's the weather? Should I bring my bikini?"

"It's hot. Very hot. Definitely bring it," I respond with a laugh. "Mom's condo has a killer pool. We'll make the most of it."

"Consider it packed," Liz says. "I'll swing by your place on my way. I can pick up anything you need."

"Would you?" Gratitude washes over me. "There are a few things I left behind in my rush." I hesitate, biting my lip before I add the detail that I don't know when I'll be returning. "I'll send you a list, if that works for you."

"Of course. I'll bring whatever. Is everything okay?" Liz asks, her tone shifting from playful to concern in an instant. "If you're not single, what have you gotten yourself into?"

"Remember me telling you about the hot doctor from the MedTalks conference?"

"No way..." she breathes.

"He was Mom's first doctor, and he lives in her building."

"No flippin' way! It's kismet. And here you thought you'd never see him again."

"I have to tell you, he's making it really hard not to fall for him." I sigh. "But he lives here, and I live in Vancouver, so we've set some rules. We'll just go on the occasional date and have incredibly hot sex until I return home."

"Wow..." I can almost hear the smirk in her words. "When do I get to meet Dr. Dreamy?"

"I'm sure you can probably meet him when you're here. When will you arrive?"

"I can leave work tomorrow at noon, so I'll be there for happy hour."

"That sounds great. Thank you. Things with Mom are... Well, it's a lot right now."

"Say no more. You just focus on your mom, and I'll take care of you— Well, Dr. Dreamy can take care of you in *that* way. I'll do the rest."

I laugh, so happy to know Liz is coming. "Thank you, and I'll send you a list," I promise. "See you soon."

"See you tomorrow, babe," she replies before hanging up, leaving me to face the day ahead with a touch more hope than before.

I park my car in the hospital parking lot and head to Mom's room. One of the nurses stops me. "Thank you for the cookie bouquet."

I smile. "Of course. My mom and I really appreciate all the work you did while she was here."

I enter Mom's room and give her a hug, but she's stiff and nervous. "What's wrong?"

"Ellen, where is George? He said he'd be here to pick me up."

Every time she calls me Ellen, a little bit of me dies inside. "He's not coming. You're going to get to ride in an ambulance over to the rehab center."

"I feel great. I don't need rehab."

"You look great," I lie. "And once you pass a few tests, they're going to send you right home with me."

She nods and seems to accept that, so I sit down in the chair. We can't leave until Dr. Chappell discharges her. It's nearly ten, and most days he's come by about now. *Where is he?*

After a few minutes, unable to sit, I pace the sterile, white corridor of the hospital. The morning drags by with the slow tick of the clock, and I alternate walking with standing watch at my mother's bedside, murmuring assurances that soon we'll be on our way to Lakeview. Her hands tremble, fingers grasping at the sheets restlessly.

"Everything's going to be okay, Mom," I whisper, though a part of me trembles with doubt.

Eventually, we get some lunch, which distracts her for a while, but it's late afternoon before Dr. Chappell eventually saunters in, laptop in hand, to explain the discharge process. He assures us that the ambulance transport is for Mom's safety, but the word *ambulance* seems to jolt her already frayed nerves.

As the paramedics wheel her out, she clutches my arm, her voice quivering. "Ellen? Why isn't George here?" Her gaze is pleading, lost in a time that no longer exists. My heart clenches.

"Mom," I soothe, stroking her hair, "Dad's watching over us, remember? But I'm here, I've got you."

But then her agitation spikes anew, her thoughts tumbling

into deeper confusion. "George must be so worried. He needs to know where I am. He'll be looking for me."

"Shh, it's okay." I kneel beside her wheelchair, trying to be the anchor in her stormy sea of memories. "I'll call George. I promise he'll know exactly where to find you."

Relief softens her features momentarily, but the paramedics are motioning me aside now. "We should get going," one of them says, his eyes kind behind the glasses perched on his nose.

"Of course." I nod, gathering my resolve like armor.

They pull the wheelchair up to the ambulance, and Mom tries to undo the seat belt. "I need to go home," she insists.

"Mom, remember, Dr. Chappell wants you to go to rehab."

"I'm no junkie." She starts screaming for help.

I reach for her hand and hold it to me. "It's okay, Mom. I'm going with you."

She quiets, though her eyes remain wide.

"Can you ride with us?" the driver asks.

I look back at the parking lot where my car is sitting and figure I can grab a rideshare back later. "Sure."

They roll her into the ambulance and being there, right beside her, seems critical now. So I climb in, taking a seat next to her, reaching again for her hand.

"See, Mom? We're going together. You're not alone." I force a smile while my insides churn with anxiety. And as the vehicle lurches forward, leaving the hospital behind, I can't help but feel as if I'm leaving a piece of myself with it, the part that believed everything could be neatly planned and controlled.

The ambulance jolts over a bump, and Mom's hand tightens around mine, her knuckles bone-white. Her eyes dart around the small space, confusion clouding her features. "I need to…" Her voice trails off, the thought slipping through her grasp.

"Mom, stay still, please." My tone is calm, but my chest tightens.

She settles back, her hand still clutching mine. The ride feels endless, each bump a reminder of how little control I have right now. I tighten my grip around her arm, protecting her from a dangerous tumble. The paramedics are focused on the road, trusting me to manage the situation in the back.

My phone buzzes in my pocket, a call to a reality I can't fully face right now. I glance at the screen — messages from work, though my boss knows today is about moving Mom. We spoke this morning to discuss implementation of the next plug-in for the electronic medical records system tonight, but I thought I'd be done before this. Probably he did too. Still, I swipe the notifications away. They can wait. Everything must wait.

Lakeview looms ahead. As we pull up, Frankie greets us at the door.

"Trinity, I've reached out to Dr. Greyson," she says, pulling me aside while the paramedics wheel Mom through the entrance.

My heart skips a beat.

Frankie reaches for me. "It's normal for memory-care patients to be very agitated when they're moved. Greyson will talk to her, and hopefully he can put her at ease."

"Of course. Thank you," I manage, still adjusting to this overlap of worlds.

Greyson arrives shortly thereafter with his doctor's coat billowing behind him like a cape. He's the epitome of confidence. He gives me a wink, but strides right past and over to Mom. With a warm smile, he asks, "Joy, how are you holding up?"

"Better now that you're here," Mom replies, a flirtatious lilt in her voice.

I wish I could disappear into the floor. I wasn't prepared for this — my mother fawning over the man I'm seeing.

"Always glad to help," Greyson responds, grinning broadly, and when his gaze shifts to mine, there's mischief dancing in his eyes, a Cheshire cat teasing its prey.

He escorts Mom to her new room, reassuring her at every

turn. She bats her eyelashes at him, and I have to clamp down on the eye roll threatening to surface. Still, even I have to admit he's impressive. This man who deftly balances charm and professionalism is the one who's shared whispered promises in the dark with me.

"Isn't he just wonderful?" Mom sighs, watching as he ensures her comfort, utterly oblivious to the complicated web of emotions tangling inside me. "And he's hot, too."

"Yep, he's...something," I agree, unsure whether I'm more annoyed with his effect on her or the fact that I'm affected at all.

Greyson prepares a dose of sedative for Mom and administers it expertly, somehow avoiding any of the panic needles can create for her. Within moments, her eyelids flutter to rest.

"Will you be bringing Trinity to the wedding?" Frankie's voice cuts through the tender scene like a poorly timed cue. She stands at the doorway, her gaze flitting between Greyson and me.

I stiffen, feeling the color rise in my cheeks. "Oh, we're not together," I blurt, leaving no room for misinterpretation — or so I think.

Greyson turns to look at me, a flicker of something passing over his face. Hurt? Disappointment? It's gone before I can decipher it, and he covers with a nonchalant shrug. "We'll work on that," he says, his tone light.

Frankie nods, undeterred. "I hope you'll come."

"Sure," I murmur, though I'm not sure of anything at all.

Seizing the opportunity to escape, I excuse myself and step out into the hallway. My phone buzzes in my pocket again, flashing a notification from my boss. My heart sinks as I realize this is likely yet another fire I have to put out.

"Hey, Andy," I say in greeting.

His voice comes through, apologetic. "I know you're busy with your mom's new location —"

"No, no, it's fine," I interrupt. "This took much longer than

I thought. Is there a problem with the rollout tonight?"

"I don't think so," he says. "I just had a quick question from IT that I wanted to run by you." He explains some technical issue with the operating system on our servers, but fortunately, it should all be fine.

"Tell them they shouldn't have to worry about that. It's solid," I assure him. "I know the migration is nerve-wracking, but this is going to be great. We've got the safeguards in place, and it should cut down on prescription shopping."

"Good, good," he murmurs, his relief palpable. "I knew you had it covered. Okay, well, I won't keep you. I appreciate all you're doing, and we'll look forward to having you back. But no pressure," he adds quickly. "You've been great about being available and getting your work done."

I press my lips together, a knot forming in my stomach. "Thanks, Andy. I'm not sure yet on the timing," I admit. "The move hasn't gone so smoothly. I need to be sure Mom's settled and determine the next steps for her care. I might be here a while."

"Of course. Keep me posted," he says kindly. "We're behind you. I hope your mother improves."

"Thank you," I whisper before ending the call.

Leaning against the cool wall, I take a moment to breathe. I'm not sure what I expected from today, but it wasn't this. The reality is that Mom may never come back to us—not mentally at least. And I, bound by love and duty, might just be anchoring myself to Paradise indefinitely.

The door to my mother's room clicks shut behind Greyson, and he turns to face me as he steps into the hallway. "The sedative has set in," he says. "Your mom will sleep through the night, and staff will be on hand for when she wakes up disoriented."

The weight in my chest grows heavier as I blink back tears. "Do you think…she'll get more of her memory back?" The words tremble as they leave my lips.

Greyson sighs. "The brain is complicated," he admits, and my heart sinks. "But right now, it's just about giving her some time."

"Thanks," I murmur. "Can you drop me at the hospital? I need to pick up my car."

"Sure, but how about dinner first?" He suggests Salt & Brick downtown, and I hesitate only a moment before nodding. It's not like I'm ready to face the empty condo yet anyway.

As we sit in the car, the silence stretches awkwardly between us. "About what I said to Frankie..." I fidget with the hem of my jacket. "I was just going by your rules."

Greyson nods, his eyes on the road. "True," he says quietly. "But it's a wedding. And you've met Frankie. I'd like you to come with me, not because of the rules we set, but because I want you there. With me."

He glances over as I consider his words, turning them in my mind. Maybe I should. What would that mean? We agreed this was temporary, a way to pass the time until I return to Vancouver. And yet, with every passing day, the idea of leaving feels less like an escape and more like a loss I'm not ready to face.

I glance at him. He's confident, steady, and so sure of where he belongs. I wish I could say the same.

We pull into a parking space close to Salt & Brick, and I finally allow myself to exhale. *Why not go with him?* It could be fun, a distraction from the chaos that's become my life.

Inside the restaurant, the staff greets Greyson like an old friend. The chef emerges from the kitchen, shaking his hand before turning his attention to me. "And who is this lovely lady?"

"Trinity, my girlfriend," Greyson says, and I resist the urge to correct him. That doesn't seem like what we talked about when we made our ground rules.

We settle into our seats and with the chef's recommendation we order the Brussel sprouts, wagyu beef dumplings, tuna tartare, and endive salad.

Greyson turns to me. "Wine with dinner?"

"Sure, and water too, please."

"Of course." The server turns to Greyson. "We have the two-thousand eleven Paradise Hill Cabernet."

Greyson looks at me. "That's a good year."

I shrug. I wouldn't know the difference between 2011 and 2020.

Greyson smiles at the server. "I think we'll have the cabernet from Black Bear Winery."

The server's brows shoot to his hairline.

"Always smart to watch the competitors," Greyson remarks.

The server nods and leaves us.

I steal a glance at Greyson, wondering if this dinner is more than just a meal, if perhaps we're tiptoeing around something deeper than either of us wants to admit. "Before I get you to dive into the whole Black Bear Wines saga or why you declared me your girlfriend to practically everyone here in the restaurant, I should tell you. I'll go with you to Frankie and Penn's wedding if you want, as long as it isn't this weekend, but I want you to think carefully, and it's okay if you decide it's better I don't. That's outside of our deal."

Greyson leans back, his chair creaking under the shift of his weight. A dimple flashes in his cheek as he smiles. "It was the easiest way to let them know we're exclusive," he explains.

I nod, caught between pleasure and caution. The label *girlfriend* resonates with a sweetness I didn't expect to enjoy so much. But this is just until Mom's settled and hopefully home in her condo. I need to remember this and keep my heart on a leash.

Our server approaches, a bottle of wine in his grasp. He presents it to Greyson for approval, but Greyson dismisses the formality with a wave of his hand. "Just serve it," he says confidently.

"Are you sure?" the server asks, a frown hovering over his brows.

"Positive," Greyson replies.

The twist of the top is followed by the sound of wine glugging into our glasses, and the server disappears.

I lift my glass, inhaling the rich aroma before taking a sip. It's good—fruity, with an oaky undertone—but it doesn't quite match the cabernet we shared the other night.

Greyson watches me taste it, a knowing twinkle in his eye. "Not as good as the last one, right?"

"Definitely not," I agree, setting the glass down.

He chuckles softly. "We've been invited to the International Wine and Spirits Competition in London in November. Black Bear Winery was as well."

"Competitive, much?" I tease.

"Of course." He shrugs nonchalantly. "It's part of the game."

I swirl the wine in my glass, and Greyson's eyes meet mine over the rim.

"Did I ever tell you that my family and the owners of Black Bear are like...well, the Canadian Hatfields and McCoys?"

I shake my head. "No, but do tell."

"Over a century of bad blood," he starts with a chuckle. "Eight generations ago, my forebears came here from Scotland. They wagon trained with other immigrants, looking for gold. My eight-generations-ago grandmother had twins, and with the lake there was a fur trade, so they stopped and decided to stay. My distant grandfather's last name was Pàrras, which is Scottish Gaelic for Paradise, so he renamed himself.

"Over time, more people came. His wife ran the general store, and he, depending on the time of year, either mined or fur trapped. They built their farm, and the Dempseys built next door. At one point they both ran for sheriff. When my ancestor won, he named the town Paradise."

"I would bet that didn't make the Dempseys happy."

"Nope. The Dempseys kept stealing cattle and developed a huge vegetable-farming rivalry. They mimicked every move we made. It was ugly. Rumor has it that if one was in the saloon and the other arrived, everyone would clear out."

The server appears and sets down our first course. "I'll bring out the plates as they're prepared, so just dig in."

With a nod, we settle in to eat, and for a time, our focus moves to the food. The courses come and go, and it's all fantastic.

"So who got your family into the wine business?" I eventually ask.

"The government had passed the Temperance Act in 1878, which prohibited the sale of wine. Four generations ago, my great-great grandfather had planted grapes for his own consumption, and he saw an opportunity. The Temperance Act wasn't being enforced yet, but he knew it was coming. He realized there was an exclusion for sacramental wine, so he planted more and more grapevines and expanded into that market. The vines by the visitor center are his original grapes."

I'm astonished by that. "Really? What did the Dempseys do?"

"They planted more grapes, too. And when the government sent people here to shut it all down, my father was already supplying the local churches with the wine, so he could continue. But the government burned the Dempseys' fields."

"That's awful." My hand goes to my heart.

He shakes his head. "They've always blamed us, and that took the rivalry up about ten notches. It's really stupid."

"Wow. So what happens if a Dempsey ends up in your emergency department?" I ask.

Greyson gives me a look of utmost sincerity. "They've come in before. And I treat them like any other patient, professional to the core."

"Good to know," I say.

Eventually, the table is cleared, and we're left with the lingering warmth of shared laughter and emptied plates. Greyson signals for the check, and as he takes care of it, a restlessness stirs within me. The night is getting on, and there's still the matter of my car at the hospital.

"Trinity, I can take you to pick up your car in the morning, if you'd like," he offers, standing and pulling on his jacket. "Let's just go back to my place tonight?"

"Okay," I agree, more out of a desire not to be alone with my thoughts than anything else.

As we step out into the evening, Greyson turns to me. "I was thinking this weekend, we could —"

"I'm sorry. I nearly forgot," I tell him as we slide into his car. "Liz, my best friend, is coming to visit this weekend. I can't wait to see her."

"What about me?"

I look at him. "It's only a few nights. We can hang out with you, but we'll probably stay at my mom's."

"You can sleep at my place."

"No, I can't," I protest. "I can't leave her alone at night."

His shoulders sag as he starts the engine. "Of course. I understand."

"Thanks," I say. "We've hardly talked since I got here, and she just broke up with her boyfriend. Maybe you have a friend, and we can go on a double date?"

Greyson nods, considering. "Maybe she'll sleep with him, and you can sleep with me."

"I wouldn't count on that. She may seem like a party girl, but she really isn't." I reach for his arm. "It's only two or three nights."

"Fine." He pulls out of the parking lot smoothly, and I lean back into the seat, not sure how I feel about him being so needy.

"Besides," I add, "it'll be nice to have some girl time."

"Of course," he agrees, the soft glow of the dashboard illuminating his profile. "Girl time is important."

Fourteen

Greyson

hen **W** we get home, I guide Trinity through my condo to my rooftop garden. Night has draped its velvet cloak over Black Bear Lake, the suspension bridge a necklace of lights that gleams against the dark water.

"Here," I say, flicking the switch that awakens the gas fireplace with a soft roar. The flames leap up, casting a warm glow on the potted ferns and flowering vines.

Trinity's eyes hold the reflection of the fire as we settle into the double chaise lounge chair that overlooks the lake. I stretch out first, offering her space beside me, a silent invitation she accepts, tucking herself against my side. Despite the heat from the fire, there's a chill in the air.

I feel the tremor of a shiver that passes through her. It's not like me to seek out closeness, to share warmth, but with Trinity it feels different. Her hair is a cascade of moonlight and shadows, releasing a scent of exotic flowers that somehow seems both wild and comforting.

"Are you cold?" I ask, already reaching for the plush blanket folded over the back of our seat.

"A bit," she admits.

I drape the blanket over us, making sure to tuck it around her shoulders. "Better?" I ask, my gaze drifting from the dancing flames to her profile, lit softly by the fire's amber light.

"Much," she replies, her breath a contented sigh.

In the silence that follows, the world outside continues on, oblivious to the small, personal orbit we've created here on this rooftop, under the stars.

Trinity's head finds a home on my chest, and my fingers trace small circles on her back, trying to spin away the tension that binds her muscles tight.

"How are you feeling about your mom?"

She sighs. "I don't know. Today was really hard. She keeps referring to me as her sister, Ellen, who passed away a few years ago. And her flirting with you has a bit of an ick factor. You didn't have to flirt back."

I can't help but laugh. "Sure, I did. It's an easy way to talk her into doing something she didn't want to do."

"I draw the line at anything more than a hug."

I pull her in close. "I'm good with that."

For a moment we watch the headlights of the cars crossing the bridge.

"You know," I murmur, "you don't have to manage everything with your mom on your own."

She shifts, lifting her gaze to meet mine, those fathomless eyes brimming with a stoic resolve. "I don't really have a choice. It's just me. No brothers or sisters to share the burden."

"Maybe not," I concede, "but you've got me. Let me help."

A sad smile plays on her lips, a harbinger of the distance she's about to place between us. "You can't," she says softly, and it feels like a door closing.

"Why not?" I ask, though I know the answer might sting.

"Because what we have, it's going to end." She sits up now, pulling away just enough to draw a boundary in the space between us. "We have an expiration date. So it would be foolish of me to rely on you for anything more than an orgasm."

Her words sting. If it was anyone else, I'd be relieved she said that, but with her, I have trouble conceiving the end. My hands, which moments ago were a source of comfort, now rest uselessly on my thighs. We both know the terms of this arrangement, but hearing them spoken aloud, they sound harsher than I expected. "Trinity..." The name is a plea, but I'm not sure what I'm asking for.

"Greyson," she replies.

I pull away gently, the warmth of our closeness fading into the night air. "We may have an end date, but until then, we're together. And whatever happens, your mother is still my patient."

Trinity's eyes, reflecting the flickering flames, meet mine. "Greyson, you were her emergency department doctor, not her GP." She sits up straighter, wrapping the blanket around herself. "I have to coordinate with her primary care doctor now. And since she's out of the hospital, you're not in the picture, medically speaking."

That hits the bullseye. Now, the distance between us feels like kilometers, not centimeters. It's clear that no matter how close we get, there's always a chasm ready to swallow the ground beneath us. She sits up and looks at me.

I sit up as well, putting my feet on the ground. "Right," I acknowledge. "Her GP will take over from here." I can feel this whole situation slipping through my fingers like the smoke rising above us.

I stand, and Trinity's shoulders tense, her posture defensive. I can feel the fight brewing in the air, it crackles with the same energy as the fire.

"You can trust me. Let me in." I take a step closer. "Use

me as a sounding board. Share the burden."

Her silence is heavy as we stand in the bubble of light cast by the flames.

"It's a bad idea. You've been fantastic, but eventually, I'm returning to Vancouver. My work, my life, it's all there. Not here. If my mom can't live alone, I'm going to have to figure out how to move her closer to me."

"I'm not sure that's a good idea. You saw what the two-mile ride from the hospital to Lakeview was like." I close my eyes. I'm saying all the wrong things. I want her to feel like she can depend on someone other than herself, and instead, I'm making it worse. But now, I have to finish the thought. "How are you going to drive her five hours to Vancouver?"

She shakes her head, and I can see on her face how badly she now wants to run out and leave me here.

"Trinity," I say calmly. "I don't want to fight, and I'm not trying to worry you." My hands fall to my sides, an intentional show of surrender, but inside, I'm in turmoil. I'm used to solving problems, fixing things. With her, it's not that simple. Her resistance isn't just a wall. It's a mirror, reflecting my own fear that no matter what I do, it won't be enough. "You don't have to go through all this alone."

Tears well up in Trinity's eyes, and she blinks rapidly, trying to keep them at bay. "I don't want to fight either." Her voice is barely a whisper, roughened by emotion. "I'm not good at letting people in." She swallows hard. "And my heart, it doesn't work like a switch you can flip on and off. I can't just open up and depend on someone who won't be here in a month."

Her words land like punches, despite their soft delivery. It's one thing to know there's an expiration date for whatever this is between us. It's another to hear her speak it aloud. I watch her struggle to maintain composure, her vulnerability laid bare under the starlit sky. It's a side of Trinity I've never seen, and it draws me to her even more.

I take her head between my hands and kiss her softly,

giving her space but not retreating. "I know it's hard. But for what it's worth, I'm here now." I see the battle she's waging — against herself, against me — and I can't stop myself from adding, "And I care. More than I planned to."

The words feel like a risk, daring her to push me away.

Without another word, I pull her into an embrace. I'm determined to wrap her in warmth, both physical and emotional. "Listen," I murmur, my lips brushing against the softness of her hair. "You're not leaving anytime soon. You'll be here for at least six to eight weeks with everything that's going on."

Her body stiffens in my arms for a moment before she leans back, looking up at me. "If that's true...I'll need to go back to Vancouver." Her voice is steady, yet it carries an undercurrent of distress. "I have a big project at work, and I'll need to be there when it goes live. I'm doing the small parts from here, but the final stage of the migration is huge, and I need to be there."

"We're not that far. You can go for a few days and then come back."

She nods, but then after a moment, her shoulders sag. "I don't have anything other than sundresses and shorts. Liz picked things up for me today to bring this weekend, but nothing I can wear to a wedding. I'll need more clothes."

I chuckle softly at her practical concerns, though I admire her foresight. "We have department stores here, too," I tease gently, hoping to coax a smile from her. "They're not quite Vancouver chic perhaps, but they'll have enough to hold you over."

There's a tentative pause, and then the hint of a smile. She steps closer, her cold nose brushing against mine. "Is that so?" she whispers.

"Absolutely," I assure her, my hands finding her waist, steadying her as the world around us fades into a backdrop.

She rises on her tiptoes and presses her lips to mine, a slow, sultry kiss that melts away the cool night air and sends a surge of warmth through every part of me.

I lean into her, enveloping her chill-bitten lips with the warmth of my own. My response is slow and steady, a silent conversation in which I try to convey the unspoken truths that words fail to capture. With each deliberate caress, I tell her she doesn't have to be perfect, that her imperfections are facets of her beauty I cherish. My hands move up her back, pressing her closer, as if to say I'm not going anywhere, not now, not anytime soon.

I feel her fingers weave into the hair at the nape of my neck, sending tingling sensations down my spine. When our lips finally part, her breaths come in uneven tremors, evidence of the emotional tumult we're navigating. She leans in, her forehead resting against mine. It's in this quiet space between heartbeats that I understand the gravity of what we are to each other, however fleeting it may be.

She pulls away just enough to look at me. "I don't want to need you," she admits.

My heart clenches. I see her struggle, the way she clings to independence like a lifeline. Beneath that, there's something else—a plea for connection, for support. Her words echo the fear of reliance, yet her body leans into mine, seeking solace.

"I know," I whisper, cradling the back of her head, fingers lost in the softness of her hair. The floral scent that lingers there is intoxicating, grounding. "But you do. And maybe I need you too."

The confession slips out, unbidden but honest. The thought of her leaving, of this delicate thing between us reaching its inevitable conclusion, twists in my gut. I need her resilience, her fiery spirit that challenges me, even as she needs my steadiness, my willingness to stand beside her in the storm. What could we be to each other?

Trinity

Liz's laughter rings through the phone, a familiar melody that tugs at my heartstrings late the following afternoon. "I'm here."

"Come on up." I smile and press the buzzer to unlock the building's front door. Slipping my phone into the back pocket of my shorts, I hurry out of Mom's condo to greet her.

The elevator dings its arrival just as I reach it, and the doors slide open. Liz stands there, a whirlwind of energy in her floral sundress. We rush toward each other, our embrace tight and lingering, as if we're trying to make up for the two weeks of distance between us.

"God, I've missed you," Liz exclaims.

"Missed you too." I've only been here a short time, but it feels like years without her. "Let's get inside. You must be exhausted."

Once we're settled in the cozy living room, I offer her a glass of wine to unwind from her journey. "Yes, please," she agrees eagerly, and I retrieve a bottle of Paradise Hill pinot grigio from the kitchen. I couldn't help myself when I picked it up.

We carry our glasses and the bottle of wine out onto the deck, the air soft against our skin. The view is tranquil, but I sense a current of anticipation rolling off Liz as she takes a sip and then blurts, "I actually didn't drive. I caught a ride with someone I've started to see. He's in town with me."

This catches me off guard, and I set my glass down. "Really?" I ask. "Is he downstairs waiting to come up?"

"No, silly." She looks away. "He grew up here."

"Who is he?"

"His name's Alaric," she explains. "He's a grad student at UBC, studying psychology. He's been doing a practicum at the hospital."

"Sounds…interesting." I tilt my head, studying her. "Is it serious?"

Liz waves a hand dismissively, a smirk playing on her lips. "We're just having fun. And what about you? You said you're not single? The guy from the MedTalks? I've been dying to know."

"It's a temporary thing until I go back home." The words feel awkward as I say them, like I'm trying to convince myself as much as her. But Greyson's not the settling-down type, even if I decide I might want to stay tangled up with him. So it's dangerous even to consider.

I can feel heat rising to my cheeks, betraying my cool exterior. Liz has always had a way of cutting through nonsense and diving straight into the deep end. She's protective. She knows my track record isn't stellar when it comes to men. I have trouble trusting, and sometimes my choices reflect that as if I'm deliberately choosing those unworthy of my heart. With Greyson, though, it's different, or at least that's what I keep telling myself. We have rules and an endpoint. This is just for fun.

No risk.

"Uh-huh." Liz eyes me skeptically.

But I brush aside her silent warnings, focusing instead on the soothing swirl of wine in my glass and the sun casting shadows across the deck.

"How long are you planning to stay tangled up with this guy?" She looks at me over the rim of her wine glass.

I chuckle. "It's not serious, Liz. I'm protecting my heart. Promise. I'm heading home as soon as Mom gets out of rehab." I'm not even sure what *home* means right now. My life is in a perpetual state of limbo.

"But when is that?" She leans forward.

"Honestly? I don't know." I take a sip of wine, savoring its fruity taste. "My boss has been great about me working remotely, but there's going to be a final install soon. He was freaking out over this weekend's integration. I should have been there."

"Job security at least, right?" Liz tries for a smile.

"Maybe." I exhale slowly. "My contract's up for renewal soon, and they're not looking to implement any more new software. Before I left, we talked about a few things, but I'm not sure what they'll have for me." The uncertainty of my professional future is another layer in all of this that I've not previously admitted to myself or anyone else.

"Promise me you won't stay here in Paradise. It's a nice place, but it's not where you belong. You've got too much going for you to be stuck in this little town with no options for work."

Paradise is small, but it hasn't felt stifling. I wonder if she's right. Or what if *home* isn't where I thought it was anymore?

I nod. "I promise. There aren't enough opportunities for growth." Paradise is a beautiful escape, but it's not likely to sustain my life.

"Good." Liz seems satisfied with that. But then she narrows her eyes. "You look tired. Have you been sleeping, or does Dr. Tall, Dark, and Hottie keep you up all night?"

Laughter bubbles from my chest. "You think you're

funny, don't you?"

She raises her eyebrows, and her question lingers in the air.

"Maybe a little of both," I admit, rolling my eyes. Sleep has been elusive, but not necessarily for the reasons she's implying. It's hard to rest when your mind is a tangle of personal and professional uncertainties. And yet, there's no denying that Greyson has been a significant distraction.

"Uh-huh." Liz's smile is knowing, and I can tell she's not buying my attempt at nonchalance.

"Let's not talk about me," I deflect, setting my wine glass down. "What about you? How's the new fling?"

Liz clears her throat. "I need to get a tan, and I saw that swimming pool out front."

I raise an eyebrow in turn. So that's how it's going to be? "What are we waiting for then?"

We head back inside, and Liz drags her suitcases down the hall into my mom's guest room. The sheer volume of luggage is comical. "I thought you were only staying the weekend?"

She laughs, unfazed by my teasing, and unzips a suitcase to pull out an array of bikinis so colorful they could rival a tropical sunrise. "We have to take advantage of this weather," she insists, holding up a swimsuit that looks specifically designed to challenge the sun's brilliance. "Pool or lake time is a must."

"Fine," I agree, already anticipating the cool embrace of the water against my skin. We retreat to our respective bedrooms to change.

When I step out, bikini-clad and ready, Liz zeroes in on my hip. Her eyes narrow slightly. "What's that bruise? Are those marks left by fingers?"

"Greyson gets a little enthusiastic," I say, brushing off her scrutiny, though I'm aware of how it sounds.

"Enthusiastic, huh?" Liz claps her hands together, her face lighting up with mischief. "Dish. I want to hear everything."

Shaking my head, I deflect her demand for gossip. "I don't

kiss and tell," I remind her firmly, though the corner of my mouth twitches. I know she won't let it go that easily, but some things are better left unshared, even with your best friend.

"Boo, you're no fun," she pouts playfully, but there's a sparkle in her eyes that tells me she'll be on the lookout for any slip-up, any inadvertent reveal. It's a dance we've perfected over years of friendship, pushing boundaries and then pulling back, always protective of each other's secrets.

"Come on," I say. "Let's catch some sun before dinner."

I hoist the pool bag over my shoulder, its contents a jumbled assortment of sunscreen bottles and fluffy towels. Liz trails behind me as we navigate to the communal pool. It's not just the lake view outside my mom's unit that makes this spot special.

We've just settled onto loungers, the sun generous in its warmth, when I hear the familiar chirp of an incoming text.

Greyson: Is she here yet?

My pulse races. It's ridiculous, really, the way a single text can throw me off balance. He makes me feel too much, want too much. And I know that is not good for me.

Me: She is. We're down at the pool. Catch up with you later?

Greyson: My brother Beckett is here, and we thought we might come down. Is that okay with you?

"Mind if Greyson drops by? He's got a brother in tow." I watch Liz's reaction closely.

Her face brightens. "The more, the merrier!"

Me: Bring your own towels. And tell your brother that Liz is seeing someone.

A few minutes later, two figures approach, strides confident, presences magnetic. Greyson hasn't bothered with a shirt, his board shorts hanging low on his hips, and there it is, that glint of metal from his nipple piercing catching the sunlight like a wink. *I wonder when he got that.* I'd love to know the story. Beside him walks his mirror image, or close enough to pass for one, which must be Beckett.

"Hey, Trinity. This is my younger brother, Beckett. I wasn't sure if I introduced you the last time you saw him," Greyson says, his voice smooth as the water that beckons a few feet away.

"Nice to meet you," I say, extending a hand.

Liz, ever the embodiment of confidence, rises from her lounger, curves hugged perfectly by her bathing suit. "Could use some help with my sunscreen," she tells me.

"I'd be happy to assist," Beckett offers, stepping closer.

Liz turns to him with a grin.

"Trinity," she says, eyeing me with a teasing lilt in her voice that I know all too well. "I could practically toast marshmallows over the heat you two are giving off."

Greyson just laughs, a deep, easy sound that ripples through the air. I feel myself blush and turn away, pretending to be very interested in the pattern of light on the pool tiles.

"And you're a doctor?" Liz asks Greyson.

"We're both doctors, actually," Beckett clarifies with a modest shrug.

"Double trouble," Liz murmurs. She turns to me, eyes sparkling. "Trinity, you didn't tell me they were also devastatingly attractive. I mean, look at them!" She gestures grandly.

"You're not wrong," I concede.

Greyson's smile is all charm. "Glad I made the cut," he says, his grin widening.

"Please stop." I groan, trying to ignore the flutter in my

stomach that his presence brings.

"Speaking of cuts, what's with the nipple piercing?" she asks.

I can't help but roll my eyes.

"You know, I have my own piercing," she mentions casually.

Beckett's eyebrows shoot up. "Oh really? Do tell." He leans closer.

He's not serious, of course — or at least I hope not — but it's enough to draw a laugh from Liz.

"Sunscreen. Now," she declares. She turns, and with a fluid motion that speaks of utter confidence, slips her bikini top over her head, baring her skin to the sun.

My gasp of surprise is drowned out by the laughter around us. "Liz!" But she just shrugs, tossing her top to the chair with a carefree grace.

"Trinity, they're doctors," she says, as if that explains everything. "If they haven't seen a pair of tits before, that's a problem."

Greyson doesn't miss a beat, his smile turning appreciative as he takes the seat next to me. "I love having the pool here," he admits. "Though I must confess, I never venture in."

"Scared you'll melt?" Liz teases, passing him the sunscreen.

"Something like that." Greyson chuckles.

A little while later, Liz has thankfully put her top back on, and she and Beckett are splashing around in the pool, laughing and having fun. Greyson lingers by my side, his voice lowering to a more intimate register. "Will you be by later tonight?"

"I already told you, I can't. I'm staying at Mom's with Liz tonight."

His disappointment is a cloud momentarily dimming the brightness of his expression, yet I hardly notice. My attention is already drifting back to Liz, who's laughing at something Beckett has said.

"Do you guys want to go out with us?" Greyson asks.

"We can't," Liz says from the pool. "We have a girls night planned."

Liz and Beckett get out of the water and reach for towels.

"All right then," Greyson says. "Have fun tonight. Liz, I'd love to take you both out to dinner while you're here, or we can do a barbecue at my place."

"We'll let you know," Liz says.

Greyson nods, and there's a subtle shift in the air as he and Beckett walk away, leaving Liz and me to the tranquility of the pool.

"You know, if you want to stay with him tonight, you can," Liz offers.

I shake my head. "I've spent almost every night with him for the last two weeks. He can manage alone for a few nights."

After a few more minutes of sunbathing, we gather our things and visit the locker room before heading back to the elevators and upstairs.

I twist the key in the lock and push open the door to my mother's condo. Liz trails behind me, her fingers still combing through damp hair from our post-pool shower.

"Okay, so what's the plan? Dress up and hit the town, or...?" I raise an eyebrow, leaving the question hanging as I toe off my sandals.

Liz flops onto the couch, stretching like a cat in the sunlight. "Honestly, I just want some downtime with my BFF. Let's order pizza, veg out, and talk about everything."

"Sounds perfect," I agree. The idea of getting dolled up again after time in the sun holds no appeal.

Our phones buzz almost simultaneously, and we exchange a look. Greyson's name flashes on my screen. "Please tell me that isn't Beckett."

Her face wrinkles. "No. I'm a PT. I don't date doctors. I know better."

I look down at my phone.

Greyson: You looked good enough to eat in the bikini today.

"Well?" I ask her.

"It's Alaric. He wanted to meet up with us if we go out tonight."

"And does that mean you've changed your mind?"

"No way," Liz says. "Order that pizza. It's a girls' night. We don't need any men to bother us."

I smile. "Agreed."

Me: Thanks. Have fun with Beckett tonight.

I dial the local pizza place and order a spinach and mushroom pizza.

Greyson: Let me know if you change your mind. I can come by and entertain you later. Winking emoji.

Me: Liz will be plenty of entertainment. I promise I'll see you after she heads out on Monday.

The wait for pizza feels shorter with Liz here, filling the space with laughter and anecdotes from work. When the delivery guy buzzes downstairs, we're ready with cash and our appetites.

We've just settled into a comfortable silence, savoring the cheesy goodness, when Liz sets her slice down and levels me with a knowing look.

"Greyson's drop-by at the pool was pretty smooth, don't you think?" she teases.

I roll my eyes, trying to keep my tone light. "He asked if you were here. I think he wanted me to meet Beckett. I saw his brothers in the garage last week, but he didn't really introduce us. He has three brothers, and I think he's tightest with Beckett."

"Uh-huh." Liz isn't buying it. "You can tell yourself it's casual, but I've seen the way he looks at you and the way you look at him when you think no one's watching. You're not just sticking around for your mom, are you? Because from where I'm sitting, this guy isn't a fling. Usually when a guy gets like this, you break it off."

Heat creeps up my neck, and I take a defensive sip of my drink to buy time. "I'm here for my mom. Greyson's just...a bonus." My voice wavers slightly, betraying more than I intend.

Liz grins, leaning back against the cushions triumphantly. "Oh, he's definitely a bonus. But don't wait too long to figure out if he's more than that."

Her words hang between us, a challenge and a warning all at once. I have to wonder if she might be right.

When we've finished the pizza, I flick off the last light, the glow of the television painting shadows across the room. Liz and I nestle into the plush comforter on my mother's king-sized bed, a fortress of pillows propped behind us.

"Okay, what's it going to be? *To All the Boys* or *The Holiday*?" I ask as I scroll through the streaming service.

"Start with *To All the Boys*," Liz suggests, wrapping her arms around one of the throw pillows. "We need something sweet and uncomplicated."

"Uncomplicated sounds perfect," I murmur, pressing play. As the opening credits roll, I'm grateful for this moment of simplicity amidst the chaos of the past few weeks.

Liz chuckles softly at the movie's first punchline, and I join her, our laughter mingling. We've done this a thousand times before, since the time when life was less about responsibilities and more about which nail color to choose for Friday night.

As the plot thickens and the characters fumble their way through teenage love, my eyelids start to droop. I'm aware of Liz beside me, her presence comforting. She's seen me at my best and worst, and right now, she's the anchor I didn't know I needed.

"Trinity, you're missing the best part." She nudges me with her elbow.

"Hmm?" I force my eyes open to see the protagonist's grand romantic gesture. "Right, sorry." A smile tugs at my lips, but the warmth of the bed is too inviting, and my resistance to sleep is futile.

With the familiar cadence of cheesy dialogue and predictable plot twists playing softly in the background, I surrender to rest. My thoughts, worries about Greyson included, dissolve into the quiet comfort of my mother's bed and Liz's steadfast company.

Sixteen

Greyson

I pace the length of my bedroom, the phone in my hand a silent accuser. The screen mocks me with its lack of new messages, an unfamiliar possessiveness taking root. I've never been territorial, but with Trinity, it's different. She's spending all her time with Liz, and a part of me—a part I don't recognize—resents that. *It's just a weekend. Get a grip.*

The phone buzzes, and I jump. It's Tarryn.

"Greyson, you have to meet me for brunch today," she says without preamble when I answer. "Zane is driving me up the wall with his chaotic management, or lack thereof."

"Tarryn, I'm not sure—"

"Please," she interrupts. "I need to vent before I lose it completely."

"Fine." I push aside images of Trinity laughing with Liz. "Paradise Grill, eleven?"

"Perfect," she says. "Thanks."

I end the call and draft a text to Trinity. The simple good-morning text I sent over two hours ago remains unanswered. The silence from her end breeds not just jealousy, but fear. Fear that every moment she spends with Liz is one less I'll have with her. Fear that, no matter what I say or do, she'll leave for Vancouver and take with her this part of me I didn't know I could give away.

With a sigh, I pocket my phone and prepare to face the day.

I arrive early at the vineyard, visitors already filling the grounds. The summer weekend crowd is in full swing, and after parking I decide to avoid the bustling entrance, slipping instead through the back way that weaves between rows of lush greenery. The scent of earth and growing things calms my restless thoughts.

As I navigate the familiar paths, I spot my father and Uncle Max ahead, bent intently over something in the vines with Mitch and Elise Anderson. They're deep in conversation, two seasoned vintners reading the land like an old, well-loved book.

"Greyson," my father calls as he catches sight of me. "What brings you out here so early?"

"Brunch with Tarryn," I answer, keeping my tone light despite the funk that's settled over me like a persistent fog. "She invited me over to catch up."

"Is it woman trouble?" he probes.

I manage a half-smile, shrugging off the question. "Nothing like that," I lie, unwilling to admit how much Trinity's absence gnaws at me. And I certainly don't want to alert Uncle Max to the real reason Tarryn called this brunch. "Anyway, what has you both so focused this fine morning?" I look over at Mitch and Elise, who have their arms crossed.

My father's expression turns somber. "It's the pinot grapes. They aren't recovering like we expected."

"We knew the early frost took their buds away," I offer.

"And last summer's fire didn't help them," Uncle Max

adds.

Dad points to the base of the vines, which are dry and barren despite careful watering.

"Damn. Life's cycle, I suppose..." Though it feels like admitting defeat. My gaze lingers on the stunted growth, a pang of empathy stirring within me. Those vines, struggling to survive, remind me of my current situation—trying to thrive when the odds seem stacked against success.

Uncle Max's fingers trace the withered vines, his eyes filled with a stubborn hope. "We should give 'em another year," he insists with a resilience born from decades tending this land.

"Elise and Mitch don't think they'll come back," Dad counters.

They shake their heads from a few paces away. Their expertise lies in coaxing life from the soil, yet they seem resigned to the loss.

"Maybe we could start fresh with some of the vines," I suggest. Uncle Max shoots me a look that could curdle wine, but I continue. "The ones by the visitor center took the worst hit. It might be time to let them go."

"Replace them?" My father mulls over my words, the furrow in his brow softening. "That would mean waiting five years for a new harvest."

"Five years..." I echo, knowing the gravity of that span. "But if the others come back next year, you'll have more possibilities."

"All right," Dad says after a heavy pause. "We'll have to consider our options."

I nod, and with a final glance at the fading vines, I turn and make my way to Paradise Grill, where Tarryn awaits.

The onsite restaurant buzzes with the clinking of cutlery and soft murmurs of conversation as I push through the glass doors, scanning the room until I spot her. She's already at our family table—a large one in the corner that's always reserved for us unless there's a big party.

"Greyson!" She smiles. "You made it."

"Sorry I'm a few minutes late. I ran into Dad and Max at the pinot vines."

Her face clouds. "What did they say?"

"Max wants to wait another year. I think Dad is leaning toward pulling them. I offered the middle ground — replace the ones next to the visitors center and wait on the others."

Megan, our server, approaches. "Good morning, Tarryn. The usual?"

"Absolutely," Tarryn answers. "Eggs benedict and a mimosa, please."

"Coming right up." Megan scribbles the order onto her pad, then looks to me expectantly.

"Black coffee," I say, "a spinach omelet and a side salad." It's a step toward the semblance of normalcy I'm craving.

"Since when do you eat that healthy?" Tarryn asks.

"Believe it or not, I'm getting too old to eat junk food and be able to make it through my shifts at the hospital." I force a chuckle. It actually really sucks.

Megan flashes a smile, promising our drinks will arrive shortly before sashaying away. She casts a wink over her shoulder, aimed directly at me, but it slides off like water on waxed canvas, unnoticed.

"Did you see that?" Tarryn nudges my elbow. "She's clearly into you."

"See what?" I ask, scanning the room absently.

Tarryn leans forward, her gaze sharpening. "Greyson Paradise, are you blind? Megan was flirting with you."

"Was she?" I feel a shrug lift my shoulders. "I didn't notice."

"Didn't notice or don't care?" Tarryn probes. Her fingers brush my arm, a gesture meant to tether my wandering focus. "Is there someone else?"

I hesitate, and Trinity's face appears in my mind, bright and beautiful, yet so heartbreakingly temporary. "It's not like that," I begin, shaking my head. "I'm seeing someone, yes, but she's only here for a few more weeks. She's from Vancouver, helping her mom out."

"Ah," Tarryn nods, her lips curving into a sympathetic smile. She doesn't press further, but her eyes tell me she understands.

I lace my fingers in front of me on the table. "Anyway, what did Zane do now?"

"I'm so angry I could spit. He keeps running to Dad with ideas and changes, and he can't even manage the tasting room schedule right."

I nod along and let her ramble. She's only looking to vent. She doesn't need me to fix her problems or offer solutions.

And then I see her. She's right here in the restaurant. That can't be an accident.

"Are you even listing to me?" Tarryn asks, following my line of sight to the entrance. "Wait. Is that her?"

"Trinity." Her name escapes on a sigh as she steps into the restaurant with Liz in tow. The mere sight of her sends something akin to an electric current down my spine, jolting me back to life.

Tarryn leans in, her voice low. "I know we have things to talk about, but go ahead, invite them over."

"Thanks," I murmur, grateful for her understanding. Pushing back my chair, I stride over to where Trinity and Liz are being escorted by the hostess.

"Greyson!" Liz greets me. She pulls me into a hug that's all warmth and welcome.

"Hey, Liz," I say, returning the embrace before turning to Trinity. Her hug is careful, tentative, like she's holding back a secret or a worry I'm not privy to. It twists something inside me, but I let it slide for now.

"Would you two like to join us?" I gesture back to the family table where Tarryn sits, watching the exchange with an unreadable expression. "We're just having brunch."

Their agreement comes readily, and I feel a swell of relief.

I lead Trinity and Liz to our table, Tarryn's smile broadening as we approach.

"Good morning! It's lovely to meet you both," she says, standing to shake hands. "I'm Tarryn, Greyson's sister."

Trinity introduces herself, returning the handshake with an easy grace.

"And I'm Liz," chimes in her best friend.

"So, what brings you out this way today?" Tarryn asks once we're all seated.

"We saw my mom earlier." Trinity beams. "She's doing really well, which is such a relief. So now we thought we'd explore the vineyard — maybe pick up a few bottles of wine."

"Sounds like a perfect Sunday," Tarryn remarks. She turns to me. "Greyson, you should give them the exclusive Paradise Vineyards tour after we eat. You know the grounds better than anyone."

I nod, catching Trinity's eye. She seems open to the prospect, and it's a chance to spend a little more time with her, away from the crowds. "I'd love to. Consider it part of the Paradise experience."

"Can't say no to that," Liz quips, her grin widening.

Before another word can be exchanged, Megan returns, pad in hand, ready to take our new guests' orders. Trinity opts for the quiche of the day while Liz goes for Belgian waffles.

As Megan scribbles down their choices, two familiar figures stroll into the restaurant. My brothers Beckett and Ryker make their entrance with typical bravado, their eyes lighting up when they spot Trinity and Liz.

"Morning," Beckett grunts, sliding into a seat beside Liz, who offers him a playful wink.

"Did you clone yourselves?" Liz teases, her gaze flitting between my brothers and me. "You all look so alike."

"Perks of the gene pool," Ryker chuckles, slipping into the booth across from her.

"Is there another one of you hiding somewhere?" Liz asks.

Tarryn laughs. "Yes, actually. Our oldest brother, Kingston. He's a bit of a hermit these days. You probably won't run into him."

"Too bad," Liz replies, a mock pout on her lips. "I was hoping to complete the set."

I watch the exchange, feeling a twinge of pride for my family and the legacy we've built here. And for a moment, amidst the laughter and light-hearted banter, all thoughts of territory and jealousy fade into the background.

A little while later, I cradle a warm mug of coffee between my hands as Megan sets down plates of steaming food.

"Trinity," Tarryn says as we eat. "Greyson mentioned that you work in hospital administration. Tell us more about that."

Trinity smiles. "Well, during his MedTalk, Greyson had some choice words about hospital administrators. I found that amusing since we're the ones making sure he gets paid." Her playful jab sends a ripple of laughter around the table, and I can't help but chuckle along.

"Touché," I concede with a grin.

She explains briefly about her work with the electronic medical records project and then volleys the conversation back toward Tarryn. "Managing the Paradise clan can't be easy," Trinity says. "How do you keep all these guys in line?"

Tarryn tilts her head back and laughs. "Oh, it's a full-time job all right, but I've got an edge. They all followed Mom into medicine, and I chose a different path. I'll be running this vineyard someday. Each brother plays his part, but I'm the conductor keeping the tempo."

"Seems like you've got everything under control," Trinity replies.

"Control is an illusion when it comes to these boys," Tarryn says, winking at me. "But let's just say, I know how to pull the right strings."

Pride swells within me. My family, with all its quirks and chaos, is bound by strong, capable women like Tarryn.

I'm leaning back in my chair, the remnants of my spinach omelet still on the plate in front of me, the salad untouched, when Trinity and Tarryn excuse themselves for a moment. Once they disappear toward the restroom, Liz slides over to the seat next to me. I know I'm in for something.

She crosses her arms. "You and Trinity. You're more alike than you realize."

The comment throws me, and I sit up straighter. "Alike how?"

She gives me a look, like I've asked the most obvious question in the world. "You're both runners."

I blink, taken aback. "I don't run."

Liz arches an eyebrow, unimpressed. "Oh, really? Tell me, Greyson, when's the last time you were in a relationship that lasted longer than six months?"

I open my mouth to respond, but nothing comes out. Liz doesn't wait for an answer.

"That's what I thought," she says, her voice softening just enough to keep it from feeling like an attack. "You keep people at arm's length, same as she does. And don't get me wrong, I get it. Life's easier when you don't let anyone get too close. No mess, no heartbreak. But it's also lonelier."

Her words settle over me, and I glance away, staring at the condensation on my glass. "It's not the same," I mutter, though even I don't believe it.

"Isn't it?" she presses. "You both want the same thing, Greyson. You want love, real love, but you're scared to trust anyone enough to let them in. You keep waiting for the other shoe to drop, for them to leave or disappoint you, so you pull away first. Sound familiar?"

I grit my teeth, my chest tightening. "What's your point, Liz?"

"My point," she says, her tone firm but not unkind, "is that you're playing the same game she is. And if neither of you stops running, you're going to lose something that could actually be real."

I force myself to meet her gaze. "I don't want to hurt her," I say quietly.

Liz's expression softens. "I know you don't," she says. "And I don't think she wants to hurt you, either. The two of you need to figure out how to stop being scared of what you might lose and start focusing on what you could have."

She sits back, grabbing her glass and taking a sip. "Trinity's not the only one who needs to take a leap here, Greyson," she adds. "You do too."

She's right—about all of it. "I care about her," I say, my voice steadier now. "And I'm not going to let her go. Not without a fight."

Liz smirks, raising her coffee cup in toast. "Good. Because if you two can figure this out, you might stand a chance. And let me tell you, Paradise, Trinity? She's worth the risk."

I clink my glass against hers. "I guess we'll find out."

Liz gives me a long, measured look before nodding. "Okay then," she says, tipping her mug toward me. "Good luck, Paradise. You're going to need it."

She sits back just as Trinity and Tarryn return.

"Hey," I say softly. "Can you tell me a bit more about the visit with your mom this morning?"

Trinity's smile falters for a split second before she regains her composure. "She seems more comfortable in the space, not so agitated. But actually, it wasn't all great, Greyson. She…she kept calling me Ellen."

"I'm sorry to hear that," I tell her. She's trying so hard to be strong, to shoulder it all on her own, and it makes me ache to think of her doing this without anyone to lean on. I want to tell her again I'll be there—for her, for her mom—but I think showing her is the best I can do.

"Thanks," she replies, managing a small smile as she reaches for her glass of water. The conversation shifts, but my mind stays with Trinity, hoping I can find a way to support her through this tough time.

"Trinity's quite something, huh?" Beckett murmurs from beside me, his voice low.

I nod, feeling the corners of my mouth twitch. There's no hiding it from my brothers, and their knowing looks are confirmation enough. All three Paradise men seem charmed by the women who've joined us today.

"Greyson, you okay?" Tarryn asks.

"Yeah, just thinking about the vineyard," I lie smoothly, gesturing vaguely toward the window and the sprawling vines.

My eyes find Trinity once more, and I see something worth the risk, worth the tangled emotions. I may not know where this path leads, but I'm prepared to walk it with care, for her sake and for my own.

Tarryn offers Liz and Trinity a tour of the restaurant, and I stay behind with my brothers. I'm nursing the last dregs of my coffee when Ryker leans in, his eyes following Liz's every move. She's got a laugh that fills the room, easy and free, and it's clear he's caught under its spell.

"Is Liz single?" he asks, a hopeful lilt in his voice.

"I'm not sure how serious she is with the guy she's seeing," I reply. "But she doesn't live in Paradise."

Ryker grins, flashing that boyish charm that's gotten him into and out of trouble more times than I can count. "Who said anything about moving here? I was thinking about tonight."

I roll my eyes. Classic Ryker, always living in the moment, never looking past the horizon for the next sunrise.

After a few minutes, Liz, Trinity, and Tarryn return, signaling the end of our brunch. The air seems to shift. We're ready to move on from the meal to the vines.

"Shall we head out for the tour?" Tarryn asks.

Trinity nods. "That sounds wonderful."

I push back my chair and focus on the opportunity ahead, a chance to share something personal, something precious — the history and heart of the vineyard.

It's a new memory to make with Trinity, one that I hope will be worth more than just a fleeting smile or a passing conversation. As we stand, I catch Trinity's gaze and offer a smile, promising to cherish these moments, however numbered they may be.

Seventeen

Trinity

Grapevines roll out in neat rows before me, coating the hillsides in shades of green against the backdrop of Black Bear Lake. Greyson's boots crunch on the gravel as he leads us into the world beyond the visitor's center. I inhale deeply — the barely sweet tang of the tiny, ripening fruit mingling with earthy undertones — and exchange a glance with Liz, who mirrors my wide-eyed wonder.

"Right here," Greyson says, stopping beside a row of pinot grigio vines, "is where it all began for my family." He gestures to the gnarled trunks, their roots deep and intricate. "Eight generations back, my ancestors settled here as gold miners and fur trappers, and they built this ranch and farm to sustain them. And farm they did, for three generations."

I trail a hand over the leaves, feeling the sun-warmed skin

of a grape between my fingers. It's as if I can touch the past, the struggles and triumphs soaked into the soil beneath my feet.

"The vines in this area are the original to land," Greyson explains. "They were planted for personal enjoyment. I don't think my ancestors ever envisioned what this is today."

"Wow," Liz murmurs.

We stroll deeper into the greenery, the clusters of grapes hanging heavy and inviting. The air is laced with the promise of fermentation, of transformation from simple fruit to complex elixir.

"Most folks think of cabernet sauvignon and merlot when it comes to BC's reds," Greyson says, plucking a leaf and twirling it between his fingers. "But there's a quiet revolution happening. Malbec is not as famous, but it's on the rise."

"Really?" I ask.

"Absolutely," he confirms. "It may not have the name recognition yet, but trust me, the time is coming."

I make a mental note to explore more malbec wines.

As we wander through the rows, I'm caught up in the romance of it all—the legacy, the land, and the lure of an undiscovered favorite waiting to be uncorked.

"These malbec grapes," Greyson says, pausing to gesture to the delicate clusters, "have their roots in French soil. They're flourishing here, against all odds."

I reach out, brushing my fingers along early green fruit, surprised by its size—such power in such a tiny package.

"Sensitive little things, aren't they?" Liz comments.

"Very," Greyson confirms. "Frost, rot, pests—they can devastate a crop. And grapes need the long, warm growing season we get here in BC to truly shine." He plucks one from the vine, holding it up to the light. Its skin is almost translucent.

"High altitudes are their friend," he continues, tossing the grape into his mouth. "This is our first crop to harvest, and they become the star of a single-varietal wine."

"Seems like they've found their second home," I muse. I'm

fascinated by these finicky fruits and the tenacity required to coax them into full-bodied reds.

"Exactly," Greyson says, leading us down another row. "British Columbia has the perfect mix for malbec—the soil, the weather patterns, even the slope of the land. All these factors contribute to the quality of the wine."

"Like a recipe," Liz adds.

Greyson smiles. "Right. You need all the ingredients to be just so. Our climate gives the grapes enough sun, but not too much. The lake regulates temperature, and the altitude..." He stops, pointing up to where the vineyard climbs the hillside. "It's high enough to make a difference without stressing the vines."

"Seems like a delicate balance," I say.

"Winemaking is part art, part science," Greyson agrees. "But when you get it right, it's magic."

We look out across the land as Greyson explains that the grapes for white wines need much more heat, so they have land on the east side of the lake where they grow those varietals.

"You sound like you wish you worked the vineyard rather than being a doctor," I note.

Greyson shrugs. "I appreciate the room in my life for both. I grew up here, but always knew I wanted to become a doctor. I love the vineyard and all that we do..." He looks over his shoulder and leans in close. "But I love being able to leave and not worry about fire season, early frosts, the lack of rain, too much rain, and all the other things that kept my father and now Tarryn up at night."

"And you enjoy your job," I add. "That helps too."

Greyson grins. "Let's head this way." He gestures toward the barns, and we head that way. "Here's where the transformation begins." Greyson points out the containers. "First, we destem the grapes. Then we crush them gently to break the skins without damaging the seeds. That's where the magic starts—the juice."

"When do you pick your grapes?" Liz asks.

"In the fall," he explains. "The grape harvest starts in late August but finishes in October. It just depends on the grape. Whites are late summer. Reds go into the fall."

We look at the shiny machinery, ready and waiting for fruit.

"Can't wait to see—and taste—the final product," Liz says.

"Patience," Greyson says with a wink. "That's another key ingredient in good winemaking."

"Good thing patience is one of my virtues," Liz quips, and I chuckle.

"Mine, not so much," I admit. Though today, surrounded by the beauty of the vineyards and the promise of what's to come, I'm content to wait, to savor each moment. After all, if the journey of these grapes teaches anything, it's that some things are worth waiting for.

"In the old days," Greyson explains, "they used to step on the grapes with bare feet. It was called grape stomping or grape-treading. We offer that at the crush celebration."

Liz's eyes widen, and she gives me an excited look.

"We host that as a fundraiser every year after all the grapes are picked. You'll have to come," Greyson says.

"Count me in," Liz agrees.

"Sounds...squishy," I comment, picturing the sticky juice staining our feet.

"Very," Greyson confirms with a chuckle. "But these days, most winemakers, including us, use machines to destem and crush the grapes."

"Less romantic, but I bet it's more hygienic," Liz remarks, and we all share a laugh.

"Exactly." Greyson nods. "And now, for fermentation and aging." He walks us over to a row of large aluminum tanks that glint under the overhead lights. "After crushing, we add yeast, which turns the natural sugars in the grape juice into alcohol."

"Science in action..." I lean closer to the tanks, the faintest hint of yeast in the air.

"For malbec, especially, reassembly is often essential," Greyson continues. "It's all about extracting the good stuff from the grape skins to give the wine its rich color and flavor."

"Reassembly?" Liz queries.

"Think of it as a mixing process," Greyson explains. "It ensures the juice stays in contact with the skins. That's where so much of a wine's character comes from."

"Like steeping tea to get the perfect flavor," I suggest.

Greyson nods approvingly. "Exactly like that," he says, and I feel a surge of pride.

"Can't wait to see what kind of 'tea' you've brewed up here," Liz jokes.

Greyson rolls his eyes, and we follow him to the next area.

"Here we are," he announces, his voice echoing slightly off the high ceiling. He moves to a stainless-steel vat and gestures toward a pump attached to its side. "To finish reassembly, this pump draws the liquid from the bottom and showers it over the top layer of skins and seeds."

We stare up at the vat doing its job.

"We're enriching the wine. Initially, we do this twice daily," Greyson continues, leading us around the vat to show the even distribution of color. "As fermentation progresses, the frequency decreases. We need less intervention and more nature taking its course."

The fermentation vats give way to a dark, cool area with rows of oak barrels, and the air fills with a heady blend of wood and wine. Greyson's boots echo on the stone floor as he leads us to the heart of the aging room.

"Here," he gestures grandly, "is where our wine takes its final form before meeting your glass."

I scan the burnished rows, each barrel stenciled with dates and notes in looping script.

"Oak barrels," Greyson explains, his fingers brushing the nearest cask, "play a critical role in shaping the final character of our malbec. We've shifted this phase to stainless-steel barrels for many of our white wines."

He taps the barrel, and it sounds a solid, promising thud. "Think of them as a finishing school for the wine," he says. "After the tumultuous fermenting phase, this is where our malbec learns sophistication."

"Is that why wine connoisseurs always talk about oaky flavors?" Liz asks.

"Yes!" Greyson nods. "These barrels introduce subtle flavors and aromas. They allow just enough oxygen to interact with the wine, softening it and giving it a smoother finish."

"The balancing act continues," I say.

"Always," Greyson affirms. "It's about enhancing, not masking. The true art is in the subtlety."

As we walk down the row, Greyson stops beside a barrel marked with a harvest date from four years ago.

"I thought you said this was the first harvest year for the malbec?" Liz asks.

"It is," Greyson replies, pointing to a small notation on the card. "This mark tells you it's our pinot variety." He gestures toward another row, then to the barrel beside it. "And this one is a pinot gris. Those grapes come from our land on the other side of the lake, where the sun exposure is different. The whites thrive in that microclimate."

Nearby, a man stands next to a small tractor equipped with a massive two-pronged fork.

"Chris is here to do his job," Greyson says. "Let's step back and watch."

Chris starts up the tractor and moves toward a group of barrels. With careful precision, he slides the fork beneath one and lifts it, rotating the barrel as he transfers it to a different stack.

"Every barrel in this cave is turned every other week," Greyson explains.

I take in the sheer number of barrels stretching into the dimly lit depths of the cave. "That's a lot of work," I murmur.

"But it's all worth it in the end," Greyson assures us as he leads us to the tasting room. He beckons us to a high counter, where empty glasses await. With a practiced hand, he selects a bottle, peels away the foil, and uncorks it with a satisfying pop. The deep, rich aroma of merlot unfolds as he pours.

"Try this," he invites, pushing a glass toward each of us. "Tell me what you find."

I lift my glass, the ruby liquid swirling with promise. I take a sip, hold it on my tongue, and search for something beyond the obvious.

Liz beats me to the punch. "Cherry! There's definitely cherry here."

"Good palate," Greyson praises before turning his gaze to me, expectant.

"Chocolate," I venture after another sip, the dark and sweet notes dancing together.

"Nice catch," Greyson says with an approving nod. Those earlier hints of spice now have context, their complexity revealed.

He pulls a card from behind the counter, glancing down at the list printed on it. "You're both right," he confirms. "Those are two signature notes among others. But wine tasting is as much about personal experience as it is about flavor profiles."

I can't help but feel a little victorious, having impressed our knowledgeable host. A small smile plays across his lips as if he's pleased by our engagement, or maybe it's just the wine talking. I swirl the wine in my glass, watching it coat the sides like silk. The bouquet of aromas hits me again, this time with a new layer of complexity.

Greyson's eyes are keen as they watch our reactions, his own glass untouched. "BC's wines have a bright future," he muses, gazing out the window toward the sprawling vines. "It's all about capturing the essence of this land, the specific conditions that nurture these grapes."

I nod, understanding now how every element from soil to sky leaves its fingerprint on the wine.

"Every year tells a new story," Greyson adds. "And we're just beginning to scratch the surface of what's possible here."

He turns and lifts his glass high.

"Cheers," we chorus, our glasses chiming together in toast.

Greyson smiles broadly, and his eyes linger on mine as he sips.

Eighteen

Greyson

J ust over twenty-four hours later, my circumstances could not be more different. The lush vineyards are a distant memory as I pace the sterile, glaringly bright emergency department, my mind racing as fast as my steps. The monitors around my patient beep in a relentless rhythm, mirroring the urgency I feel clenching in my gut as I step out of the curtain. A brittle diabetic, barely out of college and with his whole life ahead of him, is crashing before my eyes, his failing kidneys crying out for a miracle I'm desperate to provide.

"Come on, Jim," I plead with the head of the transplant team when I find him in his office. "The kid's slipping through our fingers. He needs a new kidney — now."

Jim's expression is granite hard, unmoved by the situation or my distress. "Greyson, you know the list as well as I do. There's nothing I can do until a match comes up."

"But there has to be something," I counter, not willing to accept defeat. The boy's pale, gaunt face flashes in my mind. This isn't just about saving a patient; it's about salvaging a future.

"Policy is policy," Jim retorts, his words final, cutting off any further argument.

Defeated, I watch as he ushers me out and disappears down the hall, the door swinging shut behind him with a thud. Anger and helplessness burn through me, fanning the flames of an already exhausting day.

Stripping off my scrubs in the locker room, I hurl them into the laundry bin. My energy is tight, coiled like a spring, ready to snap. I scrub my hands over my face, feeling the grit of fatigue and the weight of responsibility that never quite leaves my shoulders.

Home. The drive is a blur, my mind elsewhere. Eventually, I lock my car in the garage and trudge to the elevator, but I can't shake the sense of emptiness waiting for me inside. Trinity remains largely absent, wrapped up all weekend with Liz, and though I've shared a piece of my life with them on the vineyard tour, right now, I feel like a chapter ripped out of my own story.

The door slides open on the fifth floor, and the quiet swallows me whole as I enter. The chaos of the hospital is now replaced by a silence that amplifies the ache in my chest. I've spent all day trying to save a life, and now, all I want is to lose myself in the presence of the one person who makes me feel whole again.

It's not just Trinity's touch, though I crave that more than I'd like to admit. It's the way she sees me, not as the doctor with all the answers, but as a man trying his best to hold it all together. With Trinity, the chaos doesn't feel so heavy. She makes me believe, for a moment at least, that I don't have to carry it alone.

"Damn it, Trinity," I mutter to no one. I hate that I need her so much, hate that my independence seems to falter at the thought of her warm smile, her understanding eyes. But most of all, I hate that, suddenly, I can't seem to find equilibrium when she's not around.

But then, there she is.

"Greyson." She's appeared in the center of the living room, an ethereal vision cloaked in provocative lingerie that leaves little to the imagination. "I used the code you gave me. I hope you don't mind." Her form is silhouetted by the soft glow of the lamplight, accentuating the contours of her body. Thigh-high stockings lead to the promise of paradise, and those black stiletto pumps — punishing, merciless — are the exclamation point to the entire ensemble.

The sight of her hits me like a surge of adrenaline. My body reacts instantly, my heart pounding in my chest and my breath catching. I stand there, stunned by the sheer force of my desire.

"Trinity," I breathe her name like a revelation, my exhaustion momentarily forgotten.

"I wanted to make it up to you," she says, stepping closer, the sway of her hips an intoxicating rhythm. "For being away with Liz… And also to thank you for everything you've done for us."

Thank you doesn't begin to cover the explosion of relief, desire, and affection detonating within me. The tightness in my chest begins to unfurl as I allow myself a moment to simply drink her in. "Is this what I think it is?" My voice is rough, edged with the remnants of frustration that now seems trivial in her presence.

"Your welcome home present," she purrs. "Whatever you want," she adds, her gaze bold, unwavering. "I'm up for anything."

"Even after the day I've had?" I warn. It wasn't just long. It was grueling, testing the very limits of my patience and skill.

"Especially after the day you've had." There's a spark in her eyes, a fierce determination. "I can't wait, Greyson."

Her words soothe my spirit. With Trinity here, ready and willing to shoulder some of my burden, the evening stretches out before us, promising a much-needed escape, a chance to lose ourselves in each other and forget the world outside these walls, even if just for a few hours.

"Let's see where the night takes us." My grin widens with the prospect of all that awaits.

"Show me." Trinity steps forward, the click of her heels echoing on the hardwood. She reaches me and slips her hand under my shirt, her fingers finding the silver bar that pierces my nipple and twisting gently. A groan rumbles from deep in my throat, the sensation shooting straight to my groin.

This isn't just desire. It's a reminder that here, in this space, I'm more than my failures. I belong to her. I groan again as I feel her slick heat, so ready for me. It's intoxicating, this raw need of hers that matches my own.

Without warning, she drops to her knees, her fingers making quick work of my belt and jeans. They pool around my ankles, and I kick them aside, my entire focus narrowed to the woman before me. Her tongue traces a slow, deliberate path from the base to the tip of my aching hardness, and it's all I can do not to buckle at the knees.

"God, Trinity… You know exactly what I need. You make me feel so good," I praise her.

She looks up at me through thick lashes, and I see the smolder of her intent before she takes me deep into her mouth. The sensation is overwhelming—hot, wet, constricting—and I thread my fingers through her hair, guiding her rhythm.

"Swallow," I command as I hit the back of her throat. There's a brief moment of resistance before she complies, but then I'm lost in the pleasure of it. *Damn, she feels incredible.* "Perfect," I rasp, the affirmation torn from my lips as the pressure builds, coiling in my belly. "Just perfect."

I wrench myself from the warm haven of Trinity's mouth, my restraint teetering on the edge of oblivion. She looks up at me, her eyes glinting with a mischievous light.

"Greyson," she chides with feigned innocence, "I've been

so naughty, shutting you out while Liz was in town."

Her words, her tone, the calculated tilt of her head, all strike a chord within me, one that resonates with the need for control I've lost amidst the chaos of the emergency department.

"Maybe you should discipline me," she suggests.

I nod. "Yes, maybe I should." I stride over to one of the kitchen chairs and take a seat, my posture rigid. "Lie across my lap, Trinity."

She complies, her body a fluid motion of curves as she drapes herself over my thighs. I raise my hand and bring it down with a measured force on her bare cheek. The sound echoes sharply off the walls, and she groans.

"Again," she breathes, and I oblige, alternating the spanks between her cheeks, each slap punctuating the silence in the room.

With a growl, I slide three fingers into her, and she shudders beneath my touch, wet and ready. The realization that she's this aroused, this responsive to my discipline floods me with a possessive satisfaction.

"Go to the bedroom," I instruct firmly, withdrawing my hand. "Get on all fours, facing the lake. And don't you dare touch yourself."

She rises, her movements languid, and as she turns to go, I land another slap on her ass, a stinging reminder of my words. "Remember, no touching."

Before following her, I move to my collection of wines and select a bottle. No glasses needed tonight. Tonight is about indulgence, raw and unrefined, just like the wine from our vineyard — robust, earthy, and full of life's complexities.

Cradling the bottle, I follow her to the bedroom, anticipation coiling in my core. This is what I need — a night of hedonistic release after a day of impotence in the face of mortality. With Trinity, I reclaim a piece of myself.

I push the bedroom door open, a predator's grin curling my lips as I survey the scene before me. Trinity is on the bed, her body undulating in silent plea, each writhe and twist sending a sharp thrill through my veins. Her voice, thick with desire, breaks the charged silence.

"Greyson, please," she begs, her eyes shimmering with unspent lust. "Can't I just—"

"Shh…" I chuckle, setting the bottle down and looming over her. "I have other plans for you."

Her gaze follows my every move as I retrieve nipple clamps and a vibrator from the bedside table. I gently push the tip of the vibrator into her, and the moment it springs to life on the highest setting, her moan fills the air. The sound stokes the fire within me.

"Greyson…" She arches, pushing against the invading vibration, but I'm well versed in her body's betrayals. Without attention to her clit, she's stranded on the precipice, desperate for release.

"Patience," I breathe, teasing her breast, feeling her heartbeat race under my fingertips. Her pleas escalate into fervent begging as I affix one clamp to her nipple, her back arching at the sharp bite of pleasure-pain.

"More," she gasps, and I oblige, attaching the second clamp, reveling in the perfect mess of need she's become under my hands.

"Please, I need…" Her words dissolve into a whimper as I withdraw the vibrator and position myself behind her. My entrance is swift, uncompromising, and when I brush the vibrator past her clit in a fleeting caress, her climax tears through her, loud and shattering.

The sight, the sound, the clenching warmth around me— it all sends me careening over the edge right after her, our breaths mingling in the aftermath of our release.

With the remnants of desire ebbing slowly, I pull her close, savoring the shared heat of our bodies. Tonight, we've transcended the ordinary, and though the dawn will bring its own challenges, in this moment, we are nothing but two souls entwined in the pursuit of pleasure.

Exhaustion and satisfaction intertwine within me, lingering and full. I pull her closer, our sweat-slicked skin sticking slightly as we settle into the comfort of the sheets.

"Trinity," I murmur, my voice hoarse from earlier exertions, "I don't want to waste a single night without you. I want us to make every moment count."

She lifts her head, eyes gleaming with that tender affection that always manages to unravel me. "I'd love that," she says.

But a few minutes later, her fingers trace idle patterns on my chest, and I can tell she's tiptoeing around something—curiosity, concern, maybe both.

"What happened at work today?" she finally asks. "You seemed so far away when you came out of the elevator."

The memories of the day flood back—the sharp scent of antiseptic, the relentless beeping of monitors, the weight of decisions in my hands. "It was tough," I admit. "More difficult patients than usual. It felt like nothing I did really made a difference." I sigh. "At the hospital, I'm supposed to have control, to save lives and fix what's broken. I'm good at my job, but sometimes, I can't control everything, and I hate that."

Trinity leans in, pressing her lips to my forehead in a kiss so gentle it feels like a balm to all the day's abrasions. "Tomorrow will be a better day," she whispers, her voice steady and sure.

And in this moment, I allow myself to believe her.

Nineteen

Trinity

I watch as Greyson slicks a scoop of gel through his hair, sculpting it to perfection. The transformation from laid-back doctor to dashing groomsman is almost complete, and my pulse picks up a notch. We're getting ready for Frankie and Penn's wedding at his condo, and we've only grown closer over this past week. More than ever, I know leaving will be hard, and this week may be the week I have to pull the Band-Aid off and decide when I'm going to return to Vancouver. It all depends on what the doctor tells me about my mom's condition. No matter what, I'll be back, but I know it won't be the same.

Greyson slides into his tuxedo jacket, and my knees wobble helplessly. "You look incredible," I breathe, the words feeling inadequate for the man standing before me.

"Thanks," he says, his tone nonchalant. "But you know,

all men look good in a tux." His eyes meet mine in the mirror, a playful challenge in their depths. I shake my head. Sure, all men might look good in a tux, but Greyson looks like he's been poured into his, every line and curve accentuated to devastating effect.

His gaze drops to the sapphire blue cocktail dress he's chosen for me, the sparkles catching the light as I shift uneasily. "It's beautiful, but isn't it too short?" I question, smoothing the hem nervously.

He steps closer, his hands finding my bare arms. "You have fantastic legs," he assures me, sending shivers down my spine. Before I can protest further, he pulls me close, his mouth descending on mine in a kiss that's both a promise and a warning. His hands find the small of my back, and I gasp, breaking away with a laugh. "You can't do that at the reception," I warn, even as my heart races with the desire for him to do exactly that.

"I won't," he promises, but there's a mischievous glint in his eye that tells me it'll be a promise hard to keep.

We arrive at the church early, Greyson striding confidently ahead as I trail behind, our hands firmly clasped. Greyson's the only groomsman, a testament to his bond with Penn, and I stand aside as they pose together for photographs, the bride and groom artfully kept out of each other's sight.

I find myself caught between the joy of this moment and the ache of knowing it won't last. I tell myself it's enough, that the present has value on its own, but I'm not sure I can keep being a person who leaves when everything starts to feel real. Unfortunately, it seems that's not what I want this time.

As the church begins to fill, a sea of familiar and unfamiliar faces turns toward me. Greyson is off to attend to his duties, and I'm searching for a place to blend in when Tarryn, all smiles and radiance, waves energetically from across the room. I walk over to her pew and slide in beside her.

"Trinity! You made it—and with Greyson, no less," she exclaims, her eyes twinkling. "I've been busy playing matchmaker and trying to get all the tables arranged correctly.

Ryker and Beckett brought their latest flings. Luckily, they're sisters, so I lumped them together."

"Resourceful as ever," I reply, chuckling. "So you're doing double duty here — guest and reception site coordinator. Who did you bring along for the ride? Or are you flying solo?"

Tarryn shrugs nonchalantly, her gaze drifting over the crowd. "Who has time to meet men when there's a winery to run?" There's a lighthearted sigh in her voice, but I can sense a touch of longing too.

"Seems to me like you're not looking hard enough," I tease, scanning the congregation myself. The gender ratio seems decidedly skewed. "This place is practically swarming with men."

"Ah, but I have my eye on a certain subset." With a sly grin, she inclines her head toward a cluster of well-built men, some accompanied by dates, others sitting with the easy camaraderie of bachelors. *Penn's friends*, she mouths, and then leans in to whisper conspiratorially. "They're firefighters."

"Really now?" I raise an eyebrow, intrigued. "Well, in that case, you should take two." Our laughter mingles, a brief respite from the nerves that flutter just beneath my skin.

The organist begins a soft melody, and the crowd quiets. Penn and Greyson take their spots at the front of the church.

"Careful what you wish for," Tarryn teases, nudging me. Her laughter fades as her gaze shifts to Greyson, standing at the altar. "Looks like your wish is already waiting for you."

I watch as Frankie is ushered into the back of the church, a vision in the timeless beauty of her grandmother's wedding dress. The fabric whispers tales of a bygone era, echoing with the love and patience of those who waited through war and uncertainty to celebrate their union.

The opening notes of "Canon in D" float through the air, pure and resonant, as Frankie begins her walk down the aisle with her father. The sight of her mother, dabbing away tears with a tissue, pulls at my heartstrings, and I feel unexpectedly moved by the emotion on display.

I'm no stranger to weddings, but there's something different about this one. It's not just the full Catholic mass, which unfolds with a rhythm and grandeur that captivates me despite my unfamiliarity. It's the sense of community, the threads of shared history that weave through the pews and bind everyone here together.

As the priest finally pronounces them man and wife, the church erupts into cheers. I join in, clapping loudly, swept up in the joy of the moment.

Eventually, we follow the wedding party out of the church, and I wait patiently at Greyson's Land Rover. The parking lot slowly empties, and I feel silly just standing here, but finally, Greyson appears.

"Sorry it took so long," he says with a wave. "Photos."

"No worries. I figured as much. I could have gone over to the reception with Tarryn."

He shakes his head. "You would have hated that. She would have put you to work."

"Thank you. I'm not really wearing the proper shoes to be on my feet all night."

"Trust me, you won't be on your feet all night," he says as he helps me into the car. "But I do hope we can keep the shoes on."

I shake my head. "What is it with men and stilettos?"

He shrugs as he rounds the car. "All I know is you look damn sexy in those shoes," he explains as he starts the engine.

When we arrive at the reception, the restaurant has been elegantly transformed, with white roses on each table and as always, the gorgeous view of the vines and Black Bear Lake.

"I have to do a couple of things, but you're sitting next to me at dinner," Greyson says. "We're at a table with my brothers and sister and their dates."

"Okay. I'll manage." I wave goodbye to him as we walk into the room, and Tarryn immediately joins me as Greyson departs.

"Sorry I took off after the service," she says. "I needed to get here quickly so everything would be ready on time."

"Of course," I assure her. "This looks wonderful. But I hope you'll get to enjoy the reception at least a little bit."

Tarryn watches the firemen across the room. "I certainly plan to."

The reception is brimming with Penn's fellow firefighters. As we admire them, a tall man with shoulders that seem like they could easily carry the weight of collapsed walls, strides toward us, a glass of sparkling wine in hand.

"Tarryn, always a pleasure," he says, his voice smooth like the liquid gold he hands her. He turns to me. "And you must be Trinity."

"Why, yes, I am," I reply.

He introduces himself as Paul Berry, and it's easy to volley back the playful banter for a while, but eventually I feel like a third wheel. I should leave Tarryn to her potential conquest.

"Excuse me," I murmur, slipping away under the pretense of needing the restroom.

Inside the ladies' room, I take my time, appreciating a few moments of solitude. Then laughter echoes off the tiles as two women burst in.

"Did you see Greyson at the altar?" one gushes. "I swear, I almost marched up there to have the priest swap me in."

The other chuckles. "Well, tonight's your chance. You said you were taking him home."

"Plan to," the first confirms confidently.

They can't see me in the stall, but the notion of Greyson leaving with someone else tightens my chest, a twinge of possessiveness flaring within me. It's ridiculous. Greyson and I have an agreement—for now, at least. Yet the thought of him with another ignites something primal and territorial.

I shake it off, reminding myself this is all temporary, and anyway, just because someone says something doesn't make it so. Still, as I flush and step out, I can't help feeling unsettled.

I wash my hands and shake them free of excess water before reaching for a paper towel. The two women are still there, their eyes following me as I blot my lips and apply a fresh coat of ruby lipstick.

"Are you friends with the bride or groom?" the taller one asks.

"Neither," I reply, capping my lipstick and slipping it back into my clutch. "I'm a guest. But I've met Frankie a few times." Nonchalant, I lean against the counter. "And who do you know here?"

The shorter girl steps forward, flicking her chestnut hair over her shoulder. "We went to high school with Penn and Greyson. Cheerleaders," she adds, as if it explains everything, her pride unmistakable. "They were the basketball stars."

"Ah, that makes sense." I nod. There's a pause, a breath before the next move.

"I've waited all this time, and now, I'm going to make my move," the shorter girl says, stepping closer to the mirror. "Greyson's going home with me tonight." Her confidence is sharp, almost cutting, but I meet her gaze evenly.

"If you say so," I respond lightly. I extend my hand, staying friendly. "I'm Trinity Blaine."

"Jody Meyer," the shorter woman returns the introduction, her grip firm.

"Kristen Rogers," offers the second.

"Nice to meet you both," I say. And then, without another word, I step out into the corridor, ready to return to the celebration.

Just as I reach the main room, Tarryn materializes beside me. "Greyson's looking for you," she says with a nudge in her brother's direction.

"Ran into Jody Meyer and Kristen Rogers back there," I murmur as we walk. "They seem...interesting."

Tarryn snorts, rolling her eyes. "Dumb and Dumber from

high school." She shakes her head. "Believe it or not, they tried working at the restaurant here as hostesses. Couldn't even manage that without causing chaos."

I just nod and smile.

We step out onto the patio, which is highlighted by a blooming magnolia tree standing majestic against the setting sun, its petals drifting like soft, pink confetti. Greyson spots us and beckons me over. Frankie and Penn stand beside him, their faces radiant.

"Thank you for including me in your big day," I say as I approach.

Penn grins. "Delighted you're here. Truly."

Frankie nods, her eyes sparkling. "Wouldn't be the same without you."

I slip into place beside Greyson, his presence solid and reassuring. The photographer appears and adjusts his lens, motioning for us to huddle closer beneath the blossoms. We close the gaps and smile together, and for a moment, all the uncertainties fade away. We are simply friends celebrating love under the tender watch of nature's confetti.

When the wedding party is called away, I glide back into the reception. Tarryn's already at our table, swirling her drink and watching the crowd with a keen eye. I settle beside her just as the DJ's voice booms through the speakers.

"Please welcome the wedding party to the dance floor!"

Applause erupts, and I join in, my palms stinging slightly from the enthusiasm. The maid of honor, Frankie's younger sister, sashays into view, and Greyson, dapper and debonair, takes her hand to lead her in a dance. Their movements are fluid as if they've spent hours ensuring this moment would be remembered.

On the other side of the dance floor, Penn and Frankie come together in an embrace. There's a magic to the way they move, a poetry in motion that tugs at something wistful deep inside me.

The song ends, the dancers part, and the DJ begins directing guests toward the buffet. That's when I see Jody and Kristin, heads together, laughter sharp. They weave through the crowd, their heels clicking on the polished floor on their way to the food.

I'm about to turn away when Greyson's arm encircles my waist, his touch firm and warm. He pulls me close, and for a moment, it's as if we're the only two people in the room. The noise fades, the crowd blurs, and all I can focus on is the steady beat of his heart against my back.

"Having fun?" he whispers, breath tickling my ear.

"More than I expected," I admit, leaning into his embrace, aware of Jody and Kristin's glares. But with Greyson here, their icy stares can't touch me.

Eventually, it's our turn at the buffet, and we load our plates and then dine with Greyson's brothers and their guests. Sometimes, buffets make me nervous, but this meal is marvelous—a gorgeous salad, followed by pan-seared Chilean sea bass and grilled filet mignon with a cheesy rosemary polenta and buttery cornbread. *Yum*. Rather than a head table, the bride and groom are seated at a small table all their own, leaving the rest of us free to be more relaxed. I like it.

The clinking of silverware and the low murmur of conversation fills the air as dinner winds down. I'm still savoring the last bite when Greyson stands, and the DJ brings him a microphone, announcing it's time for his speech. The room quiets, all eyes on him.

"All right, everyone," Greyson begins. "I think it's safe to say that Penn and I weren't exactly what you'd call model students back in the day."

A ripple of laughter travels through the guests, and Penn shakes his head.

"We broke every rule we could find, and when we couldn't find any, well, we made our own." Greyson pauses as the audience grows louder, some people shouting playful jabs while others chuckle.

"Then this guy," he continues, nodding toward Penn, "decides to go off to Gonzaga and be a basketball star. Well, more like bench warmer extraordinaire."

He winks at Penn, who retorts without missing a beat, "Hey, we won March Madness my third year! And I've got the ring to prove it!"

The room erupts into laughter again.

"That's actually true," Greyson concedes. "But I've never been prouder than when Penn returned to Paradise. To become a firefighter, no less." Greyson's voice resonates through the hall, and I can see the pride in his eyes.

"And then there's Frankie," he says, his gaze softening as he looks at the bride. "I'll never forget the day Penn met her down at the waterfront. Man, did he fall for her, literally tripped over his own feet."

A collective *aww* rises from the guests, and Frankie's cheeks glow a delightful shade of pink.

"Watching them together, watching their love grow... It's the kind of thing you read about in storybooks. I wasn't sure love like my parents' existed elsewhere until I saw these two."

The room has fallen silent now, hanging on his every word.

"Let's raise our glasses," Greyson concludes, lifting his champagne flute high in the air. "To an amazing couple, to a love that defies odds, and to a future brighter than any of us could have imagined. Penn and Frankie remind me what love looks like when it's fearless, when it's worth every risk. Let's toast to that kind of love."

"Here, here!" I echo, raising my glass with a sea of others. Warmth spreads through me as I watch two people so clearly meant for each other bask in the glow of their special day.

Twenty

Greyson

The clinking of glasses and soft laughter rolls over the reception like gentle waves, and I feel a swell of contentment. Trinity's hand takes mine under the table, a silent affirmation that she's right here with me. I squeeze, grateful for her presence. This wedding has been a whirlwind of faces from the past, each one a unique reminder of my high school days.

"Hey, Greyson," Jason Bard calls to me as he navigates the throng of high school acquaintances reunited. The music shifts from nostalgic hits to something more contemporary.

"Jason! It's been ages." We exchange a quick handshake.

His wife, Julia, ever radiant, follows close behind, offering a warm smile that hasn't changed despite the years and the miles.

"Greyson, you remember Julia," Jason says.

And I do, from the handful of times she visited during college. "Nice to see you again." I nod. "Trinity, meet Jason and Julia. Jason and I practically owned the basketball courts back in the day."

Trinity stands, extending her hand gracefully. "It's lovely to meet you both."

"Likewise," Julia replies, her voice carrying the hint of a southern drawl she's picked up since moving to the States. "We've heard so much about you from Tarryn."

"Good things, I hope," Trinity teases, and we share an easy laugh.

"Absolutely," Jason assures her before turning back to me. "So, I hear you've been doing well for yourself. Still love living in Paradise?"

"Indeed," I respond with a chuckle, "and no plans of leaving. How about you? Engineering, right?"

"Yep, down in Texas now. We've got three little ones keeping us on our toes." He glances at Julia, and they share a smile.

"Three kids?" Trinity's eyes widen. "That must be quite the adventure."

"Every day's a new discovery," Julia says, her laugh light and musical. "But it's wonderful. Our own little team of engineers in the making."

"Do you like your work?" I ask, taking a sip from my glass.

"Challenging, rewarding," Jason answers with a nod. "Keeps the mind sharp, you know?"

I agree, understanding the sentiment even if our fields are worlds apart. A part of me envies his clarity, the straightforward nature of his work and the life he and Julia have created. Everything in my world seems far more complex.

Jason leans in, a curious glint in his eye. "I don't see Anita here. As close as she was with Penn growing up, I'm surprised she didn't come. Do you still keep in touch with her?" His question feels like a pebble tossed into the still waters of my past.

"Every now and then," I admit, swirling the whiskey in my glass. "She's up to her neck in work over in Toronto now. I think we're both pretty okay with the space between us."

That's true from my perspective, but it occurs to me I'm not entirely certain whether that's true for Anita or not. She does reach out every once in a while, but she's also the one who left. Who knows what she's thinking? I never really did.

I glance over and realize Trinity knows nothing about that chapter of my life. She probably deserves to, but this hardly seems the time. There's no need to complicate this night. I'll have to circle around to that later.

As Jason nods, Julia and Trinity excuse themselves to the bar for a moment. I appreciate how easily Trinity fits into this tapestry of old friends.

Before another word can pass between Jason and me, Jody Meyer appears. "Greyson, you won't believe it, I see your great-great grandfather's portrait every day!" She punctuates each word with a tap on my arm.

"Really? That's...great," I manage. *What on Earth is she on about?* "He was quite a character, from what I've heard."

"Absolutely! The true first mayor of Paradise," Jody gushes, her fingertips brushing my shoulder. She goes on and on about her new position with the city, weaving in family lore that she must realize I already know.

I nod along, acknowledging her words with a polite smile. Her touches are frequent, lingering, a contrast to the casual nature of our conversation. And while I'm flattered, my mind drifts back to Trinity, whose presence grounds me amidst the whirlpool of this wedding reception turned high school reunion.

"Anyway," Jody continues, oblivious to my wandering thoughts, "it's such an honor to be working for the city, especially when there's so much history staring right back at me!"

"Sounds like you've found your niche," I reply.

Jason has faded away — can't say I blame him — and I scan the room as subtly as I can, hoping Trinity will catch my eye and rescue me from Jody's relentless enthusiasm about municipal affairs. But when I find her, my heart clenches. Dan Tucker, with his too-wide smile and wandering hands, is leaning in a bit too close to Trinity for comfort.

"Jody, I'm sorry to cut you off," I interject. "But please excuse me." My focus narrows on Trinity, her laughter ringing out even as Dan leans in again. My stride quickens, each step fueled by the need to reclaim what's mine.

Dan's laugh carries over the music until he spots me approaching and steps back, his smile faltering. My hand finds the small of Trinity's back, a silent claim that sends an unmistakable message.

"Care to dance?" I ask her, although it's not really a question.

"Thought you'd never ask," Trinity replies, her eyes sparkling.

As we move onto the dance floor, the DJ shifts gears, and the pulsing beat mellows into something slower. Trinity slides into my arms, and it's like coming home. Her head rests against my chest, and I breathe her in, letting the world fade away.

"Jody informed me in the bathroom that she's taking you home tonight," Trinity murmurs against my shirt.

"Is that right?" I chuckle, the absurdity of the notion making it easy to dismiss. "Well, she's going to be disappointed." Visions of high school pettiness flash through my mind, reminding me why those days are best left behind.

"Did you tell her you're here with me?" Trinity asks, tilting her head up to meet my gaze.

"No," I admit. "But only because she was too busy talking about herself." I tighten my hold around her. "Regardless, I wouldn't go home with anyone but you."

"Good," she says, her tone light but her eyes serious. "That's exactly what I want."

The song ends, but we linger on the dance floor, reluctant to break the connection. Trinity's laugh is like music as she shifts and catches Jody's eyes boring into us from across the room. My hold on her tightens yet again.

"You don't need to mark your territory," she teases.

"Maybe not," I say, "but I want everyone here to know you're with me." My lips find hers in a kiss. Her knees buckle slightly, and she leans into me, her laughter melting into a soft sigh against my mouth.

"Dan didn't seem to care when I told him you were my boyfriend," she says after a moment.

"Flirting with my girl right in front of me?" I shake my head, feeling the heat of irritation flare up again. Trinity's hand slips inside my jacket, tracing the spot where metal pierces my skin, and everything else fades away. "I'm only going home with one person tonight," she whispers, and I grow taller, stronger, invincible.

As the evening wears on, we eat cake and dance, and eventually, the bride and groom return to the center of the dance floor. Frankie, glowing and beautiful in her wedding dress, calls for the single women to gather for the bouquet toss. Trinity hangs back with Tarryn, both clearly uninterested in the outdated tradition.

"Come on," I urge softly, amused by her reluctance.

"Only because you asked." She rolls her eyes, but there's a smile on her lips, a smile just for me.

Jody and her friend are jockeying for position at the front, elbows ready. Frankie launches the bouquet into the air. It arcs gracefully, a silent ballet of petals and ribbon, and then chaos erupts. Jody leaps like she's going for a game-winning catch, fingertips brushing the bouquet, but it's Trinity who ends up with it in her hands, looking as shocked as if she's caught a live grenade.

"That's not fair!" Jody's protest cuts through the laughter and cheers, but I barely hear it over the thundering of my heart. The way Trinity holds the bouquet, like a hot potato she can't wait to get rid of, only makes her more endearing.

Penn's got a cheeky glint in his eye as he motions for Frankie to drape her leg over his lap. I smile as my best friend gingerly, with exaggerated slowness, inches his hand up her thigh amidst an uproar of hoots and hollers. The crowd is eating it up, and when he triumphantly brandishes the garter, the DJ jumps in on cue, calling for all the single guys to gather 'round.

"Go on, Grey. Show 'em how it's done." Trinity nudges me. She knows just how to push my buttons.

I join the jostling crowd of bachelors, feeling a bit ridiculous. But when the garter soars through the air, instinct takes over. I'm leaping, reaching— Got it! The fabric bunches in my fist, and I land amidst laughter and backslaps.

"Looks like someone should put a ring on it!" Tarryn calls. The room erupts into a fresh wave of chuckles just as Beyoncé's iconic anthem fills the space. I can't resist pulling Trinity close for a dance, laughing all the while.

As the night winds down, Penn and Frankie make their rounds, saying heartfelt goodbyes. Frankie pulls Trinity into a hug. "Promise me we'll see each other soon?" she whispers.

"Wouldn't miss it," Trinity assures her.

"Take care of him for us, will ya?" Penn claps me on the shoulder with a grin.

"I'll do my best," Trinity replies.

As they move on, I find myself holding Trinity a little closer than before, aware of the symbolism of catching the garter and bouquet and not blind to the expectant looks from our friends. Yeah, pressure might be mounting, but looking at her, I know everything's right where it's supposed to be—for now.

I'm still riding high on the laughter and camaraderie as Trinity and I make our way through the dimly lit parking lot a little while later, her hand warm in mine. The cool night air refreshes after the heat of the packed reception.

"I'm going to take this bouquet to my mom in the morning," she says, glancing down at the unexpected trophy in her other hand.

"Your mom will love that," I respond, unlocking the car and holding the door open for her.

She slides into the seat gracefully, the scent of her perfume lingering as I close the door and walk around to the driver's side.

The engine hums to life, and we pull out onto the quiet road. Streetlights cast soft pools of light that dance over Trinity's features. She turns to me, her eyes curious. "So, what was your favorite part of the wedding?"

"Seeing all the guys from the basketball team, hands down," I tell her. Memories of games won and lost, the sound of sneakers squeaking on the polished gym floor, and the roar of the crowd flood back to me. It's a bittersweet nostalgia, knowing those days are long behind us. "It was great catching up, seeing where life has taken everyone."

"Are many of them still around Paradise?" she asks, tucking a strand of hair behind her ear.

"Actually, not many," I admit, taking a turn that leads us onto the main road toward home. "Most have moved away for jobs or family. You know how it is — small towns aren't for everyone."

She nods.

Paradise, for all its charm, can sometimes feel too small, too familiar. Tonight, though, the town feels just right — full of memories, old friends, and the promise of new beginnings. As we drive under the canopy of stars, I think about how, despite everything, there's nowhere I'd rather be than here with Trinity, in our little piece of Paradise.

We pull up to my building and park in my spot in the garage. The engine ticks as it cools in the quiet of the night. The bouquet — a vibrant tangle of colors — rests in Trinity's arms, but her expression is thoughtful, distant. I wonder if she's thinking about what comes next because I know I am. Tonight felt like a glimpse into a future I didn't know I wanted, and now, I can't imagine letting it slip away.

We take the elevator up, and I follow Trinity out into the hallway and down to her mom's condo. As soon as we enter, Trinity escapes into the bathroom. When the door opens again, she steps out in her PJs, her face fresh and clean, free of the makeup that had accentuated her features earlier in the evening. There's something comforting about her natural beauty, something real that draws me to her every time.

"Greyson," she says, "we should stay here at my mom's place sometimes. It could be fun, a little change of scenery."

"Sure," I reply. The truth is, the thought of being anywhere without her feels foreign now. The familiarity of our own space, our routines, they anchor me in a way that's hard to explain. "Let's head upstairs tonight, though."

She nods, and when we reach my place, the need for sleep nearly overwhelms me. It's been a long day. In the bedroom, the moonlight spills across the bed, casting a pale blue hue over the sheets. I change and slip under the covers, feeling Trinity's body mold against mine. Her breath is a gentle rhythm against my chest, and I wrap my arms around her, pulling her close.

"Today was..." My words trail off. Exhausting doesn't quite capture the rollercoaster of emotions, the nostalgia mixed with an underlying current of something new, something that's been growing between Trinity and me.

"Long," she finishes for me, her voice thick with sleep.

"Very long," I agree, and there's nothing left to say after that.

Our breathing synchronizes, the rise and fall of our chests creating a harmony that lulls us toward rest. As sleep claims me, the day's events replay in my mind like a silent film — the laughter, the dances, the subtle glances — all winding down to this quiet moment. Despite the pressures and expectations of those around us, what matters most is right here, in this embrace. And that means I need to reevaluate our future. Because, with Trinity, I am home.

Twenty-one

Trinity

The automatic doors sweep open with a hushed whoosh as I step into Lakeview Assisted Living. I'm here for my daily lunch ritual with Mom, but the pit in my stomach tells me something is off even before I reach the front desk. The receptionist greets me with a hesitant smile that does nothing to ease my tension.

"Hi, I'm here to see my mom," I tell her.

"Of course," she says. "But, Ms. Blaine, your mother has been moved to the memory care unit," the receptionist informs me, her eyes sympathetic yet guarded.

"Moved? Why wasn't I told? I was just here yesterday. What happened?" My heart pounds, anger and fear knotting in my chest.

"Your mother has been wandering at night," she explains. "We don't have enough staff to watch her constantly."

"And no one thought to call me?"

"Well, Frankie would be the one to discuss this with you, but she's on her honeymoon. She'll be back next week."

I nod stiffly, the information doing little to quell the turmoil inside.

She directs me to Mom's new room, in the specialized care unit. The corridors here feel different—more sterile, less welcoming. When I finally reach the right place, the sight before me tightens the vise around my heart. The flowers from the wedding I delivered to her yesterday sit cheerfully on her side table, but Mom paces the room, her face lined with confusion and distress.

"Mom?" I approach cautiously.

She turns to me, but there's no recognition in her face. "I need to speak to someone! They've locked me in, and I can't find Ellen!"

"Mom, it's okay. I'm here," I soothe, though my throat constricts with emotion.

"Ellen?" Hope flickers across her features, a heartbreaking glimpse of vulnerability.

"Yes, Mom. It's Ellen," I lie gently, guiding her to sit beside me. It feels wrong to deceive her, but right now, I'll do anything to calm the storm in her eyes.

A nurse enters, carrying a small cup with medication.

I instantly bristle. "Is this necessary?" I demand, my gaze locked on the clear plastic revealing its tiny chemical payload.

"Doctor's orders. It's just to take the edge off," she assures me.

"Off of what? Her dignity?" I want to scream, to protect my mother from this invasion, but instead, I watch helplessly as she accepts the medicine, her tears spilling over.

"Mom," I whisper, taking her hand. "I'm here, okay? You're safe."

Her sobs ebb slowly, replaced by a drowsy resignation that's almost worse to witness. I sit with her, Ellen in name only, until the sedatives pull her into an uneasy sleep. My own eyes sting with a sorrow too deep to name.

I slip out into the corridor, my heart pounding from the ordeal. I navigate back toward the front desk, searching for the acting director. When I find him, I don't even start with a greeting or an introduction. I just march over, trying hard to control my anger. "Why didn't you or Dr. Tuck call me?"

"Who's Dr. Tuck?" he asks.

"Dr. Camille Tuck is my mother's doctor. Who prescribed my mother a sleeping pill if it wasn't Dr. Tuck?"

He pauses a moment, then types into the tablet he's holding. "Our records show that Greyson Paradise was her admitting physician."

"He was, but he's an emergency department doctor. You should be dealing with Dr. Tuck."

"I'm sorry. The information we have lists Dr. Greyson. If you want to change that to another doctor…" He walks over to the reception desk and pulls out a stack of paperwork. "You'll need to fill this out and make the new doctor aware of the change."

I hold back my climbing level of frustration. "She's not a new doctor. She's my mother's GP."

When the acting director just shrugs, I rub my temples and take a breath so I don't explode. "Thank you," I say through gritted teeth. I need to talk to Greyson, and it can't wait until after his shift. I get in my car and drive straight to the hospital, though the short trip isn't enough to dissipate my anger.

I park and head into the emergency department, where I see Greyson talking to a member of the staff.

"Greyson," I say, catching his attention.

"Hey." His face changes when he sees mine. "What's wrong?"

"Mom…" My voice falters, but I push through, recounting Lakeview's actions, the medication, her tears. It pours out in a jumbled stream, my frustration barely contained.

"Hey, I approved that medication," Greyson interrupts gently. His hands are steady, professional, but his eyes hold a warmth exclusively for me. "It's to help her settle after the move. She'll be less afraid once she relaxes."

"Less afraid? She shouldn't have been moved without me knowing!" I want to shout, to demand answers, but his pager chirps, slicing through our moment.

"You're absolutely right. She shouldn't have been moved without consulting you. But it was a safety issue, and while Frankie is out, they're a little overwhelmed."

"She shouldn't have been moved. And why are you still listed as her doctor?"

He sighs and shakes his head. "It's clear things aren't exactly as they should be, and I'm sorry about that. But I feel confident your mother is safe. Can we talk about this more tonight?" He leans in, pressing a swift kiss to my forehead. "I've got four patients waiting. Sorry."

"Fine," I say, though it's far from how I feel. I watch him stride away, the door swinging shut behind him, leaving me adrift in the busy hallway.

I return to my car, and after sitting for a moment, I drive myself to a nearby coffee shop and order the biggest chocolate mocha they have. Then I sit down and read through all the paperwork they gave me at Lakeview.

I take a break and look at my work email, which is suddenly exploding with questions. I shut my eyes. *What am I going to do?* Clearly I need to get back to Vancouver, but I can't leave my mother.

Back at Lakeview, anger fuels my steps as I march straight to the administration office. The receptionist looks up, seeming startled by the intensity of my presence.

"Dr. Greyson is no longer part of my mother's care team," I inform her, setting the papers on the desk. "Dr. Camile Tuck is her physician, and any future consultations or changes are to go through her. Here is the paperwork all signed. Understood?"

"Uh, yes, Ms. Blaine," the receptionist stammers, tapping feverishly at her keyboard. "The records will reflect Dr. Tuck as the primary contact moving forward."

"Make sure they do. And I would like to be made aware of any changes to her housing or care immediately." I can't help the protective fire that rages within me. The receptionist nods again, and satisfied with the administrative capitulation, I turn on my heel and exit. I've got other fires — ones that pay my bills — to get settled.

Once back in the solitude of Mom's condo, the day's events crash over me like relentless waves. But there's no time to drown. Work needs me, and I have promises to keep, battles to wage. And somewhere in the mess, I need to figure out where Greyson fits into it all or if he even should. I don't understand how he can just cut me out of the decision-making entirely.

My fingers tremble over the keyboard, each tap echoing my frustration and disappointment. Greyson had no right to make those decisions without me. If I'd been there when they'd moved her, when they uprooted the fragile world my mother clings to, I could've softened the blow, could've held her hand and told her everything would be okay.

I try to focus on the spreadsheet in front of me, but the numbers blur into a jumbled mess. I can't work like this, not with my mind replaying the day's events on a torturous loop.

"Dammit," I mutter and open my email, my message to my boss short and lacking any pleasantries. *I need to take the afternoon as a personal day.* Send. Just like that, my cursor blinks mockingly, waiting for a response I'm not sure I want to read.

When it arrives a few minutes later, I wince. My boss's words are terse, his concern evident even through the digital divide. He might as well have typed his disappointment in bold letters. *Are you falling behind? Do you need a break? I can bring someone in.*

No, no, no. This project is mine. We're nearly at the finish line, and I won't let anyone else touch it. *Just today,* I type back fiercely, *I'll be back at it tomorrow.*

I push away from my desk, the chair rolling back with a squeak of protest. Today was meant to be productive, successful, a continuation of the high after Penn and Frankie's wedding. Instead, I'm fighting battles on too many fronts and trying not to lose myself in the process.

I pace the length of the living room, turmoil boiling inside me. Sometime later, the doorbell rings, and I fling it open to find Greyson.

"Trinity, I'm sorry," he starts, stepping inside. "I should have talked to you about your mother's medication, and Lakeview should have made you aware of the move. I didn't know you were at Lakeview when the request for medication came in."

His words do little to douse the flames of my ire. "And what about her being moved to the memory care unit?" My voice cracks. "Did you have anything to do with that?"

He hesitates, a telltale sign that there's more to this than he wants to admit. "Frankie mentioned it before she left," he confesses finally, running a hand through his hair in frustration. "They should have called you to discuss her wandering and the move, but it seems to have fallen through the cracks. I'm sorry. Frankie usually does that, and it was obviously missed."

"Missed? Fallen through the cracks?" I echo, incredulous. "I visit Mom every single day, Greyson. Why didn't someone say something? I should have been consulted." I pause, taking a deep breath to steady myself. "And Dr. Tuck, her actual GP, should have been the one to sanction any changes to her care."

Greyson's face tightens, the lines around his mouth deepening. "I understand why you're upset, but overall, this is a minor miscommunication," he says, his voice rising slightly. "I believe the move is the right call. Your mother is getting excellent care, Trinity."

"Excellent care doesn't excuse the fact that I was left out of the loop," I shoot back.

He takes a step closer, his blue eyes searching mine for understanding. "I deal with a lot at the hospital, Trinity," he explains softly. "I make it a point not to discuss patients outside of work to protect their privacy. I'm sorry the facility didn't communicate with you. They should have."

I want to melt into his comforting embrace, to let go of all the tension and fear, but there's too much at stake. My mother's well-being hangs in the balance, and I need to be her advocate, even if it means standing against Greyson.

"Privacy is one thing," I say, my voice firm. "But this is my mom. I should have known." I sigh, taking a moment to collect my thoughts. We don't disagree here, so there's no point in continuing to say the same things over and over. "I've updated the paperwork to make Dr. Tuck the primary contact for Mom's care. That's as it should be. So promise me, Greyson," I insist, locking eyes with him. "No more weighing in. You've got connections at Lakeview, and I appreciate that, but she has a doctor who knows her medical history. And then you won't feel conflicted about her privacy."

He runs a hand through his hair, a gesture of frustration I've come to recognize. "I promise, Trinity. Dr. Tuck will handle everything from here on out. And again, I'm sorry." His apology lingers in the air, the earnestness softening the anger in my chest.

"Thank you," I murmur, allowing just a hint of warmth back into my voice. It's difficult to stay mad at him when he shows genuine remorse.

Greyson shifts on his feet. "I hate arguing with you," he says, a pained look crossing his features. "Would you... Would you come upstairs for dinner? Just give me a chance to make things right."

My stomach twists, not with irritation, but hunger. I realize I haven't really eaten today. "What's on the menu?"

"Anything you want," he replies, hope in his eyes. "I'll order whatever you're craving."

"Anything, huh?" A smile tugs at the corner of my lips. "I

could go for some Thai food. Extra spicy."

"Done," he agrees as he reaches for his phone, ready to make good on his promise.

"Okay," I say, my stomach growling in agreement. "But actually, I haven't eaten all day, and maybe extra-spicy food is a bad idea. I think I'd like to go out for dinner. How about the Paradise Grill?"

He looks surprised, then pleased. "That sounds perfect."

I gather my things, and we head downstairs to the garage, the tension between us now giving way to a fragile truce. We drive over to the vineyard and walk into the warm glow of the Paradise Grill. He leads me to the family table, tucked away in a quiet corner.

"Nice choice," I comment, taking a seat.

"Only the best for you," he replies with a smile.

Before I can fully relax, the server arrives, pad in hand, ready to take our order. Greyson glances at me, then turns to her. "The salmon special looks good this evening. Perhaps we'll have two of those."

A flare of irritation sparks inside me. "Greyson, I can order for myself."

He holds up his hands. "Sorry, force of habit. The salmon is really good." He winces. "It's like I haven't learned anything today."

I'm too hungry and worn out to argue further. "Salmon special will be fine," I tell the server, my shoulders slumping. She nods and retreats.

"Trinity, I—" Greyson begins, but I shake my head.

"Let's just enjoy dinner, okay?" I suggest.

Greyson leans back, his gaze steady and patient. "Okay," he agrees, though I see the concern in his eyes. For now, it's enough that we're here together, trying to navigate the choppy waters of personal and professional boundaries. He reaches across the table to offer a comforting touch. "Trinity," he says, bringing me back from the brink of my worries, "talk to me."

I hesitate but then relent. "I'm just... I'm swamped, Greyson. The project at work is slipping through my fingers, and I can't afford to lose this job. But it's hard to focus when things with my mother are so unsteady." My words tumble out in a rush.

Greyson listens, absorbing every word like a sponge. "Starting tomorrow, we'll work harder to respect your schedule," he assures me. "Your work is important, and you shouldn't have to handle all this alone."

"Thank you," I murmur. "That means everything to me right now. But that doesn't mean doing it *for* me. I just appreciate knowing you're here."

"Of course," he replies. "You're in charge."

Light spills across the sheets as I kiss Greyson goodbye the next morning, the day's possibilities bolstered by the remnants of last night's comfort. The air is brisk as I step outside, my mind already racing with the tasks ahead. *I can do this.* I have to.

Back in the solitude of my mother's place, I bury myself in work, the relentless tick of the clock marking the pace of my progress. I speak with Andy, getting back up to speed on the final phase of the project, and together, we navigate through meetings, steering toward elusive, calm waters.

Then the buzz of the front door pulls my attention. A delivery? I check the time. It's nearly lunch, and I need to leave to go see my mother. I ride the elevator down, my curiosity piqued and stomach reminding me of its emptiness.

"Delivery from Paradise Grill," announces the guy at the door, holding out a container that smells divine. It's two green salads topped with roasted chicken, walnuts, goat cheese, and cranberries, with a side of balsamic vinaigrette. And then there's a package, wrapped neatly and stacked on top.

"Thank you," I say, taking everything from him. The delivery guy nods and departs, leaving me with these tokens of thoughtfulness that can only have come from Greyson.

Back upstairs, I set the food on the coffee table and turn my attention to the package. Unwrapping it feels like peeling away layers of concern, each fold loosening the tightness in my chest.

Within the paper lies a beautiful journal, its leather cover soft and inviting under my fingers. A nice fountain pen accompanies it, one I recall admiring last week at the vineyard's gift store. I run my thumb over its surface, the cool metal grounding me in this moment of unexpected joy.

Pulling out my phone, I snap a picture and text Greyson.

Me: Thank you for the beautiful lunch and gift.

My chest tightens with unexpected emotion. Greyson heard me yesterday. He sees me, and he's doing his best to be supportive in the way I've asked. And somehow that terrifies me, even as it's a comfort.

I stand and gather my purse and keys, ready to go see Mom when my phone chimes.

Greyson: Happy you like them. Enjoy lunch with your mom. I'm looking forward to your appreciation tonight.

A laugh escapes me.

Me: Can't wait.

The tension from earlier, the worry about work and my mother's situation, they ebb as I look at the journal again, thinking of the intimacy and laughter that await me this evening.

Everything feels a bit lighter when the burden is shared. I grab the salads and head to my car.

Twenty-two

Trinity

It's been a few days now, and Mom is less agitated about her new living situation. But I'm determined to make sure everything is right with her care, so I've been in touch with Dr. Tuck's office. That's why today, Lakeview's shuttle is idling at the curb, waiting for Mom and me. My visit is different this time. Before our lunch, we're heading to Dr. Tuck's office. I'm not just here as Joy Blaine's daughter. I'm here as her advocate, her memory when hers fails.

"Bye, Ellen," Mom murmurs to me as she shuffles off the shuttle, her tone distant.

She's done it again, mistaken me for her sister. It tugs at my heart, fraying my composure. "I'm going with you, Mom."

"Oh, that's nice of you."

We walk side by side into the clinic, her hand resting lightly on my arm. Despite the warmth of her skin, a cold current of concern flows through me.

As we wait in silence for Dr. Tuck, my thoughts drift to Greyson. Despite our occasional hiccups, he's the tender touch that soothes my furrowed brow after long days. It's nice to have a partner in all of this. Could I stay in Paradise a while longer? The idea blooms.

But ambition is a relentless force, and it soon pulls me back to reality. This project is difficult to manage entirely remotely, and then there's my vision of someday leading a hospital, shaping healthcare. That dream requires more than remote work or a job in a small town. It demands a claim staked firmly in the ground of boardrooms and policy debates in the city.

A moment later, my mother's name is called, and a nurse guides us into the office. We're settled in a room, and just moments later, Dr. Tuck appears.

"Joy, Trinity, nice to see you both," she greets us, her bright glasses a splash of color against the clinical backdrop. She's upbeat, but I can't help wondering if it's just the precursor to bad news.

Dr. Tuck motions for me to take a seat behind Mom, her eyes soft as she turns back to face my mother. "How are you feeling today, Joy?" she asks, notepad at the ready.

Mom sighs, the sound heavy. "I'm fine," she insists, but there's a tremor in her voice that suggests otherwise. "I miss my condo, though. It's too loud at Lakeview."

"What kept you busy yesterday?" Dr. Tuck's question is gentle, coaxing.

Mom nods eagerly, brightening a bit. "I got Trinity off to school," she starts confidently. But then her assurance crumbles like a cliff's edge into the sea. "I read a book most of the day, did some light housework, and then I made dinner for..." She trails off, her eyes clouding over, searching the room for a name that's slipped through her fingers.

"Before making dinner for...?" Dr. Tuck prompts.

"Ah, it's on the tip of my tongue. I can't remember his

name." Mom's hands flutter like trapped birds.

From my seat, I catch Dr. Tuck's glance. I give a small, involuntary headshake. None of those things happened yesterday, and my heart aches for her, for us.

"It sounds like you had a good day," Dr. Tuck comments.

Mom relaxes and nods.

"Why don't I listen to your heart and lungs?" Dr. Tuck guides Mom to the exam table, and the stethoscope moves gently across Mom's chest, listening to stories only hearts can tell while her lungs whisper secrets with each breath. Dr. Tuck's professionalism is a blanket of calm, but beneath it, I sense her concern.

"Your heart and lungs sound good, Joy. You can go back to your chair now," she says.

As Mom returns to her seat, her gaze suddenly finds me, surprise on her face. "Trinity, when did you get here?" she asks as if seeing me for the first time.

"Just now, Mom," I lie smoothly, the words leaving a bitter aftertaste.

"Fit as a fiddle," she declares, turning to Dr. Tuck. "I'm ready to go home."

Dr. Tuck nods, acknowledging the spirit behind the assertion. "You're close, Joy. But I'd like to try a new medication to help with your memory."

"Long as I write things down, I manage just fine," Mom counters.

"That should work well with this treatment," Dr. Tuck assures her, and I can see Mom relax slightly, her need for control met with understanding.

I watch them, these two women—one fighting to preserve her mind, the other working to mend it—and I'm caught in the crossfire of hope and reality.

"Okay, Joy, you're all set for today," Dr. Tuck says, scanning the charts one final time.

As Mom shuffles back to the waiting area, Dr. Tuck grasps

my elbow, drawing me aside. Her voice lowers to a confidential murmur. "Trinity, I'm concerned about your mother's memory. It's not rebounding as we'd hoped after the stroke, and I think it's wise that's she's receiving the added support of a memory care unit." She pauses, assessing my reaction. "I'd like a neurologist to evaluate her—Dr. Luke Dunham is excellent. And as I said, we'll try a different NRI medication. It may provide more benefit than the current one."

A knot forms in my stomach, but I manage a nod. "Should I start preparing for…for her to stay at Lakeview permanently?"

Dr. Tuck places a reassuring hand on my shoulder. "Not yet. Let's see what Dr. Dunham advises first."

"Thank you," I muster, grateful for her blend of compassion and candor.

Exiting the office, I find Mom sitting patiently, a faint smile gracing her lips. She recognizes me instantly, and something warm flickers inside me. "Ready to go home, Mom?"

"Always ready when you are." Her voice is stronger now that she's free from the weight of medical scrutiny.

The shuttle ride back to Lakeview is quiet, but just as I settle into the rhythm, my phone vibrates. Greyson's name lights up the screen.

"Hey, how did it go with your mom?" he asks when I answer.

"Dr. Tuck is switching her meds, and we're getting a consult with a neurologist too—Dr. Luke Dunham."

"Luke Dunham? He's top tier. Your mom's in good hands." Greyson's assurance lifts a weight off my shoulders.

"Thanks, Greyson. That means a lot." I watch as Mom gazes out the window, lost in thought or memory.

"Let's grab dinner after my shift ends," Greyson suggests.

"Sounds perfect. Six thirty?" I'm ready to enjoy the evening with him.

"Six thirty it is. See you then."

I hang up and turn to Mom. The sun casts a soft glow over

her features. Today has been kinder than most, and for that, I am thankful.

Back at Lakeview, I ease Mom into a chair at a table in the dining area, ensuring she's comfortable before I join her for lunch. The murmur of other residents and the clinking of cutlery form a familiar soundscape as we eat. Mom's more present today, her eyes bright and focused on me; it's a small win that buoys my spirits.

"Trinity, this is nice," she says. "We don't get to do this very often."

I smile, swallowing the lump her words bring to my throat. "Thanks, Mom. I agree." My heart hurts. We do this every day.

Still, I savor the warmth between us, pushing aside thoughts of medications and doctor's appointments. As lunch wraps up and Mom's attention begins to drift, the reality of my situation creeps back in. I kiss her forehead and promise to visit tomorrow, leaving her with one of the caretakers.

Back in the solitude of her condo, I fire up my laptop, the screen filling with a barrage of unread emails and unfinished tasks. Before I took Mom to Dr. Tuck, I managed to tick off only a fraction of my to-do list. Now, with Greyson's impending visit as my deadline, I hunker down, fingers flying over the keys, determined to make a dent in the workload.

The hours slip by in a blur of spreadsheets and conference calls, the afternoon sun casting shifting patterns across the wooden floors. A glance at the clock tells me it's nearing six, and I can almost feel Greyson's presence, his easy smile and the way he instinctively knows how to ease the tension from my shoulders.

My phone pings with an incoming text, and I reach for it, expecting the usual message confirming our dinner plans. The words that greet me are a jolt back to reality.

Greyson: Big boating accident. Not sure when I'll be out.

Don't wait up.

I stare at the screen, disappointment a bitter taste in my mouth. Yet concern for him and the victims quickly pushes my feelings aside.

Me: Stay safe. I've got plenty to keep me busy. We'll catch up later.

Setting the phone down, I refocus on the task at hand, diving back into the endless stream of work. Each report, each email, is another step toward the future I'm building for myself, and I know it will make a difference for countless others.

Yet even as I use this extra time to further catch up on our impending transition to electronic medical records, part of me longs for the simplicity of a shared meal with Greyson, for the chance to forget, if only for a moment, the weight of ambition and obligations resting on my shoulders.

The phone's ring cuts through the silence of the condo. I hesitate, the number unfamiliar, but I've learned that calls from Lakeview often come cloaked as unknowns for privacy's sake. I swipe to answer.

"Trinity Blaine speaking."

"Hey, it's Tarryn Paradise," comes the unexpected voice on the other end, not a resident or nurse from Lakeview, but Greyson's sister. "Greyson told me he's swamped at the hospital and you're buried in work. He asked me to stage an intervention."

A laugh bubbles up. "That sounds like him. But really, I'm okay. There's just so much to do."

"Come over. Elise and I are making pizzas, and we've got some excellent wine calling your name. It'll be fun," she cajoles, her voice warm and inviting.

I hesitate, weighing duty against the lure of good company and wine. "Well, when you put it that way, how can I refuse?"

"Perfect! See you soon!" She explains to me how to get to her house at the vineyard, and my excitement grows.

Ending the call, I stand, pushing back from the table with a decisive motion. Work will always be here. The prospect of unwinding with Tarryn and Elise—and the promise of wine—outweighs my professional goals, just this once.

I call a rideshare and step into the evening to enjoy the late summer air, still warm as it kisses my cheeks. The drive takes us up the hill at the vineyard to the address Tarryn gave me.

It's a picturesque scene, a quaint cottage nestled amid the rolling expanse of vineyards stretching toward the horizon. The rich aroma of earth and growing things fills my senses as I step out of the car. Gravel crunches underfoot, making my arrival obvious even before the car pulls away.

"Hey, you made it!" Tarryn greets me as I reach the door, her arms open in welcome. "So glad you came."

"Thanks for inviting me." I return the smile.

"This is my place." She sweeps her hand toward the cottage nestled among the vines. Then she points to another dwelling, half-hidden by trees. "And that one over there will be Elise's someday. She's staying with me for now until our fathers decide it's time to retire."

"Sounds cozy," I reply, taking it all in—the serenity of the vineyard, the camaraderie waiting inside, the softening sky above us. For a moment, I let myself simply be here, present and untethered from my usual constraints.

"Come on in. Let's get you that glass of wine." Tarryn leads the way, and I follow, ready to embrace whatever the evening has in store. "Elise should be here shortly. She's doing something with the cab vines and her father."

A few minutes later, we settle on Tarryn's back porch, the wooden planks warm beneath us as we face the sprawling vista of grapevines cascading toward Black Bear Lake. She grins, a mischievous twinkle in her eye, and I can't help but chuckle.

"Am I missing something here?" I probe. "Feels like there's more to this than an impromptu pizza night."

Tarryn waves away my question with a casual flick of her wrist. "Nothing at all. Just happy for some girl time without Greyson hovering," she says.

But I remain unconvinced and file this away to ask Greyson about later. As the sky begins its slow transition to dusk, bathing everything in soft gold, I take a deep breath.

"Ready to make some pizza?" Tarryn pulls out dough and an array of fresh toppings from a cooler by her side.

We rise and stand before the granite counter in her outdoor kitchen, and I press and stretch the dough, the rhythm soothing, the aroma of fresh basil and garlic already filling the air. It's therapeutic, the rhythm of kneading, and I lose myself in the simple task.

"Wow, you've got the real deal here," I say, nodding to the pizza oven that radiates welcoming heat. "You must be serious about your craft."

"Ah, this old thing?" Tarryn laughs. "My oldest brother, Kingston, installed it back when he lived here with his wife. Now, he's divorced and living across the water in Black Bear, rattling around in that big house of his."

"Sounds...lonely," I murmur, sliding my margherita pizza onto a peel.

"Maybe," Tarryn acknowledges with a shrug. "But I remain grateful for the improvements he made here. Tonight, we have good company and excellent food on the way."

We slide our pizzas into the oven, and then I cradle my wine glass, feeling the smoothness under my fingertips as Tarryn pours a deep ruby wine to refill my drink. "This pinot," she says, "is from our last good harvest. The frost this year was unkind to the grapes."

I bring it to my nose, savoring the rich aroma before taking a sip. It dances on my tongue—notes of cherry and earth. "It really is incredible."

Tarryn's smile is wistful as she leans back against the porch railing, holding her own glass. "Enjoy it. This bottle is one of the lucky survivors."

The conversation shifts then, as natural as the transition from day to dusk, and Tarryn's gaze meets mine. "So, what's going on with you and Greyson?"

I pause. "I'm here for my mom," I explain, swirling the wine in my glass, watching it cling to the sides. "Once Mom's settled, I'll need to head back to Vancouver. That's the plan, and I've always been good at sticking to plans."

"But that doesn't answer my question," Tarryn presses, tilting her head. "About Greyson?"

My shoulders rise and fall with a resigned sigh. "We're having fun. But there's an expiration date on this...whatever it is." At least, that's what I keep reminding myself. When I think about leaving, the idea feels more and more like losing something I didn't realize I wanted.

"Trinity, I think he likes you more than you realize."

"That's not possible," I counter quickly, too quickly maybe. "It's wishful thinking on your part."

She nods, but I detect a knowing look in her eyes. "I'd love to see my brothers settle down, eventually. Might mellow them out a bit."

I chuckle, and part of me wonders what it would be like with Greyson if there wasn't an impending end date. But then I wonder if I'd be here at all. That's not what I came for, and that's not usually what I do. It's not why I've let Greyson get close. In some ways, the end date makes this possible at all.

Elise arrives and pours herself a big glass of wine as she joins us.

"Everything okay?" Tarryn asks.

"Yes. Dad's worried that he saw some aphids. We don't see any sign of them on the vines, but he wants to plant some rose bushes to be sure."

"What do rose bushes do?" I ask.

"The aphids will eat at the rose bushes first. Once we see them there, we'll order ladybugs to eat them right away." Elise takes a big sip of her wine.

"Wow, who knew there was a battle going on all the time," I say with a laugh.

Elise raises her glass in toast. "Tell me about it."

When the pizza's ready, we shift gears to focus exclusively on that. As we eat, laughter breaks the silence of the night, a sound as rich and deep as the wine we've soon drained from two bottles. Tarryn's collection is impressive, but it's the company that makes the evening sparkle. She and Elise keep me laughing, and I feel more relaxed than I have in quite some time. As night falls, the air turns crip, yet the warmth of camaraderie keeps the chill at bay.

I reach for my glass, adding just a splash more wine, and set it gently on the table as I savor the remnants of flavor lingering on my palate. Stars begin to dot the heavens like pinpricks of light through a vast curtain.

"Is that Greyson?" Elise asks, peering into the darkness as headlights sweep across the vineyard.

The rumble of an engine grows closer, then dissolves into the click of a car door opening and closing. Moments later, Greyson emerges from the shadows, his presence like a final missing piece falling into place.

"Sorry I'm late," he says, pulling off a scrub cap to reveal disheveled hair, evidence of his hectic day at the hospital.

"Perfect timing," Tarryn replies with a grin. "We saved some dough for you."

Greyson rolls up his sleeves, revealing forearms toned by long hours of intense work. He takes the dough and shapes it into a perfect circle.

"Was the boat accident as bad as you expected?" I ask.

He spreads a dark sauce over the crust before layering on red onions, bacon, chicken, and cheese. While he works, he tells us about the chaos that hit his emergency department — too much alcohol, too many people. Two drowned, and several others will carry lasting injuries. Once his pizza is in the oven, he pours himself an Italian soda, then sits beside me, reaching for my hand and giving it a gentle squeeze.

"Greyson, how serious are you about Trinity?" Tarryn asks, going the direct route this time.

He glances at me, his expression softening in a way that makes my pulse quicken. "I'm serious enough to know I'm not ready for this to end."

The words hang in the air, and for a moment, I'm not sure if I want to laugh, cry, or run. Usually, when a guy says something like this, I use that as my excuse to flee. But this time I don't do any of those things. I just hold his gaze, letting the weight of what he said settle somewhere deep inside me.

"Trinity and I..." He starts, then pauses, searching for the right words. "We're enjoying the time we have together."

He looks at me again, and something unspoken passes between us. A recognition of the temporary nature of what we share, yet a connection that runs deeper than either of us expected.

"Tarryn," I interject, feeling the need to manage expectations, "we've set boundaries. There's an end date to this, but that doesn't mean we can't remain friends. I have to go back to Vancouver for a week or so for my job, but I'll always be back until I know what my mom needs, until I have her stable." My voice holds a note of finality, even as my heart quietly questions the truth of my words.

"Friends," Greyson echoes softly, his gaze lingering on mine before he turns back to the oven. He slides the cooked pizza out onto his plate, and the aroma of melting cheese and barbecue sauce fills the air.

"Here's to new friendships and moments we'll remember." Tarryn lifts her glass.

"Cheers," we all say in unison, clinking our glasses together.

And as we sit under the starlit sky, the laughter resuming, I let myself get lost in the here and now, knowing that whether friendship or something more, what matters is the connection we're creating, one slice of life at a time.

Twenty-three

Greyson

On Sunday morning, I wake to the sensation of warmth enveloping me, a pleasure so intense it borders on the surreal. Trinity is sliding down onto me, her movements a hypnotic rhythm that draws a low groan from my throat. My eyes flutter open to the sight of her breasts bouncing in time with her slow, steady pace, the best method to prolong the ecstasy that's building within me. We've spent the better part of the last three days in bed in my condo — with just a few quick breaks here and there for basketball and visiting her mother — and it seems we're both insatiable.

"Good morning," she purrs, a wicked glint in her eye.

"Morning," I manage. "You should wake me up like this every day."

She smiles at that, and the way she rides me — controlled and deliberate — tells me she knows exactly what she's doing to me. My hands find their way to her hips, but she quickly captures them, her fingers interlocking with mine. "Keep those hands to yourself, or I might have to tie you up."

But restraint isn't something I'm good at, not when it comes to her. As she leans forward, I seize the opportunity, my mouth latching onto her nipple with an eagerness that borders on desperation. She gasps as I suck her deep into my mouth. When she attempts to rise, I refuse to release her, keeping her nipple taut between my lips. Her response is immediate and intense. Her pussy clamps down hard. *God, I love how responsive she is.*

The connection between us is electric, each movement and countermovement drawing us deeper into a shared space where only we exist. It's moments like these, where the world outside our embrace ceases to matter, that I'm reminded just how much I need her in my life.

My muscles tighten with anticipation, and I lock my knees around Trinity's hips as I shift. In one fluid motion, she's beneath me, her back pressed to the sheets that still hold the warmth of our slumber. The transition from rider to ridden doesn't faze her. Her eyes are alight with the thrill of it.

I hoist one of her legs over my shoulder, granting myself deeper access as my fingertips find her clit, circling with a practiced touch that elicits a chorus of breathy moans.

She reaches for the piercing that seems to serve as a conduit for our electric connection. Her fingers tweak it just as my control frays at the edges, and I'm gone, spilling into her as she clenches around me, following me over the edge into blissful oblivion.

We're panting, out of breath, and clinging to the remnants of ecstasy. She rolls away, a sly smile curving her lips. "My plan was to finish you off with my mouth."

The mere suggestion sends an eager pulse through me, and I can feel myself stirring again. But after a moment she bounds out of bed, and soon, the steam from the shower clouds the room, wrapping around Trinity like a shroud as she steps in. I linger on the edge of the bed, watching her silhouette through the frosted glass, admiring the efficiency with which she moves. Even on a Sunday, Trinity is all about precision.

"Need help with those hard-to-reach spots?" I call as I push myself off the bed and pad across the cool tile floor.

Trinity's laugh rings out above the patter of water. "I fell for that line once, Greyson Paradise," she retorts. "And all you did was play with me."

Her accusation is nothing short of inviting, but I hold back a chuckle, leaning against the door frame. "And here I thought you enjoyed my hands-on approach."

"Very nice, but I need to get some work done today." She turns slightly, the movement casting ripples through the water cascading down her body.

"Of course," I say, though I can't resist slipping into the shower behind her. Droplets cling to my skin instantly, merging with the remnants of our early morning activities. Her dedication to her work is one of the many things I admire about her, even if it means resisting the urge to pull her back into a world where only we exist.

"Let me at least make sure you're thoroughly rinsed off," I offer, my voice pitched low, a compromise between my desire and her determination.

After a few minutes we trade places, and she leaves the bathroom while I finish in the shower. Wrapping a towel around my waist, a conversation begins to form in my mind. We've talked a bit this weekend about Trinity's mother, but she only gave me a quick update. She'd been disappointed by her encounter with Dr. Dunham, which wasn't surprising to me. Luke is the best bet for helping her mom, but I probably should have warned her. As a neurologist, he doesn't always have the best bedside manner. I don't want her to think his lack of reassurance means there's no hope for improvement. But I also don't want to steer her mind to worry about her mom if she needs to focus on the last phase of her migration project today.

Then all my thoughts are cut short by unexpected voices in the kitchen, where Trinity went to make coffee. My heart lurches into my throat. *This can't be happening.* Not now.

With a burst of adrenaline, I yank on a pair of sweatpants and race toward the source of the commotion. The scene unfolding before me is like a car crash in slow motion, impossible to look away from yet filled with impending doom.

"You need to leave. Greyson doesn't do repeats or breakfast with anyone but me." Anita's voice is sharp, her attitude entirely out of place.

"Who do you think you are?" Trinity's reply is incredulous, her stance defiant, her wet hair a dark curtain around her shoulders.

"He's my fiancé," Anita states, attempting to lay claim to territory long abandoned and never entirely hers.

Trinity's face falls, her eyes wide with disbelief and hurt. My heart lurches, and I spring forward. This is a moment I can't afford to lose control of.

"Stay where you are," I tell Trinity. I turn to Anita, striving to keep my tone even. "What are you doing here?"

"I told you I'd be here this morning," she reminds me, her words a punch to the gut. She's right. She did say that, in an email I skimmed and promptly ignored. But she's been back in town before and never showed up at my condo like this.

"Anita…" The name sits heavy on my tongue, weighted with a history that is long in my rearview mirror. My gaze flickers between the two women, the past and the present colliding in a storm I never saw coming. "You should've called," I insist, but it's too late.

Trinity's eyes, once filled with warmth and intimacy, are now cold with betrayal. For a moment, I think she's going to say something, but instead, she presses the elevator button. The doors open, and she steps inside without a word, her shoulders squared as if bracing herself for the blow that's already landed.

"Trinity, wait!" But the doors close on my plea, sealing her from my sight. I can't believe she just left, not that she deserves any of this. I don't blame her one bit for getting out of here. But I can't leave things this way.

I move to go after her, but I'm ensnared by Anita's sudden embrace. "I've missed you so much," she murmurs into my chest. The scent of her perfume, once familiar, now strikes me as invasive, a reminder of a world I no longer inhabit.

"Anita, you should've called before letting yourself in," I repeat. She pulls back, her gaze searching mine, but there's no mention of Trinity. No acknowledgment of the storm she's stepped into. It's as if Trinity were nothing more than a wisp of smoke, easily dispersed and forgotten.

My heart beats a frantic rhythm, each thud echoing Trinity's name. I have to go after her. I have to make this right. I clear my throat. "Anita, this isn't a good time. You need to go."

"Greyson, we've been in touch this whole time," Anita insists, her eyes wide. She seems undeterred by my words and by the absence of warmth in my tone. "I'm back now, and we can start planning our wedding."

Her assumption hits like a punch to the gut. Confusion races through me as I meet her gaze. "We're not getting married, Anita." I don't understand why she would think that. I never proposed, even before she left town.

Anita and I were high school sweethearts, and for a while, we talked about getting married, but that's all it ever was. We stayed together through university and my medical school in Vancouver, and even into my residency, but then she moved east to Toronto, chasing her own aspirations. I've heard from her now and again over the past few years. Whenever she visited her parents, we'd catch up, and we still exchange birthday calls. But we haven't been in a relationship since she left. Toronto seemed to be where she wanted to stay, and she didn't seem to care what I thought about that.

She blinks, taken aback. "But we never broke off our

engagement."

My eyes widen. "We weren't engaged, Anita. And it's been nearly three years," I remind her. *How can she believe we still had a relationship?* "You chose to leave everything behind."

"Greyson, you can't mean that." Her voice is soft, pleading. "We've always loved each other. I waited for you — to finish college, medical school. We had plans."

"Plans that changed when you left," I counter. The memory stings, sharp and fresh. "You were gone without a goodbye."

"Left?" She recoils as if struck, anger flaring in her eyes. "I needed to follow my dreams and know that Paradise is what I always thought it was."

"You've been alone because you chose to be," I reply, my voice rising. "Text messages don't count as being there for each other."

"Greyson —" she starts.

But I've heard enough. "I'm glad you're home," I interject. "Your parents must be thrilled, but I..." My voice trails off. I've moved on from what we had, and I thought she had too. How could I have missed this?

"Please," she whispers, reaching out as if to bridge the gulf between us. "Don't do this. Don't throw away what we had."

"Anita," I begin, steadying my resolve. "What we had was beautiful, but it's in the past. I've moved on." The words are a quiet declaration of independence, a release from the ghosts that have haunted me.

"Moved on to where? To who?"

But I owe her no answers, not anymore. My heart is elsewhere, racing away in an elevator I didn't catch in time. I step back, putting distance between the past and my present.

"Anita." Her name feels foreign on my tongue now, like it belongs to someone I used to know. "We loved each other once, but that was a long time ago. We haven't been part of each other's lives for years now. I've fallen in love with someone else." As I say them, I know those words are truth. I'm now connected only to the woman who's taught me what it means to feel alive again. "There's nothing between us anymore."

Her face crumples, tears welling up. It's a familiar sight, one that once would've unraveled me, had me scrambling to comfort her. But not now. "You used to manipulate me with those tears," I note. "You will always be an important part of my path, but the past is where you belong."

She opens her mouth to argue, but I turn away, urgency propelling me toward the elevator. I can hear her following, her voice escalating as she tries to reason with me. "Greyson, you're wrong! I'm here now, ready to work through everything with you."

The ding of the elevator arriving cuts through her pleas. I step inside, making a clear choice. Her words fade into the background, muffled by the closing doors. All that matters now is reaching Trinity.

But what if I'm too late? What if Anita's presence has already undone everything we've built? I can't think that way. I have to believe in what we have, what we know about each other. And I know I can't let her turn away, not without a fight.

Twenty-four

Greyson

When the elevator opens, I dash down the hallway, propelled by a mix of dread and urgency. My fist hammers on her mother's door—once, twice. There's no answer. "Trinity! Please! Open up!" A frustrated *Fuck!* bursts from my lips before I can stop it.

"Greyson Paradise!" The rebuke comes from behind me, and I spin to see Mrs. Henley from across the hall, her eyes narrowed behind her spectacles. "Language!"

"Sorry, Mrs. Henley." I rub the back of my neck, chastened.

She huffs, disappearing behind her door, leaving me to grapple with my racing thoughts. *Where could Trinity have gone?*

Without another moment's delay, I retrace my steps. Anxiety twists inside me. The elevator doors open, and there's Anita, crumpled on my living room couch, sobbing into her palms.

"Anita..." My voice trails off, unsure what comfort I can offer when my mind is focused on getting her out of here.

She looks up. "Greyson, please —"

"Anita," I interrupt, softer now, even though impatience is a live wire beneath my skin. "You know we've been over for a long time. I don't know why you're doing this."

"Please, Greyson, take me back," she pleads. "I waited for you to follow me, but I know now that your heart is here. So I'm back." Her voice breaks, and she rises to clutch my hand.

Her words twist something in me, but not the way she wants.

"That's not really what you want. You know that's not right."

She reaches for me, but I pull away. She's not going to change my mind.

"Listen to me," I say, disentangling my hand. "I care about you, I do. You'll always have a place in my heart, but I'm not in love with you. You need to move on."

"But —" Her plea is cut short by another sob, and it takes every ounce of my resolve not to comfort her.

"Trinity," I admit, the name feeling like a confession. "I need to go find her, so you need to go. And I need my key fob back from you."

Anita's crying intensifies, but she fumbles in her purse and hands me the small, metallic object. Our fingers brush, a final contact, as I accept it.

"Thank you," I whisper, pocketing the fob. Guilt gnaws at me, but I need to find Trinity and make things right. "Take a moment if you need to, but then please go."

I leave Anita behind, her sobs echoing in my ears as I make a beeline for the garage. The cool air hits me like a splash of sanity, and I whip out my phone to call Trinity. It rings into the void, unanswered, and something inside me tightens with unease.

"Dammit," I mutter. Decision made, I start my car and steer toward Lakeview, clinging to hope that she's there, that I can make her understand.

But the parking lot at Lakeview is half-empty, and there's no sign of Trinity's car. My heart sinks a little more, but I push through the doors of the facility and head straight to the memory care unit where Joy, Trinity's mother, resides. The scent of antiseptic mixed with something faintly floral greets me, doing nothing for my anxiety.

"Joy?" I call softly as I approach her, noting the vacant look in her eyes today.

"Who's asking?" Her voice is cautious, distant, as if she's speaking from another world.

"It's Greyson Paradise. I'm looking for Trinity, your daughter." I watch for any flicker of recognition, any sign that might lead me to Trinity.

"Trinity?" She furrows her brow. "I don't know a Trinity."

Desperation tightens my throat. "Maybe...maybe Ellen? Your sister? Have you seen her today?"

"Ellen..." Joy's lips tremble slightly. "Haven't seen Ellen in years. Who are you again?"

"Greyson," I repeat, feeling utterly defeated. I thank her and step away.

On the way down the hall, I stop a nurse to ask if she's seen Trinity. She shakes her head. I don't know what else to do. Back in my car, my hands shake as I dial Trinity's number again. This time, I leave a message, my voice raw.

"It's me. Greyson. Please, just talk to me. I'll explain everything. I'll fix everything. You have to know what you mean to me, how you've changed everything I thought I knew about love and life. I need you to believe that this, us. It's worth fighting for."

I hang up, the silence around me more profound than before. All I can do now is wait, hope, and fight this sinking feeling that I've lost something irreplaceable.

Twenty-five

Trinity

My tires crunch on the gravel as I pull up to Tarryn's cottage. The car door shuts with a heavy thud, and Tarryn waves from the porch, her smile at odds with the storm brewing inside me.

"You're back." She holds up a cup of coffee. "You just missed Elise. She's already out in the vines."

I nod, my throat tight with words I can't yet unleash about some woman calling herself Greyson's fiancée.

She looks at me a moment, perhaps waiting for an explanation, but then she smiles brightly. "Come in! Let's get you some coffee." She ushers me into the warmth of her home.

She's soon rambling about a new blend she's trying as she scoops grounds into the coffeemaker, but my mind remains elsewhere, snagged on the image of Anita in Greyson's kitchen. My curiosity, a gnawing creature in my belly, keeps me rooted here when every instinct screams at me to flee.

"Smells good," I manage to say as the coffeemaker starts.

"Wait till you taste it!" Tarryn replies.

We wait in awkward silence until finally she hands me a mug, the steam curling up like a gentle question. Stay or go?

We carry our coffee over to the living room, where overstuffed couches and an array of colorful pillows beckon. This room definitely has a woman's touch, the opposite of the stark, modern lines that men seem to be drawn to.

Tarryn again seems to be waiting politely for me to offer some reason for being here, but again, I dodge the direct approach. "Did you redecorate after Kingston moved out?" I ask, tracing the pattern on a throw pillow with my finger.

Tarryn laughs. "Oh, I did. Can you believe he had everything in leather, black, and ivory? Very contemporary, but not cozy at all. I prefer the lived-in look."

I smile, despite the ache in my heart. "I do too."

As I settle back into the soft cushions, the warmth from the coffee cup seeps into my palms. Maybe staying for a little while won't be so bad. After all, there are questions that need answers, and for now, Tarryn seems like the only link to understanding what's happening with Greyson—and with me.

Tarryn's suggestion that Greyson would finance a redecoration at his place snaps my attention back to her. "Anita probably has other ideas," I mutter.

"Anita?" Tarryn's voice cracks like thin ice underfoot. "Is she coming back to town?"

I nod. "She showed up this morning. In his condo." Bitterness coats my words. "She kicked me out."

"She kicked you out?" Tarryn leans forward, her eyes wide, reflecting shock and something akin to fear.

"Yep."

"Damn her," Tarryn hisses, the curse sounding foreign on her usually cheerful lips. She shakes her head. "I can't believe she had the nerve to come back. The whole family despises Anita

Lowe. Not one of us could see what Greyson saw in her." Her gaze sharpens, fixing on me. "He's over her. I'm sure of it. What did he say when she appeared?"

"Nothing. He didn't say much of anything. He told her it wasn't a good time, but I didn't stick around after that." My voice is hollow, echoing the emptiness spreading through my chest.

"Greyson cares about you, Trinity. You know that, don't you?" Tarryn's conviction is palpable. "He was worried sick about leaving you alone last night when he had to work late after the boating accident. That's why he wanted you with me. He wouldn't have done that if you didn't mean something to him."

Her words are meant to comfort, but Greyson's concern for me now feels like salt rubbed into the rawness left by Anita's unexpected appearance. What's worse, I can't shake off the image of hurt in his eyes as I walked out, the same ones that had gazed at me with such warmth not long ago.

"Tarryn…" I start, my throat tight, but I trail off. If I want to know the backstory here, I need to ask Greyson, and I'm not ready to do that.

I stand, my limbs stiff. My heart aches, but I have to focus on what's ahead. "Tarryn, I need to get back to Vancouver." My voice trembles despite my efforts.

"Vancouver? Now? I thought you weren't leaving until next week." Tarryn's brows knit together.

"Yeah." I avoid her gaze, looking instead at the worn comfort of the overstuffed couches around us. "It'll be a few weeks before Mom's next appointment with the neurologist, and my boss is… Well, he's not thrilled about how long I've been gone."

"Can't it wait?" Tarryn pleads, reaching out as if she could physically anchor me to Paradise. "Stay a little longer, please. Don't leave with things like this."

I shake my head. "The last part of my project at work is about to be deployed, and I need to be there for it." I force a smile. "I'll call you when I'm back in town to visit Mom, okay?"

"Trinity…" Tarryn stands, closing the distance between us. "Don't leave because of Anita. Stay in Paradise."

"I wish I could," I whisper, feeling the lie settle on my lips. The truth is, I need to escape. Paradise feels suffocating. Every corner reminds me of Greyson — his touch, his voice, the way he looked at me like I mattered. Leaving isn't just about Anita. She's just a wake-up call. I have to protect what's left of me before I lose myself completely.

"Promise me you'll call?"

"I promise," I tell her.

Tarryn wraps her arms around me. "Trinity, listen to me," she says, pulling back to meet my eyes. "You and Greyson…you're meant to be together. We all see it. You're good for each other."

"Tarryn —" I protest, but she cuts me off.

"I mean it. Greyson loves you, which makes us sisters."

Tears leak from my eyes as I shake my head. "I've always said it wouldn't last forever. Anita is just a reminder that I've been here too long and it's time to go."

"Anita's nothing but a ghost from his past," she counters. "Don't let her haunt your future with Greyson."

Her words stir something within me, a flicker of warmth amid the chill of doubt. Even so, I know the road back to Vancouver is calling. After a quick stop to check on Mom, I need to be on my way.

Twenty-six

Greyson

I grip the steering wheel, knuckles white, as I cross the bridge back to Paradise Hill. My mind is a tempest, churning with thoughts of Trinity and the mess Anita has caused, that I caused by not telling Trinity about Anita.

Driven by some sliver of hope, I steer my car toward the vineyard. Maybe Trinity sought refuge there.

Tarryn spots me the moment I step out of the car, her fury unmistakable. "Greyson! What the hell? How could you let that woman kick Trinity out of *your* house?"

Her words freeze my heart, but I don't have time to wallow. "Tarryn, it's not like that," I assure her. "I was in the shower. By the time I realized she was there, Anita had already…" I trail off, the words catching in my throat.

"Trinity left." Tarryn's eyes soften with concern before hardening again. "She went back to Vancouver for work."

"Vancouver?" My heart sinks. "She wasn't planning on going back today. For how long? When is she coming back?"

"She told me she'd call the next time she comes to town." Tarryn shakes her head and walks back inside, leaving me to grapple with the magnitude of my mistake.

The drive back to my condo is a blur. When the elevator opens on the fifth floor, the sight that greets me steals my breath. Anita, bare as the day she was born, sprawls across my couch, a smirk on her lips.

"Anita, get dressed and get out," I demand, my voice cold.

"Come on, Greyson," she whines, tears welling up again. "Can't we just—"

"No!" I cut her off. I grab her clothes and stuff them into her bag, tossing it into the open elevator. "I can't say it any other way. It's over. I'm in love with someone else. Not you."

Naked and defeated, Anita gathers what's left of her dignity, steps into the elevator, and vanishes.

I dial Trinity again, the ringtone echoing around my apartment. Voicemail. "Trinity, it's Greyson. Please, just talk to me. I'll explain everything. I just… I need to hear your voice and see you."

I sit down and stare into space, frozen and overwhelmed. Perhaps I sleep, perhaps I just shut down, but the next thing I'm aware of, the sun is casting long shadows across my condo. The walls feel like they're closing in on me, suffocating me with the silence of Trinity's absence. My phone lies abandoned on the coffee table, its screen dark and unresponsive.

The elevator's soft ding startles me, and I drag myself up, hoping against hope that it's Trinity. But when the elevator doors slide open, Ryker stands there.

"Tarryn filled me in about Trinity," he says, exiting the elevator. "How are you holding up?"

"Not great," I admit.

Ryker surveys the room, his gaze pausing at the crumpled cushions where Anita laid earlier.

"Trinity went back to Vancouver," I say. "She left because of Anita." I can't meet Ryker's eyes. "I should've made her feel secure here with me. I should have told her about my past with Anita."

Ryker doesn't speak, but I see the question in his eyes. *Why didn't you?*

"Trinity…she's different," I continue. "There's something about her that just fits. I never wanted her to leave."

"If you'd told her about Anita, she wouldn't have been able to send her packing so easily," Ryker finishes for me, nodding in understanding.

"Exactly." I run a hand through my hair. "Now, she's gone, and I'm left wondering why I let that happen. I can't believe I didn't see it coming."

"Greyson." Ryker places a hand on my shoulder. "Only you can fix this. You can't let her slip away over a misunderstanding."

"Yeah," I whisper. "I know."

I turn away from him, looking out the window at the fading light, wondering how I'll bridge the distance between Paradise and Vancouver, between the life I thought I wanted and the future that now seems so uncertain without Trinity.

I pace the length of my condo. Paradise, with its familiar streets and the faces I've known all my life, feels claustrophobic now, like a beautiful cage that's suddenly too small.

"Why are you here?" Ryker asks after a while. "You could live anywhere in the world. Why Paradise?"

The question hits an unexpected nerve, and my anger simmers. "Why do you live here?" I shoot back. I've never questioned it before, the deep roots I have in this place.

He shrugs. "I like it here. But if something were to happen, if I got a head of cardiology position at a major hospital or I fell in love with someone who doesn't want to be here, I'd leave."

His words knock the breath out of me. *Move? Leave Paradise?* The very thought sends a jolt through my system.

"Never thought about it. Even when Anita left for Toronto." I admit. "The winery is here. I've never wanted to live anywhere else."

Ryker studies me for a long moment, and I can see the gears turning in his head. He doesn't know Trinity — not really — but he understands more than enough. "Oh. I thought you were in love with her."

"I'm not in love with her!" I yell, my frustration mounting as I deny what I've already said is true. But I want to tell her before I tell the world. It's bad enough I told Anita before I said anything to Trinity.

"Trinity's important to you," he amends. "Don't lose out on something great just because you're tied to a place. You say you don't want to live in Vancouver, but what's more important? The where or the who?"

His question is like a splash of cold water. What am I willing to sacrifice? My comfort zone, my town, for her?

"Think about it," Ryker says, his hand on the doorframe. "If she's the one, figure out what you're willing to do to prove it. You've always been good at fixing things. It's time to fix this. That is, if you want her."

With that, he turns to call the elevator, but his words linger long after he's gone, planting a seed of determination I can't ignore.

Can I let go of the life I've always known? The answer isn't clear, but the image of Trinity Blaine's face — the way she laughed, the way we were together, the depth of her understanding — makes my heart lurch with longing. There is no one else like her.

I lean my head back, close my eyes, and allow myself to imagine a different life. One that might not be set against the backdrop of Paradise but is nonetheless filled with the light of Trinity's smile. Suddenly, there are more possibilities than I ever considered.

Twenty-seven

Trinity

O n the long drive back to Vancouver, the road stretches ahead like a chasm between what I had in Paradise and the emptiness waiting at home. The hum of traffic feels louder than ever, and my thoughts keep circling back to Anita, the intruder who shattered the morning's peace. Why didn't Greyson tell me she was coming? Was it a lapse or something worse? The memory of his arms around me last night, the way he whispered my name like a promise, feels like a cruel contradiction now. I want to believe him, but the doubt Anita planted refuses to let go.

Shaking my head, I try to dismiss the gnawing questions, to focus on the road, the mountains rising around me as I cross the threshold back into city life. It's only when I reach the familiar outline of the Vancouver suburbs that a different kind of panic sets in. I left my phone at my mother's when I stopped to say goodbye.

For a moment, I consider turning back, but then resignation settles over me. I'm already here, and it's just as well. I don't want to hear the apologies, the excuses, or the silence that might be even worse. Greyson, Tarryn, my mother — they all feel like parts of a dream I'm desperate to wake from.

Then it comes to me. I'll call Lakeview and give them my office number since I'll be living at work this week. And I can order a new phone. My old one was three years old. I'll handle that once I'm done with the software migration.

So I press on, ignoring what I left behind and trying to focus on being back in the bustling city, where starting tomorrow morning, I can throw myself into work and the parts of my life I can still control.

The next morning, as I head into my office, the city crawls at a snail's pace, each red light mocking me as I inch forward. Four lights to get through this intersection — ridiculous. I can't help but long for the simplicity of my mother's dining room table, where I could walk to work, sometimes in my pajamas. Now, I'm back to my hour-plus commute.

"Need to swing by Martin Wireless," I mutter as I work through my mental to-do list. I need to be reachable all the time. Any other thought was just avoidance. As of now, Lakeview can't reach me when I'm not at the office, and that's just not responsible, no matter who I do or don't want to talk to.

Finally, I pull into the familiar employee lot at North Vancouver General Hospital. Stepping out, I stretch, trying to shake off the tension from the commute. I sling my bag over my shoulder and set my sights on the hospital's entrance, steeling myself for the final push on the electronic medical records migration.

My cubicle is waiting for me as I enter—a photo of my parents and me smiling from the desk, a stack of reports waiting for my attention. I tuck my personal effects into their usual nooks before heading to the communal freezer, frozen meal in hand, my plan for the late nights ahead.

Back at my desk, I'm greeted by a wave of enthusiasm. "Trinity Blaine! You're back just in time," Andy exclaims, his grin wide. "I'm so glad you're here!" He buzzes around me, pulling me toward the center of activity. "We're so close, Trinity. This final push for the migration—it's all hands on deck."

"Happy to be here." I smile, but I really can't put words into how I feel.

"Do you have a minute?" he asks after a moment, gesturing to his office.

"Of course." The words are automatic, my feet already moving me toward his office before my mind fully registers the interruption. The door closes behind us with a soft click.

"Before your day gets started, I wanted to ask how your mother is doing?" he says, a softness to his voice that tugs at the freshly stitched wounds in my heart.

"Memory care," I say. "They're managing her condition, but it's tough when she doesn't recognize me."

He nods. "My father went through the same thing," he confides. "I get it. And I appreciate you being here, but if you need to get back to Paradise for a while, we'll understand."

But how can I leave? Work is the only constant I have left. "I still need this job," I admit, voicing my fear—unemployment, drifting, losing the ground beneath my feet.

"Maybe we can find some projects you can do remotely," he offers.

That's generous, but it's also a detour from the path I've planned for myself. Running a department, running a hospital— that's the dream. And I don't know how to waver from it. Right now, I'm standing at a crossroads with no signs to guide me.

"Thank you," I tell him. "I have a lot to think about." Despite everything, he's at least given me an option. And that's more than I had before.

"I know you're ambitious, but someone once told me life is all about juggling balls," he adds. "Some, like your career, are rubber. When you drop them, they bounce. But others, like your family, are glass. When you drop them, they shatter. You've had a tough year. Think about what you really want."

His revelation roots me in my seat. I open my mouth, but then close it again. I don't know what I want to do. "Thank you. That gives me a lot to consider."

Andy smiles and slaps his hands on his thighs. "Well, you've got a big week ahead. Let me know what you need from me. You've got this."

I nod, and his rallying cry sends me back to my cubicle with renewed purpose. It's time to dive back into the work that's been waiting for me. I'm ready.

I plop into my chair, and the red voicemail light winks at me. Guess I should start there. I press the playback button, bracing for the onslaught of demands and questions, but it's Liz's voice that fills the silence first, a bit concerned, asking about dinner plans we never made. I had called and told her about Anita and that I was returning to Vancouver, but then I left my phone and she never heard back from me.

The message ends, and another begins, this one ensnaring my heart in a tangle of emotions. *Greyson*. His voice stirs a storm within me, and tears pool in my eyes.

"Trinity, I'm sorry for calling your work. I... I've been trying to get ahold of you," he starts, his voice laced with regret. "Anita had no right to do what she did, asking you to leave. It was wrong. I can't get through on your cell phone, so I'm just going to tell you this here..."

My breath catches as he delves into their history, unraveling tales of youthful promises with Anita, vows that lingered like ghosts. I press a trembling hand against my heart.

"I should have told you about her, about all of it," he admits. His voice cracks. "She's not my fiancée. She had a fob to my condo because she never gave it back when she left three years ago. I miss you. I don't want us to be over. Please call me."

I have to take a moment to breathe when the message ends. He's giving me a chance to bridge the gap between us, but the question remains — can I do it?

We knew my return to Vancouver was a countdown to our end. My life is here. His life is there. Yet now, with his voice lingering in my cubicle, I feel torn. What if Greyson is worth risking everything for?

I swipe at the moisture on my cheeks, willing away the tears Greyson's voice has conjured. I draw in a shuddering breath and let it out slowly, deliberately. My desk, littered with notes and reminders, beckons me. "Once this integration is done," I murmur. "Then I'll have time to figure this all out."

Shaking off his message, I rise from my chair. The project needs me. And I need it.

I head to the conference room to meet with the IT team, and the door swings open before I can reach for the handle. They have bagels, coffee, and a box of my favorite donuts, TimBits.

"Welcome back!" says Jocelyn Rider, one of my coworkers. "We missed your bright and shining face."

"This is so sweet of you," I say looking at everyone. Suddenly, I'm glad I'm here and ready to make a difference. "Shall we take this thing live?"

"Absolutely," they chorus.

Over our food, we divide up tasks and make plans to keep each other up to date before we return to our cubicles to take care of the work.

I slide back into my chair and I settle noise-canceling headphones over my ears, ready to ward off any distractions that threaten my focus. The Gantt chart for the project stares back at me, a mess of deadlines and dependencies that are almost complete.

My gaze locks on the first task on my list, double-checking that all the codes and forms have been updated in the system. I've pulled out the files and started working down the row when a steaming cup of coffee materializes before my eyes. I blink up, momentarily disoriented, and Liz's concerned face swims into view. I pull my headphones off.

"Gotcha," she says with a wry smile, tilting the cup toward me.

"Thanks," I murmur.

"I've been calling your name for a solid minute." She chuckles. "You were so deep in your mind, I thought I might have to send a search party."

"Sorry, just—" I gesture vaguely at my screen. "—busy. These things are amazing for blocking out the world." I hold up my headphones.

"Looks like it." She glances at the chart with an appreciative nod. "That's some serious dedication."

I take a sip of the coffee, grateful for the interruption, even if I hadn't realized I needed it.

Liz's eyes scan mine. "It's past lunchtime, and you need a break," she says, her voice firm. "Come on, let's take a walk."

I glance at the clock. It's nearly two in the afternoon. My stomach growls. A break does sound good. I nod, setting the coffee down and pushing back from my desk.

We weave through the maze of cubicles, and then our steps echo as we head down the corridors of the hospital. Familiar faces move past, but my mind is once again elsewhere. Freed from my focus on work, it's now replaying the voicemail that's been haunting me since this morning. I force my attention to the present, to Liz.

"I'm sorry I didn't get back to you after we talked about dinner. I left my phone at my mom's, and I've not had any time to replace it."

"I get it." She wraps her arm around my shoulder and

squeezes me tight. "Don't worry about it. I'm worried about you, but you'll tell me when you're ready."

Liz and I push through the doors to the outside and into the small park with several paths that abuts the hospital. We meander down one of the trails, soaking in vitamin D.

"Greyson called," I blurt.

"Really?" She looks over at me. "What did he have to say?"

I swallow hard, the memory of his voice making my heart ache. "He's sorry about Anita, and they're not engaged... And he said he's not ready for us to be over."

Liz's eyebrows shoot up. "Wow, that's...a lot. Are you okay?"

I shrug. "I don't know. I just can't see the way forward."

"Hey," she cuts in, reaching over to take my hand in hers. "You don't have to figure it all out this second. Let's just enjoy our break, okay?"

"Okay," I agree, managing a small smile. Inside, I'm a whirlwind of emotions, each one clamoring for attention. *What if I've been too afraid to consider whether I'm ready to let him in or let him go for good?*

"With everything that's happened—your dad, your mom's illness, and this monster project at work finally coming to a head after three long years—it must feel like you're carrying the weight of the world."

I nod. "A little bit." The truth is an understatement, but it feels safer than admitting how close to the edge I really am.

"And in the middle of this hurricane, you managed to fall for Greyson." Liz's tone is gentle, but her words strike with the precision of an arrow.

I stiffen. Denial rises like a reflex. "I didn't fall for him," I say quickly.

Liz gives me that look, the one that says she knows me better than I know myself. "Come here." She stops and opens her arms. Despite myself, I lean into the embrace she offers.

"Greyson's apology sounds like he's in love with you too," she whispers.

I want to argue, to pull away and tell her she's reading it all wrong, but instead, a sob lodges in my throat, betraying the turmoil inside.

Twenty-eight

Greyson

I'm staring at the ceiling, as I have been for some time, when my alarm sounds. The bed feels so empty without Trinity. It's time to face the day, yet I can't remember closing my eyes last night. Coffee is going to be my lifesaver. Fortunately, there's no emergency shift to tackle, just a staff meeting, which requires my presence, but not necessarily my attention.

Why the hell hasn't Trinity called? There's an ache I can't shake. I tell myself it's just the silence, but it's more than that. It's the way her absence feels like a piece of me has gone missing, leaving only the emptiness of what I didn't say when I had the chance.

After the meeting, where I managed to nod and smile at the right moments, I drift back home. The condo feels too quiet, which is saying something for a man who's typically relished silence. That's when Kingston shows up, entering my living room with that all-too-familiar look of concern on his face.

"Everything okay?" he asks.

"Fine," I lie, because admitting anything else feels like opening Pandora's box. "What's up?"

He raises an eyebrow. "You missed Sunday dinner. And Tarryn mentioned something about your girlfriend having a run-in with Anita and hightailing it back to Vancouver yesterday."

His words hit like a sledgehammer. Hearing someone else recount my life back to me makes it more real, more final. I keep my face neutral, though. I can't let Kingston see the turmoil underneath.

"Trinity had to handle some stuff back in Vancouver for her work," I say with a nonchalance I don't feel. I rise and lean against the cool glass of the window, staring into the evening sky.

"We all think Trinity is a catch," he presses. "She must have become pretty special to you."

A ghost of a smile flickers across my lips. "Yeah, I like her," I admit. "Anita had no right to boot her out like that." My fingers curl into fists at the thought.

"How did Anita get into your place, anyway?"

"She had a key fob she never gave back. It's been so long that I'd forgotten."

"Where is Anita now?" He looks around my condo.

"I assume she's at her parents', but I don't know." I return to the couch and devote my attention to the sports channel.

"Why do you think Trinity didn't stand up to Anita and tell her off?"

There's an edge to Kingston's question that digs at me.

Looking away, I let out a long breath. "We had an understanding. She was here for her mom, and when the time came for her to return to Vancouver, we'd be done. And I never said anything to her about Anita, so for all she knew, maybe I had been hiding a fiancée this whole time." I scrub my hand over my face.

"Her mom's still here, isn't she?"

I nod slowly. "She is. She's at Lakeview now in the

memory care unit."

"Man, that's tough." Kingston moves to the kitchen and makes himself an espresso. "So, what's the deal? Is that it? Are you in love with her?"

I sit silently, watching the muted television. Kingston just waits for me to respond.

"I feel more than I should," I confess. "But in love? No way. I don't fall in love."

"Didn't you love Anita?" he probes, his stare unsettlingly perceptive.

Shaking my head, I chuckle without humor. "Thought I did. But when she left for Toronto, it didn't faze me. Not really."

"And Trinity heading back to Vancouver? How does that feel?" he persists, pushing me into a corner.

My shrug is meant to be dismissive, but instead, it's heavy, loaded with unspoken truths. Silence stretches between us as I battle with the honesty I owe myself.

I watch Kingston stride to the window and look out at the view. "I was in love with Cara," he muses, tilting the espresso cup to his lips. "When she left to go to London, I told her I'd go with her. I would have moved Renew Motion wherever she wanted to live. But she told me the only person she wanted to go with her was Mark."

His best friend. I can't even comprehend that kind of betrayal.

But our situations aren't the same. "Easy for you to say," I scoff, my temper short. "You've got your own company and work from home. You're not tied down."

Kingston sets his cup on the counter with a clatter, confusion knitting his brows together. "But there are hospitals in Vancouver, right?"

"Of course." I sound defensive. The fabric of the couch bunches under my fingers as I grip it tighter. "Hospitals are everywhere. But this — " I gesture to the view of Paradise outside my windows. " — is where *my* job is. And our family."

"Greyson, man…" He shakes his head. "Your job's not tethered to this town alone. And we're family regardless of where you live."

Why is everyone so quick to leave Paradise? We've spent eight generations in this town.

Ryker and Kingston's words band together and echo in my head, pressing against the wall I've built. The truth is there, staring me down, but I can't let it win. Not yet.

Kingston sits on the couch next to me. "Seriously. What's the difference if you're an ED doc here or in Vancouver?" His eyes are sharp, probing for a crack in my defenses.

I avoid his gaze. "Not much," I admit. "Bigger population out there, might be more exciting. Probably fewer accidents with farm equipment." A bitter laugh escapes me.

He chuckles. "Yeah, wouldn't want to miss all the tractor rollovers."

"Ha-ha," I shoot back.

"Why not go there for a bit?" he suggests. "See how things might turn out with Trinity?"

The image of her face, bright and smiling, flits across my mind, and I push it away. "And leave Tarryn without any backup at the vineyard? Skip out on family dinners? Just abandon my condo?" The words tumble out, a litany of excuses masking my fear.

Kingston rolls his eyes, the gesture so familiar it almost eases the tightness in my chest. "C'mon, the family will survive. It's not like you can't drive or fly back whenever you want." He pauses, giving me a pointed look. "Hell, I'll swoop in with the chopper if you're that desperate to have dinner with us."

I can't suppress the snort that follows, imagining Kingston landing on some downtown street just to ferry me home. The absurdity of it lightens the conversation, but the weight of his words lingers.

"You can always move back. Paradise General will always take you."

I rise and retrieve a beer from the fridge, then lean against the kitchen counter while Kingston moves to the barstool across from me. He's all casual confidence, a stark contrast to the restless energy I'm trying to suppress.

"Business going good?" I ask, hoping to steer our conversation away from my turbulent thoughts.

Kingston nods. "It's moving. Got a couple of patents pending on the new knee replacement devices," he says. "We have more orders for the knee lined up than we can get made."

"Sounds like a big deal." I try to sound enthusiastic, but it falls flat.

"It is. Scheduled two surgeries next month. They'll be recorded, used for demos. Maybe I'll be a YouTube influencer..." He grins with a twinkle in his eye.

"Must be nice, creating something that changes lives." I admire that about him, the way he makes his mark, tangible and vital.

"Speaking of changing lives..." His voice trails off as he glances at the clock on the wall. "I should get going. I don't want to fly in at night." He pushes himself up with an ease that makes me envious of his unburdened conscience.

"Right. Safe flying," I say, but he's already heading for the door, a man forever in motion.

He waves as the elevator doors close, and I find myself pacing the same path he just walked, back and forth, back and forth, until on a sudden whim, I snatch my phone from the coffee table and dial Griffin Martin's number. Griffin and I were in residency together, and if there were any openings in Vancouver, he would know.

Griffin answers almost before it rings. "Could this be Paradise?" He launches into "Almost Paradise" from the *Footloose* soundtrack.

"Good to hear your singing hasn't improved," I note.

"What's happening, man? You going to speak at another MedTalk?"

"Naw. I'm actually wondering if you've heard of any ED spots open up your way."

"Hmmm...interesting," he says. "My boss is a great guy. I'd be happy to introduce you. We're always looking for new blood."

Griffin's suggestion pulls me toward possibilities I hadn't let myself consider. "Thanks, I will let you know. I need to move a few things around on my schedule first. I'm not sure of anything yet."

"Great. Well, just say the word, and while I have you, you can be one of the first to know. Tori is pregnant."

I laugh, and the sound is surprisingly genuine. "That's amazing news! Congrats, man!"

"Thanks," Griffin replies. "We're over the moon about it."

"Is Tori going to keep working after the baby arrives?" I ask.

He sighs. "We're not sure yet. The biggest issue is our living situation. Our condo on False Creek isn't exactly kid-friendly, you know? But we love living in the middle of everything and close to the hospital."

"Planning on a hockey team, are you?" I chuckle, trying to imagine Griffin, once the most eligible bachelor at med school, as a family man.

Griff laughs too, but it's tinged with a bit of anxiety. "No, no twins or triplets. But we do want a few little ones running around eventually."

"Sounds like a plan. I'm thrilled for you. And thanks for offering to connect me with your hospital. I'll figure out my schedule and see how things feel."

Even as I say it, I wonder what I'd be leaving behind and if Trinity's world will ever truly fit with mine.

"Great. Let's set it up. And Greyson? It's good to hear you're considering a change. Sometimes, that's exactly what we need."

"Thanks." I end the call and sink back into my chair,

staring at the ceiling. For the first time since Trinity left, excitement flutters in my chest, a tentative bird testing its wings. *I can always move back.*

And maybe Kingston was right. Maybe this is just what it will take to get Trinity back.

I glance at the clock, its hands inching toward dinner time. The silence of my phone mocks me. There's still no word from Trinity. But she's probably swamped with her project going live, I realize. She really did have a reason she was returning to Vancouver. I should give her space, but I can't help myself. I miss her.

With a resigned sigh, I pull out my phone and open the meal-delivery app. My fingers move with purpose as I scroll through the options, selecting the salad similar to the one we shared last time at Paradise Grill. She loved it.

Hope this isn't as good as ours, I type in the notes section. *But you need to eat. And...I miss you.* There's so much more I want to say, but I leave it at that. My thumb hovers over the send button as I picture her smile. In the end, I order it to be delivered to her at the hospital in Vancouver.

I toss the phone aside and unmute the TV. TSN sports highlights roll across the screen, a litany of victories, defeats, and near-misses. I'm only half-watching, my thoughts lost in a whirlpool of what-ifs and maybes. Every so often, I check the app, following the virtual progress of the salad from the restaurant to the delivery service.

When the notification pops up that the meal's been delivered, a small sense of accomplishment washes over me. At least I've done something for her today, even if it's just ensuring she doesn't skip dinner. I lean back into the couch and let the endless loop of sports fill the room, a familiar backdrop to an unfamiliar restlessness.

Then my ringtone slices through the haze of sports stats and commentator banter. The screen says North Vancouver General Hospital. *It's her.* I snatch up the phone, my heart kicking against my ribs.

"Greyson," she breathes when I answer, and just like that, the room feels less empty.

"Trinity." I revel in the sound of her voice. "Did you get the salad?"

"Thank you for dinner," she says, her tone warm. "I left my cell phone at my mom's place on my way out of Paradise. I ordered a new one. It should be here tomorrow."

"Ah, that explains the silence." My attempt at lightness doesn't fully mask the relief flooding through me.

"Yeah, I'm sorry about that. And I got your message at work. Thank you for that. I've been thinking about how I want to respond, but it's been crazy with the project launch."

"Understandable." I lean back, imagining what she might look like in her office.

"I'm really glad we're reconnected, Greyson." Her voice softens. "My days will be long until we go live next weekend, so maybe we can talk and catch up properly after that. Sound okay?"

"Sounds good, Trinity. I'd like that." I try to keep my tone even, but there's a hopeful edge to it.

"Okay then, goodnight."

"Goodnight." And she's gone.

I drop the phone beside me, a smile on my lips. I suddenly feel warmer in the cold places her absence has carved out. I think there's still a chance for us. She's going to come back to me, even if it's just her voice on the line for now.

Twenty-nine

Trinity

I lift my glass, the crystal catching the dim light of Boulevard's chandeliers like tiny stars captured in a delicate curve. Last weekend we got the migration completed with only a few hiccups, and then I slept for two days. It's Wednesday now, and Liz insisted we go out to celebrate.

She raises her glass to mine. "To the end of a marathon," she toasts. "It's all over." A proud smile spreads across her face, as if the success of the project is partly her own.

I can't help but laugh. "Sure, it's 'all over,'" I air quote, "until the untrained ones start clicking where they shouldn't, and the system throws a fit." I laugh. "But at that point it will be tech support's responsibility."

Liz shakes her head.

"Yeah, the hard part is done," I continue. "I'm excited to think about something else for a while."

"So, what's next for you?" Liz asks. "Go back to see your mom and Greyson in Paradise?" Her question reminds me of the gulf that still exists between Greyson and me, despite the comforting routine of the nightly dinners he's been sending. I haven't yet had the energy to tackle a full conversation with him.

"Next?" I echo, swirling the wine in my glass before taking a sip. Its richness feels like a celebration in itself. "I think more sleep. Then…I'll figure it out."

"Has the hospital offered you another contract?" Liz probes.

"They've mentioned it." I pause. "I still have a month or so of finalization to do with the electronic medical records system, plus writing the final report about the process — what worked and what didn't." The thought is daunting, yet there's a completeness to it, an ending I both crave and fear.

"Ever thought about looking for something closer to your mom?" Liz swirls her wine with a casual air that doesn't quite mask the intent behind her words.

I blink. "Closer to Mom?" I repeat, astonishment creeping into my voice. "Liz, you're the one who's always touted the merits of staying here, in Vancouver. The job market, the opportunities…"

She nods, but there's a knowing look in her eyes. "Sure," she concedes, "but you also have options now. Your boss offered you projects you can work on remotely, right?"

"True," I admit. "I worry that veers away from my path, though — the CEO track."

"Doesn't have to be forever." Liz's voice is gentle, yet insistent. "You could work remotely or see what Paradise has in the administration area. That could give you exposure to how other hospitals operate, add to your experience."

I consider her words, letting them roll around in my mind like the wine in my glass. The idea isn't without its appeal — flexibility, new perspectives, being closer to Mom, and maybe others… But it isn't the path I've long envisioned.

"Why the change of heart?" I ask, shifting my gaze to meet hers. Liz's shrug is nonchalant, but there's a spark in her eyes that wasn't there before.

"Paradise isn't the same place we used to camp in when we were kids," she says, a wistful smile curving her lips. "It's grown, changed. Alaric is going to move back to Paradise…" Her voice trails off, but the implication hangs between us.

"Sounds intriguing," I reply, and I realize something in me longs for what Liz has seemingly found — a connection, a possibility, a reason to look beyond the skyline of our bustling city. "I don't know what I want," I confess. "But I know that if I'm going to invest in someone…it has to be going somewhere, not just filling time." I want a relationship that's a journey, not a detour, a partnership with purpose and direction.

Liz smiles and raises her glass in toast. "Let's see where the road takes us," she murmurs, and I nod. "Sometimes, the best destinations are the ones you never planned on finding."

I swirl the remnants of my wine. It's a small celebration, just Liz and me at Boulevard, but it feels momentous. The weight of the past three years is lifting with each sip. "Mom might be moving out of memory care," I tell her, recounting my conversation yesterday with Dr. Dunham, Mom's neurologist. "But I'm not sure if I'm being too optimistic."

Liz's eyes soften. "It's good to hope."

"Maybe." I chew on my lip, thinking about Mom's neurology appointment next week. I'll need to be there, regardless of the outcome.

"Enough about me, though." I lean forward. "Tell me more about what's happening with Alaric."

She lets out a laugh. "The sex is mind-blowing, the best I've ever had." A blush creeps up her neck. "But honestly, he's like a yo-yo, hot one minute, distant the next. Too many mixed signals."

"Sounds exhausting," I murmur. "But maybe you're just still working through things? Otherwise, you know what they say. The right guy is out there somewhere."

"Right." Liz snorts. "Make sure you don't overlook what or who, you might already have." Her words land gently, but they linger, a reminder that sometimes the answers are closer than we think.

"Maybe," I concede, the thought tickling the back of my mind like a feather. But now's not the time for what-ifs or maybes. Now's the time for celebrating victories and for cherishing the friendships that have carried us through storms.

"Cheers to mixed signals and hopeful futures," I say, raising my glass once more. Liz clinks hers against mine, and together, we drink to the messy, beautiful uncertainty of life.

At the end of our evening, I slide into a rideshare. My heart is warm, full from the evening's laughter and Liz's unwavering support. I lean my head against the cool window, watching Vancouver streak by. Memories of my father, his steady presence that's now just echoes in time, mingle with my mother's fragile smile in her care facility. Without Liz, those moments of loss would have been unbearable.

In the darkness of the car, I allow myself a moment of gratitude, for her, for the resilience life has forced upon me, and for the strength to celebrate tonight after years of relentless work.

My phone buzzes. *Greyson.* His name still sends a jolt through me. The screen lights up with his message.

Greyson: How did it go?

A small smile curves my lips despite the knots that twist in my gut. I type back swiftly, thumbs dancing over the keys.

Me: It's done. Now comes the bug hunt, but that's not on me.

I almost hear his chuckle, see the crinkle around his eyes.

Greyson: Are you around tomorrow?

Me: Sleeping till noon. But free after that. I add a sleepy emoji.

Greyson: Great. I'm coming to Vancouver, and I want to see you.

My heart stops for a moment as the rideshare turns onto my street. We've danced around each other since I left Paradise — messages, nightly dinners, a connection neither of us has fully severed.

Me: Okay.

What does he want? An apology, a fresh start, or something else entirely? I'm not sure which answer scares me more.

Greyson: See you then.

As the car pulls up to my building, I gather my things, anticipation and anxiety intertwining.

"Thanks," I tell the driver, stepping out. I don't look back as I make my way to the entrance, my mind already racing toward tomorrow, toward Greyson, and the uncertainty of what his visit might bring.

My fingers hover over the screen, the little blinking cursor in the message box mocking me. I swallow the lump in my throat.

Me: Where do you want to meet?

Greyson: How about L'Abattoir in Gastown? Drinks, maybe dinner?

Me: Sure.

The word feels too small for the swarm of butterflies battering against the walls of my stomach.

Greyson: Does 6 work?

Me: Yes, 6 works. See you there.

I hit send, trying to keep my breathing steady.

Home greets me with silence as I push open the door. I kick off my shoes and stumble toward my bedroom, my lingering exhaustion suddenly tangible in my limbs.

I face-plant into my bed, not even bothering to pull back the covers. My eyes close, and I'm out like a light, the need for sleep claiming me wholly.

When my eyes blink open, sunlight is streaming through the blinds, casting lines across my sheets. I fumble for my phone on the nightstand. *9:07 a.m.* I was supposed to sleep until noon. But here I am, awake, robbed of a few more hours of oblivion. But I know it's the excitement of seeing Greyson tonight.

I lace up my running shoes, anticipation in my limbs. The apartment is too still, and I need movement, need to feel the pulse of the city under my feet. I step outside and start off toward Kitsilano Beach.

My breath comes in steady puffs. Tankers line up in the harbor waiting for their turn to unload their goods. The rhythm of my run syncs with the heartbeat of Vancouver, a city that's as much a part of me as the blood in my veins. Even so, Greyson's presence lingers. It's not just the thoughtful dinners or his texts. It's the way he's learned how to steady me, even when everything else feels out of control.

What if tonight changes everything? What if it doesn't?

Surprisingly, the idea doesn't sink claws of panic into my chest. Instead, it feels like possibility, like freedom. Maybe a change wouldn't be so bad. Maybe I could tell my boss I'm open to a new contract that lets me work closer to Mom until she's stronger.

An hour slips by unnoticed, and I slow to a walk, endorphins humming through me. I return to my apartment, peel off my damp running gear, and head straight for the shower. Steam fills the room, and as I lather shampoo into my hair, I smile, thinking of Greyson's thoughtful dinners, his care for me even when we're apart.

Wrapped in a towel, I pick up my eReader and open a spicy romance. I make myself a cup of tea, curl up on the sofa, and lose myself in the pages.

But even the pull of a good story can't keep my mind from wandering to tonight. To Greyson. What does this mean for us? What if this is just the goodbye we never had? Or are we rekindling something that never quite extinguished?

Thirty

Greyson

I settle into a utilitarian blue plastic chair in Mercy Hospital's cafeteria, the aroma of strong coffee in the air. Across from me sits Chance Devereaux, Chief of Emergency Medicine, and Griffin. Instead of the stern interrogation I prepared for, the vibe is unexpectedly laid-back, their smiles warm and inviting.

"Greyson," Chance says, sliding a tray of sandwiches toward me, "we're not just looking for a set of skilled hands here at Mercy. We're looking for someone who can dive into the weeds with us."

Griffin chuckles, his eyes crinkling. "It's a family here. We fight, we laugh, we save lives together."

As I take a bite of turkey on rye, Chance continues. "We see around one hundred and fifty-six thousand patients annually," he says, his tone matter-of-fact.

I nod, absorbing the heft of those numbers as my gaze shifts to the bustling cafeteria. Around us, staff moves with purpose. "You must be a well-oiled machine," I comment.

"Sure, but even well-oiled machines need constant maintenance," Griffin notes. "Especially with the three twelve-hour shifts we ask of all our docs each week. It's demanding work but rewarding."

Chance's expression sobers a fraction. "We could always use more nurses, though. We're running with eighteen now."

I nod, understanding the strain understaffing can bring. The knowledge settles in my gut, heavy but not unwelcome. Here, I could make a difference. I'd be needed. And if being needed also means I can be closer to Trinity, Mercy might just become my new home.

I swirl the ice in my nearly empty glass, watching as Chance Devereaux's eyes light up. "You haven't seen anything until you've worked a night shift here at Mercy," he says, a grin tugging at his lips.

"More happens at night?" I ask.

"Absolutely," Griffin chimes in. "It's like the city saves all its surprises for us until after dark. And don't get me started on full moons."

"Superstition or not, it does seem to hold true." Chance leans back, arms crossed over his chest. "On those nights, the ED becomes a theater where the bizarre and chaotic take center stage."

"Full moons," I repeat, shaking my head with a chuckle. "We find the same in Paradise, although, somehow, I suspect it's rather tame in comparison."

"Wait until you've seen it," Chance advises with a knowing look.

I consider this, the challenge of the unknown sparking more excitement than fear within me. Trinity loves the unpredictability of her city. Maybe I can find the allure in it too. I did go to med school here.

Chance's demeanor shifts, and he adopts a more business-like tone as he addresses the logistics of the position. "In terms of patient load, you might see anywhere between fifteen to twenty patients on a shift, depending on the day and what rolls through those doors."

"Sounds intense," I say.

"Intense, but manageable, especially with your experience," Chance assures me. "Initially, we'd start you on day shifts, which admittedly do pay less. But with what you bring to the table, you'll be making what you're used to, salary-wise."

The mention of compensation brings a stark reality into focus—the cost of living in Vancouver. It's a steep climb from what I'm accustomed to in Paradise. But when I think of Trinity, of the life we could build here, the numbers lose their edge.

"I'm fine with that," I confirm.

"Good to hear," Chance says as he nods. "I hope you'll consider it. Mercy could use someone with your dedication."

"Thanks," I reply, feeling the weight of the decision settle firmly on my shoulders. It's a weight I'm ready to bear.

Chance leans back. "What's pushing you to leave Paradise?" he probes.

My palms feel suddenly clammy against the cool surface of the table. It's the question I've been preparing for, the one that cuts closest to the bone.

"I met someone," I explain, the words tethered to the pulse of my heart, which quickens at the mention of her. "Her life is here in Vancouver. And she means everything to me."

There's a moment of silence as the information sinks in. I watch their reactions, see the understanding dawn in their eyes. Chance nods, and Griffin's posture relaxes.

He chuckles softly. "Welcome to the club, man."

Their camaraderie warms me from within, and I can't help but smile back.

"Guess we're all fools for love in our own ways," Chance adds with a wink.

We stand and gather our trash from the tabletop. They lead me out of the cafeteria, past the buzz of hospital life that never truly quiets, and into the emergency department, the doors swinging open to reveal the controlled chaos within.

"Take a look around, Greyson," Chance gestures expansively.

I step into the flow, dodging an EMT barreling through with a gurney. Nurses pivot gracefully among the stretchers lined up as if in battle formations, each patient an individual story waiting to unfold.

Griffin points out the trauma bays, where the most critical cases are sent, a dance of life and death played out under harsh white lights. We weave through the packed space, and I'm introduced to snippets of lives in progress—a mother clutching her child's hand, a young man with a bandage wrapped around his head, an elderly woman with eyes clouded by confusion.

"This is what we do," Griffin says proudly. "And we do it well."

"We could use your expertise," Chance reiterates, clapping a hand on my shoulder.

I nod, taking it all in—the sounds, the sights, the unmistakable pulse of urgency that permeates the air. It's a far cry from Paradise, but it's not unfamiliar, and the challenge ignites something within me.

"Looks like a place I could belong," I confirm. And as the tour concludes, the thought of Trinity's smile, the life we might share here, fills me with a sense of purpose I haven't felt in years.

Chance turns to me with a congenial smile. "Thank you for coming in today." He extends a hand, and between his fingers is a business card. "If you're interested in joining us, we'd be thrilled to have someone with your qualifications on board."

I take the card and slip it into my pocket. As our hands part, there's a sense of finality. It all depends on what happens tonight. "Thanks, Dr. Devereaux. I'll let you know."

With a nod, he steps back, allowing me the space to

process everything I've seen today. Griffin puts his hand to his face in the shape of a phone and mouths, *Call me.*

Turning on my heel, I make my way out of Mercy Hospital, the sliding doors giving way to the world outside. The air hits differently here, heavy with the hum of life and the hint of salt water. It's so different from the tranquil peace of Paradise.

My thoughts move to Trinity, her laugh, the way it warms me like sunlight breaking through clouds. I think of her determination, her fire, and the way she makes me want to be someone worthy of standing beside her. For her, I'd trade the comfort of Paradise for the unknown, no matter how daunting it feels. I could get used to this relentless energy. For her, I would embrace the unfamiliar, dive into this ocean.

The decision settles within me like the last piece of a puzzle clicking into place. Yes, it's different here — intimidatingly so — but the thought of being with Trinity, building something real and tangible, gives rise to a courage I hadn't known lingered in my veins.

The skyline of Vancouver stretches out before me, a sea of glass and steel reflecting the golden light of the sun. It's beautiful, in its way, though a stark contrast to the rolling hills of Paradise Hill, the vineyard, and the life I've always known. I can see Trinity's world, her life, and for the first time, I realize how small mine feels in comparison. I take a deep breath. This is a drastic change. *What comes next?*

I love her. I've never been more sure of anything. But I also know I've been asking her to fit into my world, to change her life for me. And that's not fair.

She's shown me that love isn't about safety. It's about risk. It's about stepping into the unknown because the person you're stepping with is worth it.

So I'm moving here. To Vancouver. To be with her. If she'll have me.

She's my life now. The vineyard will survive without me there so often. The hospital will find someone else to fill my shoes. But I can't imagine my life without Trinity. I don't want to.

For the first time, the idea of leaving everything I've ever known doesn't feel like a loss. It feels like a leap.

Thirty-one

Trinity

The vintage lights of L'Abattoir cast the golden glow of gas lanterns over the cobbled streets, their reflections dancing on the rain-slick pavement in the Gastown neighborhood. The rideshare drops me, and I try to run between the raindrops. I'm a few minutes early.

I spot Greyson immediately, his back to the wall in the bar, scanning the room with that attentive gaze. Seeing him after everything that has happened is like a glimpse of sunlight after relentless rain. He springs up when he notices me, a smile blooming across his face as if he can't quite believe I'm here.

In three long strides, he's at my side, enveloping me in an embrace that's both familiar and foreign. I inhale deeply. The scent of his cologne engulfs me, a mixture of cedar and something indefinably him. My heart flutters despite my resolve, and warmth rushes through my veins.

"Trinity," he murmurs, voice muffled against my hair. "You look fantastic."

"Thank you," I say, pulling away before the comfort becomes too much. We follow the hostess and slide into a booth, the leather cool and smooth beneath me.

His drink arrives shortly thereafter, a lowball glass holding an amber liquid that catches the light. The server turns to me. "And for you, miss?"

"Sunshiny Day, please." The words roll off my tongue after studying the menu earlier, trying to anticipate every detail of this evening.

"Interesting choice," Greyson says once we're alone. "What's in it?"

"Rum, pineapple, lemongrass…"

"Sounds sweet," he replies, the corners of his mouth turning up in a smile that used to make my knees weak. "Just like you."

I force a smile, ignoring the pang in my chest. Sweetness may not be enough to hold together what distance and circumstance have strained. I need to remain clearheaded. I take a deep breath and prepare myself in case what I receive tonight is closure, not rekindling. But still, a part of me thrills at his compliment, yearning for the simplicity of our past before reality intruded, before Anita and work and my mother's illness forced our hands.

"Greyson…" I start, ready to steer us toward the conversation that looms, but I stop myself. Let's let him tell me why he's here. I don't need to jump the gun. For now, we're just two people, sharing a drink. I pick up the menu and force myself to comprehend the words printed there.

My drink arrives, and Greyson gives me the update on his family and the vineyard. He's also been stopping in to see Mom, as a friend, though, he's quick to clarify, not as her doctor, according to my wishes. He feels like she's improving, which is great news, but then he shifts uncomfortably in his seat.

Maybe he doesn't know how to tell me we're through. He inhales deeply, his chest rising like he's about to dive into uncharted waters. "Trinity, I'm sorry," he begins, and there's a tremor in his voice that resonates with something deep inside me. "About Anita...I am." His brow furrows, then smooths out as determination takes over. "But then again, I'm not. She—"

I brace myself, ready to deflect whatever justification he's about to offer.

"—she made me see the truth." His gaze never wavers from mine as if he's willing me to understand. "I'm in love with you."

The confession hangs in the air, and for a moment, I forget to breathe.

"I knew I didn't want you to leave yet, but..." His voice cracks ever so slightly. "What I'd failed to realize is that I *never* want to be away from you."

The tenderness in his eyes threatens to unravel me. But I can't just cave. I'm not built to be someone's afterthought. "We agreed at the beginning," I say firmly, though my heart pounds a rhythm of longing.

He reaches across the table, and I put my hand in his, warm and reassuring. "You don't have to move back to Paradise," he says, cutting off my retreat before it can start. "I've got a friend from medical school working at Mercy Hospital here. I met with the emergency department head this afternoon, and they're looking for someone. The job is mine if I want it."

My mind whirls. *Is he serious? Moving for me?*

"Trinity, I'll do whatever it takes to be with you," he continues. "I'll be right here until you have no doubt how much I love you."

I sit stunned. Could it really be this simple? Greyson's willingness to uproot his life stirs something deep inside me, equal parts awe and fear. What if his sacrifice becomes a burden? What if I can't live up to the expectations of a love so unwavering? But even as doubt creeps in, his steady gaze soothes my fears, at least for the moment.

My throat tightens, words lodged somewhere between my heart and my lips. "I...I don't understand," I manage to whisper.

He leans forward, resting his elbow on the table's edge, a soft intensity radiating from him. "I want to be with you, Trinity. That's what I'm saying. If you're staying in Vancouver, then so will I. I'll work here, live here, whatever it takes, as long as we're together."

I blink at him, half expecting him to laugh it off, to say *gotcha* and ease the weight of his declaration. But there's no humor in his gaze. "Is this some kind of joke?" I ask, though the tremor in my voice betrays my hope that it isn't.

"No joke," he says, giving my hand a squeeze. "I love you. And if you're not there yet, if your heart still needs convincing, I'll be here. I'll wait for as long as it takes."

I chew on my lower lip, his words swirling in my mind. Could I trust this? Trust him? Every instinct screams at me to protect my heart, but then the defenses I've clung to for so long begin to waver. I have to focus on what's real, not what I'm afraid of. "What about your family? Your life in Paradise?"

Greyson's eyes soften. "They'll understand. They'll support me," he assures me. "Besides, it's only a short flight away or a quick drive home."

"Well...I'm working on securing a remote position, so I can be in Paradise for a while, until my mom is better or, at least, more stable." I still don't know for sure which it's going to be.

He nods. "Then we'll stay in Paradise until you're ready. If you want to find a job in London, we'll go there. The NIH is always looking for doctors," he says. "I'll find work and follow you wherever you want to go."

His sheer determination finally dismantles the walls I've built around my heart. He's offering me not just love, but a partnership to face whatever our future holds.

"Okay." I nod slowly, and something warm begins to bloom inside me, hope mingling with gratitude and a tinge of awe at this man who wants to chart our course together.

Greyson stands, pulling me to my feet and into a firm, decisive kiss, a silent pledge that echoes in the space where our breath mingles.

Pulling back, he gazes down at me, a playful twinkle returning to his eyes. "I've got my eyes on the beef tartare," he announces as if nothing else in the world could be of more importance at this moment.

"The cod looked good to me," I reply, finally allowing myself a small smile.

He flags down the server with a casual wave, and we place our orders, sealing our decision with the mundane act of choosing what to eat. And yet, there's nothing ordinary about tonight. Because even as we navigate the menu, we've also negotiated the contours of a future that suddenly feels wide open.

The breeze swirls around us as we ascend the concrete steps leading to my apartment, a three-story walk-up nestled in the heart of Kitsilano. Greyson's hand rests lightly on the small of my back, a touch I've missed more than I care to admit.

"Never thought I'd find myself in a neighborhood this hip," he quips, his breath forming clouds in the crisp night.

I roll my eyes at his attempt at humor, a familiar dance between us. "You're just fine," I assure him, unlocking the door. It swings open to reveal my one-bedroom sanctuary, cozy with its compact kitchen and living room. A sigh of relief escapes me. At least, it's clean.

He follows me inside and takes a seat on the worn-out couch that has been my companion through many solitary evenings. His presence already makes it feel less lonely. But I don't know what to do with myself. "Would you like some water? I think that's all I have."

"Come here," he says softly, crooking his finger, beckoning me closer.

A current runs through me at his words. I cross the room, feeling the weight of his gaze on me. As I stand before him, my fingers find the hem of my dress, lifting it just enough for me to straddle his lap.

"I've missed you," he whispers, his voice laced with an emotion that grips my heart and refuses to let go. He leans forward, his teeth catching the delicate spaghetti strap of my dress, tugging it down my shoulder with a tantalizing slowness.

His lips find the softness of my breast, and a shiver courses through me, a mix of desire and the aching vulnerability. My body responds of its own accord, hips pressing down against the undeniable evidence of his desire. The sensation sends a wave of heat coursing through my veins, and in this moment, I am acutely aware of how much time we've wasted apart. But even as coherent thought becomes difficult for me, I realize that, like he explained earlier, this challenge was important for both of us. It's pushed us to see that what we have is real.

Greyson's mouth works its magic, awakening every nerve ending with the warmth of his tongue, and I'm home. Despite the doubt, the hurt, and the distance, this is where I belong, — in the arms of the man who holds my heart.

Greyson's arms wrap around me, and he lifts me from the couch. The world tilts as he carries me through over the threshold and into my bedroom.

He lays me down with reverence, and I watch, breathless, as he slides off the last barrier to our intimacy. My thong, a flimsy piece of fabric, is no match for his deft fingers.

On his knees now, Greyson worships at the altar of my body. I am splayed open before him, vulnerable yet empowered by his desire. His tongue flits across my clit, a whisper of sensation that builds to a crescendo with each flick and suckle. He takes me deep into his mouth, and I am lost to the waves of pleasure that crash through me, relentless and all-consuming.

"God, yes," escapes my lips as his fingers plunge inside me, finding a rhythm that drives me toward the edge. Every stroke, every curl is a step closer to oblivion. And then, the climax shatters me, a starburst of ecstasy.

As tremors ripple through my spent body, Greyson stands, practically ripping away his clothes. His raw masculinity is on full display, and my gaze locks on his cock — stroked by his own hand, ready.

He pushes into me, and a guttural groan vibrates from the depths of his throat. His body is a testament to restrained power, muscles taut as he enters me slowly, inch by inch. I gasp at the sensation. I stretch to accommodate him and feel complete, so utterly possessed.

"Trinity," he breathes.

With each thrust, I become more acutely aware of how we fit together. My fingers find his chest, trace the contours of his skin, and play with the barbell through his nipple. A tweak elicits a sharp intake of breath, and a deliciously pained expression crosses his face for a moment before he plunges deeper inside me. "God, I've missed this...missed you," I whisper against his lips, capturing them in a searing kiss.

"Never again," Greyson vows between fervent kisses, his movements becoming more insistent. "I never want anyone but you."

The space around us shrinks until there's nothing but the sound of our bodies colliding, an urgent rhythm that echoes off the walls. The world beyond is lost in the haze of our reunion.

And with every slap of skin on skin, with every shared breath, I know this is where I'm meant to be, in the arms of the man who has become my heart's true north.

The next morning, the light in my condo is dim, the soft hum of the refrigerator filling the silence. Greyson left early this morning to return to Paradise, and I've been sitting in this worn leather armchair for what feels like hours, my journal open on my lap. The pen in my hand hovers over the page, poised to write, but the words won't come. Because I don't know what to say. Or maybe, I don't want to say it.

I stare at the blank page, its emptiness mocking me. It feels like a metaphor for everything I've been avoiding—my future, my feelings, Greyson.

Greyson.

Even thinking his name makes my chest tighten. The weight of everything he's offered me, everything he's asked of me, presses down like a stone. He wants us to stay together, to build something together. He wants me to trust him. And that's the hardest part.

Trust.

I set the pen down, my fingers curling into fists. While I'm thrilled with the possibilities this opens for us, trusting someone means letting them in, letting them see the cracks and imperfections I've spent years hiding. It means giving them the power to hurt me. And after everything, after the years of building walls and convincing myself I was better off alone, I don't know if I can.

But then I think of Greyson.

The way he looks at me, like I'm the answer to a question he didn't know he was asking. The way he challenges me, frustrates me, makes me laugh when I want to scream. He doesn't just see me. He sees through me. And that's terrifying.

Because what if he's wrong? What if I'm not the woman

he thinks I am? What if I can't be enough for him, for his life, for this…thing we've built?

But what if I am?

The thought slips in, uninvited, and I can't shake it. What if I'm enough? What if I don't have to do this alone anymore?

I close my eyes, pressing my palms against my knees. The truth is, I'm tired. Tired of pretending I don't need anyone. Tired of holding everything together with both hands and pretending it doesn't hurt when things fall apart.

Greyson isn't asking me to give up who I am. He's asking me to let him in, to let him help carry the weight. And I want that.

I pick up the pen again, my hand trembling as I write the words that have been circling in my mind.

What if trusting him doesn't make me weaker? What if it makes me stronger?

The tears come then, hot and fast, spilling onto the page. I let them fall. I let myself feel the fear and the hope and the ache of wanting something I've spent so long convincing myself I didn't need.

When the storm has passed, I wipe my eyes and stare at the words on the page. They feel like a question and an answer all at once.

Trusting Greyson is a risk. But it's a risk worth taking.

Thirty-two

Greyson

The dogs surround me as I park in the family driveway. I sit down on the concrete and am attacked by slobber, wet noses, and tongues. You'd think they don't get any attention the way they're behaving, but I know the truth. These four Humane Society rescue mutts are replacements for all my parents' children, but I like to think they're better behaved.

"What are you doing on the ground?" Mom asks.

I scramble to my feet. "They were the welcoming committee, and I couldn't resist."

Tarryn walks out of the house. "Have you got a minute?"

"Sure," I tell her.

Mom waves us off, and I follow Tarryn into the vines. I know it's serious if she wants to talk out here.

The late-afternoon sun bathes the vineyard in warm light.

Tarryn is a few steps ahead, her long strides eating up the dirt path between rows of vines. She hasn't stopped talking since we left the main house, her voice sharp with frustration.

"Uncle Max is driving me insane," she snaps, tossing a glance over her shoulder. "He keeps calling me with 'suggestions' about how to '*maximize profits.*' As if I haven't been running this place for the last five years."

"Max has always been good at giving advice he wouldn't follow himself," I say, keeping my tone neutral. Family politics have never been my strong suit, and Tarryn's complaints about Maximus are as old as the vines themselves. He's always been a meddler, but lately, his meddling feels...pointed.

"It's not just annoying. It's disruptive," Tarryn continues, her arms crossed. "He's got half the staff second-guessing me because they think he knows better. And don't even get me started on his pitch to turn part of the vineyard into a wedding venue. A wedding *venue*, Greyson. Not just the Grill to hold a reception."

I suppress a smirk. "To be fair, some vineyards do well with that kind of thing."

She whirls around. "Do you want to run this place? Because if you think you can do a better job, be my guest."

"Relax," I say, raising my hands. "I'm just saying, he's not entirely wrong about diversifying."

Tarryn groans and turns back to the path, muttering something under her breath. I let her vent, knowing she needs to let it out before she explodes. That's Tarryn—stubborn, fiery, and as protective of this vineyard as if it were her child.

We round a corner, Tarryn stops abruptly, her hand shooting out to stop me. "What the hell is that?"

I follow her gaze to a cluster of vines a few rows over. At first glance, they look fine, but as we move closer, the damage becomes clear. The leaves are curled and browned at the edges, the grapes shriveled and dry. It's subtle but unmistakable.

"This can't be right," Tarryn mutters, crouching down to

inspect the nearest vine. "These were fine last week."

"Maybe it's a pest," I suggest, though the words feel wrong even as I say them. Something about the damage doesn't look natural.

"No," Tarryn says, shaking her head. "We've been monitoring for that. This isn't pests, and it's not disease. It's…something else."

The sound of footsteps crunching on the path comes up behind us. Elise approaches, her face shadowed with concern. "What's going on?"

"Look," Tarryn says, gesturing to the damaged vines. "This isn't normal."

Elise kneels beside her and presses her fingers to the base of one vine, frowning. "Damn," she mutters. "This looks deliberate."

"Deliberate how?" I ask, stepping closer.

She points to a faint puncture mark at the base of the vine. "Here. Looks like someone might have injected something. It's subtle, but it's there."

Tarryn's frustration morphs into something colder, sharper. "Are you saying someone sabotaged the vines?"

Elise stands, brushing dirt off her hands. "That's exactly what I'm saying."

My stomach tightens, and I glance at the rows of healthy vines surrounding us. The vineyard has always felt like a fortress, a symbol of stability and legacy. The idea that someone would target it—target us—feels like a violation.

"This isn't the first thing that's gone wrong," Tarryn says quietly. "The equipment breakdowns, the chardonnay vat turning to vinegar…and now this. It's starting to feel like more than bad luck."

Elise nods, her expression grim. "I'll send samples to the lab and see if we can figure out what was used. In the meantime, we need to be careful. If this gets out, it'll tank our reputation before we can get ahead of it."

I cross my arms, my jaw tightening. "Do you think it's the Dempseys?"

Elise shrugs, but there's a flicker of unease in her eyes. "Could be. They've never made it a secret how much they hate this place. But it could just as easily be someone trying to stir the pot."

Tarryn exhales sharply, her frustration bubbling back to the surface. "Great."

I place a hand on her shoulder. "We'll figure it out. Whoever's behind this, they won't get away with it."

Tarryn nods. "Yeah. We'll find them. Please don't say anything about it at dinner? I want to look into it before everyone starts weighing in."

"Good idea."

I follow Tarryn and Elise back to the house, and the aroma of roasted chicken and herbs like a comforting hug as we enter. It's been too long since I've had Mom's cooking, and even longer since we've all sat at this table together.

"Greyson, you made it just in time!" Mom exclaims.

"Wouldn't miss it," I reply, returning her smile. I take my place among the familiar faces—Tarryn, Kingston, Beckett, Ryker, and Dad.

As we dig in, Tarryn's eyes are on me, bright with curiosity. "So, Greyson, how was Vancouver?" she prompts.

"Vancouver was…enlightening," I begin. "Trinity is moving back to Paradise for a while."

"Really?" Kingston perks up. "How did you pull that off?"

"Actually, I interviewed at Mercy Hospital, and they offered me a job," I admit. "I'd be willing to go there to be with her. But turns out, for now at least, she wants to be closer to her mom, and I guess…" I pause, feeling the gravity of my next words, "she's good with us staying together."

A collective exhale moves through the room, and I realize just how invested they all are in this part of my life. It's strange but heartwarming. I lean back and bask in the familiar teasing and laughter that follows, the warmth of home. I wasn't entirely certain they didn't care for Anita until she'd moved away. But with Trinity, they've clearly been fans since the beginning, and I can see how different that feels.

I spear a piece of roasted potato, and just as I'm about to pop it into my mouth, Beckett leans forward, his gaze sharp and inquisitive.

"Would you really have moved to Vancouver?" His question turns all eyes on me.

For a moment, I hold everyone's attention. "Yeah," I say with a nod. "For Trinity, I would. And if she decides she wants to go back there in the future, or to Toronto, or the African jungle, for that matter, I'll pack up and go without a second thought."

A murmur ripples across the table, and from the corner of my eye, I catch a glance between Mom and Dad.

"Really? You'd just leave Paradise behind?" Tarryn asks, but before I can answer, the conversation escalates around us.

"Wouldn't be the first time someone chased love across the map." Mom's voice cuts through the chatter. We all turn to her. "Your father chased me down on Vancouver Island, where I was working in a small community as a doctor." She looks to Dad with a fondness that has spanned decades. "He stayed with me for a year until we decided to move back here to Paradise, and that's when I started my own practice."

Dad smiles. Love, it seems, has a way of carving paths we never expected to tread, paths that lead us not just across cities, but into the very heart of what it means to be family.

I push my plate aside, still conjuring the image of Dad as a young romantic, chasing after Mom like something out of an old love story.

"Wait, why haven't we heard this story before?" Tarryn demands.

Dad chuckles. "Well, kiddo, had your mother decided to stay on the island, I would've handed the vineyard over to Max and found another job," he says, nodding toward the window as if Uncle Max might be working among the grapevines right now.

"Ha! He must've been rooting for you to stay put then," Tarryn quips.

Dad shrugs. "Max was just fine running his own ventures. Besides, Grandpa hadn't retired yet. But anyway, for me, this place—" He spreads his hands wide, encompassing more than just the dining room. "—this is home."

I watch him, understanding a bit more about the sacrifices woven into the fabric of our family.

Beckett folds his arms. "So, sacrificing for love..." he muses, casting a glance around the table. "Would any of the rest of us do something so bold?"

Ryker snorts. "Depends on the woman."

It's Kingston who ends the debate with a statement that rings like a gavel in a courtroom. "If you aren't willing to give up something big for a woman, you don't love her," he says with quiet conviction.

A hush falls over the table, and as I clear my plate, a thought lingers. For Trinity, I'd do anything. But what does that look like? Sacrifice isn't one big decision made in a vacuum. It's the small, everyday choices. And for her, I'm ready to make every one of them count.

Over dessert, Tarryn tells us about the crush party she's planning in a few weeks—live music, grape-crushing competitions, and food trucks galore. She's given us all jobs and responsibilities. "We're going to have a great time!" she declares. "You should be sure to bring Trinity."

I assure her I'll make the invitation, though Tarryn will likely invite her herself.

When everyone's finished, I help Mom clear away the dessert plates. "Tarryn's buzzing like a bee in springtime," I chuckle, stacking plates with care in the kitchen. "She can't wait for Trinity to join our circus of a family."

Mom wipes her hands on a dishtowel. "Just make sure Trinity isn't overwhelmed. Your brothers and this business can be a lot to take in. But she'll find her place here," Mom says confidently.

I turn to the sink, sleeves rolled up, ready to tackle the mountain of pots and pans.

"Speaking of which," Mom adds, "when does she come back?"

"About a month," I tell her. "She's wrapping things up in Vancouver, and then she's all yours to interrogate."

A knowing smile dances across Mom's lips. "Oh, I have no doubt we'll get along famously." She laughs. "I raised you boys to speak your minds. I expect nothing less from a woman brave enough to join this family."

"Trust me, she's got no problem there," I assure her, plunging my hands into the sudsy water.

The rhythm of washing and drying becomes a meditative dance between mother and son until finally I dry the last dish and place it in the cupboard. I look at the time and tell Mom I'm headed out, but then I turn to find Kingston leaning against the door frame, a hint of a smile on his face. Mom scoots past him into the other room.

"Hey," he says quietly as I shrug into my jacket. "Glad to see you took my advice for once."

I nod, adjusting the collar. "Yeah, chasing Trinity felt right. Thanks." A pause hangs between us. "I know I said this a long time ago, but I'm really sorry it didn't work out with Cara." While Kingston was working on building their new house, she was busy with his good friend.

Kingston looks away, his jaw clenching. Silence stretches, his lack of an answer speaking volumes. He's always been the fortress among us, walls built high, especially after his heartbreak. "Take care," he says finally, stepping back as I open the door to the cool night air.

"See you. Thanks again for the good advice," I reply, stepping into the darkness.

The drive home is quiet, and as soon as I'm through the

front door, I pull out my phone and dial Trinity. My heart picks up speed when she answers.

"Hey. I just finished dinner with the family," I tell her, imagining her face on the other end of the line.

"Sounds cozy. How did it go?" Her voice engulfs me, and I'm reminded of the way she leaned into me the first night we danced, uncertain but trusting. That memory feels like a promise, one I intend to keep.

"Good, good. My parents are excited to meet you when you move here. Is that okay?" I ask, already knowing her answer but needing to hear it.

"Of course, Greyson. I'd be happy to," she replies.

"Great. It'll mean a lot to everyone, especially Tarryn. She's looking forward to having another woman at the table," I chuckle, sinking onto the couch.

"I don't think she needs a friend at the table. I think she wants to look out for me," she clarifies, and I can almost see her playful smirk. "Either way, I'm looking forward to it."

"Can't wait for you to be here. Paradise isn't complete without you." With her here, it'll truly be home. "Are you going to give notice to your landlord?"

"I own the apartment, so I guess I'll need to get it ready for sale."

"Why are you going to sell it?" I ask. "I think you should keep it."

There's a brief silence before she responds. "Are you worried I'm not going to be happy and will want to come back?"

My heart lurches into my throat. "What? No way. I was just thinking it would be a great place to stay when we go back."

"I don't think I can afford that. It's expensive. And if I'm living in Paradise..."

"Listen," I interject, the solution clear in my mind, "you could move in with me. Your mom can figure out her place when she's ready. And I'll pay half the mortgage for your Vancouver place. It's worth it to have that option available." Generosity and practicality blend in my offer. I'd be happy to pay the entire mortgage, but I know she'd refuse.

"Half the mortgage?" Her voice lifts, hopeful and surprised.

"Absolutely," I confirm. "It's a smart backup plan. Vancouver's housing market is doing nothing but going up, and keeping your place gives us options."

"Okay," she says after a moment, her voice soft with gratitude. "We can do that. I could always make it a rental, and the rent would cover the mortgage."

"Whatever feels right for you." My heart warms at the thought of sharing my space with her, making a home together, even temporarily. "Can't wait for you to be here," I tell her again.

"What would you do if I were there right now?" she asks, a playful lilt in her voice.

A deep sigh escapes as I close my eyes, imagining. "I'd give you a whole-body massage, start with your shoulders, work down your arms, and then your legs…" My voice drops lower, each word measured and heavy.

"Greyson…" She draws out my name, a moan threaded through it, and I know she's feeling every word.

"Would you like that?" I tease.

"Very much," she breathes, and I imagine the flush of her cheeks, the way she'd arch into my touch.

"Are you…touching yourself?"

"Yes," she whispers, and that word sends heat coursing through me.

"Good." My voice is a husky murmur. "Because I can't wait to do that for you in person. Very soon." I pull my shirt off and drop my jeans, leaving me in my boxers. I settle into bed, phone still clutched in my hand, and switch the call to FaceTime.

Suddenly, she's right there on my screen, a vision of wanton need. She's in a little T-shirt, and I'm already hard, throbbing with anticipation.

"See what you do to me?" My fingers wrap around myself,

stroking firmly as I angle the phone to give her a full view.

"God, Greyson," Trinity says, her voice laced with longing. "I wish I could be there."

"Do you?" I grunt, thumbing the slick bead of pre-cum that has gathered at the tip. "What would you do?"

"I'd kneel before you," she says, eyes locked on the movement of my hand, "and take that drop with my tongue."

The thought alone is almost enough to undo me. "Yeah? And then what?"

"Then, I'd suck you deep. Worship you with my mouth." Her words are like fire against my skin.

"Fuck," I groan, feeling the pressure build. "You'd love that, wouldn't you? My cock filling your mouth."

"I'd stop only to suck your balls," she adds, and though my eyes are closed, I can hear the smile in her voice.

"Trinity," I hiss, tension ratcheting up. "I'm so close."

"Where do you want to come, Greyson?" she asks.

"Your tits," I rasp, the image of marking her as mine pushing me over the edge. "I want to claim you."

Her moan reverberates through the phone, electrifying my senses, and with a few more urgent strokes, I reach my climax. The rush of release is intense, and as I spill onto my chest, I hear her own cries of pleasure.

The afterglow is warm, comforting even through the miles that separate us. We lie together, connected by our phones, silent save for the sound of our breathing slowly returning to normal. It's not long before she's drifted off, and I follow suit, the distance between us momentarily forgotten.

When the harsh blare of my alarm jolts me awake at five thirty, she groans softly through the phone. "The bed's cold without you," I murmur.

"Have a good day at the hospital," she mumbles. "I'm going back to sleep."

"Can't wait to have you here," I whisper again before ending the call, the promise of her warmth in my bed fueling me for the day ahead.

Thirty-three

Trinity

A few weeks later, with fall firmly underway, the burst of afternoon sunlight through the window by my cubicle feels like a promise, a golden seal on this new chapter that's about to begin. I'm practically vibrating with excitement as I stuff the last of my reports into my messenger bag. My contract for the migration of our electronic records software is complete. And next week, I start my new contract with the hospital, working remotely from Paradise.

Lakeview Assisted Living and I had a call earlier, and they informed me that my mother is doing better — much better. They are planning to move her out of the memory care unit and into a room with a view that could rival any postcard picture.

I glance at the clock, counting down the minutes until my phone appointment with Dr. Tuck. She'll tell me what needs to happen next, what milestones Mom has to hit before she can move back home. That thought propels me into action, and I power down my computer with a definitive click.

"Come on, Dr. Tuck," I mutter under my breath. When it comes to being on time, she's about as reliable as snow in Vancouver, a rare occurrence that throws everything off balance when it happens. But today, I don't mind the wait. It's cushioned by hope and good news.

The ringtone finally cuts through the silence, and I answer with a smile on my face. "Dr. Tuck?"

"Trinity, hi. I apologize for being late. I just got off the phone with Lakeview Assisted Living."

"Of course, I understand. Busy day?" I ask, already flipping open my notebook to jot down her advice.

"Always. Listen, they explained their plan to return your mother to assisted living, rather than memory care, and I know they've already discussed it with you. I really wish they'd discussed it with me first."

Her statement catches me off guard, a curveball I didn't see coming. "I see. Are you not in agreement with this plan?" I frown, confused.

"It's not that I disagree — your mother is definitely making progress — but I worry their decision is driven by internal concerns, rather than your mother's mental state. These places are in high demand, and I wonder if they're looking to maximize their population," she says.

Concern prickles at the back of my neck, replacing the excitement I felt moments ago. This isn't just about a room change. It's about my mother's well-being, her future. "Dr. Tuck," I press, trying to keep my voice steady. "Lakeview has been so optimistic. They say she's responding well to her medication, and it's all very promising." I shuffle papers on my desk. "But now, I need to better understand why you're concerned. My hope for our conversation today was to learn about the milestones my mother needs to reach so we can consider bringing her home."

There's a brief pause, and Dr. Tuck takes a deep breath. "Trinity, it's good that your mother is showing improvement with the new medication, but..." She trails off.

"Go on," I urge, my heart sinking.

"Well, it's the ankle monitor that bothers me," she explains. "It sends an alert if your mother tries to leave the building at night. But if Lakeview is worried she might wander, then shouldn't that indicate that she's not ready to leave memory care?"

"An ankle monitor?" My voice cracks. "I didn't realize..."

"Trinity, Lakeview is one of the best facilities we have, but even the best struggle with staffing shortages, especially overnight."

"Right," I murmur. I clutch the phone a little tighter, my heart hammering. "I will have to speak to Lakeview again about this decision, but my question remains. What other steps does Mom need to take before we can consider moving her home?"

She pauses a moment. "Trinity, full recovery from the kind of stroke your mother had could take years. And some patients are never entirely the same." The words hit me like a punch.

I swallow, trying to push past the lump forming in my throat. Mom has gotten so strong physically, striding through the gardens, her step counter often boasting close to five thousand steps a day. But that strength disguises the insidious nature of her condition.

"Memory loss...it's a cruel kind of departure," Dr. Tuck continues softly. "It unfolds right in front of you, taking pieces of the person you love. I'm not sure your mom is suited for independent living at this point."

"Thank you, Dr. Tuck," I manage to say. "I'll get more information from Lakeview so I can make a good decision about Mom's move out of memory care. I appreciate your perspective." I end the call before my tears can make their grand entrance.

I breathe for a moment, getting my emotions back in

check. I'm about to dial Frankie at Lakeview to get to the bottom of this when my phone rings in my hand. It's Greyson.

I freeze for a moment, and I almost push the button to dismiss his call, my instincts telling me I need to handle this myself. *But why would I do that?* I can let him in without giving up control, and his perspective could be valuable here. If Mom's not going to be leaving Lakeview, it's even more important that she receives the correct care.

"Hey," I answer, forcing cheerfulness into my voice.

"Hey," he says. "I'm glad I caught you. I know you were talking with Dr. Tuck today, and I wanted to tell you that Frankie mentioned Lakeview moving your mom back to a regular assisted-living room. I told her I couldn't weigh in on that, but I wanted to be sure you were aware of it so you could discuss it with Dr. Tuck."

Despite everything, a ridiculous smile breaks over my face. *This is what it feels like to have a partner.* "Thanks, Greyson. I talked with Lakeview earlier today, and they are very enthusiastic about that option. But then I spoke to Dr. Tuck, and she's not entirely comfortable with moving Mom out of memory care. So I'm at a bit of a loss."

There's a beat of silence before he responds. "Okay, let's talk it through," he says. "What are Dr. Tuck's concerns?"

I explain the ankle monitor and Dr. Tuck's view on the wandering at night and possible staffing or space issues at Lakeview, as well as her thoughts on Mom's long-term prognosis. I confess that I'm not sure whether to be optimistic about Mom's memory or more realistic. "I just don't know what's actually possible and what's right for her at this point."

"I have seen improvement in recent weeks," he assures me. "And having more opportunities for interaction and stimulation can only be helpful to her progress. Frankie seems confident that Lakeview can manage, and I trust her," Greyson says. "They aren't short-staffed, and they'll be vigilant. But if you want to keep her in memory care, that's what we'll do."

We bounce the idea back and forth a few more times, and by the end of our conversation, I feel like Dr. Tuck's concerns are based more generally in her experiences, not on experiences with Lakeview in particular.

"Your mom will be happier with the freedom to step outside whenever she wishes — within reason, of course. But the gardens, the lake...they're therapeutic," Greyson reminds me.

The image of Mom strolling through blooms, face upturned to the sun, eats at my resolve. "Fine," I relent. "But if the alarm goes off at night — even once — she goes back to memory care."

"That seems reasonable," he says. "Feeling better?"

With a sigh, I realize I am. "Thank you, Greyson. I appreciate you taking the time to sort through this with me. Hopefully, Mom won't be disrupted so much by the move this time, and this will be a positive step forward."

"I think it will," he assures me. "And if things need to change again, we'll make sure we get it right."

My phone buzzes, and a text pops up.

Liz: I'm leaving the hospital now. See you soon.

"I need to run," I tell Greyson. "Liz and I are meeting for a nice dinner this evening before we leave in the morning."

"Enjoy," he tells me. "Can't wait to see you soon."

We say our goodbyes, and I call a rideshare to take me over to the Fish Counter. Liz is going to drive with me back to Paradise tomorrow, thank goodness, and this dinner will be a thank you in advance. Keeping my apartment here in Vancouver is going to be my excuse to escape often to see her, but it won't be the same as seeing her every day.

When I arrive, Liz has already been seated. I slide into the booth across from her.

"Ready for Paradise?" she asks.

"Ready as I'll ever be," I reply, fiddling with a napkin. The trailer is packed with essentials and memories and locked in the garage, ready to be hitched to my car.

"Good," Liz nods. "We're going to have so much fun." Her voice holds something more than camaraderie, but she doesn't elaborate, and I don't press. She's a closed book when she wants to be.

We talk about the drive, the weather forecast promising a clear path. And we discuss the logistics of what I'm going to put in my mother's condo. I don't tell her my concerns about moving in with Greyson right away. I don't want her opinion to influence me. I'll just have to sort that out after I arrive. But I'm glad that at least for now, my mom's place is an option. And I do still wonder about the life I'm leaving behind here. Will I be able to pick it back up, or is this the beginning of something entirely new?

"Thanks for coming with me," I say after a pause, and Liz simply smiles.

We order dinner and agree to meet early so we can avoid the weekend traffic getting out of Vancouver. We're both nervous about driving the trailer on the narrow city streets.

Liz and I eat our perfect fish and chips, and then we hug goodbye, as tomorrow is an early morning. Each item I've placed in my bags feels like a farewell—to the safety of routine, to the city that's been my anchor. Paradise awaits, but with so many uncertainties ahead.

Thirty-four

Greyson

'm
out.

I about to check Mr. Henderson's chart when my phone buzzes in the pocket of my scrubs. I fish it

Trinity: We're on the way! See you soon. ☺

A smile pulls at my lips, warmth spreading through me. I wish I could be there beside her, watching the landscape change as we drive into Paradise, but I'm glad Liz is keeping her company. Safety in numbers and all that.

"Dr. Greyson!" Nurse Janet's voice yanks me back to reality. "We've got an incoming emergency. Woman lost three toes mowing her lawn in sandals."

"Understood," I reply, putting my phone away. My mind shifts gears—sandals, lawnmower. I can almost paint the bloody scene before the victim even arrives.

I stride through the bustling ER, reaching the ambulance bay just as the siren's wail crescendos. The ambulance doors swing open, and the gurney emerges, the patient pale against the red-streaked bandages.

"Vitals?" I ask, assessing the damage as we move into trauma one. She's unconscious, the pain likely too much for her to stay awake through the blood loss.

"BP's low, eighty over fifty. Pulse is thready," one of the paramedics rattles off. "She passed out right after the neighbors called nine-one-one."

"Start two large-bore IVs and get her typed and crossed for four units," I direct, my mind racing. "We'll need to clean the wound and assess the damage before deciding if she needs surgery immediately or if it can wait until she's more stable."

The team moves seamlessly together, and I'm right there with them, hands steady as I work to stop the bleeding and save what's left of this woman's foot. In moments like these, everything else falls away and my focus narrows to the life in front of me, dependent on my skills, my decisions. And for a while, I forget about the waiting, about Trinity and her journey to me. There's only this, the fight to keep another person whole.

Then the wail of sirens fills the air again. I've barely got the lawnmower patient stabilized when the radio crackles with the next crisis — a pedestrian struck by a car. My heart rate surges. These cases are always bad.

"Dr. Greyson," a nurse calls as I move toward the bay doors, "the ambulance is two minutes out."

"Thanks, Mara."

When the doors burst open, it's chaos. The paramedics wheel in a young girl, no older than sixteen, her leg mangled and twisted unnaturally. Her face is ashen, eyes squeezed shut against the pain or fear or both.

"Hit by a car," one paramedic says over the din. "Driver seems drunk. He's on the bus coming in behind us. Not a scratch on him."

"Got it." I don't have time to curse the driver's recklessness. Right now, this girl needs all of me.

"Let's get her into trauma two," I bark. "I need full scans, a vascular consult, and let's prep for possible surgery!"

The team mobilizes, as I assess her leg, the grim possibility looming that she might lose it. My hands are steady, though my heart isn't, not when someone so young faces such a life-altering event.

"Greyson," my brother Beckett's voice cuts through the turmoil. "I'll run a tox screen on the driver."

"Thanks," I mutter, hardly looking up from my work. Trusting Beckett to handle it, I focus on saving what's left of this girl's future.

Hours bleed into each other, and eventually, the adrenaline fades, leaving exhaustion in its wake. It's only when the pace finally slows that I remember Trinity. Slipping into the staff lounge, I check for updates, hoping for good news.

But when I see her text, disappointment grips me tight. It took her over an hour just to get out of Vancouver? Traffic must be hell. I cringe. If this keeps up, I might actually beat her home, and that thought sits like lead in my stomach.

"Come on," I whisper, as if she can hear me. "Drive safe, but please, hurry."

An hour later, I stumble out of the hospital, the weight of forty-plus patients' fates still lingering on my shoulders. But it's over for today, and I push through the exhaustion because Trinity is back. As of about twenty minutes ago, my Trinity is here in Paradise.

I yank off my scrubs and jump into the shower in the staff locker room, letting the hot water sluice away the grime. When I emerge, Kingston is there with Beckett and a few others from the team. They're all laughs and plans, already halfway to their night out.

"Come grab a drink with us," Beckett urges.

"Can't," I reply, raking a towel through my damp hair.

"Trinity is here."

Understanding morphs Kingston's smile into a knowing nod. "Say no more."

With a wave, I sling my backpack over one shoulder and make for the exit, my eyes on the clock.

Back home, I pull quickly into the parking garage and race to the elevator. But as I scan the rows of cars, disappointment crashes over me. She's not here. There's no sign of her car.

"Damn it," I mutter, thumbing my phone. Maybe she went to see her mother? Maybe she sent another message, an update I missed in the flurry of traumas?

Nothing.

I unlock the door to my condo. The silence inside feels heavier than usual, like the room itself is holding its breath. I wanted her things here, her books on the coffee table, her jacket on the chair, a sign that this space was no longer just mine but ours. Without them, it feels incomplete, like me.

I pull out my phone and call her number. She picks up on the first ring.

"Hey, where are you?" I ask, trying to keep my voice light.

"Downstairs, in my mom's condo," she replies, and I can hear the bustle of movement and conversation behind her voice.

"Oh! Okay, I'll come down." I try to mask my letdown with enthusiasm. I had hoped to have her to myself, but at least she's here in the building.

"Great! Liz's friend is about to show up too," Trinity adds.

"Got it. I'll order some Thai food for us all," I say before we hang up.

After a quick call to order dinner for four, I get in the elevator and head down to Trinity's mother's condo.

I walk in, and there are boxes everywhere. It's a maze. "Where are you?" I call into the void of cardboard. I want so much to hold her and whisk her off to bed so the world will be right.

She peeks around a row of boxes. "I'm right here."

I rush to her, and she wraps her arms around my neck. Her kiss is a soft promise of more to come.

"How was the drive?" I ask.

"Fine once we got out of Vancouver. But traffic was slower than we expected, so it took longer," Trinity says.

"That and I had to go to the bathroom a few times," Liz adds with a laugh as she appears from the bedroom.

We talk a little more about the trip, and thankfully, it was uneventful. The tourist season has ended. The nights are getting cooler, and the grapes are nearly all picked, which means fewer people are coming this way.

The buzzer sounds, and dinner has arrived. Trinity buzzes it up.

"Who's this friend you're here to see?" I ask Liz.

"Oh, wait until you meet him. He's—"

There's a knock, and I open the door, expecting the Thai food delivery. But instead, standing there is one of my family's arch enemies—Alaric Dempsey.

"You deliver food now?" I ask.

"No!" Liz says as she jumps into his arms.

Then I notice the delivery driver behind him. With a tip and my thanks, he's soon on his way, leaving me to focus on Alaric Dempsey making out with Trinity's best friend. His presence pulls up memories I've spent years burying—schoolyard rivalries, veiled competition, and the uneasy truce we've maintained. He's not a man I want anywhere near Trinity or her friends.

"Greyson," he says when he finally comes up for air. His surprise mirrors mine, though I bury it under a layer of civility.

"Alaric." I acknowledge him with a nod. "Didn't expect to see you here."

"Likewise," he replies, and there's a challenge in his eyes.

"Are you two friends?" Trinity asks.

"We were schoolmates," I answer, choosing my words carefully.

Alaric nods in agreement as we continue assessing each other. We've both changed, but some histories refuse to stay buried.

"Let's eat," I suggest, ushering everyone to the table where the smell of Thai spices promises a welcome distraction. I catch Trinity's eye and force a smile. Tonight is about her return, not old grudges or unexpected guests.

As we eat, Liz laughs easily, recounting their road trip, while Alaric's gaze lingers too long on Trinity. Across the table, she meets my eyes, her smile soft, as if trying to reassure me. But the knot in my stomach doesn't loosen.

"So, how did you land a condo in this building?" Alaric asks between bites, his gaze fixed on Trinity.

She chuckles. "It's not my condo. It belongs to my mom."

"How did you and Greyson meet?" he asks.

What is this, an interrogation? His questions are setting off all my warning bells. My business is no business of his.

"We met at a MedTalks conference in Victoria, and then I actually ran into Greyson again here in the emergency room." She tilts her head toward me, a smile on her lips.

"Small world," Alaric muses.

"Liz, how did you and Alaric meet?" I ask, feigning casual interest.

Liz leans forward, her hands wrapped around her wine glass. "It was at this bar downtown," she begins, her cheeks flushing. "I was supposed to meet this guy, but he stood me up. Then Alaric stepped in, like some kind of knight in shining armor." Her eyes find Alaric's, and there's a warmth there that makes my stomach twist.

"Is that right?" I say. I force a smile, nodding as though I believe every word.

When we've finished eating, Trinity and Liz clear the dirty plates, insisting Alaric and I stay seated and catch up.

"Funny, isn't it?" Alaric says finally, his tone casual in a way that sets my teeth on edge.

"What's funny?" I ask.

Alaric smiles faintly, a slow, deliberate thing that doesn't reach his eyes. "How fragile everything is. One moment, it's thriving, and the next, it's gone. Makes you think about the long-term value of things."

I narrow my eyes. "If you've got a point, Alaric, make it."

He shrugs, feigning nonchalance. "I'm just saying, the vineyard's been through a lot lately, hasn't it? The loss of the pinot vines this year, the fire that got dangerously close to the north fields last summer... It must be hard to keep the books balanced with hits like that."

My jaw tightens, and I set my glass down with more force than necessary. "We're managing just fine."

"Of course you are," he says smoothly, his smile widening. "For now. But how many more setbacks can Paradise Hill take before the losses start adding up? Sometimes, holding onto something because it's tradition doesn't make sense in the long run."

There it is. The subtle dig, the implication that our family's legacy is a sinking ship. I've heard it before, mostly from Max, but coming from Alaric, it feels different. More like an attack.

"We're not going anywhere," I say evenly, meeting his gaze. "No matter how much some people might want us to. And I think our invitation to the International Wine and Spirits competition in November supports that."

Alaric raises an eyebrow. "I wouldn't dream of suggesting otherwise," he says. "But it's worth considering all the options. Especially when the land itself might be more valuable than the grapes it grows."

I lean forward, my hands flat on the table. "What are you getting at, Alaric?"

He holds up his hands in mock surrender, his expression carefully neutral. "Nothing, Greyson. Just an observation." But the glint in his eyes says otherwise.

I sit back, my shoulders stiff. Alaric may claim innocence,

but he knows more than he's letting on. I'm sure of it. And I'm going to find out what.

Liz and Trinity return, and Alaric checks his watch. "We should get going," he tells Liz.

"Of course," I reply. The sooner he leaves, the better.

"Thanks for the dinner, Greyson. It was great catching up," Alaric says as Liz gets her coat. "I'll look forward to seeing you in London in November."

"Are you coming to celebrate our win?"

He shakes his head. "No, we are competing as well, and this time your family can't pay off the judges."

"I can't wait," I assure him.

As they head for the door, I watch Alaric's back and vow to keep an eye on him, for Liz's sake.

The door clicks shut behind Liz and Alaric, and Trinity turns to me. "Paradise really is a small world, huh?" she muses.

I manage a shrug, keeping my face neutral. "Yeah, it can be," I say, veering away from the topic before it goes any deeper. The old feuds that go back generations with Alaric's family are like scars, always there but better left concealed. "So, about all your stuff here in your mom's place…"

Trinity laughs lightly. "I tend to overpack. And now, I have no idea what to do with everything." She gestures helplessly, but her eyes are bright with amusement. "This seemed like the best place for it all to explode."

"Hey, don't worry about it." I breathe an internal sigh of relief, as it seems she still plans to stay with me. "We'll make room for whatever you need at my place. I've cleared out half my closet. There's a storage room, and I have two guest rooms. We'll figure it out. There's no rush." I take her hand in mine, squeezing gently.

"Thank you." She kisses me softly.

"Come on…" I beckon with a tilt of my head toward the doorway, feeling the weight of the day's fatigue pulling at me. "Let's head up and call it a night."

She gathers a few things, and we lock up her mother's place, taking the elevator upstairs to mine.

"I'm a little tired," I warn her. "But I have big plans for us." I wink, and she smiles.

Thirty-five

Trinity

Greyson and I haven't been very social with others in the week since I returned to Paradise. It seems we have a lot to catch up on. But I am visiting my mom every day, and I'm also finding my footing with my new contract with the hospital back in Vancouver. They're building a new wing, and I'm in charge of making sure the disruption to care is minimal. Greyson seemed surprised that wouldn't just happen naturally. I've determined, yet again, that as long as things work well, doctors are pretty oblivious. They don't know how much work goes into making sure that happens.

But today, it's the weekend, and we're headed to the crush fundraiser at the vineyard. I'm looking forward to seeing Tarryn and the rest of his family again.

As we drive past rows upon rows of lush grapevines, Greyson's voice is tinged with pride. "This event is a big deal around here. We're hosting it to benefit Backpack Buddies this year, a program that helps kids take food home to their families who are in need."

I glance out the window, feeling my anticipation build. "Sounds incredible," I reply.

The car rolls to a stop behind the family home. We step out, and together we ascend the hill toward the event, the sound of chatter and laughter growing louder with each step.

The scene that greets us is organized chaos. The event isn't open yet, and everyone is scurrying around, preparing. Vendors are setting up booths, the food trucks are busy doing prep, and people everywhere are waving and calling out directions. Greyson spots his parents in the thick of it and insists on introducing me.

His mother's laughter reaches my ears before I see her. And then Greyson waves as we approach. "Mom, Dad, this is Trinity," he says, beaming.

His mother envelops me in a hug so warm and encompassing it feels like coming home. "Welcome, dear! Call me Vicky," she says.

Trace, Greyson's father, follows with a firm handshake, his weathered skin a testament to years of hard work. "You're in good hands with this one," he says, nodding toward Greyson, his gaze steady.

"Any of the rest of the family here?" Greyson asks, scanning the crowd.

Trace gives a look that's equal parts amusement and resignation. "Everyone but Beckett. You know your brother, probably trying to make an entrance."

"Or just lost track of time," I quip.

Greyson chuckles.

"Always late," Vicky adds, shaking her head fondly as if tardiness is an endearing trait only Beckett could get away with.

It's clear they're a family stitched together by love and gentle teasing, a family I'm beginning to feel a part of, even if just on the periphery.

"Let me show you around," Greyson suggests, and I nod, ready to immerse myself in the heart of Paradise Hill.

He leads me toward the large stage where a microphone stands, waiting for the day's serenades. "Rebel Luv will be rocking us later." He grins, pointing to the band's vintage-style poster tacked up on a nearby tree. The name alone promises a throwback to slicked-back hair and guitar twangs that I can't wait to hear.

I survey the circle of food trucks nearby, each one with a quirky name emblazoned on its side in bold, colorful letters — Green Machine, Cone Zone, Wok This Way, Burger Bus, Taco 'Bout It, and BBQ Bandit. The aromas mingle in the air, a heady perfume of sizzling spices and sweet desserts. My mouth waters.

Then Tarryn, a whirlwind of enthusiasm, charges toward us with arms flung wide. "Trinity!" she exclaims, nearly tackling me in a fierce hug. "Welcome home! When you start planning your wedding, count me in! I started as the event planner here when I was fifteen. I know all the ins and outs." Tarryn beams.

"Whoa there, Tornado Tarryn." Greyson chuckles, stepping between us with a playful wag of his finger. "Give her a chance to breathe. She just got here."

"Trust me, if you don't want half the guys here hitting on her, you'd better lock it down," Tarryn teases, waggling her eyebrows.

"Tarryn!" Greyson groans.

I pat his arm. "We're not quite there yet," I tell her. "But I'll remember you're the go-to for planning."

"Promise?" Tarryn's smile is bright.

"Cross my heart," I affirm, and for a moment, I'm swept up in the possibility of a future filled with love and laughter, right here in this little slice of paradise.

I'm still basking in Tarryn's warm welcome when a voice cuts across the parking area.

"Did I overhear someone's getting hitched?" The man

who approaches wears an easy grin.

Greyson's expression tenses for a split second before he turns to me. "Trinity, you remember my older brother, Kingston." He gestures to the man with the playful smirk.

"Nice to see you again." Kingston extends a strong hand that swallows mine in a firm shake. "Glad to see Grey took my advice on locking down a good one."

Before I can process the comment, another figure joins us, bearing a striking family resemblance.

"Ryker, it's nice of you to join us," Tarryn says.

A third, whose features echo the familial lines, trails behind him. "Our cousin Zane," Greyson adds.

We exchange pleasantries, their warmth drawing me in immediately.

"Everything looks incredible, Tarryn," Kingston remarks, sweeping a hand toward the festivities.

"Doesn't it?" Tarryn beams and accepts their compliments with a flourish. "Couldn't have done it without your help," she says, including them all in her gratitude.

The moment is punctuated by a sudden swell of sound as the front gates open, unleashing a stream of eager attendees into the venue. Children's laughter ricochets off the hills, mixing with the chatter of adults. Tarryn seizes the opportunity, her voice carrying over the crowd.

"Everyone, make sure you hit the Grape Stomp! The little ones will start in half an hour, and trust me, it's the highlight of the day."

"Wouldn't miss it," Greyson assures her, a smile stretching across his face.

"Congrats again, Tarryn," I add, feeling swept up in the communal spirit that seems to thrive in this place.

She hurries off, and Greyson and I weave through the bustling crowd, his hand a reassuring presence at the small of my back. The air buzzes with laughter and chatter, the scent of ripened grapes mingling with a medley of savory aromas wafting from food trucks stationed like colorful sentinels at the perimeter.

We continue on, drawn by a chorus of giggles and splashes. At the Grape Stomp, children clad in swimsuits and goggles cluster eagerly around barrels overflowing with plump grapes.

"Let's hang back a bit," Greyson suggests, smiling as we find a spot to watch from a safe distance.

After a few minutes, Tarryn takes the makeshift stage. She explains the rules, and then says, "Each one of you gets ice cream from Cone Zone after! And I've got special gift bags for you brave stompers!"

Her words are met with cheers and clapping hands.

"Ready... Set... Stomp!" Tarryn commands, and the barrels erupt into chaos. Legs flail, grapes burst, and juice begins to flow. One little girl hesitates, a crinkle of distaste marring her brow.

"Come on, honey, make some grape juice!" Her mom encourages, and the girl's reluctance transforms into exuberant stomping.

"Who knew making juice was such hard work?" quips a boy, earning laughter from onlookers.

The timer winds down, and the children peer into their respective bottles, assessing their liquid accomplishments.

"Look at them go," Greyson says. "Reminds me of my first stomp."

As the timer buzzes, we drift away from the joyful pandemonium. I'm getting more than just a glimpse into Greyson's childhood. I'm becoming a part of his present, wrapped up in the traditions of Paradise Hill and the heart of its community.

We're caught up in the ebb and flow of the crowd when a familiar voice cuts through the hum of conversation.

"Trinity!"

I turn, and there's Frankie, her smile bright. She sweeps me into an embrace that feels like homecoming. "Your mom's doing so much better since we moved her out of memory care," she says, pulling back but holding onto my arms.

"Thank you for helping with that," I reply. "I have to agree. I have lunch with her every day, and she's sharper than I've seen her in a while."

"Every good day is a blessing." Frankie nods.

We share another moment of small talk before the flow of the party pulls us in separate directions. Greyson takes my hand, guiding me through the crowd. As we pass a group laughing over glasses of wine, I catch sight of Beckett leaning against a barrel, the sunlight catching the gold hints in his hair.

"Beckett!" Greyson calls as we approach.

"Hey, look who's gracing us with her presence," Beckett says with a grin, pushing away from the barrel to greet us. Beside him stands a woman whose smile rivals the brightness of the day.

"Trinity, this is Sara Demetrius," Beckett says, gesturing toward her with a casual hand. "Nurse extraordinaire from the hospital's labor and delivery department, and she's also my best friend's little sister."

"Nice to meet you," Sara says as she shakes my hand. "Welcome back to Paradise!"

"Thank you, Sara. It's great to be back," I reply.

"Greyson's is all the better for it," Beckett adds.

We chat briefly, exchanging pleasantries, and then Greyson and I continue our stroll, leaving Beckett and Sara behind. Greyson rolls his eyes, a smirk playing at the corner of his mouth.

"He's slept with half the hospital, huh?" I tease, nudging him with my elbow.

"More like the whole thing," Greyson retorts, shaking his head. "He never learns. But hey, that's Beckett for you — heartbreaker, lifesaver, and perpetually tardy."

We laugh, the sound mingling with the chords of a guitar tuning up on stage, and I feel a deep sense of contentment. Here, amidst family and friends, the complicated threads of life seem simpler, woven together by the shared joy of this moment, under the wide-open sky of Paradise Hill.

We spend the afternoon eating and tasting wine, and I'm sure I've met half the town. I'm exhausted by the time it's over and more than ready to go back to Greyson's and relax.

"Tarryn, it was incredible," I tell her as the crowds dwindle.

"Thanks so much, Trinity. It means the world to hear you say that," she replies, tucking a loose strand of hair behind her ear.

"Fantastic job," Greyson chimes in.

"Next year will be even better," Tarryn calls as she's whisked away by a volunteer needing her attention.

Leaving the bustle of the festival behind, Greyson and I make our way down the hill, the vineyard sprawling out before us like a patchwork quilt. New memories nestle themselves within the old, and warmth settles in my soul. The thought of leaving Vancouver still feels like shedding a part of myself, yet every step through these vines pulls me closer to something I continue to realize how much I've needed.

Thirty-six

Greyson

The past two weeks with Trinity have shifted something in our relationship. I've made every effort to show her I am trustworthy, solid, here for whatever life brings our way. We've laughed together, lounged together, just done the basics of life—making space for each other in our worlds, finding a shared world we have in common. It's mundane but also pretty incredible.

And somehow, in the middle of all that quiet consistency, I think she's started to breathe easier. She told me the other day that being together doesn't feel like she's giving something up. It feels like she's choosing something better. That might be the best thing anyone's ever said. And I'm hoping it's a foundation we can build on.

This evening, the air smells of earth and blooming wildflowers as I lead Trinity up the gentle slope of the vineyard.

The sunset is painted in streaks of gold and pink, the kind of sky you don't soon forget. I look over at her, the way the light catches her hair, the easy rhythm of her steps. She belongs here, even if she doesn't see it yet.

"It's beautiful," she says, her voice soft as we reach the crest of the hill. I nod as I take in the view. The rows of vines stretch endlessly below us, a patchwork of greens and browns, the heart of my family's legacy. I've walked these hills a hundred times, but tonight feels different. "My parents, their parents, all of them poured their lives into this place," I say, slipping my hands into my pockets to keep them steady.

She turns to me, her brow furrowing slightly. "It's a lot of pressure to carry."

"It is." I meet her gaze, the weight of what I'm about to say anchoring me. "But it's not about the vineyard. Not really. It's about what it stands for—family, growth, resilience. That's what matters."

Her lips curve into a small smile, but I see the questions in her eyes. She thinks this is about the feud, the sabotage, all the things we can't control. It's not.

"I didn't bring you here to talk about the vineyard," I say, stepping closer. My heart is pounding. "I brought you here because this place— It's where my family has built something lasting. And I want to build something lasting with you."

Her eyes widen, and she takes a small step back, her hands clutching the hem of her sweater. "Greyson…"

"I know it's fast," I say quickly, holding up my hands. "And I know we're still figuring things out. But, Trinity, you've changed everything for me. You've made me see that life isn't about control or perfection. It's about the mess, the risk, the leap. And I want to take that leap with you."

She's silent, her gaze darting to the horizon where the sun dips lower, casting the sky in shades of crimson. For a moment, I think I've misjudged. Maybe I've pushed too hard, too soon.

But then she looks back at me, her eyes bright with unshed

tears. "Greyson, you drive me crazy," she says, her voice trembling. "You're stubborn, impossible, and you make me question everything I thought I wanted. But…you're also the best thing that's ever happened to me."

I reach into my pocket and pull out the small velvet box, opening it to reveal the ring. The diamond catches the last rays of sunlight, glinting like a promise. "So what do you say, Blaine? Want to risk it all with me?"

She laughs through her tears, her hand flying to her mouth. "You're ridiculous," she whispers, but there's no hesitation as she steps closer. "Yes, Greyson. Of course, yes."

Relief crashes over me, and I slide the ring onto her finger before pulling her into my arms. She fits perfectly, like she was always meant to be here, in this place, with me.

We sit on the hilltop as the last light fades, her head resting against my shoulder. The vineyard below us is quiet, but my thoughts are restless. The sun slowly disappears into the lake.

"What do you think about the sabotage?" she asks after a while.

I sigh. "I think it's easy to blame the Dempseys," I tell her. "Our families have been at odds for so long, it's second nature. But…I don't know. Something about it doesn't feel right."

She tilts her head to look at me. "Interesting. I wasn't sure about Alaric at first, but he's kind of won me over. He looks at Liz like she hung the moon, so he can't be all bad. Though I know there are more Dempseys than just him."

"Yeah," I agree. "They're a lot of things, but I don't see them as saboteurs."

Her brow furrows, and I can see the gears turning in her mind. Trinity doesn't like loose ends, but this one is going to have to wait. "We'll figure it out," I say, reaching for her hand. "Together."

She nods, her expression softening. "Together," she repeats.

As the stars begin to dot the sky, I feel a strange sense of calm. The feud, the sabotage — it's all unfinished, but for the first time, it doesn't feel like a burden. Because now, I have Trinity.

Thank you for reading *Dr. Greyson*. I hope you enjoyed Greyson and Trinity's story as much I did. If you want a peek at their future, you can download it here:

https://dl.bookfunnel.com/xectq4qt3k

And here is a sneak peek at Beckett's story:

Dr. Beckett

Sadie

Rain pelts down relentlessly, as if the heavens themselves are weeping for my plight. I stand at Beckett Paradise's door, shivering, feeling cold droplets seeping through my jacket to touch my skin with icy fingers. My luggage is piled at my feet, a sad testament to my current life, packed in haste, a chaotic collection of everything I thought I'd need when I stormed out of Alex's place.

I hesitate, my finger hovering over the doorbell. Am I really this desperate? Desperate enough to ask Beckett for help, the grown-up boy who spent our childhood finding new and creative ways to terrorize me? The boy who once locked me in the treehouse for an entire afternoon just because he could? The same Beckett who had no issue making my life a living hell every time our families got together?

I take a step back, my breath coming fast and uneven. *Maybe this is a mistake.* Maybe I should turn around and figure something else out. Sleeping in my car suddenly doesn't seem so bad. At least, it doesn't come with the added humiliation of asking Beckett for a favor.

But then another gust of wind howls through the night, sending a shiver straight to my bones. I have nowhere else to go. My pride is the only thing standing between me and warmth, and at this point, it's already in tatters.

Before I can talk myself out of it, I press the doorbell. The chime echoes behind the heavy wood barrier, the sound nearly swallowed by the storm. My heart thumps, and I brace myself for the inevitable scowl that awaits me. When the door creaks open, it's exactly what I get.

Beckett appears, a creature roused against his will — shirtless, tousled, and definitely not happy to see me. His sleep-creased features shift from irritation to outright disbelief, his blue eyes narrowing. He fills the doorway, broad and imposing, radiating the kind of energy that makes lesser people back away. Too bad for him, I'm in no position to run.

A muscle in Beckett's jaw ticks. "What the hell are you doing here, Sadie Calloway?"

"I had nowhere else to go," I inform him.

Beckett exhales, rubbing a hand down his face. I see the exact moment he resigns himself to this situation — the subtle shift in his shoulders, the flicker of irritation that turns into something more resigned.

"Get in before you drown on my doorstep," he mutters, stepping aside.

I want to say something, anything that might explain why I am here, drenched and disheveled, but the words lodge in my throat, stubborn as stones. Instead, I meet his gaze squarely, letting the suitcases speak where my voice fails me.

With a muttered curse, Beckett steps aside as I shuffle past him, my soaked sneakers squeaking against the hardwood floor. I desperately try to ignore that his scrub pants are hanging low on his hips, and his chest is a washboard. Instead, I drag my bags into his house, water pooling beneath them.

"Are you serious?"

I swallow hard. "No, I'm just testing how waterproof my luggage is."

His scowl deepens. "Jesus, Sadie."

A clap of thunder cracks through the night, and I flinch. I won't beg. If he wants to kick me right back out, fine. I'll figure something out.

But he doesn't.

"Make yourself scarce," he mumbles, scratching the stubble on his cheek. "And don't think this is a sleepover that turns into a weekender."

I roll my eyes. "Please, like I'm thrilled about being here."

"Could've fooled me."

My fingers curl into fists. "I'll be gone soon enough."

"Good."

But neither of us moves, we just stand there staring, the tension thick.

Beckett sighs, shaking his head as if trying to dislodge reality. "Guest room's down the hall. Towels are in the closet. Try not to flood the place."

He turns on his heel and disappears, likely already counting the seconds until he can call my brother, Caleb, and wash his hands of me. But I also know something he doesn't. Caleb won't have an easy fix this time.

I drop onto the guest bed, my wet clothes clinging to me uncomfortably. The room is unfamiliar, but somehow, the scent of Beckett is everywhere—clean, crisp, and a little like cedarwood. I rub my hands up and down my arms, trying to will warmth back into my bones, but it's useless. My fingers are stiff, my body aching from the cold.

I should move, get up and take a shower. Or at least change into something dry. But exhaustion weighs me down, my mind spiraling as I think about Caleb, half a world away, completely unable to help me right now. Even if he wanted to fix this, there's nothing he can do from the other side of the globe.

I'm stuck for the foreseeable future.

Eventually, I force myself to my feet, my body protesting. The bathroom is small but spotless, and I peel off my wet clothes with shaking hands. The hot water stings at first, sharp pinpricks against my chilled skin, but soon enough, the warmth seeps into my muscles, loosening the knots of tension.

I press my forehead against the cool tile, my chest rising and falling as I try to keep my thoughts from running wild. *This is temporary.* It has to be. Beckett doesn't want me here, and I don't want to be here any longer than necessary.

But as the water rushes over me, washing away the grime and the worst of the night, I can't ignore the truth.

Temporary or not, for now, I have nowhere else to go.

Sunlight peeks through the blinds, its soft intrusion a huge shift from the storm that raged last night. I'm perched at Beckett's kitchen counter, one leg swinging idly as I cradle a mug of coffee between my hands. The oversized T-shirt I borrowed — or commandeered, depending on who you ask — hangs off one shoulder, the fabric warm and smelling faintly of his cologne.

Footsteps shuffle behind me, and Beckett's grumble of irritation is my greeting. He makes a beeline for the coffeemaker, pouring himself a cup with an air of desperation.

"Morning." I sip my coffee.

He doesn't answer right away, but his gaze flickers to me — more specifically, to the oversized shirt hanging off my frame.

His shirt.

His scowl deepens. "You're really making yourself at home, huh?"

I sip my coffee, feigning indifference. "It was either this or dripping all over." Yes, I have bags with me. No, I did not pack effectively.

His eyes narrow, like he wants to argue, but instead he focuses on his coffee, taking a slow sip as he watches me over the rim.

His phone rings, and Beckett glances at the caller ID, mutters another curse, and answers. "Caleb," he says.

I tense, curling my toes against the cold tile floor. This is it, the moment Caleb tells him to kick me out. I texted Caleb last night to tell him where I was. He sent back a slew of curse words, and I turned my phone off.

Beckett's expression shifts from annoyed to stunned. His eyes flicker to mine, and I straighten up, suddenly self-conscious.

"Yeah, she's here," he says, his tone cautious. I watch Beckett's jaw tighten as he listens, his grip on the phone tightening until his knuckles turn white.

"Are you serious?" His voice rises. There's a long pause, and then he sighs heavily. "All right, all right, I'll keep her away from Alex. Yeah, I get it. Do whatever it takes."

I freeze, coffee forgotten. The room feels smaller somehow, the walls inching closer. Beckett ends the call and slams the phone down on the counter. He rubs a hand over his face, clearly at a loss.

"What did Caleb say?" I ask.

"Damn it, Sadie." He groans, meeting my gaze. There's something—concern, maybe even fear—before his eyes harden again. "What is Alex up to, and how deep are you in it?"

"I don't want to talk about it." I turn away from him, racing through how I can explain what happened and why I left in the middle of the night. I can't even describe it myself. "It's none of your business."

Beckett breathes in and out noisily, like a bull ready to charge. "Your brother wants you to stay here until he returns—"

"Oh, I'll be out of your hair faster than that."

"No." Beckett has a no-nonsense vibe now. "You will do as Caleb and I say."

"You're not my keeper."

"According to Caleb, I am."

I shut my eyes in frustration. I knew I shouldn't have come here.

"Your brother has given me specific instructions to make sure I do whatever it takes to keep you safe from Alex. Do you know what that means?"

I swallow, my throat suddenly dry. "Trouble," I whisper. Here I am, wearing his T-shirt, sipping his coffee, and now bound to him by a promise he never wanted to make.

Thank you

To every reader who has picked up one of my books — thank you. Your reviews, your messages, and your continued support mean the world to me. Every note of encouragement, every kind word, always seems to arrive right when I need it most. The more you share and review, the more the algorithms share my stories — and I'm endlessly grateful for that.

To my husband — my muse, my soul mate, and my greatest supporter — thank you for reading every book and standing beside me through it all. And to my two boys, thank you for pretending to be interested in Mommy's kissy books (even though I know you'd rather not hear about them at all). Your love is my foundation.

Publishing may feel like a solo sport, but it truly takes a team. I'm so grateful to my brilliant developmental editor, Jessica Royer Oken, whose insights and talent make my words sparkle.

And to my incredible proofreading team—Courtnay, Linda, Iris, Nancy, and Diana—thank you for catching all the sneaky little typos that try to slip through. Your sharp eyes and dedication make every book better.

With all my heart, thank you.

Books by Grace Maxwell

Men of Mercy
Doctor of the Heart (Paisley & Davis)
Doctor of Women (Nadine & Michael)
Doctor of Sports (Eliza & Steve)
Doctor of Beauty(Laine & Jack)
Men of Mercy Box Set

Mercy Medical Emergency
Doctor Delight (Tori & Griffin)
Doctor Bossy (Amelia & Kent)
Doctor Rebel (Lucy & Chance)
Doctor Enemy (Ava & Roman)
Previously released as *A Doctor for Valentines* **in "Love is in the Air, Vol 3"**
Doctor Tyrant (Hailey & Christian)
Mercy Medical Emergency Box Set

Brothers Paradise
Dr. Greyson (Trinity & Greyson)
Dr. Beckett (Sadie & Beckett)